Get your face stuck into
The Clown's Pie

A moist slice encrusted with the batter bits of issues 94-99

Licked into shape by Alex Collier, Chris Donald, Simon Donald, Graham Dury, Stevie Glover, Davey Jones, Ian McKie, Sheila Thompson and Simon Thorp.

With additional self-raising ingredients from Guy Campbell, Simon Ecob, John Fardell, Ray Fury, Lew Stringer and Brian Walker.

ISBN No. 1-90 2212-37-1

Published in Great Britain by
IFG
9 Dallington Street
London EC1V 0BQ

First Printing October 2001

Printed in Great Britain

AN AUDIENCE WITH Roger Mellie

ROGER MELLIE

ARE YOU READY, YET, ROGER? THE SHOW STARTS IN TEN MIN...
ROGER!?

PASS ME THE 'SUN' WILL YOU, TOM! I'M OUT OF BOG ROLL
TOILET

I'M FARTING FIZZY GRAVY IN 'ERE, TOM. I'VE HAD THE BLOODY TRUMPETER'S LIPS ALL DAY
TA!
TITS ALL OVER THE SHOP
IT'S NOT LIKE YOU TO BE NERVOUS, ROGER.

OF COURSE I'M NERVOUS, TOM. THIS IS THE BIG ONE! "AN AUDIENCE WITH" YOURS TRULY.

TOP OF THE SHOWBIZ TREE, THIS.

IT'S NOT THE GREAT UNWASHED OUT THERE. IT'S THE TOUGHEST GIG OF ALL... PERFORMING TO MY SHOWBIZ PEERS, TOM.
SOME OF MY CLOSEST MATES WILL BE OUT THERE, TONIGHT.

DES,.. BRUCIE... TARBY... THAT PUFF WHO DOES THE THING WITH THE SUPERMARKET TROLLEYS
OH, BY THE WAY
HERE'S THE QUESTIONS FOR THE AUDIENCE. MAKE SURE THEY STICK TO THE SCRIPT. ANY AD LIBS AN' I'M FUCKED

I WAS HERE FOR "AN AUDIENCE WITH JERRY SPRINGER" AND HE WENT DOWN LIKE 'DR. MENGELE'S MAGIC ACT AT A BARMITSVA

HOLD ON, ROGER...
THESE QUESTIONS... CHRIST!

"ROGER. I HEAR YOU'VE GOT A TEN-INCH COCK! WOULD YOU LIKE ME TO SUCK IT AFTER THE SHOW?"
YEAH! THAT ONE'S FOR DANI BEHR. WHATEVER YOU DO, DON'T GIVE IT TO CLAIR RAYNOR, EH!?

AND WHAT'S THIS!? "DO YOU HAVE ANY FANNY FARTING ANECDOTES ABOUT SUE LAWLEY?"
HA!
WAIT 'TILL THEY HEAR THAT STORY, TOM. IT'S FUCKING DYNAMITE!

AND WE END ON THIS ONE
"WE KNOW YOU DON'T LIKE TO TALK ABOUT YOUR CHARITY WORK...
...BUT IS IT TRUE YOU RECENTLY GAVE £100,000 TO A LOCAL CHILDREN'S HOSPITAL?"

WE GET STEPHEN HAWKING TO READ THAT ONE OUT. I PAUSE, SAY "NO COMMENT" AND GIVE A LITTLE SLY WINK TO CAMERA 2
THEN I'LL GO OVER AND STICK A £50 NOTE IN THE POOR CUNT'S TOP POCKET... AN' ROLL CREDITS.

CUE TEARS AN' CHEERS! I'LL BE A TRIUMPH, TOM... BE ABLE TO NAME MY FUCKIN' PRICE AFTER THIS...

... AND DOUBLE IT!

OH, I'D BEST WARN YOU, TOM. I'VE GOT A COUPLE OF GREAT CANNIBAL GAGS LINED UP, ONLY THEY'RE NOT TOO P.C. SO MAKE SURE YOU GET A SHOT OF TREVOR McDONALD LAUGHING OR I'LL GET MY WRISTS SLAPPED
PSST! CAN I HAVE A QUICK WORD, TOM?

WHAT?... YES!.. HOW MANY?.. BLOODY HELL!

IS THERE A PROBLEM, TOM?
ERM... NOT REALLY, ROGER... ERM... JUST A FEW EMPTY SEATS IN THE AUDIENCE, THAT'S ALL

EMPTY SEATS? HOW COME? I THOUGHT WE INVITED ABOUT A THOUSAND NAMES
NEVER MIND, ROGER. YOU'LL BE A TRIUMPH. JUST GO OUT THERE AND KNOCK 'EM DEAD.

SHORTLY...
WELCOME TO "AN AUDIENCE WITH ROGER MELLIE"... AND HERE HE IS... ROGER MELLIE!
THANK YOU...
AN AUDIENCE WITH
CLAP! CLAP! CLAP! CLAP! CLAP!

THANK YOU. WELL LET'S GET STRAIGHT ON, AN' THE FIRST QUESTION IS FROM MY OLD MATE, GARRY BUSHELL...

AUDI
WIT
..WHERE ARE YOU, GARRY?

I'M OVER HERE, ROGER!
HIYA, GARRY! FIRE AWAY!

ROGER... I HEAR YOU'VE GOT A TEN INCH COCK...

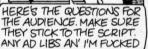

It's the quiz that sorts the Men from the Boys in Blue

Are YOU a COPPER?

"IF you want to know the time ask a policeman," so the saying goes. But if someone asked YOU the time, would you know if you were a policeman or not? With many of today's cops wearing plain clothes, like Inspector Morse and DI Jack Frost, you could be a bobby without knowing it. Wearing a full police uniform is no indication either, you might simply be going to a fancy dress party. The only way to find out the truth is to help yourself with your own enquiries by answering the following questions. Take down anything you say and use it in evidence to find out whether *YOUR* jobby is a *BOBBY*.

1 One night you spot someone in a cloth cap and a stripy jumper shinning down a drainpipe with a sackful of candelabras. How many times would you say 'Hello' to him?

a. Once
b. Twice
c. Three times

2 You arrive at the scene of a hit-and-run accident. The victim is a young black lad who has been knocked off his bike and is unconscious. What is the first thing you do?

a. Check for vital life signs and put him in the recovery position.
b. Ask if anyone took the registration number of the vehicle involved.
c. Slap him till he comes round, ask where he stole the bike from and throw him into the back of a police van.

3 You are trying to teach your pet dog to sit and stay on command, but after a few hours he is getting bored and losing concentration. What do you do?

a. Give up and take him for a walk.
b. Speak to him in a loud voice to show him who is boss.
c. Hang him by his collar over a fence and kick him to death.

A police dog.

4 Early one morning, you find yourself first at the scene of a break-in at a newsagents shop. The owner has yet to arrive. What do you do?

a. Call the police and guard the shop to prevent further looting.
b. Hurry past, it's nothing to do with you.
c. Go inside and stuff your uniform with fags, and sell them later to work colleagues from your locker at the station.

5 Your young son comes home from school and reports that he has done quite badly in a spelling test. What action would you take?

a. Humorously laugh it off, telling him Shakespeare was unable to spell.
b. Sit down and calmly discuss the problem.
c. Take him down to the cellar, wrap him in a mattress, and beat him with a length of rubber hose.

DOCTOR. MY HUSBAND'S HAD A STROKE.

6 At work, your boss discovers that you have been systematically incompetent and dishonest. You are looking at certain dismissal and a possible prison sentence. What course of action would you take?

a. Resign in disgrace and accept your punishment.
b. Deny all charges and try to ride the storm.
c. Accept early retirement on the grounds of 'ill health' with a fucking big lump sum and a full pension.

7 In the bathroom one morning, you notice that the toothpaste tube has been squeezed from the middle, and the top left off. What course of action do you take?

a. Replace the cap and think no more about it.
b. Make a joke of it over breakfast, hoping the culprit will get the message.

The police yesterday.

c. Lock each member of the family in a separate room and keep them awake for 5 days. Disorientate them with violent 'Nice & Nasty' mood swings and lead each one to believe that the others have made signed statements blaming them. When their spirit is broken, hand them a brief and innocuous statement to sign, the last two pages of which are blank, and to which you later add a fabricated confession.

7 You go into a shop to buy a hat. What sort do you choose?

a. A trilby hat.
b. A baseball hat.
c. A tall, black tit with a metal nipple.

8 Driving home from the pub, you are pulled over by a police car and breathalysed. The roadside test proves positive. What do you do?

a. Admit the offence and vow to change your ways.
b. Contest the result and demand a blood test at the station.
c. Flash your warrant card at the officer and drive merrily on your way.

9 What sort of person were you at school?

a. Studious and academic.
b. Sporting and competitive.
c. A big racist bully, pickpocket and thief with no friends.

10 What do you consider the most important skill you bring to your profession?

a. An ability to organise and work as a member of a team.
b. The capacity to solve problems quickly and imaginatively.
c. Being over 5 foot 10.

Tall and proud, a member of the Metropolitan police. How do you measure up?

HOW DID YOU DO?

MAINLY A'S: Oh, dear! You are fair, honest, hardworking and you always try to do the right thing. You are certainly not a copper, and never will be. There is no place in the police force for the likes of you.

MAINLY B'S: You are not definitely a copper, but on the other hand you are not definitely not a copper neither. You are somewhere in between. Perhaps you're a traffic warden or a security guard in Top Shop.

MAINLY C'S: Congratulations! You're the Fuzz. Tirelessly pounding the beat in your big, shiney shoes, you impartially dish out justice to young and old, black or white, paying particular attention to the young and black.

BILLY BOTTOM AND HIS ZANY TOILET PRANKS

AAH! WHAT A LOVELY DUMP. NOW TO WIPE ME ARSE

SOD IT! I'VE RAN OUT OF SHIT PAPER

SUPERMARKET
FRUIT
SHUFFLE! SHUFFLE!

THAT'S £40 PLEASE
BUGGER!..
I'VE FORGOT ME WALLET!

I'LL TRY TO WALK WITH ME CHEEKS APART SO I DON'T SPREAD IT AROUND TOO MUCH
SHUFFLE! SHUFFLE!

SHORTLY...
SUPERMARKET
WALLET
SHUFFLE! SHUFFLE!

BLOODY MARVELOUS. YOU NEVER RUN OUT OF PAPER WHEN Y'VE GOT RABBIT TODS, DO YOU? SOD'S LAW, IT IS.
ONLY EVER RUN OUT WHEN Y'VE GOT SHITE LIKE CREAM FUDGE

THERE YOU GO, LOVE!
SORRY..
WE DON'T DO BARCLAYCARD

OUTSIDE...
CASHPOINT
'URRY UP, PAL. ME RING PIECE'S ITCHIN' LIKE BUGGERY 'ERE

'ERE YOU ARE, LOVE. FORTY QUID CASH!...
NOW TO BUFF UP ME BROWN EYE

BUGGER IT. I'M TOO LATE. IT'S GONE AND DRIED ON ME ARSE

YOU DON'T MIND IF I SWAP THIS LOT FOR SOME 'WET WIPES' DO YOU, LOVE?
SHUFFLE! SHUFFLE!

SNATCHED!

Couple's heartache as baby is stolen

A couple who's new born baby was snatched from a hospital maternity unit by a woman posing as a nurse, faced an agonising wait whilst the search for a newspaper willing to pay for their story continued.

Maureen Cretis, 32, had given birth to daughter, Chloe, just eight hours before she was taken. Max Clifford was alerted when the baby's father, Stephen, 34, found her cot empty.

snatch

Their nightmare began about an hour after the snatch when Mr. Clifford informed them that immediate negotiations with papers in the local area had drawn a blank.

muff

He expressed his fears that the search for the tabloid may have to be extended to the rest of the country.

At an emotional press conference this morning, Stephen Cretis appealed for help.

"This is a complete nightmare" he said. "My heart goes out to anyone who has ever tried to sell a story to the papers." Fighting back tears, he added "I appeal to the editor who wants our story, whoever you are, please, please, give us the money now."

Cifford - yesterday

Benson & Hedges
CLOWN FAGS

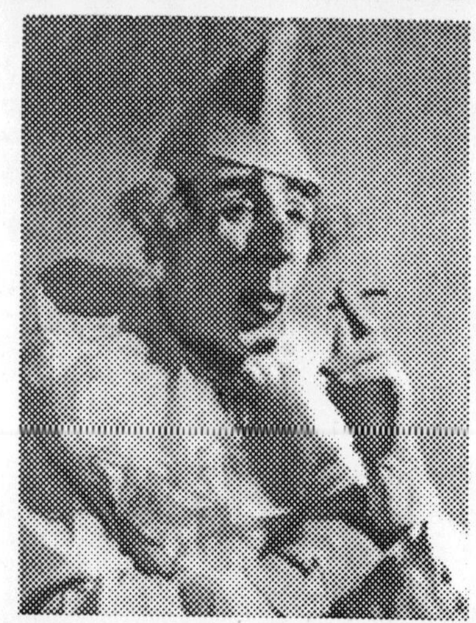

Government Health Warning

SMOKING FAGS CAN MAKE YOUR CAR DOORS FALL OFF

6mg Tar O.5mg Nicotine 3mg Custard Pies

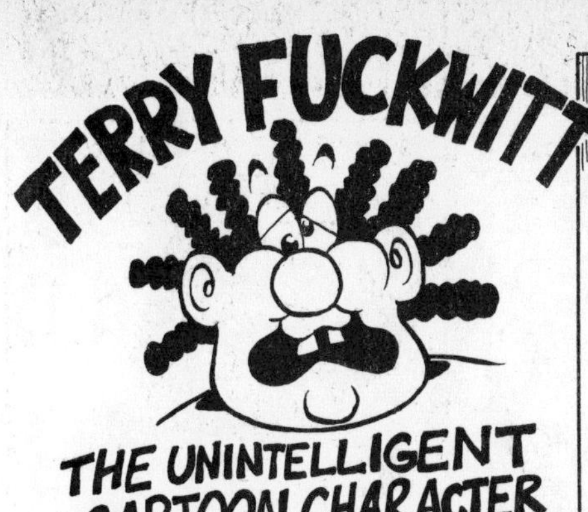
TERRY FUCKWITT
THE UNINTELLIGENT CARTOON CHARACTER

FUCK ME! I HAVEN'T GOT A CLUE.

AND YOU'VE GIVEN ME YOUR FINAL ANSWER?
YES.
A: The Eiffel Tower
C: The Cutty Sark
B: George Washington
D: Pigshit

YOU'RE SAYING THAT THE KIND OF SHIT THAT COMES OUT OF A PIG'S ARSE... IS ... THE CUTTY SARK?
ERM... YES.

IT'S THE WRONG ANSWER ... YOU'VE JUST LOST ONE MILLION POUNDS! I'M AFRAID THE AUDIENCE WAS NO HELP TO YOU.
ITV
PAY Terry Fuckwitt
FUCK ALL POUNDS
& FUCK ALL PENCE

ERM...
ERM...
FUCK ME!
GO WOLF GO!

FUCK ME! I KNEW I SHOULD HAVE GONE 50/50!
NOT ACTUALLY LIVE
T.V. STUDIO

HELLO TERRY. I'M GOD.
CAN YOU FUCKING BELIEVE IT!

I'M ON THE BOG AT THE MINUTE, AND I'VE LEFT THE OVEN ON. I DON'T WANT MY FINDUS CRISPY PANCAKES TO BURN...

ALL I ASK OF YOU MY SON, IS THAT YOU TURN THE OVEN OFF FOR ME... IF YOU DO THIS, YOUR SOUL SHALL BE CLEANSED AND YOU WILL LIVE IN MY KINGDOM FOREVER. AND 100 TONS OF GOLD.
OFF
ON

TERRY. I'M THE DEVIL.
I'VE GOT A BETTER IDEA. WHY DON'T YOU SELL ME YOUR SOUL FOR THIS DRIED-UP LITTLE DOG-SHIT?

ERM...

SO...
AAAAIIIIEE!!
HA! HA! HA!
HA! HA! HA!
RIIIP!
KRIIIP!
RIIIP!
KRIIIP!

200 BILLION YEARS LATER...
I'M BEGINING TO THINK I SHOULD HAVE TURNED THE OVEN OFF.
HA! HA! HA!
HA! HA! HA!
RIIIP!
KRIIIP!

YOUR TOP 100 Borderline

In issue 95, we asked you to nominate your Borderline Boilers, the kind of birds who are no oil paintings, but still manage to wet your palate. And you didn't let us down, sending in your favourite 'certain angle stunners' from stage, screen, sport and pop. Such was your response that we've been able to compile a chart of your top 100 rub-a-tug-boats - the Monkey Wenches that tighten your nuts.

1 Ginger Spice

Bitter and lonely ex-Girl-Power knicker flasher

Ginger Spice Geri Halliwell, despite being a porker-faced attention-craver of indeterminate vintage, is nevertheless, thanks to her big tits, what a lot of blokes really, really want. "I'd love my cock ***'2 become 1'*** with her ginger fanny," says Viz reader, the Rev. James Foucault, of Truro.

2 Anne McKevitt

Tiny carrot-topped Scott mott

She may need a ladder to paint the skirting board, but this strangely attractive bit of skirt is a welcome decoration to the Top Ten, and narrowly misses being your Top Dog.

"She's okay by me." writes T. Sinclair of Stoke. "I wouldn't mind being the wallpaper in her changing room when she's stripping. And I'd provide my own paste."

4 Monica Lewinsky

Ex-Whitehouse intern & Presidential spam flautist

Monica Lewinsky is a 'jizzy-frocked' testosterollercoater. You look at her and think 'she's alright'. Then you notice how fat she is. Then you remember she swallows.

"Chubby or not, I'd like to pop my slick willy into her oval orifice, I can tell you," writes J. Cursitor of Bristol.

3 Jilly Goolden

Elfin wine-guzzling gobshite

Petite, bubbly and very thirsty, Jilly has probably got the tiniest tits on telly but she's guaranteed to squeeze the juice out of any man's grapes.

"Despite her being a stuck-up batty old trout, I wouldn't mind giving her something to roll across her tongue. It might not burst with fruit, but it would certainly have a long finish and provide an excellent accompaniment for cheese and fish," writes J. Stonehill of London.

5 Charlie Dimmock

Bra-less peanut-smuggling TV gardener

Bonnie Bint Charlie is everybody's darling. With her dugs bouncing as she digs, there's healthy stalks of rhubarb springing up in every middle-aged viewer's Y-front garden.

"She might look a bit like a bloke, but I wouldn't turf her out of my flower bed, and that's for sure. Mind you, I'm desperate," confesses Mr. B. Gervasio of Lincoln.

6 Sian Lloyd

David Coulthard-jawed weather-girl

With her 'Tales-of-the-Unexpected' style hand-movements, and her ***'go to bed'*** eyes, Sian gets men's weathercocks spinning in her direction. "Granted, she's a bit long in the tooth" writes Mr. Gusset of Edinburgh, "but have you seen the size of her gob? I reckon you could get it in up to the nuts with room to spare. I'd probably send a few 'scattered showers' in her direction if she was up for it."

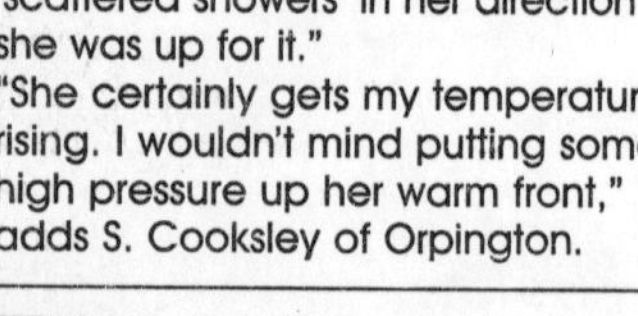

"She certainly gets my temperature rising. I wouldn't mind putting some high pressure up her warm front," adds S. Cooksley of Orpington.

7 Sue Barker

Ex-tennis pro & TV presenter

Woof! Woof! Sweet Sue was the darling of the Centre Court in the late seventies and romantically linked to Cliff Richard, if such a thing is possible. Despite her 'Lord Snowdon-like' face, it's 'A Question of Spurt' whenever she's on the telly. "I'm sure she'd make a racquet if I smashed my balls into her service box. And I'd soon have her love deuces flowing with a skilful forehand stroke. Ace!" writes Bertie from Merseyside.

8 Carol Vorderman

Leggy TV maths brainbox

Cambridge educated Carol reaches number 8 in our countdown of the top 100 'Happy Shopper Beauties'. And with a third class maths degree and second class looks, she adds up to a first class borderline boiler. "She's never off the telly," writes Phil Crowther of Bolton. "So I'm consonantly on the bonk."

Boilers

9 Sophie Dahl
Sexy cake monster

Sophie's your choice at number 9. A top class model and real stunner, who's voracious eating habits leave her with one foot in the boilerhouse. "After a hard day's work, there's nothing I'd like more than a long lie down on a well upholstered Sophie," says Turtle of Chiswick.

10 Helen Mirren
Ageing nymphet

Voted the sexiest woman in the world back in the sixties, the intervening decades have battered her once riveting looks and now she's a bit of a boiler. However, time has not withered her enthusiasm for getting her kit off, which we suspect may account for her prime position in your Top 100 Blart Chart.
"Unlike her namesake Helen of Troy, her face could only launch about three ships. Mind you, she could launch my skin boat any time she liked. Up her snatch," says Viz reader Ian Oxton of Dundee.

11 Fergie
Toe-gobbling Duchess of Pork

12 Barbara Windsor
Bubbly cockney EastEnders landlady

13 Anneka Rice
Wide-arsed, toothsome T.V. personality

14 Cheri Lunghi
Kenko Coffee woman

15 Anna Ryder-Richardson
Tiny-titted bone-bag

16 Maggie Philbin
Swap Shop ex-Mrs. Cheggers

17 Ruby Wax
Gobby Yank

18 Julia Somerville
Poor man's Anna Ford

19 Tina Turner
Wobbly-thighed lip curler

20 Katie Puckrick
Stunner (next to Hufty)

21 Margi Clarke
Frightening Street Star

22 Cheryl Baker
Crusty batch loaf

23 Suzi Quatro
Leather-clad moustachioed Rocker

24 Gina McKee
Lovely high-class actress - but nose and jaw not quite right

25 Venus Williams
Tennis elbow workout

26 Miss Brahms
Seventies semi-sexy stropstress

27 Niamh Cussack
Heartbeat missus

28 Letitia Dean
Blousy EastEnders heavy-weight

29 Carol Patterson
Zippy-mouthed actress out of EastEnders

30 Suzie Dent
Dictionary corner bookworm

31 Fern Britten
Meaty, beefy, big and bouncy

32 Felicity Kendal
Cabbage patch doll-faced actress

33 Celine Dion
Horse-faced Titanic warbler

34 Liza Tarbuck
Shopping bag

35 Kate Mulgrew
Male-voiced Star Trek actress

36 Meg Matthews
Noel's spouse blarty

37 Gillian Taylforth
Roadside assistance

38 Lily Savage
Scouse comedienne and leggy game show hostess

39 Anne Robinson
Slopey-faced watchdog

40 Patty Cauldwell
Fag-raddled hag

41 Dolly Parton
Enormous-titted Country singer

42 Gabrielle
Pop Dr. Hookalike

43 Lesley Joseph
Birds of a Feather nightmare

44 Goldie Hawn
Horny golden oldie

45 Camilla Parker-Bowles
Royal Bint

46 Maria Aitken
Cow-eyed convict's sister

47 Steffi Graff
Game,set and snatch

48 Honor Blackman
Dried-up Pussy Galore

49 Diane Keen
Wank-gesture coffee ad star

50 Linda Bellingham
Confessions film tit-out OXO mum

51 Anita Dobson
Brian May poodle-alike

52 Joan Collins
Room for four noses

53 Jill Gascoigne
Gentle Touch bossy boots

54 Carol Barnes
Anne Nightingale lookalike newsreader

55 Anne Nightingale
Carol Barnes lookalike D.J.

56 Henry Sandon
Overweight pottery dish

57 Barbara Streisand
Boz-eyed big-nosed songbird

58 Sue Lawley
Desert Island dish

59 Kate O'Mara
'Happy Shopper' Joan Collins

60 Cyndi Lauper
Loopy fun girl

61 Joan Bakewell
High class tart

62 Amanda Barrie
Coronation Street Cleopatra

63 Debbie Harry
Blondie bombshell (defused)

64 Sally Gunnel
Sporty half-a-gadge

65 Paula Yates
Hughie Green's pop-tart daughter

66 Sally Magnussen
God-bothering Viking crumpet

67 Debbie McGee
Conjuror's moll

68 Tracy Thorne
Everything but the Nicholas Lyndhurst lookalike

69 Emma Thompson
Posh luvvie

70 Cerys Mathews
Horny Welsh dragon

71 Alice Beer
Sunken-faced TV watchdog

72 Kirsten O'Brien
Aardvark's sidekick

73 Sue Cook
Nothing to write home about

74 Bette Midler
3 big hooters

75 Anne Diamond
Rough-cut gem

76 Lorraine Kelly
Full Scottish breakfast babe

77 Rula Lenska
Husky-voiced Minder wife

78 Joanna Lumley
Not so purdy these days

79 Toyah Battersby
Lardy mardy teen temptress

80 Molly Ringwald
Not so pretty in pink

81 Emma Freud
Intellectual wingnut

82 Penelope Keith
Parrot-faced pretend snob

83 Sally Whittaker
Sparrow-faced actress

84 Samantha Janus
Rough as a badger's arse

85 Lisa Stansfield
Towbar-conked Lancashire lark.

86 Michelle Collins
Old-faced youngster

87 Suzanne Danielle
Turkey titted Carry-on crow

88 Tara Palmer-Tomkinson
Tiny-titted toff

89 Jayne Torville
Frosty ice-queen

90 The Girls out of the Human League
A brace of Yorkshire slappers

91 The tall one out of Bananarama
The tall one out of Bananarama

92 Delia Smith
Tea-time treat

93 Grace Jones
Scary Amazon

94 Michelle Smith
Drug-free swimmer

95 Anabelle Giles
Posh stick insect

96 Bunny Campione
Road show antique

97 Anni-Frid Lyngstad
Dark haired one out of ABBA

98 Princess Stephanie
Royal tattooed gadgy-wife

99 Jamie Lee Curtis
Buoyant-knockered actress

100 Shirley Bassey
Old flingtits

Remember, next year, many of these borderline boilers may have strayed across the border into no-man's land. So keep your nominations coming in, and we'll publish an updated list of your tastiest slightly-off cheesecake next year.

LetteRBOcKs

It's the page that's always funny, But never seems to pay out money

A fiver for every letter we publish. (In fact, it's already in the post)

Letterbocks
Viz
PO Box 1PT
Newcastle upon Tyne
NE99 1PT

viz@viz.co.uk

Star Letter

*I read in an article recently that one third of road accidents are caused by people who have been drinking too much, and one quarter are caused by people driving too quickly. It doesn't take a genius to work out that too thirds are therefore caused by people who have not had enough to drink, and three quarters by people who drive too slowly. This means that people who drive quickly whilst over the limit are twelve times safer than those who are sober and obey the speed limit.

David Clayton
My Bog

Put down boy

*People say that every dog has its day. How right they are. We got a dog for Christmas, got bored with it and had it put down on Boxing Day.

Graeme Kenna
Wallasey

*"Nobody ever comes to Cyprus just once", so the tourism advert says. My dad did. He was ran over and killed by a bus in Limmasol on the first day of his holiday.

I. Porterfield
Sunderland

Roll up, roll up

*I've just had a massive shit, then noticed that there isn't any toilet paper. If either of my parents, who are avid Viz readers, happen to be reading this, could you please throw a toilet roll up onto the landing.

J. Tudor
Sheffield

*What a load of rubbish this new 'foil wrapped bread' is. It's supposed to last for 7 days. I ate mine in two. Do I win £10?

Chris Pether
e-mail

YOU'VE BEEN FOUND GUILTY BY THIS COURT, OF STEALING THINGS YOU SAID YOU BOUGHT, I'LL SENTENCE YOU AND SHED NO TEARS, YOU'LL GO TO JAIL FOR SEVEN YEARS

JUDGE

IT'S POETIC JUSTICE

Up, up and away

*Following his latest farcical failure to fly around the world in a balloon, Richard Branson reports that his wife is encouraging him to have another attempt. Well if I was married to a billionaire who looked like a cross between Noel Edmonds and Mr. Shifter the PG Tips chimp, I'd be egging him on too. In fact I'd be blowing his next balloon up before he'd had the chance to dip his last one in the sea.

Mrs. T. Currie
Sheffield

Red flag week

*I expect Tony Blair is very relieved that his 'honeymoon period' is over. My wife had one of those, and it really pissed on my fire, I can tell you.

S.S.
Glossop

*I think it's a disgrace that the hard shoulder on motorways is reserved for broken down vehicles or accident victims. Why should irresponsible motorists who can't be bothered to look where they're going or service their car enjoy the privilege of their own lane? It's madness gone mad. I suggest that in future the hard shoulder should be reserved for cars with a full service history, and no dents.

Mark Glover
Coventry

Monumental error

*Britain is littered with war memorials dedicated to "those that have laid down" and "those who have fallen" during two world wars. Has anybody considered building a monument to the poor sods who weren't bone lazy or too clumsy to keep their footing and who actually got shot?

W. Donachie
Dundee

A MOUSE'S head mounted on a Blue Peter badge makes an ideal hunting trophy for a sporting cat.
J. Montgomery, Hilton

GIVE your children ideal 'Riverdancing' practice by pinning their sleeve cuffs to their trouser pockets and sending them out on icy days.
James Thompson, Tiverton

WOMEN. When paying for petrol with cash always carry 3p in change as you will invariably go over the 'tenners worth' which you intended to buy.
Dave Potts, Cramlington

ENCOURAGE your teenage sons to read more by leaving books in black bin bags under the garden hedge.
J.T.,Thropton

MICE. Toothpicks make excellent snooker cues-
ELEPHANTS. Snooker cues make excellent toothpicks-
TOOTHPICKS. Mice make excellent elephants-
SNOOKER CUES. Elephants make excellent mice, etc.
A. Bond, Greenwich

CAULIFLOWERS make ideal 'brains' for vegetable Frankenstein monsters.
Joseph Tams, Torquay

SPRINKLE cat litter on the sofa whenever granny comes to call. This will alleviate smells in the likely event of any geriatric leakage.
John Tait, Thropton

BUY a meal from Marks & Spencers then eat it. If you are still hungry afterwards, take it back and say that it wasn't big enough.
S.T., Newcastle Polyversity

FOOTBALL managers. Avoid unsightly yelling from the touchline by equipping your players with pagers and discreetly using a mobile phone to contact them. The pagers could also be used by the supporting crowd, to send messages of congratulation to any goal scorers.
Sir Giles T. Ardenflesche, Kensington

A HULA HOOP inserted into a small hole drilled in a door provides an inexpensive security viewing device.
J. Tomacnevski, Tromsk

BIG ISSUE publishers. Save time and distribution costs by introducing a subscription service. Every week, interested readers could receive a copy by post and there'd be no need for innocent shoppers like me to have to circumnavigate tramps on every street corner to avoid buying it.
Rob Thompson, e-mail

FRESHEN up your mouth and remove even the most stubborn of stray pubic hairs after a night on the fuzzy clam by brushing your teeth with Immac cream.
John T., Morpeth

∗If my vicar genuinely believes that it is better to give than to receive, why doesn't he put his hand in his pocket and stick £100 on the collection plate next Sunday? The congregation can do the receiving for a change.

G. Salmon
Sheffield

∗New Labour promised that the New Year's Honours list would represent the people's choice, and they haven't let us down. Who can forget the nationwide clamour as the public rose up and with one voice demanded that Michael Scholar, the Permanent Secretary to the Department of Trade be made Knight Commander of the Order of Bath?

Martin Chivers
Southampton

∗Why does Prince Naseem get a gong just because he's good at punching people? I'm brilliant at it but the most I've ever got is 200 hours community service.

A Woodward
Sheffield

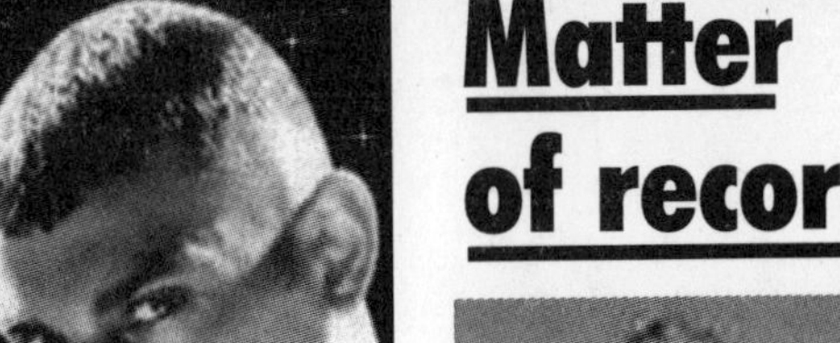

Matter of record

∗Note to Richard Branson. People who successfully set aviation records, Charles Lindbergh, Alcock and Brown, Louis Bleriot etc., tend to do it on their first attempt.

David Young
Sunderland

Principle objection

∗According to boffins, for every action, there is an equal and opposite reaction. Bollocks. I recently ran over an old woman, and she didn't get up and run over my car.

D. Sisson
Kirby

WELCOME to the brand new game where if you're lucky YOU could get to kick millionaire television game show host Chris Tarrant as hard as you like right up his fucking jacksie.

The rules are simple. We ask you an easy multiple choice question. If you answer it correctly, you could plant a hobnail boot up Chris Tarrant's chocolate starfish. If you want to play, simply send £5 cash to our usual address, then answer the following question.

What is a fish?

Is it *(a) a bird?*
Is it *(b) a mammal?*
Is it *(c) an insect?*
Or is it *(d) a fish?*

Write your answer here .... then turn to page 31 to see if you win.

OI! KEEP IT DOWN! SOME PEOPLE ARE TRYING TO SLEEP!
DEAF INSTITUTE

The Adventures of MAJOR MISUNDERSTANDING

BUSHELL ON THE DOCS

I was against euthanasia until I tried it for myself... *now I've changed my mind*.

OAP-LESS! That's what I always thought of euthanasia. A group of stuck-up docs sticking their noses and syringes in where they weren't wanted, and knocking off our old folk before their time.

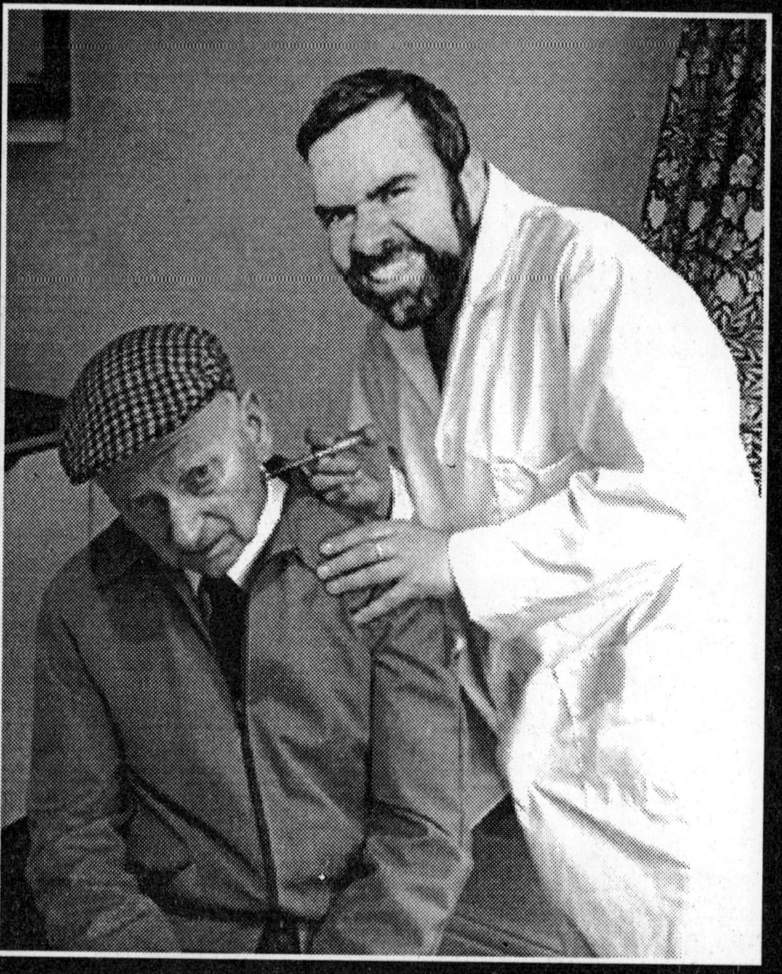

GET STUCK IN...Garry gets ready to euthanase some old bloke

Don't get me wrong. I'm not some bleeding-heart liberal with a rose-tinted view of the old.

By GARRY BUSHELL

I know they're not the kindly, twinkly-eyed grandparents you see in the Werther's Originals advert. I was brought up in the middle of London, and I've seen the havoc a Chelsea Pensioner can cause to a queue of people trying to get on a bus.

Even so when I was invited to go along and see a mercy killing for myself in a Staffordshire nursing home, I went along not expecting to have my opinions altered one bit.

How wrong I was.

The first thing that struck me was the pageantry. There can be few more stirring sights on an English summer morning than a group of physicians in their splendid white coats and shiny stethoscopes gathered in the lobby of a nursing home.

My second surprise was how friendly everyone was, standing round laughing and joking over a glass of sherry.

My third surprise was that they weren't all toffee-nosed doctors.

"All sorts of people turn out to follow the action at a mercy killing," said Wendy Hardboard, a ward orderly. "There are nurses, consultants, physiotherapists - even a couple of airline pilots and a lorry driver. It's very much a social occasion."

A very social occasion. I hardly have time to finish my sherry and we're off.

The doctors stop at the end of the first corridor. Nothing seems to be happening. Then suddenly, a flash of beige from the breakfast room and the chase is on.

The baying doctors pick up his unmistakable scent and set off in hot pursuit. I'm caught up in the excitement as the pack careers along the corridor, knocking furniture and visiting relatives flying.

Our prey is a sly old fellow, surprisingly fast, and is heading for the safety of the day room.

"Most old people get away," says euthanasia enthusiast Edward Chipboard, as we try to work out our old man's likely route. "The ones we do catch tend to be the weak, senile or the terminally ill."

We finally run down our quarry. He's cowering in the corner of the dining room, whimpering, his rheumy eyes filled with terror. He knows he is beaten. The chief consultant moves in for the kill with his syringe.

It's exciting for sure. But is it right?

"Euthanasia isn't cruel," insists Chipboard. "This way, the end is relatively quick and painless. It's certainly a lot kinder than allowing them to linger on up to a very old age."

I thought I'd be spending my day with a bunch of murderous hooray henrys. But what I saw changed my mind.

Euthanasia may not be everyone's cup of tea, but one thing is for certain -

The people who oppose it are slushy, mis-informed, sentimental, misguided Marxists.

And if you accept that the aged population has to be controlled, which everybody does, then anaesthetic overdose is far less cruel than the alternatives - smothering them, pushing them down the stairs or attacking them with hammers.

Next week Garry says - Bring back old-fashioned variety. And shoot all the puffs.

MILLIE TANT and her radical conscience

DING! DONG!
DING! DONG!
DING! DONG!
DING! DONG!

OKAY! LET'S HAVE A NICE BIG GROUP PICTURE, WITH THE HAPPY COUPLE AND ALL THE BRIDESMAIDS.
MILLIE! MILLIE! THAT'S YOU TOO!

AS I HAVE ALREADY SAID, JAYNE, I AM NOT AT ALL HAPPY ABOUT BEING DRESSED AS A MALE MASTURBATION FANTASY!
CLUMP!
CLOMP!

ON SECOND THOUGHTS, LET'S NOT BOTHER WITH THE BRIDESMAIDS... THIS LENS COST 150 QUID.

OOH. I DO LIKE A NICE WEDDING.
PAH! YOU'RE NO BETTER THAN A SLAVE TRADER!
OH DEAR. AM I?

OF COURSE YOU ARE! PRESIDING OVER A CEREMONY GIVING RELIGEOUS CREDENCE TO THE ENSLAVEMENT OF A WOMAN. SHE IS NO MORE THAN HIS PROPERTY. TO DO WITH AS HE WILL.

DO YOU TAKE THIS WOMAN? THOSE WERE YOUR WORDS. TAKE! TAKE!... BELIEVE ME HE WILL TAKE HER... IN A CEREMONIAL RAPING RITUAL TONIGHT! FORCED AGAINST HER WILL, DE-FLOWERED AS MILLIONS OF HER SISTERS BEFORE HER!...
!
PROD! PROD!

..FORCED AGAIN AND AGAIN TO ENJOY... I MEAN ENDURE, THE ENGORGED PHALLUS AS IT THRUSTS IN AND OUT, IN AND OUT, IN AND OUT, FASTER AND HARDER, FASTER AND HARDER, IN-OUT, IN-OUT, SHAKE IT ALL ABOUT, HE DOES THE HOKEY-COKEY AND HE TURNS AROUND, THAT'S WHAT IT'S ALL ABOUT!...
...erm... SISTERS.

HEAVE! HOOOH! HEAVE! HOOOH! HEAVE! HOOOH! HEAVE! HOOOH! HEAVE! HOOOH! HEAVE! HOOOH!

SHORTLY...
HERE GOES!
TOSS!

KLATTER!

IT'S ME! IT'S ME! IT'S ME! I'M NEXT! I'M NEXT!...
SKIP!
...ERM...

BOOOMPH!

FRU T. BUNN the MASTER BAKER & HIS GINGERBREAD SEX DOLLS

RUN FOR YOUR LIFE!
A TRUE STORY OF MEN WITH GUNS
The Berlin Olympics of 1936 provided Adolf Hitler with the perfect opportunity to show off his so-called master race. But one man, the recently selected British sprinter Brad Travers was determined to prove him wrong.
On the first bend Travers took an early lead

OK BRAD, JUST KEEP RUNNING ALONG THE TRACK.
But Travers' ears were burning
Meanwhile the German bench were discussing an early switch of tactics.
WHISPER,WHISPER...

Under starters orders.
DREI, ZWEI, EIN!
HERE GOES...

CRIKEY, THAT WAS CLOSE!
From the midday sun a low flying Messerschmitt took the British athlete by surprise, a ricochet catching his calf.

The German runner was closing in fast.

WATCH YOUR STEP HERR BRITISHER, HA HA.

HMM, I WONDER WHAT HE MEANT BY THAT?

Moments later he found out exactly what he meant as a land mine exploded sending him 15 feet into the air.

HAPPY LANDINGS, HA HA.

Within seconds he was back in the race and closing in on the rest of the field.
HMFP!

With the finishing line in sight the British athlete pulled ahead.
IF I CAN JUST...

As Travers crossed the line, he disappeared beneath the tracks of a German Panzer, but not before he had secured the Gold Medal.

1
2
3
Brad Travers went on to receive the Victoria Cross and, with his Olympic ambitions in ruins, Hitler decided to try full scale war instead.

The end

JOHNNY FARTPANTS
THERE'S ALWAYS A LOUD BANG IN HIS UNDERCRACKERS...
...AND A PAPER HAT

CHRISTMAS MORNING...
HEY, GREAT! IT'S BEEN SNOWING!

IN FACT, I'M SO HAPPY I COULD SING...

IN THE LANE, SNOW IS FALLING, AND MY ARSE SMELLS APPALLING, IT'S CHRISTMAS AGAIN, AND I CAN'T REFRAIN, FROM FARTING IN A WINTER CHUNDERLAND

ON MY PLATE, IS A PLUM-DUFF, THAT WILL BREW UP A BUM-GUFF...

WITH TWIGLETS AND NUTS, ROTTING MY GUTS, I'M FARTING IN A WINTER CHUNDERLAND
B-R-RAAAP!

THE FAMILY WATCH THE BOND FILM ON THE TELLY, GATHERED ALL AROUND THE YULETIDE LOG...

SUDDENLY THE AIR IS RATHER SMELLY, LUCKILY THEY THINK IT IS THE DOG
PFFSSSS SSSSSS
YIPE!
BOOT!

I'LL GO OUT, CAROL-SINGING, THOUGH MY RING WILL BE MINGING. THEY'LL GET QUITE A FRIGHT, WHEN I PUMP "SILENT NIGHT," FARTING IN A WINTER CHUNDERLAND
?
QUACKETY-QUACK!

THEN NEXT DOOR, AT THE VICAR'S, I BLOW OFF IN MY KNICKERS...
A-ROO-GA!

HE'S PRAYING FOR AIR, BUT WE JUST DON'T CARE. WE'RE FARTING IN A WINTER CHUNDERLAND

THE NEIGHBOURS BUILD A SNOWMAN IN THE GARDEN, THE BIGGEST AND THE BEST ONE IN THE TOWN...

THEN WITHOUT A PLEASE OR BEG YOUR PARDON, I'LL POINT MY ARSE AT HIM AND FART HIM DOWN
BRAP-AP-AP-AP-AP!
ON THE FROZEN DUCKPOND I'LL GO GLIDING, POWERED BY MY ARSE I'M SURE TO WIN...
FINISH
F-WOOOF-VROOOM!
TO STOP THE LOSERS GIVING ME A HIDING, I'LL FART AND MELT THE ICE SO THEY FALL IN
G-ROAR!
LATER ON, I'LL SEE SANTA. AFTER TWELVE TINS OF FANTA...
GROTTO
GURGLE!
BLOIK!
RUMBLE!
GLOOP!
CHUFF THE BEARD OFF HIS FACE, IT'S SUCH A DISGRACE, FARTING IN A WINTER CHUNDERLAND
BLART!
IN THE STREET THE SALLY ARMY BRASS BAND, IS RAISING CASH FOR OLD FOLK AND THE POOR...
OOM-PA!
OOM-PA!
TOOT!
PARP!
I JOIN IN WITH A BLAST OF METHANE GAS AND, THEY'RE FALLING DOWN LIKE FLIES UPON THE FLOOR
BOOM-PARP!
(RUMP-ET VOLUNTARY)
WALKING HOME, THROUGH THE SNOW, WITH MY ARSE CHEERS A-GLOW, I'M HAPPY TO SAY, I'VE SPENT THE WHOLE DAY...
...FARTING IN A WINTER CHUNDERLAND!
SHORTLY...
I'M SURE I SAW HIM COME INTO THE PARK. HE'S GOT TO BE AROUND HERE SOMEWHERE
YES, I CAN SMELL A BEEFY EGGO
OO-ER!
THERE HE IS!

ravey davey gravy
LARGE AS YOU LIKE IN
IBIZA

Bidip!.. Blidip!.. Blidip!..
PARP! Blidip! Blidip!
Blidip! HONK!

HEY! I'M IN IBIZA TRANCE ORBIT!
YEAH! IBIZA RAVE ON!
Blidip!.. Blidip!.. Blidip!
PARP! Blidi TOOT!

Blip! Blip! Blip! Plip
BLAM! BLAM!
I'M IN THE PLACE, I'M OFF ME FACE!

BLAM! BLAM! BLAM!
Plip! plip! plip! plip!
AN' WHAT PHAT SOUNDS!
YEAH! CHUNKY!

Blidip!.. Blidip!.. Blidip!.. Blidip!..
SQUARP!.. Blidip!.. Blidip!..
HEY, WE WERE ON OUR WAY TO 'ES PARADIS' AN' WE HEARD YER SCHWINGING CHOONS
HONK!
COME IN!.. HANDS ON!

Blidip!.. Blidip!.. Blidip! QUACK! PARP!
Blip!.. HONK! QUACK! Splapadappada
BLAM! Bidip! Blidip! Blidip! Blidip! SQUIT!
HEY, YER PIPIN' SOME FULL SPEC SOUNDS
CHEERS...
MING! MING! MING!
...TELL YOU WHAT THOUGH, BOD... IT'S THE LAST TIME I EAT PAELLA

Christmas Day TV Choice

your essential guide to what's on TV this Christmas...

Christmas Day:

9.00 BBC1: Kilroy Lively debate-Today's subject, TV presenters who go on Daytime telly shitfaced. **9.30 BBC2: Celebrity Changing Graves** Anne McKevitt jazzes up Les Dawson's traditional oak coffin with some leopard print fun-fur and a pot of funky coloured paint, and Laurence Llewellyn-Bowen transforms Bill Owen's staid casket into a Louis XIV fantasy palace whilst Handy Andy nicks the corpse's watch and wedding ring. **11.00 BBC1: Sleep Tight** Not-very-good-but-she's-blonde vet Trude Mostue puts down the pets of the stars. **12.30 BBC1: Christmas Sporting Bloomers** Four mundane clips of footballers' mistimed passes are spun out by means of interminable slow motion repeats and Terry Wogan's lame linking banter into this two hour Christmas Day spectacular. **2.30 BBC2: Can't Think of an Original Programnme, Won't Think of an Original Programme** Two commissioning editors battle it out to dish up a single creative thought. Presented by Ainsley Harriot. **3.00 BBC1: HRH The Queen** Miserable old cow talks wank in a dead posh voice. **3.15 BBC1: Brown Bread** A new bittersweet sitcom from the pen of Carla Lane, set in the chapel of Rest at a Liverpool Cancer Hospital. **4.00 ITV: Not Doing Much** Hermitage docusoap. It's Christmas day and Dominic is staring at the wall of his cave. Suddenly, nothing else happens. Narrated by Peter O'Sullivan. **4.30 ITV: You've Been Decapitated** More hilarious fire brigade videos of industrial accidents, introduced by Lisa Riley wearing a flamboyant multicoloured tent to disguise her planetoid girth. **5.00 ITV: Wheel of Fortune** The Same shit as all year, but streak of piss John Leslie wears a Santa costume in the picture in the TV Times. **5.30 BBC1: Helicopter Police Doctor Vet** Nettleship, the unconventional antique dealing mountain resue pathologist with marital troubles is back for a new series. Stars Nick Berry, or if wet, Kevin Whately. **7.00 ITV: Emmerdale** Mandy tells Zack that Seth Armstrong is Amos Brearley's dad, and spurned lesbian Zoe Tate eats Marlon's herion and jumps off the Woolpack. **7.30 ITV: Coronation Street** Emily Bishop tells husband Ernie that her nephew Spider, is really Gail Tilsley's lovechild by Albert Tatlock. Meanwhile, Les Battersby rapes Minnie Cauldwell six ways, including arse, and she throws herself off the Rovers onto a big spike. **8.00 BBC1: Eastenders** Dirty Den confesses to Ethel's dog, Little Willie that Pete Beale is the father of the taxi driver he murdered in Germany forty years ago. Grant gives Phil the BBC's first pre-watershed lesbian kiss, and in a fit of jealousy, Dot Cotton jumps 80 feet from the roof of the Queen Vic, through a flaming hoop and lands in a bath of acid only 8 inches across. **8.30 Ch4: Brookside** On his cannibal deathbed, Sinbad confesses to Mick that he caused only 6 of the 14 explosions in the Close this year. Meanwhile Max, in a strait-jacket and padlocked upside down in a milk churn is trying to come to terms with Jimmy Corkhill's sex-change revelation that Barry Grant is not the father of Heather Haversham's two-headed snake baby. After eating dynamite, Ladies and Gentlemen, a blindfold Anabelle Collins is shot from a cannon over the Great Pyramid of Cheops, landing in a flaming thimbleful of deadly poison balanced on unicycling Ron Dixon's nose. Meanwhile, a phonecall brings unwelcome news for Terry. **9.00 BBC2: Panorama** - Is TV dumbing down? Presented by Dale Winton and Maureen from Driving School. **9.30 BBC1: Before They Were Born** Angus Deayton ambushes the stars with more hilarious footage of their mother's embarrassing ultrasound scans. **10.15 BBC1: Last of the Birds of a Grave and Horses** An hour and a quarter of Christmas hilarity with all your favourite catch-phrases, as BBC contract sitcom writers once again get the chance to prove that 25 minutes is the ideal length for a sitcom. **11.00 BBC2: Charlie Dimmock's Pneumatic Drill Masterclass** Seasonal fun with the big-titted gardener. **11.45 Ch5: Hallelujah! It's Raining Spunk** 1992 TVM. Erotic Drama.

Rogue Trader Shot Dead

By our financial staff, a man who, if he knew half as much as he pretends he knows, wouldn't have to write a shitty newspaper column to pay his bills

Police marksmen last night shot dead a rogue trader after he ran amok on the floor of the London Stock Exchange.

There was a desperate scramble for the exits as the 13 ½ stone bull trader careered across the trading floor, trampling several stockbrokers and causing damage estimated at tens of thousand pounds.

ferried

Trading was halted for 3 hours whilst a fleet of ambulances ferried the dead and injured to nearby hospitals.

trawlered

The rogue trader was eventually cornered near a basket of foreign currencies and killed with a single shot to the head.

Stock Exchange - massacre

A spokesman for Kleinwort Benson Clearing Bank said. "It's a great shame.

frigated

"These normally placid creatures usually spend their day roaming the floor looking to make vast profits for doing nothing. We suspect this one may have been financially wounded by falling gold prices and had come in search of a six figure bonus."

FELIX
AND HIS AMAZING UNDERPANTS

HI, READERS. I LOVE A GOOD SCARY FILM, ME.
ROXY
ALL THIS WEEK: THE BLAIR WITCH PROJECT

ROCK-HARD ICE CREAM £10 A TUB
I'M SORRY EVERYONE, BUT THE POPCORN MACHINE HAS BROKEN DOWN!
WATERED DOWN COLA £6
KNACKERED
BOO!
!

DON'T WORRY. WHY NOT POP THE KERNELS IN MY UNDERPANTS?
...I'LL HEAT THEM UP BY RUBBING THE CHEEKS OF MY ARSE TOGETHER!
GOOD IDEA, FELIX!

OKAY. STAND BACK.

SHORTLY~
RUB! RUB! RUB!
HOW ABOUT THIS FOR "BUTTOCK-KISSED" POPCORN, EH?
REGULAR, PLEASE.
POP! POP! POP!
ME NEXT.
YES THEN ME!
HOORAY FOR FELIX!

IZZY WIZZY, LET'S GET BUSY! CACKLE! CACKLE!
CRIPES! THIS FILM REALLY IS SCARY!

EXCUSE ME. I'M ABSOLUTELY TERRIFIED OF THIS FILM. WOULD YOU MIND IF I HID IN YOUR UNDERPANTS UNTIL THE SCARY BITS ARE OVER?
NOT AT ALL. I'D BE DELIGHTED!

ACTUALLY, WE'RE ALL TERRIFIED. WOULD YOU MIND IF WE ALL HID IN YOUR UNDERCRACKERS?
ER, NOT AT ALL. THE MORE THE MERRIER.

COME ON! COME ON! MOVE RIGHT DOWN TO THE BACK OF THE PANTS, PLEASE!

SHORTLY~
EXCUSE ME. IS THE SCARY BIT OVER YET?
NO, NOT QUITE.

HEY! THOSE UNDERPANTS ARE IN BREACH OF FIRE AND SAFETY REGULATIONS!
EH?

IT'S DARK IN THERE, IT'S OVERCROWDED, IT STINKS, IT'S SWEATY, AND THERE'S NO ROOM TO BREATHE!

HMM! YOU'RE RIGHT...

SKIDDERS NIGHTCLUB
SORRY, PAL. NOBODY'S ALLOWED INTO THESE PANTS WEARING TRAINERS!
NEW YEAR'S EVE MILLENIUM ADMISSION PRICE £2,500
GPD. ST. SD. DJ. AC/LEW STRINGER.. VIZ 99

Who killed

IT is now four months since the cold-blooded doorstep slaying of People's Presenter Jill Dando. And still the police seem no nearer to catching her killer. So we've asked Britain's best known ex-policeman (apart from Geoff Capes) to try and crack the case.

In an amazing series of interviews, **JOHN STALKER** uses his vast experience as deputy Chief Constable of Greater Manchester and garage door salesman to pick the brains of four famous T.V. detectives in the hope that their unconventional approach may help shed light on this bewildering case and enable him to finally name Jill's killer.

"**I HAVE** always had the greatest respect and professional admiration for **Lieutenant Columbo**. With his tenacity, intuition and his squinty eye for detail, he always gets his man. So I asked him how he would go about solving this 'Whodunit?'"

"**AS ANY** police officer will tell you, the most important part of a copper's equipment, after a canister of C.S. gas and a big stick, is his sense of humour. No matter how tragic and appalling the crimes that confront him, he must never lose the ability to have a good laugh. That is why I admire **Inspector Jacques Clouseau** of the French Surete."

Case No.1

Investigator: **Lieutenant Columbo**
Status: **L.A.P.D. (Homicide)**
Channel: **ITV**

"This is typical of the cases I handle," the glass-eyed, cigar-chomping sleuth told me. "A high-profile celebrity victim and no obvious motive. If I were investigating this case, the finger of suspicion might point at a fellow star. For the sake of hypothesis, somebody like, oh, I don't know, Sir Cliff Richard, for example.

"When I first interview him he would be cooperative and helpful, even to the extent of signing a record for my wife, Mrs. Columbo. After the interview, I'd leave, only to reappear almost immediately, ruffling my hair and looking puzzled, to ask one more question about Sir Richard's movements on the morning of Miss Dando's death. This time, after I leave, Cliff's smile would fade and his expression would harden. I would then begin to badger Sir Cliff, turning up unexpectedly to ask him more questions. I'd appear unannounced at music rehearsals, or interrupt a game of tennis in the grounds of his Weybridge mansion, shambling across the lawn in my raincoat saying there were still one or two things 'bugging me'. By now, Cliff would have become quite terse, eventually turning openly hostile.

"Finally I would confront Cliff with a flimsy web of circumstantial evidence and supposition, at which point it would be game, set and match to me."

Case No.2

Investigator: **Inspector Clouseau**
Status: **French Surete**
Channel: **BBC 1**

"I would arrive at Gowan Avenue. My attention would be drawn immediately to a man with a minkey," the inspector told me at his Paris headquarters. "I would question him and he would mock my accent, whilst Mlle. Dando's killer made his getaway behind me; I might even hold up the traffic, enabling him to make good his escape in a blue Range Rover.

"I would report to my superior officer, Inspector Dreyfuss, who would twitch unconvincingly, as I outlined my ill-conceived theories on Mlle. Dando's murder. He would become confused between a real pistol and a novelty cigarette lighter on his desk, shooting the end off his nose as a result.

"A combination of farcical circumstances, including being blown up by a berm whilst dressed as Toulouse Lautrec, and knocking over a large rack of precariously poised long clattering things in the presence of a supercilious butler, would eventually somehow lead to me being convicted of the murder, whilst the real perpetrator escaped over the alps in a convertible Rolls Royce."

Dan-do?

Stalker's Telly 'tecs search for Star's assassin.

"**AFTER** 25 years at the sharp end of coppering, and more recently selling garage doors, if I have learned one thing it is this: That no motive is too far fetched, no matter how ghastly the crime. Never more so than in this case, where none of the facts seem to add up. A perfect case then for Scooby Doo and the kids in the Mystery Machine."

"**JIMMY NAIL'S** Spender is a no-nonsense North East copper. Like his name suggests, James Aloysious Bradford, is as hard as nails and twice as good at acting, and he has a distinct advantage over other T.V. detectives. For, as writer, director and producer, Jimmy can choose who the villain is going to be, no matter how ridiculous and implausible the plot, or laughable the dialogue. So I asked Crocodile Shoes himself how he would 'nail' Jill Dando's killer."

Case No.3

Investigator: **Scooby Do**

Status: **Independent Investigator**

Channel: **Cartoon Network**

"By coincidence our brightly coloured van would run out of gas during a thunder-storm, right outside the old Dando place," Fred told me. "Myself, Daphne, Velma, Shaggy and Scoob would go inside in search of clues. Whilst in the basement, Shaggy would discover a revolving bookcase, from behind which would emerge a sweaty man with a mobile phone. Scooby would then jump into Shaggy's arms, and the sweaty man would chase them along a very long corridor, passing the same objects at regular intervals." "Like, yeah!", Shaggy contin-ued, "Then we would, like, drop a net onto the sweaty man, and tie him up, whilst waiting for the police to arrive, before removing his sweaty man mask, to reveal... the estate agent!" "It would turn out that the estate agent who was selling Miss Dando's home had dis-covered an abandoned gold mine in the basement. He had dressed up as a sweaty man with a mobile phone and shot the 'Crimewatch' presenter on the doorstep, in order to scare off potential buyers. At this point, whilst being led away, the estate agent may well suggest that he would have got away with it, too, if it hadn't of been for us meddling kids.

Case No.4

Investigator: **Jimmy Nail**

Status: **Plain clothes detective**

Channel: **BBC 1**

"I've got the perfect plan," said Jimmy, "I'd hide up a tree and wait for the murder-er to walk past, then jump out and shout, 'Bastaaad!' Then I'd run faster than a train and chase him in a hot air balloon."

Well, we've looked at the clues through the eyes of four very different T.V. detectives; one a maverick scruff in a raincoat, one a comedy Frenchman who's been dead for 18 years, one a cartoon dog and the other a Geordie twat. It's time for me to name the killer.

Who killed Dan-do?

There is no obvious answer. But one thing's for sure. With me, former Deputy Chief Constable John Stalker, and all my fictional police friends on the case, the killer, or killers, whoever he, she, or they, is or are, will not be sleeping well in his, her, or their bed, or beds, tonight.

THE ADVENTURES OF THE SANDWICHES AND THEIR ATTEMPTS AT WORLD DOMINATION

SOON...

LATER...
BAH. FOILED AGAIN
TIN WRAP

THE ADVENTURES OF IAN PAISLEY

"IT'S THE WAY I YELL 'EM!"

RIGHT!.. MISS WORLD SASH, MICKEY MOUSE GLOVES AND JUVENILE JAZZ-BAND DRUM!!!

I'M ALL SET TO MARCH DOWN THE GUVAKKY ROAD!

WAIT A MINUTE!..
WHERE'S MY STAN LAUREL HAT!?!

HELL FIRE AND DAMNATION!!!
IT'S BEEN ATTACKED BY PAPIST MOTHS!

SO...
HAT SHOP

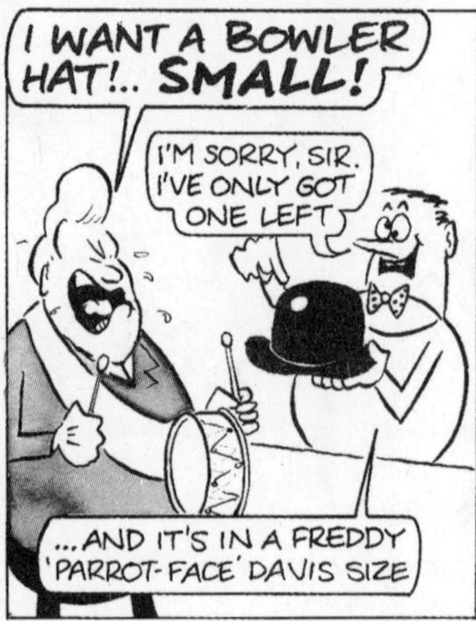
I WANT A BOWLER HAT!.. SMALL!
I'M SORRY, SIR. I'VE ONLY GOT ONE LEFT
...AND IT'S IN A FREDDY 'PARROT-FACE' DAVIS SIZE

CLANG! TISH! CLANG! TISH!

BONK!

PARAMILLINERY
BOWLERS · BERETS BALACLAVAS

GIVE ME A BOWLER HAT!.. SMALL!!!
SORRY, SIR! I'VE SOLD OUT OF BOWLER HATS COMPLETELY...

...KENNY BALL & HIS JAZZMEN ARE PLAYING AT THE CITY HALL TONIGHT!... HE BOUGHT MY ENTIRE STOCK!
KENNY BALL and his Jazzmen
TONIGHT AT THE CITY HALL

BACK HOME...
DON'T WORRY, SON. YOU'RE BOUND TO FIND ONE SOME--WHERE...
...HERE! LOOK IN THE ORANGE PAGES

YOU'VE GOT A SMALL BOWLER IN STOCK... AND YOU CAN DELIVER!
...GREAT!!!
BOWLERS FOR SALE ALL SIZES

CLANG! TISH! CLASH! TISH! HA!
HA! HA! HA! HA! HA!
FRED TRUEMAN
HA! HA! HA!
OH, NO! NOT THAT KIND OF SMALL BOWLER!

OH, NO! NOT **THAT** KIND OF PUNCHLINE! ← READER'S VOICE

BIFFA
LOVE
HATE
BACON
VIZ 96
Shibe ST·GPD·DJ

WHO'S A PRETTY FUCKER THEN? WHOOO'S A PRETTY FUCKER? WHO'S A PRETTY LITTLE FUCKER?

HOW! WHAT THE FUCK'S GANNIN' ON IN HERE?
EH?!
ARE YE QUEERIN' UP THAT BORD, BIFFA?
NAAH FATHA. I'M TEACHIN' IT TU TAALK.

GIZ IT HERE! NEE-ONE'S HAVIN' QUEE-AH PETS IN THIS HOOSE!

ME BUDGIE!
Y'BASTAD! YUV TORNED IT'S FRIGGIN' NECK!
SNAP!

NOW THEN SON. YE DIWEN'T WANT PUFFS' PETS NOW D'YU? BUDGIES ARE PINK, LIKE LASSES KNICKERS, AN' THEY FUCKIN' GAN 'TWEET' AN' THAT.

YE WANT A BORD THAT'S AALL GREY AN' DORTY, AN' EATS TAB ENDS AN' DOG SHITE.

BIFFA. WE'LL GERRUS SOME PIDGEONS. PIDGEONS ARE NAILS. THEY'RE FOR MEN!
AYE FATHA! WUZ CAN RACE THE FUCKAZ!
AYE SON. BUT FORST WUZ'LL NEED A CREE FOR TU KEEP THE FUCKAZ IN.

SO, SHORTLY...
HOW, FATHA! MUTHA'S GANNA TEK A FUCKIN' RADGE WHEN SHE SEES THIS!
DIVVENT BE SUCH A SOFT SHITE BIFFA, SON.
MUTHA'S WARDROBE
KEEP THE FUCK OOT
BIFFA + FATHA'S PIDGIN KREE
MUTHA'S FROCKS
LET'S GAN AN' GET WURSEL'S SOME PIDGEONS OFF GREY'S MONUMENT.

AND...
FATHA! D'YU THINK THEY'LL FLY AALREET AFTA YE STUNNED THEM WI' YA BOOT-END?
WHY AYE, THEY'LL TEK OWT MAN, THEY'RE GEORDIES.

READY!... STEADY!... GAN!

HOY!
FLUTTER!
FLAP! FLAP! FLAP!
FLUTTER!
FLUMP!
PLUMFF!

FUCKIN' HELL FATHA! THAT WAS SHITE.
AYE. YA REET. THESE ISN'T RACIN' PIDGEONS. THESE IS FUCKIN' FIGHTERS THESE CUNTS.

GAN ON LIRRIL BORD! THAT 'UNS JUST CAALED YA MUTHA A WHOO-AH!
GAN ON KIDDA! HE'S FUCKIN' SPILT YA MILLET!
GOAD! GOAD!

GAN ON!... GAN ON!... FUCK 'IM MAN!
GAN ON! GET STUCK IN! FUCK THE LIRRIL FUCKER!
FLUTTER!

WHAT THE FUCKIN' HELL'S GANNIN' ON HERE?!!
LESS IT THE PAIR O' YEZ! FIGHTIN' LIKE FRIGGIN' BAIRNS!
FLUTTER! FLUTTER!

STOTT!

HOW MUTHA! YE'VE KILT WOR FUCKIN' BORDS!
DIVVEN'T WORRY, SON. I WAS THAT RADGE WHEN I SEEN ME BYOOTIFUL WAADRURBE THAT I LAID A GEET BIG EGG MESEL.

LOOK SON! IT'S ABOOT TU HATCH!
HAD ABOOT. LAST TIME I GOT A EGG YA BOOT COME OOT OF IT AN' FUCKED US IN ME LUG!
BIFFA SON. THAT WOZ A EASTER EGG. THIS IS A REAL EGG WHAT I'VE LAID OOT ME AAN FANNY.

KRACK!

TWEET FUCKIN' TWEET, Y'LIRRIL CUNT.
HO! HO! HO!

THE FAT SLAGS

DING-A-LING!-A-LING!
-A-LING!-A-LING!-A-
SNORE!

JESUS! LOOK AT THE TIME! I'LL HAVE TO GET GOIN'
EH!? WHAT'S THE RUSH, BAZ, LOVE?

I'VE GOT T'MEET THELMA AT THE CLAP CLINIC... THE DIRTY BITCH HAS GOT A DOSE
URGH! WHO DID SHE GET IT OFF?
ME

EEH! THE ROTTEN GET! HE MIGHT 'AVE TOLD ME HE WAS SERVIN' UP SPOTTED DICK...
GRACE BROS GB GRACE BROS
WELL, HE'S FRIGGIN' KNOWN LONG ENOUGH. I MEAN, I GAVE IT 'IM THREE WEEKS AGO
...ME TWAT'S ITCHIN' LIKE BUGGERY
SALE
SALE PLEASE Q HERE

ANYWAY, COME ON. DOORS'LL BE OPENIN' SOON. WE'VE QUEUED F' TWO WEEKS. WE DON'T WANT THESE GREEDY GETS PUSHIN' IN
AYE! THAT FUR COAT'S AS GOOD AS MINE...

...SO EITHER OF YOU TWO GET TO IT BEFORE ME AN' I'LL FUCKIN' WELL KILL YER!
THEY'RE OPENIN' UP, SAN! QUICK!
SALE

ROAR!!
CHINA HABERDASHERY FUR COATS

OOH, YES I LIKE MINK. I THINK I'LL HAVE THIS
MINE!.. MINE!.. MINE!..
REAL MINK
£200

...MINE!..
...SO FUCKIN' LEAVE IT!!
OOOF!

EEH, SAN. WORRA FUCKIN' BARGIN' Y'D SET YER 'ART ON THAT, 'ADN'T YOU, EH? YOU'LL LOOK GREAT!
AYE!

WAIT 'TILL THEY SEE YOU IN IT AT THE DOG AN' 'AMMER KARIOKE NIGHT
AYE. AN' I CAN'T WAIT T' WALK ROUND ALDI IN IT ...I'LL FEEL LIKE LADY SHITE, I WILL
GROAN!

QUICK!.. STUFF IT IN YER BAG

STUFF! STUFF!

I CAN'T RESIST A BARGAIN... I'M TERRIBLE. I SAW SOME SHOES IN CLARKS LAST WEEK, TWENTY QUID OFF, AN' I'D NICKED SOME THE WEEK BEFORE... FULL PRICE!
EEH! I WAS FUCKIN' SICK!

OOH, WHILE WE'RE 'ERE, I'LL TAKE THEM KNICKERS BACK BAZ GORRUZ F' CHRISTMAS...
THEY'RE FAR TOO SMALL!
Lingerie
GOOD IDEA

'ERE, I WANT ME MONEY BACK F' SOME KNICKERS I GOT AS A PRESENT OFF BAZ. THEY CUT UP ME ARSE TOO MUCH
CERTAINLY, MADAM. DO YOU HAVE THEM WITH YOU?

AYE!

'ERE THEY ARE!

I'M SORRY... I... ER... CAN'T ACCEPT... ER ...THOSE
WHY!? HE DEFINITELY GOT 'EM FROM 'ERE... LOOK... THAT'S ONE OF YOUR SECURITY TAGS, IN'T IT?

SECURITY TAG... ER... YES... I'LL JUST GET OUR... ERM... REFUNDS MANAGER!
RIGHT!

SHORTLY...
SECURITY

RIGHT THEN. LET'S 'AVE A LOOK IN THIS BAG, SHALL WE, LADIES?
IF Y' WANT

WELL, WELL, WELL... WHAT'S THIS?
DUNNO... NEVER SEEN IT BEFORE IN ME LIFE!
NEITHER 'AVE I...
...AN' ANYWAY, WE WAS GOIN' T' PAY FORRIT!

AW, COME ON... LERRUZ GO... ME MAM'S DYIN' IN HOSPITAL.
AYE! SO'S MINE!
SAVE IT F' THE COPPERS, GIRLS. THEY'LL BE 'ERE ANY MINUTE!

'ELLO! 'ELLO! 'ELLO! WHAT'S ALL THIS THEN?
I APPREHENDED THESE TWO WOMEN IN POSSESSION OF A FUR COAT...
A FUR COAT, EH!? COME ON... IN THE VAN!

HEY! I'VE ALWAYS FANCIED A BLOKE IN UNIFORM... TELL Y' WHAT, LERRUZ GO AN' I'LL POLISH YER HELMET FOR YER, EH?
AYE! AN' WHILE SHE'S DOIN' THAT, I'LL GIVE YOU A BLOWJOB

SORRY. THAT WON'T WORK ON ME. I'M TAKIN' YOU IN. IT'S PEOPLE LIKE YOU THAT BUMP PRICES UP, AND HONEST PEOPLE LIKE ME END UP PAYIN'
ALRIGHT! ALRIGHT! P.C. SHIRT LIFTER!

OH! COULD I TAKE THE FUR COAT, SIR? IT'LL BE NEEDED FOR EVIDENCE
OF COURSE! HERE IT IS, OFFICER

OH!... ERM...

...YOU 'AVEN'T GOT ONE A COUPLE OF SIZES SMALLER, 'AVE YOU?
EH!?
...THIS ONE WILL FUCKIN' BURY MY MISSUS

TINRIBS
OIL
11-YEAR-OLD TOMMY TAYLOR HAD A FANTASTIC ROBOT FOR A PAL

IT'S A LOVELY SUNNY DAY CHILDREN – SO INSTEAD OF LESSONS, WE'LL TAKE A TRIP TO THE ZOO
ZOO ENTRANCE
HOORAY. I LOVE THE ZOO – HOW ABOUT YOU, TINRIBS?
HEAD MASTER
HI. I'M BARBIE. I LOVE YOU VERY MUCH

WAIT A MINUTE – THIS HOT SUNNY WEATHER IS MAKING ME IRRITABLE AND BAD-TEMPERED
TICKETS
HEAD MASTER
SO INSTEAD OF GOING TO THE ZOO, YOU WILL ALL RETURN TO SCHOOL FOR TEN HOURS OF LONG DIVISION FOLLOWED BY A SADISTIC BEATING

MY ROBOT CHUM WILL COOL YOU DOWN, HEADMASTER
HEAD MASTER
SQUIT!
FIRST, I STICK TINRIBS' ARMPIECE THROUGH THE END OF MR SNODWORTHY'S TONGUE
AWK!

THEN I WIND IT ROUND AND ROUND LIKE AN AEROPLANE PROPELLER
TWIST TWIST TWIST TWIST
HEAD MASTER
EK! AK! IK! EEK!

WHIRRRRRRRRR
THERE, YOUR OWN PERSONAL TONGUE-POWERED 'ELECTRIC' FAN
GNNN!
AH! LOVELY COOL BREEZE. WELL DONE TAYLOR

THANKS TO TINRIBS, I'M IN A GOOD MOOD AGAIN
ZOO
TICKETS
HEAD MASTER
SO WE'LL GO TO THE ZOO AFTER ALL

I'M AFRAID THE DEPRESSED MONKEY WILL NOT BE MASTURBATING TODAY, AS IT HAS CHEWED ITS OWN ARMS OFF OUT OF BOREDOM
DO NOT FEED THE DEPRESSED MONKEY FRANTICALLY MASTURBATING IN A CONFINED SPACE
ZOO
HOW DISAPPOINTING

MY ELECTRONIC BUDDY CAN PROVIDE A REPLACEMENT MONKEY – WITH MR SNODWORTHY'S ASSISTANCE
ZOO
?!
SEE – TINRIBS' RUBBER-GLOVE HANDS MAKE IDEAL MONKEY FEET...

...AND HIS TOW-ROPE MAKES A SMASHING TAIL
HEAD MASTER
EXCELLENT! A MOST CONVINCING MONKEY-SUBSTITUTE. GET IN THE CAGE AND START WANKING, MR SNODWORTHY
B-BUT HEADMASTER...

HA! HA! LOOK AT THE DIRTY MONKEY PLAYING WITH ITSELF!
ZOO
HEAD MASTER
JERK TOSS
OO! OO! OO! OO!
OH, THE HUMILIATION

GRR! THAT DRATTED ROBOT IS CAUSING ME ENDLESS PAIN
DANCING BEARS
PERFORMING SEALS
CLAMBER
I'LL FIX HIM ONCE AND FOR ALL WITH THIS POWERFUL MAGNET

HEH! HEH! I'LL DANGLE MY MAGNET OVER THE TIN TWIT AS HE PASSES BENEATH
CREAK
IT'S MAGNETIC FIELD WILL BUGGER UP THE DELICATE WORKINGS OF TINRIBS' COMPUTERISED BRAIN, AND CAUSE HIM TO MALFUNCTION

SNAP!
YIKES! THE BRANCH HAS BROKEN

THUNK!
YOW! I'VE LANDED NECK-FIRST ON A JAGGED SOUP-TIN
IT'S SEVERED A MAJOR ARTERY

HOY! CAN'T YOU READ? PUT THAT BLOOD AWAY AT ONCE!
DO NOT TEMPT THE VAMPIRE BATS
ZOO
Squeak
Squeak
choke
YOU'RE DRIVING THE VAMPIRE BATS INTO A FEEDING FRENZY

SHORTLY
HI. I'M BARBIE. I LOVE YOU VERY MUCH
DO NOT FEED THE PARROTS AND BOXING KANGAROOS
SQUAWK
"HI-I'M BARBIE"
HA! HA! LISTEN, TINRIBS – THAT PARROT IS IMITATING YOU

..."I LOVE YOU VERY MUCH"
SNARL
SOUNDS LIKE THAT STINKING ROBOT IS IN HERE
NO ENTRY
THIS TIME I'M GOING TO POUND THE CYBERNETIC CRETIN INTO A HEAP OF RUSTY SCRAP

TAKE THIS YOU METAL MORON
CLONK!
WOW! THAT'S NOT TINRIBS – THAT'S A BOXING KANGAROO!

HI. I'M BARBIE. I LOVE YOU VERY MUCH
PUNCH
KICK
THUMP
HURT
HA! HA! THAT'S RIGHT, TINRIBS: IF THOSE KANGAROOS KEEP HITTING MR SNODWORTHY, THEN ZOONER OR LATER HE PROBABLY WILL DIE OF MASSIVE INTERNAL INJURIES

SOCCER SHOCKER!

New commitment rate hike kicks players where it hurts

By our sports staff, a fat red-faced drunk

PROFESSIONAL footballers were reeling last night after the Chancellor of the English Football Association raised the players' commitment rates for the third time this year. A rise of 50 percentage points means that all players must now give 250 per cent effort each time they take the field.

Kegan: Thousand per cent.

League

The decision was taken to bring the FA into line with the Bundesleague, which raised its own rate last week.

"We had little choice but to take this action" said David Davies, the only man left at the FA. "No one likes to raise commitment rates, but we must take these steps if we are to remain competitive in Europe."

Fathom

But many amateur clubs fear that this is beyond their players' means. "All our players hold down full time jobs." said Phil Castiaux, secretary of Blyth Spartans. "They cannot possibly go to work during the week and then give 250 per cent on a Saturday. The level should be capped for part time players. They cannot be expected to give much more than 170."

Britain enjoyed a stable 100 per cent rate throughout the seventies. But in 1982 it was raised to 101 per cent by Trevor Francis during a controversial summing up on Match of the Day. The eighties saw the rate creep up to 110 per cent.

Chain

The highest ever commitment rates occured on 'Black Saturday', when comments by Kevin Keegan sent rates spiralling. The part-time England coach promised to give a thousand per cent in his new job, causing many clubs to panic and set their own commitment rates. By the end of play that afternoon, the rate had reached an unsustainable 10,000 per cent. Officials at Lancaster Gate finally stepped in and restored sanity by announcing a standard rate of 200 per cent.

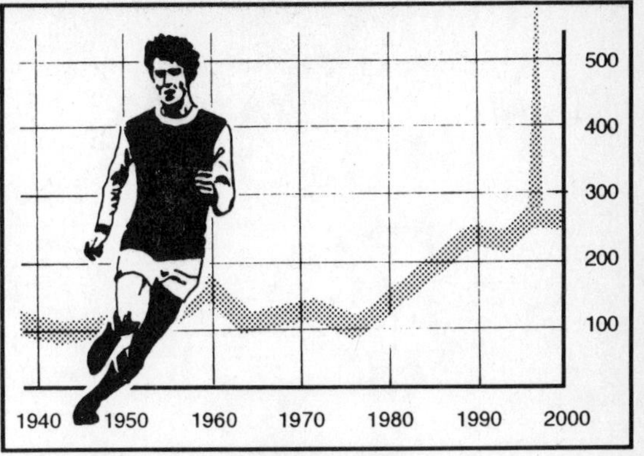

A graph yesterday.

We called Keegan at Bisham Abbey, to see how his 1000 per cent commitment to the England job was going, but we were told he was probably at Fulham F.C. that day. "If he's not there, you might catch him at his racing stables in Hampshire or perhaps at home in Durham," the cleaning lady told us.

THE *WHEEL* SECRET BEHIND YOUR FELLAS LUNCHBOX

YOU can tell what a man packs in his lunchbox by watching how he holds his car steering wheel, researchers advised women yesterday.

BOTTOM of the lunchbox league is the anxious motorist who drives with one hand on the wheel and the other hovering over the horn. Verdict: "Dull and unimaginative packed lunch, limp cheese sandwiches, non-branded chocolate biscuit and a scotch egg."

Christie: Obligatory in lunchbox article.

STEER CLEAR of the man who grabs the wheel with both hands at exactly the same height.

Verdict: "No appetite for lunch. A bag of crisps, a flask of tea and he's happy untill teatime."

BETTER is the guy who holds the top of the wheel with two hands close together

Verdict: "Adventurous sandwiches on unusual breads, fancy salads and little tomatoes, a Mr Kipling cake and a bag of Quavers."

BORING. Those who drive with both hands firmly clenching the bottom of the wheel.

Verdict: "Same packed lunch every day. Ham, cheese and pickle sandwiches on Mother's Pride, raspberry yoghurt and an apple."

BEST EATERS drive with one hand at the 8 o'clock position and the other at 2 o'clock, says the Aston University study, which looked at the driving habits of 7 men, then asked their wives what they liked in their sandwiches.

Verdict: "Doorstep sandwiches packed with filling, 2 sausage rolls, a can of pop, a Mars bar and a family bag of Cheesy Wotsits. And another sausage roll."

STUDENT GRANT
HIYA! TARQUIN! LISTEN - I'M ON MY ONE-2-ONE - THIS IS A TERRIBLE LINE - CAN YOU CALL ME BACK..? I'M ON 005690 6147... CIAO!
DIDDLE-EE DEE DEE DE-DEE DEE... DIDDLE-EE DEE DEE DE-DEEE... DEE DEE DEE DEEEE DE-DEE DEE... DIDDLE-EE DEE DEE DE-DEEE...
HIYA... YEAH. THIS IS A MUCH BETTER LINE. LISTEN - CAN YOU GET ME A BAG OF NUTS TOO..?
BAG OF NUTS? NIL PROBLEMO AMIGO.
MUCHO OBLIGADO AMIGO.
THEATRICAL FLAP!
BRRRRRR!
OH, FACK!
SORRY... NO NUTS BUYING CRISPS... WHAT FLAVOUR... TARQUIN 8:38pm
PAGERS 2000
TAP-TAP.. TAPPITY-TAP.. PRESS
DEE DEEDLE-EEDLE-EEDLE DEEE... DA DEEDLE-EEDLE-EE DA-DEEE DEEE DEEE... DA DEE DEE DEEEE...
HIYA GRARNT! ...SALT AND VINEGAR?... RIGHT. CIAO!
HEY! WHERE'VE YOU GUYS BEEN?
BRUNO'S BEEN TO HAVE HIS TONGUE PIERCED!
WOW! LET'S HAVE A LOOK
CLANG!
NLLLLTH! NLLTH! NLLLLLLLTH!*
WOW! THATS SOO-OOO COOL! DID IT HURT?
*HELP! I'VE CAUGHT THE STUD IN MY FRONT TEETH.
AND HOW MUCH DID IT COST?
NLLLLTH! NLTH! NLLLLLLTH! NLLLTH!*
* CHRIST! NO, REALLY. IT'S REALLY HURTING AND MY MOUTH IS FILLING WITH BLOOD.
YOU'RE RIGHT, BRUNO. IT IS A MARK OF INDIVIDUALITY. THAT'S WHY I'M GOING TO GET ONE JUST LIKE YOURS.
ME TOO.
AND ME.
SO...
Welcome to THE SPUNKBRIDGE BODY-ART Consultancy
I'M JUST PHONING GRARNT ON MY UP-2-YOU TO SEE HOW HE'S GETTING ON - BUT ITS A TERRIBLE LINE AND I CAN'T UNDERSTAND A WORD HE'S SAYING.
* LASER AUTOCLAVE
* PAINLESS
* BY APPOINTMENT TO ROYALTY
CONSULTING ROOM
GGGLLTH!! GRLLOOUGHTH!! BLUUURGH!!

Matthew Shight

★ *RED* faces at Pinewood Studios, where six-footer **Ewan McGregor** is starring in *Moulin Rouge*, a film about titchy painter Toulouse-Lautrec. Height worries?
"No, you stupid cunt. I'm playing another character. Now get out of my fucking bathroom." quipped my old chum.

RAY OF SHIGHT

I WENT to see my super-star pal, **Madonna** at the Hammersmith Odeon last week. After a wonderful gig, I went backstage where she opened her heart exclusively to yours truly. "Who's this asshole? How did he get past security?" she gushed.

★ *GUESS* what. Neither 007 star **Pierce Brosnan** or **Scary Spice Mel B.** were anywhere to be seen in Soho's trendy *Titanic Bar* when I stood on a box to look through the window last night before running away when a policeman came.

BIG Breakfast star **Johnny Vaughan** has to get up very early in the morning, according to my spies at *Channel 4*. Johnny who used to present the programme with **Denise Van Outen** and now shares star billing with bra model **Kelly Brook**, must get up at 5.30am at the latest.
"He probably has an alarm clock", one insider at **Bob Geldof** - who was married to **Paula Yates** - **'s** ex-TV company told me.

Liam's back-lane bust-up

INDICATES: Fish shows where winds will be high

POINTS: Moves hand upwards

Storm Warning!

THESE EXCLUSIVE pictures show the most dramatic moments from this Saturday's edition of the *Weather Forecast*. I can reveal that weatherman **Michael Fish** points his finger at an area of low pressure over the North of Scotland and a band of rain moving in from the South later. Shocked viewers will also see the veteran meteorologist predict gusting winds and blizzards across the south.
The dramatic episode ends with Fish, who is married to his real-life wife, **Mrs. Fish**, summarising Sunday's weather and looking ahead to the early part of next week. But if you want to know the long range forecast, you'll have to tune in.

OASIS wildman Liam Gallagher, whose rocky marriage to Patsy Kensit has kept him in the headlines for all the wrong reasons, has made a fool of himself yet again.

For 20 extraordinary minutes, he berated me in the back lane of his £7 million Chalk Farm mansion.

Our paths crossed whilst I was rummaging through his £200 dustbins. "Not you again, you little cunt. It's three in the morning."

"For fuck's sake leave me alone" he yelled, humiliating himself. His ridiculous shouting woke up neighbour **Rowan Atkinson**, who once stabbed me in the face with a fork whilst I simply tried to go through his pockets at a showbiz barbecue, thrown by my old pal **Elton John**.

"Liam," I explained, "I'm just looking for any old rubbish to fill my column tomorrow." After a further tirade of abuse, during which he slurred his words, he borrowed my mobile phone to make a call. Minutes later, Liam and I were joined by my old mate **Bonehead** and a couple of minders.

Gallagher: Embarrassed.

"That's it! You're fucking dead," they joked, before pinning me to the ground and cutting my trousers off with a Stanley knife. Liam, then made a complete laughing stock of himself by ramming a broken lemonade bottle up my arse.

"Stick that in your fucking column, you little wanker," he laughed. Well, Liam, that's just what I've done. So who's sorry now?

CARPETING FOR MATT

WHAT an honour this lunchtime for your illustrious scribe. Returning from loitering outside **Gordon Ramsay's** top eaterie, where pop bad boy **Robbie Williams** once lightheartedly spat in my face, I was called into the Editor's office. "Shight, isn't it? You're fired. Clear your desk and fuck off," quipped my best mate, **Mr. Moron**.

KNOW ANYTHING THAT MIGHT FILL THIS COLUMN? ABSOLUTELY ANYTHING. JUST AS LONG AS IT TAKES SOME SPACE UP. CALL ME ON 09090 400 915

LetterBocks

The page that's as hairy as the Queen Mum's mary

Star Letter

● They say that good manners cost nothing. Bollocks. I sent my daughter to a posh finishing school in Switzerland, and it cost me twenty bastard grand.

J. Morgan
Wigan

● I wish the irresponsible makers of ITV's "Don't Try This At Home" would stress the title of the show a little more. Only the other day I arrived home to find my wife and children attempting to drive a Mini Moke across a rope bridge suspended between two hot air balloons at 30,000 feet. With a snake in their pants. On fire. Etc. In our living room.

John Tait
Thropton

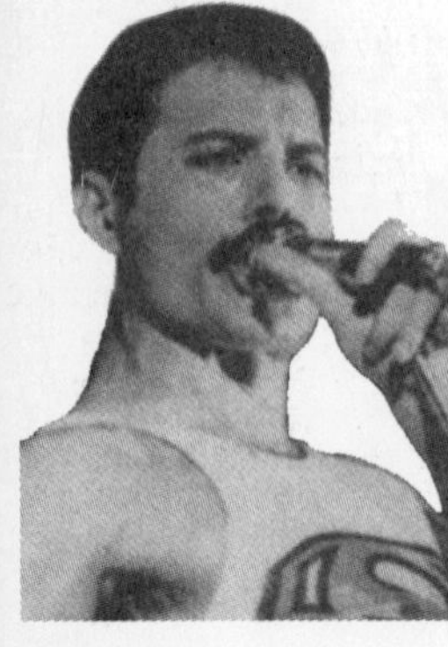

● If, as Freddie Mercury claimed, fat bottomed girls make the rocking world go round, isn't it about time that the city of Derby received some recognition for its contribution to astrophysics?

Neil Sedgwick
Nottingham

● As it will probably be the last opportunity I get, I plan to spend New Year's Eve 1999 wanking over internet filth. Do any other readers have special plans for seeing in the new Millennium?

Neil Weatherall
Dunstable

Viz
PO Box 1PT
Newcastle upon Tyne
NE99 1PT

viz@viz.co.uk

● I spotted Jimmy Hill, not in Viz but on this saucy seaside postcard where, in response to an enquiry about cucmbers, Jim humorously alludes to the size of his penis and implies a sexual attraction to the female customer.

Miss S. Hall
& the sandwich boy
Jesmond

● I had to laugh the other day. It was in the script.

Noel Edmonds
Crinkly Bottom

Pop the question

● If it's true what they say, *"Once you pop, you can't stop"*, why the fuck are Pringles tubes resealable?

A. Bean
Sudbury

● Bearing in mind the outcome of recent murder investigations, might it not be an idea for the police launching new ones to simply hold a press conference and arrest the first person who starts bubbling?

C.L.
Fife

● In Holland Park the other day I passed the headquarters of the Esperanto Society - who campaign for the world-wide adoption of their own universal language. However, I couldn't help wondering what language they would use to shout out of the window if the building caught fire. I somehow think that *"Assisti! Assisti! Propra domo est je fajr,"* would not be the first phrase that sprang to their big fat hypocritical lips.

S. Dennis
Clifton

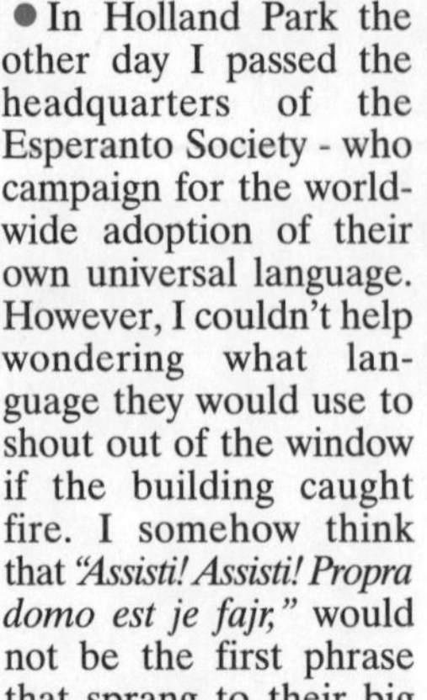

Bag Daddy

● Why do our media and politicians often refer to the evil Iraqi dictator Saddam Hussein simply as 'Saddam'? You could hardly imagine Iraqi TV broadcasting a message to the people of Baghdad saying "Last night we were bombed again by Bill and Tony".

Neil F. Mayell
London SE12

● Surely there was no need to move the News at Ten to make way for all-action Hollywood blockbuster movies. Trevor MacDonald could simply have read the news whilst on fire, being blasted through a large pane of sugar glass by a huge fireball explosion, flailing his arms and legs pointlessly. In a vest.

M. Radcliffe
Ipswich

Den of iniquity

● "Not so Dirty Den now," says Leslie Grantham on that new soap ad. It must be good if it's washed the blood off his hands.

Big Bean
Edinburgh

Animal magic

● The other day, while throwing all my belongings out onto the lawn and crying hysterically, my wife accused me of behaving like an animal. I ask you, what animal on earth is capable of lying under a glass-top coffee table and having a wank while his wife's sister has a dump on it? Women, eh?

CWAL5
e-mail

Honourable member

● In response to your request for readers with dicks which resemble celebrities. I have the good fortune to be circumcised, and by the addition of a miniature pair of spectacles, fashioned from a pipe cleaner, I can transform my member into a dead ringer for right-wing labour MP and unfounded cannibal rumour victim Gerald Kaufman.

Graham Brook
Wilmslow

OFFICE managers. Keep sexual harassment complaint forms in the bottom drawer of your desk. That way, every time a female employee needs one of the forms, you'll get a terrific view of her arse.

Edward Hitler
e-mail

THE BILL. The vast majority of houses have back doors. Don't look so bleeding surprised every time anyone escapes out of one.

S. Holmes
London W1

MANAGERS at Byker Shell station. Why not hire an aged deaf fuckwit as your night-time attendant and fit sound proof glass to the serving hatch. That way you can ensure that all your customers get a six pack of bog roll and a Lego model instead of the 20 cancer sticks they bloody well asked for in the first place.

Blagwedge
Byker

AVOID the expense of commissioning expensive portraits of your family by simply popping along to the local police station and saying that you've been mugged. Describe your loved one in detail to the sketch artist, and when they've finished ask if you can keep a copy.

David Barnett
Gospel Oak, London

TRIM the wings off a bat with kitchen scissors and, hey presto, a pug-faced, big-eared, slovenly field mouse.

Buzz
Herts

RUN a length of string through an Edam cheese. Hey presto! A delightful aromatic candle which will fill your home with the smell of burning cheese.

J. Tait
Thropton

SKIERS. Don't wipe your bums for the duration of the holiday. In the event of an avalanche this will greatly increase your chances of being located by sniffer dogs.

S.S.
Bunny, Notts

WHEN running or taking vigorous exercise, always increase your breathing rate to compensate for the body's additional oxygen requirement.

H.N. Loops
Belfast

GARRY Bushell. Prevent attacks by homosexual vampires by sprinkling your buttocks with holy water and shoving a clove of garlic up your arse.

Saucer 51
e-mail

Miriam

SOLVES YOUR PROBLEMS

Dear Miriam... **MY husband and I went on a two day motor tour. On our return we noticed that the figures for the mileage of the second day were the same as those for the first day but in the reverse order, and the difference between the two days' runs was one-eleventh of the total. How far did we travel in two days? Please help me, Miriam.**

* YOU travelled 99 miles, 54 on the first day and 45 on the second.

LETTER OF THE DAY

Dear Miriam... **I am a corn merchant and I have 21 sacks of grain - 7 full, 7 half full, and 7 empty. I wish to divide them equally amongst my three sons. How can I - without transferring any portion of grain from sack to sack - do this so that each son shall not only have an equal quantity of grain, but also an equal number of sacks? I am at my wits end.**

* THIS can be done in two ways. A and B each take 2 full sacks, 2 empty and 3 half-full, and C takes 3 full, 3 empty and 1 half-full. Or, A and B each take 3 full sacks, 3 empty, and 1 half-full, and C takes 1 full, 1 empty and 5 half-full sacks.

Dear Miriam... **I have a terrible problem and I don't know who to turn to. I am a pig farmer and I have put my pigs into 4 different clover fields. In the 2nd are twice as many as the 1st. In the 3rd twice as many as in the 2nd, and in the 4th twice as many as in the 3rd. The total number of pigs is 105. Please, please tell me how many are in each field.**

* Relax, Tom. There are 7 pigs in the 1st, field, 14 in the 2nd, 28 in the 3rd and 56 in the 4th.

Fox, chicken and sack of corn crossing river in one boat
0898 6060

FAST to SLOW and WIND to KITE in 4 moves
0898 7070

5 equilateral triangles with 9 matches
0890 8080

Fish anagrams
0890 9090

Calls cost 50p per minute

Crooner Phil in crocodile shock

SINGER Phil Collins has vowed never to record a song about crocodiles. For the slap-headed pop millionaire is a real-life Captain Hook.

Like the pirate in Peter Pan ugly Collins, 46, is terrified of the razor-toothed reptiles. So much so he demanded record company bosses write a clause in his contract excusing him from writing or performing songs about, or including references to, crocodiles.

Phil Collins (above) will not try rocking the crockodile rock - his feet just can keep still. thank you very much.

false

Over the years crocodile rockers have made a fortune singing about the snap happy creatures. In 1973 Elton John's 'Crocodile Rock' soared to number 5 in the charts. The ivory tinkling arse tickler celebrated by snapping up 2,000 pairs of crocodile skin shoes the very next day.

waterloo

A chubby young Geordie schoolkid was so inspired by seeing Elton's extravagant footwear on Top of the Pops, that 20 years later he wrote a song about it. Plank actor Jimmy Nail's 'Crocodile Shoes' was a massive hit, and launched the Easter Island Statue headed star's singing career.

paddington

Yet Phil Collins refuses to take the bait. "It would be easy for Phil to write a song about crocodiles and make a fortune, but he was never one for taking the easy way out", said one record company insider.

winnie the pooh

Ironically Collins's phobia does not extend to alligators. And just as well! For the stocking faced star, whose hits include 'In the Air Tonight', is a keen alligator breeder and keeps a dozen of the scaly croc lookalikes in a giant cuckoo clock fastened securely to the wall at his Swiss mountain home.

WHO WANTS TO KICK A MILLIONAIRE UP THE ARSE?

Continued from page xx.

The correct answer was *(d) a fish.*

Check your answer (on page 11) with the correct answer above. If they match, congratulations! You have just won a kick up the arse... of someone who has got *£100*.

Go out and find someone who has got £100, then kick them up the arse. Once you've done that, buy the next issue of Viz and there'll be another question for you to answer. *Get that one right and you double your prize - you get to kick someone who has got £200 up the arse!*

Keep getting your questions right and in a mere 15 issues time you could be kicking millionaire Chris Tarrant up his smug, money-spinning backside.

NB. If you got the wrong answer, don't worry. You can play again by sending another £5 to us at the usual address.

Remember me this way...

Young Bunty Twinkle was the most popular girl in the Alpine Ballet Boarding School, where she was the head ballerina. Imogen Tibbs and Bibi Bartlet were her closest pals.

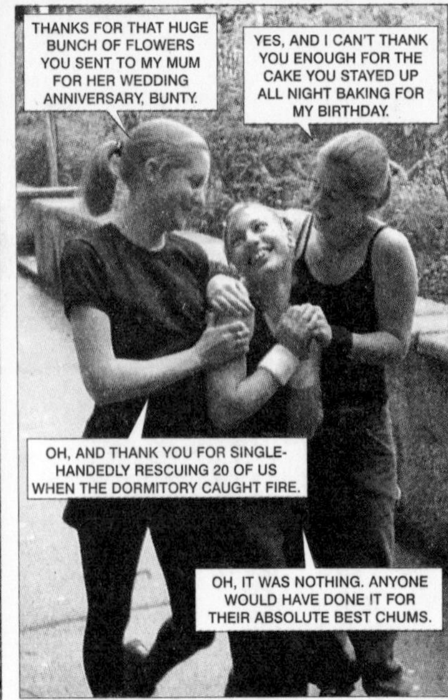
THANKS FOR THAT HUGE BUNCH OF FLOWERS YOU SENT TO MY MUM FOR HER WEDDING ANNIVERSARY, BUNTY.
YES, AND I CAN'T THANK YOU ENOUGH FOR THE CAKE YOU STAYED UP ALL NIGHT BAKING FOR MY BIRTHDAY.
OH, AND THANK YOU FOR SINGLE-HANDEDLY RESCUING 20 OF US WHEN THE DORMITORY CAUGHT FIRE.
OH, IT WAS NOTHING. ANYONE WOULD HAVE DONE IT FOR THEIR ABSOLUTE BEST CHUMS.

Shortly...
GOSH BUNTY, YOU'RE SO KIND, AND SELFLESS. I WISH I COULD BE AS POPULAR AS YOU.
BIBI'S RIGHT, EVERYONE LOVES YOU BUNTY. WE COULDN'T FACE A WORLD WITHOUT YOUR FRIENDSHIP.
WE'D NEVER SMILE AGAIN IF YOU EVER DIED.

DON'T WORRY CHUMS, I'M NOT PLANNING ON DYING JUST YET HO! HO! HO
HO! HO! HO
NEXT!

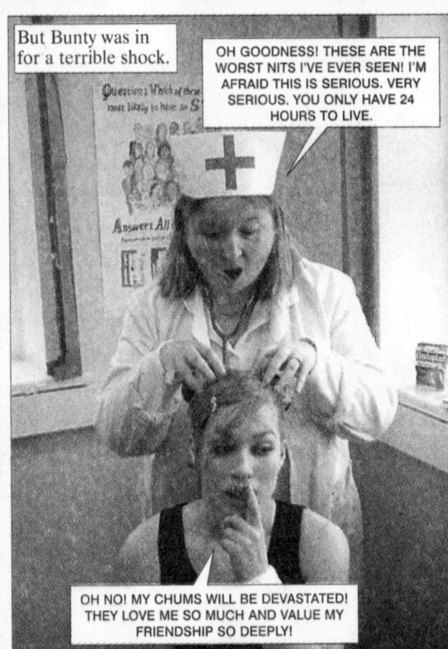
But Bunty was in for a terrible shock.
OH GOODNESS! THESE ARE THE WORST NITS I'VE EVER SEEN! I'M AFRAID THIS IS SERIOUS. VERY SERIOUS. YOU ONLY HAVE 24 HOURS TO LIVE.
OH NO! MY CHUMS WILL BE DEVASTATED! THEY LOVE ME SO MUCH AND VALUE MY FRIENDSHIP SO DEEPLY!

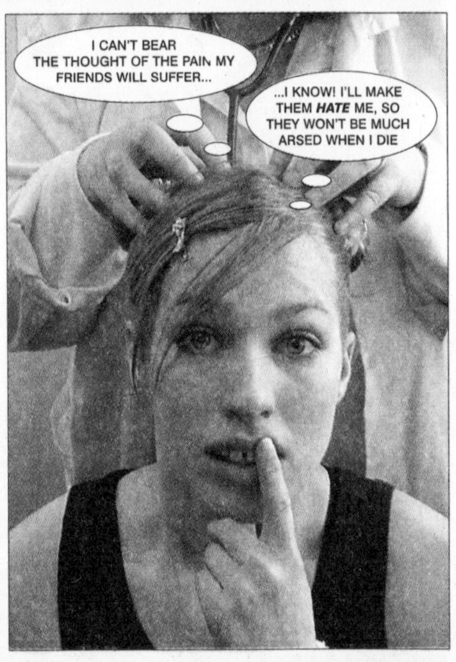
I CAN'T BEAR THE THOUGHT OF THE PAIN MY FRIENDS WILL SUFFER...
...I KNOW! I'LL MAKE THEM *HATE* ME, SO THEY WON'T BE MUCH ARSED WHEN I DIE

So...
NOW THEN, FOR HOMEWORK, I WANT YOU TO DO THIS SUM.
OH GOSH! I'M USELESS AT MATHS! YOU WOULDN'T HELP ME, WOULD YOU, BUNTY?

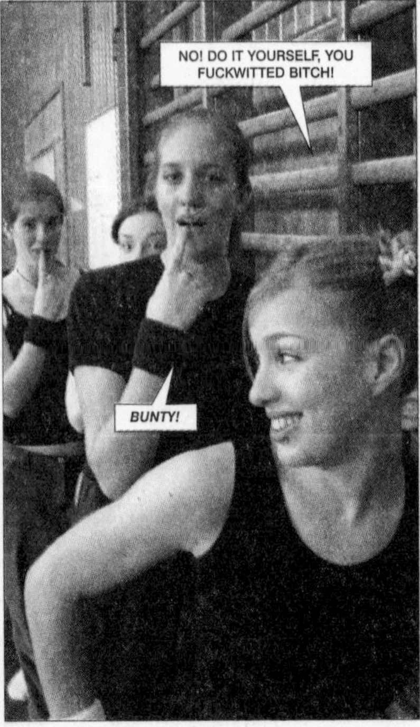
NO! DO IT YOURSELF, YOU FUCKWITTED BITCH!
BUNTY!

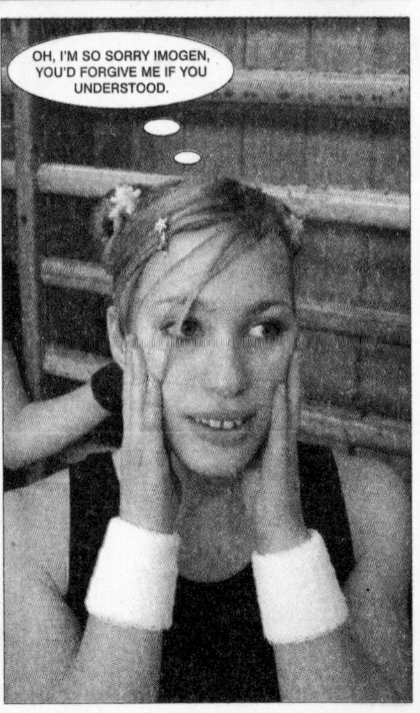
OH, I'M SO SORRY IMOGEN, YOU'D FORGIVE ME IF YOU UNDERSTOOD.

Continued over

Throughout the day Bunty forced herself with a heavy heart to behave rudely towards her friends...
I'M SO SORRY!
GLUG!
FLUSH!

I DON'T WANT TO DO THIS!
TRIP!

TAKE *THIS!*
BIFF!
UGH!
PLEASE FORGIVE ME!

At lunchtime.
UUURGH! SOMEONE'S DONE A POO IN ONE OF MY SANDWICHES!
YES. THAT WAS ME, TURD-BREATH. DO YOU WANT TO MAKE SOMETHING OF IT?

WHAT'S UP WITH BUNTY? SHE'S JUST NOT THE LOVELY GIRL SHE USED TO BE.
YES. I'M STARTING TO REALLY HATE HER.

OH, BUNTY! I'M GLAD I'VE CAUGHT YOU. I MADE A MISTAKE THIS MORNING. I GOT NITS MIXED UP WITH CANCER. SORRY.
YOU'RE NOT GOING TO DIE AT ALL.
GREAT! NOW I CAN TELL MY CHUMS WHY I'VE BEEN SO BEASTLY ALL DAY.

...SO YOU SEE, THAT'S WHY I'VE BEEN SO HORRIBLE TO YOU BOTH. CAN YOU EVER FORGIVE ME?
OH MY BUNTY! CAN YOU EVER FORGIVE *US?*
FORGIVE YOU? WHATEVER DO YOU MEAN?

OH, BUNTY. YOU MADE US HATE YOU SO MUCH THAT WE DECIDED TO KILL YOU.
SO WE POISONED YOUR FLASK OF TEA.
CHOKE! SPLUTTER!

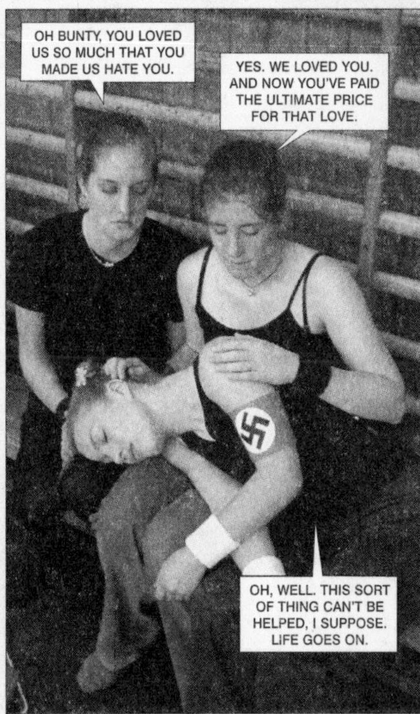

OH BUNTY, YOU LOVED US SO MUCH THAT YOU MADE US HATE YOU.
YES. WE LOVED YOU. AND NOW YOU'VE PAID THE ULTIMATE PRICE FOR THAT LOVE.
OH, WELL. THIS SORT OF THING CAN'T BE HELPED, I SUPPOSE. LIFE GOES ON.

The end

QUACKING GOOD VALUE!

1 RRP £16.99 Offer price £1.00

2 RRP £14.99 Offer price £1.00

BLUE EGGS

3 RRP £10.99 Offer price 50p

4 RRP £29.99 Offer price £2.00

5 RRP £22.99 Offer price £2.00

COUNTS AS ONE CHOICE

CHOOSE any 5 from only 50p each (+p&p)

6 RRP £16.99 Offer price £1.00

7 RRP £16.9 Offer pric £1.0

8 RRP £14.99 Offer price £1.00

9 RRP £20.99 Offer price £1.50

COUNTS AS ONE CHOICE

10 RRP £29.95 Offer price £2.50

11 RRP £9.99 Offer price 50p

SEXUALLY EXPLICIT

12 RRP £15.99 Offer price £1.00

13 RRP £14.98 Offer price £1.00

14 RRP £11.99 Offer price 50p

FEATHERBACK EDITION

15 RRP £9.99 Offer price 50p

16 RRP £17.99 Offer price £1.50

17 RRP £14.97 Offer price £1.00

WEBBED FEET

18 RRP £12.9 Offer pr £1.0

19 RRP £15.98 Offer price £1.50

POINTY ARSE

20 RRP £11.99 Offer price 50p

21 RRP £11.99 Offer price 50p

22 RRP £11.99 Offer price 50p

COUNTS AS ONE CHOICE

23 RRP £25.00 Offer price £2.50

To: *Duck of the Month Club*,
PO Box 50, Slimbridge, Glos.

Please accept my application and enrol me as a member of the Duck of the Month Club and send me the 5 introductory birds whose numbers I have indicated in the boxes provided. I will be charged only the special introductory offer prices, plus a total of £1.65 towards postage and packing. As a member, I will receive approximately every month (ie. every other day) a free Duck of the Month Club magazine. I understand that the quality of the Ducks offered in these magazines will spiral downwards as sharply as their price rockets upwards, and I will inevitably find myself buying large quantities of unwanted ducks that I cannot afford and will never look at. My only obligation is to buy everything from these magazines, and that the minimum length of membership is for the rest of my natural life. If after this period I wish to cancel, I can do so by giving one month's notice in writing.

Membership is subject to acceptance. We may consult a sinister credit reference agency to see how deeply and for how long we can shaft your arse.

Name ....

Address..

....

Signed..

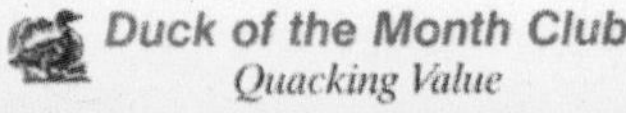

AT LAST! A DIFFERENT KIND OF DUCK CLUB

A club that promises you the best and very latest ducks at a fraction of high street prices. From the best-selling Buff Orpington and Miniature Appleyard to the classic Khaki Campbell and Welsh Harlequin. From the Lavish East Indian Drake and Abacot Ranger to the spicy Blue Swedish and Chocolate Runner, you're sure to find what you are looking for in Britain's largest Duck Club.

MEMBERSHIP HAS ITS REWARDS

Our buyers ensure that the selection of waterfowl we offer is the latest and best, and all our ducks carry huge discounts - of up to 40% off duck shop prices.

SELECT YOUR DUCKS NOW

To become a member of the Duck of the Month Club, simply choose any 5 of the superb items shown here from ONLY 50 PENCE EACH! (+ p&p) but SEND NO MONEY NOW. We invite you to examine the ducks in your own home for 10 days before you decide to keep them. Should you choose not to keep them, simply twist their necks, return them to us, your membership will be cancelled and you will owe nothing.

8ACE THE THIRSTY FAMILY MAN

A WANT T'BE A COMPLETE MAN. THAT'S WOT F-FFUCKIN' GOD WANTS... F-FFUCKIN' *HIM*... BIG MAN... WANTS ME TO TRY THE ACE.

WELL THAT SEEMS TO BE IN ORDER. SIGN HERE HERE AND HERE. YOUR HOME IS AT RISK IF YOU DO NOT KEEP UP THE PAYMENTS.

AYE PAL. THAT'LL BE F-FFUCKIN' CHAMPION.

CAN YER NOT SEE, LUV? A'VE LEARNT ME LESSON. A SHALL NEVAH EVAH EVAH TOUCH THE ACE AGAIN... A'LL SHOW YER WOT A CHANGED MAN A AM... A'LL GO AN' GET SUM CHIPS FOH TO STOP THE BAIRNS SKRIKING...

...THEH ONE FORTEH NINE.

THE MODERN PARENTS

John Fardell '99

November 5th
Now, we've called this emergency meeting of the Ethically Aware Parents' Committee to discuss a very serious issue.....
Yesterday, it came to our attention that some of our young people have been pooling their personal allowance money and buying fireworks...
That's awful! These evil by-products of the arms industry should be banned!
Absolutely! Apart from being terribly dangerous, they glorify missile technology.
And it's not just the rockets... The Catherine wheel is a sick representation of an instrument of misogynist torture!
COMMUNITY CENTRE
DISCOVER YOUR INNER TREE SPIRIT
DOLPHIN TAPESTRY PROJECT Volunteers welcome

Obviously we discussed the issue with the young people and democratically decided that they should hand over these fireworks to us so that we can dispose of them responsibly... Malcolm's stored them downstairs in the Community Hall for now...
I hope you've locked them up, Malcolm...
Well I don't actually believe in the concept of locking things up from young people... It discourages moral responsibility... I'm sure Tarquin and the others won't abuse the trust I've placed in them not to remove the fireworks from the cupboard...
It's outrageous that Guy Fawkes' Night should still be allowed at all! These lager-loutish British festivals are terribly offensive to people from different cultures...
Yes, we should be adopting quiet, meditative festivals like Divali instead.

And Guy Fawkes' Night is particularly offensive to the ethnic Catholic community... We shouldn't be celebrating the execution of a Celtic freedom fighter.
Absolutely... Guy Fawkes was a pacifist... He was only trying to blow up the English parliament to stop them taking over the druidic sisterhood of Celtic nations...
Wasn't Guy Fawkes Spanish?
Ah well then, he'd have been a Moor at that time, wouldn't he?... He was a black activist trying to stop the slave trade.
I read that he was a gay rights campaigner. He was framed because he was having an affair with Christopher Marlowe.
No no no! He was framed by the Pope because he fought the Catholic Church's bigoted attitude towards Third World birth control. It's all to do with the Knights Templar and the Freemasons..

Anyway, it's definitely an offensive festival....
Why don't we hold our own festival tomorrow night instead? We could have a Celtic Pagan Fire Festival!
Oh yes!.. We could wear giant wickerwork costumes and juggle flaming torches and do primitive free drumming...
Actually, I don't think we should be using real fire at all... At a time when villages are still being burnt and fire-bombed in places like... like... Bosnia and... um... places, it seems very inappropriate.

Wendy's absolutely right!.. We know that the ancient Pagan societies used fire in a *caring*, *spiritual* way but nowadays flames have too many connotations with *male violence* ...
We have to consider the feelings of any *refugees* living near here ...
And the concerns of the *flammophobic community* ...
I know! Why don't we create a piece of *fire dance*, in which the flames are represented by *movement* and *costume*?
Oh *yes!* I could wear my orange silk wrap which I brought back from Bali ...

And our World Rhythm percussion group could improvise the music.
Look, this is a Tai Chi fire gesture ... You have to *feel* the *upward flow* of *energy* ...
Do you think we should get some of the young people to join in?
I don't know ... I think us adults should perform it as a *surprise* for them.
Yes ... Anyway, Tarquin and Guinevere are very busy at the moment ... We've *finally got them interested* in Feng Shui ... They've spent the whole afternoon moving bits of our furniture and stuff downstairs.
Gosh, so have Mhairi and Zak! They've even been taking *some* of our things into the garden ... It's so *sweet!*

Anyway, that's agreed then ... We'll hold a *non-violent*, *non-explosive*, *non-inflammatory* festival of *expressive choreography* and *peace* ...
Absolutely! ... I'm sure the young people will *love it!* ...
Community Centre
GENUINE HEALING CRYSTALS
ORGANIC MASSAGE OILS
SUSTAINABLE SOURCE PINE FUTON
BREW YOUR OWN NETTLE WINE KIT
GARLIC
PARAFFIN
PARAFFIN
PARAFFIN
ASSORTED FIREWORKS
GIANT FIREWORKS SET
SSSSSSSSSS

ALDRIDGE PRIOR

THE HOPELESS LIAR

NOT ME.
NO.
NO.

SCREEECH!
THUMP!
?

I THINK HE'S UNCONCIOUS.
SOMEONE CALL AN AMBULANCE!
IT LOOKS BAD.

LET ME THROUGH. I'M A DOCTOR.
BUS

ME TOO, BUT I'M ONLY A JUNIOR HOUSE OFFICER. I'M COPING, BUT I'VE ONLY JUST QUALIFIED. CAN YOU TAKE OVER?
NO PROBLEMS MATE. I'M A TRAUMA BUS-VICTIM SPECIALIST OF 40 YEARS STANDING. I SAVE LIVES FOR BREAKFAST, PAL.

HIS HEAD SEEMS A BIT LOOSE ...ERM... THAT'S GOOD.
SHOULD YOU BE DOING THAT?
SURELY THERE'S A POSSIBILITY OF SPINAL CORD DAMAGE? YOU COULD PARALYSE HIM.

DON'T WORRY ABOUT THAT. I FOUND A CURE FOR THAT JUST LAST WEEK.
A CURE FOR PARALYSIS? WHAT IS IT?

IT'S A PILL. ABOUT SO BIG. PINK. WELL, TOP HALF'S PINK, BOTTOM HALF'S ORANGE. A HUNDRED POUNDS EACH.

CRACK! POP!
OH... ERM... ANYWAY, THEY'VE GOT OLYMPIC GAMES AND EVERYTHING NOW. RAMPS INTO SHOPS.
I WAS IN THEM DISABLED OLYMPIC THINGS MESELF LAST YEAR. I WON THE ONE-LEGGED HIGH-JUMP. TWENTY-FOOT I JUMPED. WORLD RECORD.

BUT YOU'VE GOT TWO LEGS.
SHUT-UP FOR GOD'S SAKE! THIS IS MY HUSBAND DYING IN YOUR ARMS. HE'S A CATHOLIC. HE MUST HAVE THE LAST RITES...
... IS THERE A PRIEST ANYWHERE?

FUNNY YOU SHOULD SAY THAT, AFTER THE OLYMPICS I WENT TO LORDS, THAT CATHOLIC CRICKET GROUND. ME LEG GREW BACK. MIRACLE. I BECAME A PRIEST. THEY'VE ASKED ME TO BE POPE NEXT YEAR.

'COURSE I USED TO BE JEWISH. NO. NOT JEWISH. THEM WITH THE TOWELS ON THEIR HEAD. I WAS ONE O' THEM. IS THAT THE ONES WHO WANTED TO KILL SALMAN RUSHDIE?
MUSLIMS?

YEAH, MUSLIN. THAT WAS ME. IT WAS ACTUALLY ME THAT KILLED SALMAN RUSHDIE.
BUT HE'S STILL ALIVE.
NO. NOT MUSLIN. BUDDHIST.

STOP THIS! FOR PITY'S SAKE! THE LAST RITES... PLEASE.

ERM... POST MORTEM... ERM... DOMINOES... MONOPOLY-IUM... ERM... I CLAUDIUS... STATUS QUO...
BUY STUFF
EAT THINGS
NER! NER! NER! NER! NER!

THIS IS JOHN. R.T.A. VICTIM. PEDESTRIAN STRUCK BY BUS. MULTIPLE INJURIES. PULSE EXTREMELY WEAK. BREATHING SHALLOW AND IRREGULAR.
RIGHT. LET'S BLUE-LIGHT HIM TO FULBY GENERAL!

OKAY! HE'S ABOARD!... LET'S MOVE!
SLAM!

DON'T MIND IF I DRIVE DO YOU? ONLY I CAN GET THIS CRATE THERE FASTER THAN ANY OF YOU LOT. I WAS A FORMULA ONE DRIVER, YOU SEE. AND THAT'S TRUE THAT.
?

I DROVE FOR THAT TEAM WITH THE YELLOW CARS. Y'KNOW, BIRDS WITH BIG TITS. I USED TO TEST-DRIVE ALL THE FASTEST FORMULA ONE CARS BEFORE ANY OF THE FAMOUS DRIVERS EVEN GOT TO SEE THEM.
CHUG! CHUG! VRR!
VRR! CHUG! NASH!
OF COURSE FORMULA ONE'S ALL A CON. IT'S JUST DONE WITH SCALEXTRIC CARS. ALL FILMED IN A BARN IN BERKSHIRE.

AN HOUR LATER...
OF COURSE IT SHOULD'VE BEEN ME, BUT I GOT THE 'FLU AND NEIL ARMSTRONG TOOK MY PLACE. HE'S NEVER THANKED ME. I HAVEN'T SPOKEN TO HIM EVER SINCE.
CHUG! GRIND!

EVENTUALLY...
OH WELL, WE'VE LOST HIM I'M AFRAID
I FEEL SOME OF THESE NECK INJURIES ARE INCONSISTENT WITH A ROAD TRAFFIC ACCIDENT. IT'S REALLY RATHER STRANGE.
I WAS THERE. A PIANO FELL ON HIM AS WELL... ERM... AND A BIG DOG CAME ALONG AND SHOOK HIS HEAD ALL OVER THE PLACE.

EXCUSE ME. IT'S OUR SON. HE WENT IN THERE. DO YOU KNOW HOW HE IS?
OPERATING THEATRE
WAITING ROOM

YES. I'M THE SURGEON. I'VE JUST FINISHED OPERATING ON HIM. IT'S A GOOD JOB HE GOT ME, I'VE BEEN WORKING IN REVOLOUTIONARY BIONICS FOR YEARS NOW. I'M HAPPY TO TELL YOU THAT HE'S SITTING UP IN BED TELLING JOKES.
OH. AND HE'LL BE ABLE TO RUN AT SIXTY MILES AN HOUR.

OPERATING THEATRE
VIZ 95

SID the SEXIST

THURSDAY'S

ADVENTURES of JACJAC

Cub reporter Jacjac and his dog Silvery are helping the vicar put together the Christmas issue of the parish magazine...
There. My article is finished.
Blistering barnacles! Have a cup of tea.

Oh dear. I hope it's not too late to include my advert.
THE MYTH OF THE HOLOCAUST by Jacjac aged 11.
Of course not, Miss Spindle. It can go on the back cover.

I did it last year and raised enough money to buy four sticks and and a guide dog.
SATURDAY 1st DEC. MISS SPINDLE WILL BE HOLDING A HOME MADE CHRISTMAS CARD SALE AT MARLINSPIKE VILLAGE HALL
All money raised will go to buy guide dogs and white canes for the blind.

Hmm!?

Next day...
Knock! Knock!

Morning, lady. Can I have a glass of water?
Of course you can, my poor man. Just wait there, I'll go and...

Shortly...
Ooh, my... What..?

Who are you? What do you want? I've got no money, honestly I've not.
Shut it, lady. Unless you want me to black the other eye.

I didn't find a thing, Silvery... and that's all the evidence I need!
Woof.

Are you sure you are alright, Miss Spindle? You must have had a nasty shock.
Yes I'm fine, Vicar. He didn't steal the Christmas cards I made, and that's all I'm bothered about.

Continued over

Well, they are lovely cards, Miss Spindle. I'll have one myself.
There you are, Vicar, the last one. That'll be fifteen pence, please.

There! £58.25. That's enough to buy another guide dog and half a dozen white sticks.

Later that day...
Come on then. Off to the blind institute.
OPEN
PETS

Not so fast, Miss Spindle.
Hello Jacjac. What's the matter?
Constables Timpson and Timpson. Arrest her.

Now then, Jacjac, what's this all about?
My question precisely, Timpson.

Well, Constables. It's simple. Old Miss Spindle has been making and selling these cards in aid of the blind for years.
Yes. Do carry on.
Well, in all that time she has never applied to become a registered charity.

But it's still not illegal for individuals to raise money for charity, Jacjac.

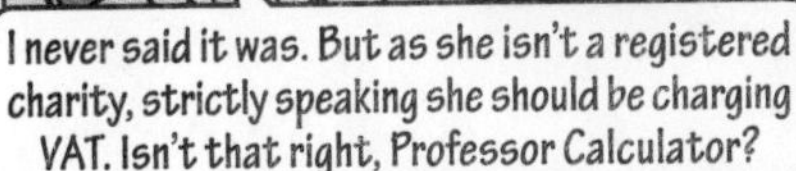
I never said it was. But as she isn't a registered charity, strictly speaking she should be charging VAT. Isn't that right, Professor Calculator?

Sort of, Jacjac. VAT liability depends on Miss Spindle's Gross turnover for the quarter. If it exceeds the excise threshold, then duty is payable, but she must not automatically assume that it is not.

And when I tied her up and ransacked her house, I could find absolutely no evidence of correspondence with the Customs and Excise.
Well, Jacjac, we don't know her financial circumstances, so it's a bit of a legal grey area...

Absolutely, but we'll give you the benefit of the doubt. We'll lock her up until the new year and sort it all out then.
But what about the things she's bought? They have been bought with money that may be liable to Value Added Tax surcharge.
Hmm! Your right, Jacjac. We'd better sort that out.

Where are you going, Jacjac. Don't you want to watch us drown the dog?
Yes, and burn the sticks?
No time for that, constables. I've got to write a detective story for the next parish magazine.

MARLINSPIKE PARISH NEWS
CHARITY FRAUDSTER EXPOSED BY BOY REPORTER!
Jacjac Honoured by Mayor
LOCAL SPINSTER'S CHRISTMAS DAY PRISON SUICIDE
INSIDE:
DOGLESS BLIND MAN BLUNDERS OFF CLIFF - DASHED TO PIECES.

Tasha Slappa's Mam
TASHAS MOTHER + HER MATE ARE GETTING READY TO GO OUT...
REET, NOW THE FACE PACK IS ADMINISTERED YER HAVE TER LEAVE IT FUR FIFTEEN MINUTES
EH? FIFTEEN MINUTES DURNT THEY KNA AAH'VE GOT A GEET BUSY SUR-CHAL LIFE?
PONDS MUD FACE PACK
WHEY, IT SAYS HERE YER CAN CARRY ON WITH YER LIFE AS USUAL WHILE IT SETS.
FUCKIN' THINK SUR AN' ALL. AAL FINNISH OFF THE IRONING AND MEK SOME DINNA, THEN.
PONDS MUD FACE PACK
SOON...
EEH! AAH THINK ITS FUCKIN' WORKIN' BETTY!! AAH CAN FEEL ME PORES AAL URPENIN' ITS GEET FRESH AND REEJOOVINATING
AYE- YER SKINS GANNA LOOK FUCKIN' LUSH
SIZZLE! POP! FRY!
LARD
ONCE YER PUT YER SLAP ON
ARE Y' OOT ON THE PULL THE NEET THEN BETTY?
WHEY AYE.
WELL AAH HURP YUR HAPPY WITH SECOND BEST, 'COS I AM AN' AAL.
EEH!! WHAT ABOOT YER TONKA? AAH THOUGHT YEE WUH DEED HAPPY WITH HIM.
SUR DID AAH, BETTY, TURNS OOT HE'S SOME SORT OF A BASTAAD
EEH!! WHAT DID 'EE DEE?
HE TELT US HE WOULD AALWAYS BE THERE FORROS AND HE WANTED TO MOVE IN AND MEK A COMMITMENT
EEH!! WHAT A BASTAAD! WHEY- YER BEST OFF RID. FIND YERSEL A PROPPA BLURK THE NEET, ONE WHATS NOT AFRAID TO GIVE YER A PROPPA HIDING
AYE- AAH CANNOT BE DEEIN' WITH NEN OF THAT TONKA I'M NOT READY TO SETTLE DOON YET. I'M TOO YOUNG MAN, AAH'VE STILL GOT ME WHOLE LIFE AHEAD OF US
AYE- YER DIVVINT WANT NEN COMMITMENTS
WHAAAAAAAA!! WHAAAAAAAAA!!
THAT'LL BE ONE OF YOUR BAIRNS WANTING ITS NAPPY CHANGED
AYE, WHEY IT CAN FUCK OFF WE RUN OOT LAST TUESDAY AND I'M NOT GETTING ANY MORE TILL THE MORRA
WHAAAAAAAAAA!!! WHAAAAAAA!!!
FUCKIN' SHUT IT DARREN!! YER DAD'LL BE IN FROM THE PUB LATER ON
AYE, AND YER'D BEST HURP THE TOON HAVE WON
HOWAY, LETS GET WUH BUS
IN TOWN...
HOWAY MAN! LET WUH IN!
KIST
SORRY GIRLS, YOU'RE TOO YOUNG
GAN ON MAN! LET WUH IN AND WE'LL SUCK Y' COCK!
SORRY LASSES, IT DOESNT WORK LIKE THAT
FUCKIN' DID LAST WEEK
AYE, AND I'M NOT CHUCKIN' ME MUCK DOON THE SAME GOBS TWO WEEKS RUNNIN' NOW FUCK OFF!
BAALDY BASTAAD!!
HA! THAT'LL SHOW YER! PEOPLE YOUR AGE SHOULDNT BE IN TOWN
HA!
SWAGGER!
-AND WHERE THE FUCK D' YER THINK YEE ARE GANNIN'
EEH! GET THIS ONE BETTY!! AAH KNEW THAT FACE PACK MUST OF MADE US LOOK YOUNGER!
-HAD ON LOVVER, AAH'VE BRONG ME PASSPORT...
SORRY LOVE, BUT MY BADGE SAYS THAT I'M EMPLOYED UNDER THE EQUAL OPPORTUNTIES ACT AGAINST DISCRIMINATION TO TELL ANY BOOT UGLY OLD DOGS TO FUCK RIGHT OFF
NOW PISS OFF TO THE BINGO GRANNY, BEFORE AAH LAMP YER ONE.
SUDDENLY...
SKRIIIIIK! DOOR SECURITY 27- WE THINK SOMEBODIES JUST WALKED PAST "YELP" WEARING TRAINERS. REQUEST BACKUP TO MERCILESSLY KICK HIM SHITLESS DOON A BACK ALLEY, OVER- SKRIIIIIK!!
TRAINERS?! THE FUCKIN' BASTAAD!
HOWAY JIMMY! URPEN SEASON!! SOME CUNTS WEARIN' FUCKIN' TRAINERS!!
AAH CAN FEEL THE FUCKIN' TEST FILLIN' ME EYES UP- AAH DURNT THINK I'LL BE ABLE TU RESTRAIN MESELF FROM HOOFIN' HIS HEED IN
KIST
MEANWHILE, INSIDE...
YOU DONT EVEN KNOW ME- YOU SAY THAT I, BLAH BLAH BLAH YOU DONT UNDERSTAND ME
OI!
TWO LAGERS!!
GASP!
BAR STAFF
LAGER
LEMONADE
NIP!
AALREET GORGEOUS, ARE Y' GETTIN' US A DRINK AN' AAL?
!?
GET IN! I'VE FUCKIN' SCORED!
...ERM... AYE, I'LL GET YER A DRINK, BUT WHAT'LL I GET IN RETURN?
EEH! Y' SAUCY DEVIL!! I'M URLD ENOUGH TO BE YOUR ...erm... SISTER
ARRRGHHH!! FUCKIN' JESUS!
BUT...
HERE MAN BETTY, FORGET HIM, WE WERE JUST WARMIN' UP... LISTEN MAN, IF WE HAVENT SCORED WITH A HUNK BY THE END OF THE NEET, I'LL BUY THE FUCKIN' DRINKS IN
THE END OF THE NEET LATER...
AALREET GORGEOUS- I WANT A LONG HARD MEMOIRABLE SHAFTING OFF YOU
AYE! AND AAH WANT A NUMB FANNY WITH YER BIG, THROBBIN' COCK!
ALLRIGHT GIRLS, RIGHT AWAY!
THAT'LL BE £7 PLEASE
KIST COCKTAIL BAR LIST!
SEX ON THE BEACH // HANGING BALLS
SAND UP YOUR CRACK // NUMB FANNY
LONG HARD MEMOIRABLE SHAFTING
THROBBING COCK
KNEE IN BOLLOCKS
FLOPPY SAGGY TITS
RED RAW BELL
KNOB CHEESE
SHES FUCKIN' PAYIN'
BAH!

SID the SEXIST
TYNESIDE'S SILVER-TONGUED CAVALIER
TITS OOT for the lads

ARE YE GERRIN' THE NEXT ROOND IN THEN, SID?
NAAH. I CANNAT STOP. I'VE GORRA GAN TU THE LIBRARY.

THE LIBRARY?!!
WHAT THE FUCK FAWA?!
PHHTT!
PHFFT!

THEY HAVEN'T PUT A BAR IN HAVE THEY, SID?
DIVVEN'T BE FUCKIN' DAFT MAN. I'VE GOT ME REASONS.

TEKKIN' YER FUCKIN' FANCY FAWA-EYED READIN' BOOKS BACK!
GEROFF MAN!
WHO'D Y'THINK YE ARE LIKE? BAMBA FUCKIN' GASCOIGNE?
PRESTO
WRESTLE!

'PIRATE OF MY HEART' BY BARBARA CARTHORSE? WHAT'S THIS? YER FUCKIN' WANKIN' STASH?
AYE IT'S IN LARGE PRINT 'COZ AALL THE TUGGIN'S SENDIN' HIM FUCKIN' BLIND!
PRESTO

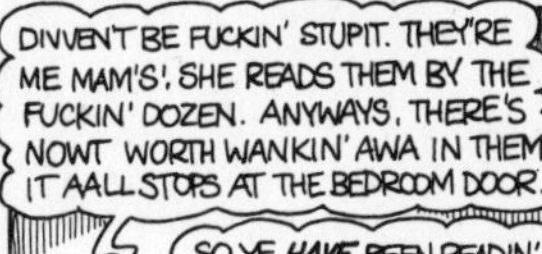
DIVVEN'T BE FUCKIN' STUPIT. THEY'RE ME MAM'S. SHE READS THEM BY THE FUCKIN' DOZEN. ANYWAYS, THERE'S NOWT WORTH WANKIN' AWA IN THEM. IT AALL STOPS AT THE BEDROOM DOOR.

SO YE HAVE BEEN READIN' THEM THEN?
ERM...
HA! HA!
HO! HO!

PIPE DOON. PIPE DOON LADS. I'LL TEK THEM BACK FOR YE, SID.
YE? GAN TU THE LIBRARY?! HAVE YE GONE FUCKIN' MENTAL? THE FUCKIN' LIBRARY'S FOR PUFFS AN' TRAMPS!
AYE. I THINK THE PAIR O' THEM NEED THEIR FUCKIN' BUMPS FELT.
LISTEN MAN, IF I GAN TU THE LIBRARY IT'LL BE ME THAT FEELS THE BUMPS...
...LADY-BUMPS THAT IS.

EH? WHAT'S HE ON ABOOT?
LIBRARIANS MAN. THINK ABOOT IT... THINK ABOOT IT...
...FILTHY.

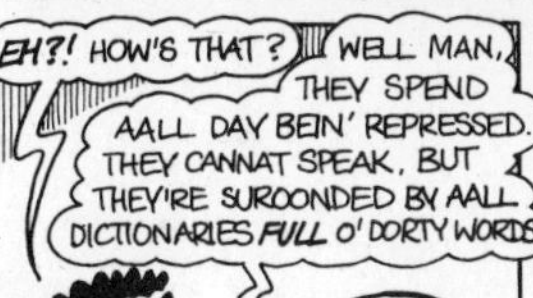
EH?! HOW'S THAT?
WELL MAN, THEY SPEND AALL DAY BEIN' REPRESSED. THEY CANNAT SPEAK, BUT THEY'RE SUROONDED BY AALL DICTIONARIES FULL O' DORTY WORDS.

AALL THEM BOOKS ABOOT SHAGGIN' AN' COCKS AN' AALL THAT. AN AALL THEM JAPANESE WANK BOOK THINGS.
AYE, EROT... ERM... EROT- IKKA.
AYE... 'NIPPLE- NOUN. THE PAP OF THE BREAST'. Y'KNAA, LIKE 'PAPS' MAN, Y'KNAA, TITS.

IT'S AALL TU DEE WI' REPRESSION MAN, Y'SEE ONCE THEY GET THEM GREY SUITS AN' SPECS OFF AN' THAT, THEIR PIES ARE LIKE A BOILIN' CAULDRON O' FANNY BATTA!
I SEE... LIKE, THEY'VE BEEN COOKIN' IN THEIR AAN JUICE AALL DAY LANG.

AYE, THEY'D FUCK OWT - LIKE CATHOLIC LASSES IN THE SIXTH FORM AN' THAT, Y'SEE, WHEN THE PURP TELLS THEM IF THEY DEE SEX AN' THAT THEY'LL BORN IN HELL, IT JUST MAKES THEM WANNA DEE IT AALL THE TIME.

AYE. TELL SOMEONE NOT TU DEE SUMMIK, AN' IT JUST MAKES THEM WANNA DEE IT MORE.

AYE. LIKE DRINKIN' BLEACH.

HERE I GAN! HERE I GAN!
LIBRARY

CAN I HELP YOU?
AYE... ERM... ERM...

ARE YOU AFTER ANYTHING IN PARTICULAR?
GUMPH! ERM... AYE ...AYE... ERM...
LIBRARY

DO YOU FANCY A THRILLER? JUST NICE FOR A LONG COLD NIGHT.
ERM... ERM...
IF ITS AN OVERSIZED ONE WE'LL HAVE TO GO INTO THE STOCKROOM.

DO YOU KNOW EXACTLY WHAT YOU WANT?
ERM... AYE, AYE... YE COULD SAY THAT!

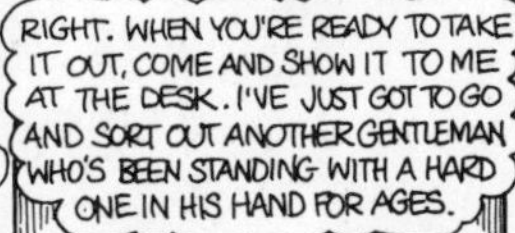
RIGHT. WHEN YOU'RE READY TO TAKE IT OUT, COME AND SHOW IT TO ME AT THE DESK. I'VE JUST GOT TO GO AND SORT OUT ANOTHER GENTLEMAN WHO'S BEEN STANDING WITH A HARD ONE IN HIS HAND FOR AGES.

JESUS.

SHORTLY...
RIGHT PET. I'M READY.
EXCELLENT. JUST PUT IT ON THE COUNTER AND I'LL DEAL WITH IT.
ERM... IF YA SURE THAT'S HOW YE WANT IT... HERE GANS....

IN COURT...
THEN THE DISGUSTING PERVERT EXPOSED HIMSELF TO ME. I'M NOT SURE IF IT WAS ERECT, IT WAS TOO SMALL TO TELL.

STUDENT GRANT

WELL HERE WE ARE. GLASTONBURY. WE MADE IT.
YEAH. THAT WAS SOME HITCH.
RIGHT FROM OUTSIDE YOUR GATE, GRANT.

THANKS DAD.
DON'T MENTION IT. GIVE ME A RING SUNDAY NIGHT AND I'LL COME OVER AND PICK YOU UP.

WOW! IT'S JUST SO ALTERNATIVE.
THAT'S WIGHT. IT'S A WEVOWUTIONAWY SPACE OUTSIDE THE CAPITAWIST SYSTEM.
YEAH. ANARCHY!
QUEUE HERE

£400 PLEASE. DO YOU HAVE AMERICAN EXPRESS?
CASHPOINTS NANNY VILLAGE MERC CAR PARK CORPORATE HOSPITALITY

RIGHT. ANY OF YOU LOT CARRYING DRUGS?
NO.

DO YOU WANT TO BUY SOME? TEN QUID A BAGGY - AND IT'S GOOD SHIT.
WHAT SORT IS IT?
ERM... COW.

GREAT SCORE, GRARNT!
WE CAN WOLL IT UP INTO A BONG. THEN WE CAN HAVE A TOKE ON IT.

SO...
...I'LL DO THIS, ACTUALLY. I'VE SMOKED MORE DOPE GRASS SPLIFFS THAN YOU LOT PUT TOGETHER.
RUSTLE
CRINKLE
CAMERAS PLEASE DO NOT STEAL.

WATCH ME AND LEARN.
CLICK!

SUCK!

FFT FFT FFT

BLAAAAARGH!!!

WOW! IT'S THE ULTIMATE HIGH! YOU'VE ALL GONE PSYCHADELIC GREEN!
DON'T HOG THE DRUGS JOINT, DADDIO! MY TURN NEXT.
THEN ME!

10 MINUTES LATER...
MAN - I AM CHILLED TO THE MAX.
ME TOO ACTUALLY.
WOW! THAT IS GOOD STUFF. NOW WE'RE ALL MELLOW, LET'S GO OUT AND CATCH A POP GIG.

Why do we pay through the nose for electrical goods?

GREEDY SHOPS PUT THE SQUEEZE ON CONSUMERS

British shoppers are being lured by manufacturers into paying way over the odds for their electrical goods.

A study has revealed that on average we are paying £800 more than we need to for our household appliances. Items retailing at £1000 or more in the high street are readily available for only £20 just a short walk away - that's an incredible saving of £980. Britain's consumers are being ripped off because they don't know that identical branded goods are available at hugely discounted prices in their local pub. With the same specifications as the shop bought models, the only difference is that they have had their plugs cut off and sometimes contain small fragments of broken glass.

The biggest price difference we uncovered in our survey was for a £1800 Del Computer which we bought from a heroin addict in the Red Lion for £20 cash.

HOW THEY OVERCHARGE US

MODEL	SHOP PRICE	PUB PRICE	SAVING
Philips 32" widescreen TV	£999	£20 (Red Lion)	£970
JVC MD70R Micro HiFi	£349.99	£20 (Nag's Head)	£329.99
Olympus C900Z digital camera	£499.99	£20 (The Blubell)	£479.99
Panasonic Nicam video	£249.99	£20 (King's Arms)	£229.99

IT'S TIME TO FIGHT BACK!

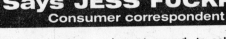

Says JESS FUCKRAD
Consumer correspondent

WE HAVE sat back and allowed ourselves to be ripped off for far too long.

The fact is that Manufacturers and shops are conspiring together to keep prices artificially high. It is up to the British public to say enough is enough. We must make a stand and demand a better deal.

Unless shops are willing and honest enough to sell us big tellys for £20, we should vote with our feet and take our custom elsewhere. Mark my words, if we keep paying these ridiculously inflated prices, they'll keep charging them.

Whatever they tell you, they are lying. It's time they put OUR money where THEIR mouth is, and told the truth for a change.

RONAN the BARBARIAN!

A 'PUNNY' headline thought up in a Fleet Street pub yesterday lunchtime sparked a desperate search for a story to match it.

EXCLUSIVE!

Keating (above) - civilised, and reporter Nick Gates (below left) overcome at press conference

Boyzone headline sparks desperate search for story.

But as journalists across the country last night combed their brains, hopes ware fading that a vaguely appropriate 600-word article would be cobbled together in time.

Sun editor David Yelland said: "The fact that Ronan Keating lives such a squeaky-clean lifestyle is hampering the search, but we are leaving no stone unturned."

Singer

Hopes were raised briefly when a sub-editor walking his dog remembered that the Boyzone singer once rode a motorbike.

Hillman

The lead was followed up, but ended in disappointment when it turned out that Keating had always obeyed the speed limit and shown courtesy to other road users.

Riley

At a hastily arranged press conference, a tearful Nick Gates, the reporter who thought of the headline made a direct appeal to Ronan Keating: "Please, wherever you are, do something a bit barbaric.

Sunbeam

"Trash a small hotel room or have a fight outside a nightclub. Even if it's just posing for photographs in a Viking hat, please do something so I can use my headline."

Eggs not eggs- *claim*

EGGS aren't eggs! And that's as sure as eggs are eggs, *which they aren't!*

That's the conclusion of a report by leading egg-head scientists at the University of Miami who have spent the last three years looking at what eggs are.

But if they're not eggs, what are they?

"No one can say for sure," says the report's author Professor Dwight Kolchinsky. "All we know for certain is that they ain't eggs."

A PINT AND A FIGHT

A *GREAT* BRITISH NIGHT

Issued by the Licensed Victuallers Association

GILBERT RATCHET
I'M OFF TO HAVE A CHAT ABOUT RELIGION WITH THE VICAR, READERS
THE VICARAGE
I FIND THAT IT HELPS TO SOOTHE MY TROUBLED SOUL

AH GILBERT, YOU FIND ME IN A BIT OF A QUANDRY. I HAVE JUST URINATED THROUGH MY PENIS...

...BUT I DAREN'T SHAKE OFF THE DRIPS BECAUSE THE BIBLE FORBIDS US FROM HANDLING OUR PRIVATE PARTS. PROBABLY.

NO WORRIES, VICAR
I'LL INVENT A HANDS-FREE PREPUCE-PULLER TO WAGGLE YOUR LITTLE FELLER DRY.

SEE — THE SPRING-POWERED ARM WILL GENTLY TUG THE TIP OF YOUR TADGER, THUS DISLODGING ANY DEWDROPS
START
GREAT! START IT UP, GILBERT

YANK!
OOPS!
START
I MUST'VE SET THE SPRING TO PULL A DISTANCE OF EIGHT FEET INSTEAD OF EIGHT MILLIMETRES

NICE GOING, GILBERT. AN EIGHT-FOOT LONG FORESKIN IS PRECISELY WHAT I NEEDED...
...YOU LITTLE TIT

BUT NEVER MIND THAT NOW. I HAVE MORE PRESSING THEOLOGICAL MATTERS TO ATTEND TO
START
WHAT'S VEXING YOU, VICAR?

MY VICARAGE IS BEING HAUNTED BY THE H-H-H-HOLY G-GHOST
WOOOOOOO WOOOOOOO
CHATTER CHATTER
BLESS YOU MY SON, WOOOOO
BRRR! I'M SHIT-SCARED OF GHOSTS ME, GILBERT

NEVER FEAR, REVEREND
HOLY WATER
WE'LL PERFORM AN EXORCISM ON THAT BOTHERSOME GODLY GHOUL — USING MY PATENTED "EXORCISE BIKE"

KEEP PEDALLING, VICAR — YOU'RE DOING SWELL
SCOOP
SPLOSH
HOLY WATER
=GASP= IN NOMINI PATRI DOMINOES SOLITAIRE =PANT=

EEYARRGH! MY ELONGATED "POLO-NECK" HAS GOT TANGLED IN THE SPOKES
HOLY WATER
CHEW GRIND MANGLE

OH CRIKEY! I CAN'T GET THE VICAR'S FLUESKIN OUT THE BICYCLE WHEEL
AND THE HOLY GHOSTS ARE ALL COMING TO GET US

WOW! I'VE PULLED THE WHEEL LOOSE
CLONK!
OUCH! MY HEAD
HERE! WHO'S THAT BEHIND MY SOFA?

IT'S THE ARCHBISHOP — WITH A SET OF 'HOLY GHOST' STRING PUPPETS
SO THOSE SPOOKS WEREN'T REAL AFTER ALL

THAT'S RIGHT. MY PLAN WAS TO FRIGHTEN YOU AWAY FROM THE VICARAGE SO THAT I COULD STEAL ALL YOUR TEA AND STICKY BUNS
AND I WOULD'VE GOT AWAY WITH IT IF IT WASN'T FOR THAT MEDDLING KID

GOOD WORK, GILBERT. WE'VE BEEN AFTER THIS CROOKED ARCHBISHOP FOR A LONG TIME
CHURCH POLICE
THERE'S A REWARD FOR HIS CAPTURE — A 24-CARAT GOLD WATCH
GREAT!

INEVITABLY
THERE. JUST EAT THOSE 24 "CARATS" WHILE YOU "WATCH" SPANDAU BALLET PERFORM THEIR SONG "GOLD" ON TELLY
=MUNCH= BAH!
ALWAYS BELIEVE IN YOUR SOUL...

RAT BOY
EEH, THAT WAS A GOOD EASTENDERS, I WONDER WHATS ON THE OTHER SIDE...
CLICK!
Telly
GONE!
WHAT YE FUCKIN' LOOKIN' AT, EH? EH? FUCKIN' MINE THIS.
Y' FUCKIN' BITCH
OOH DEAR. I'D BETTER PHONE THE COUNCIL
HELLO- IS THAT THE COUNCIL? COULD YOU SEND SOMEONE ROUND? I THINK I'VE GOT A RAT-BOY
SO...
ALRIGHT LOVE, VERMIN CONTROL
OOH GOOD. YOU'D BETTER COME IN
COUNCIL VERMIN CONTROL LTD.
SO YOU THINK YOU'VE GOT A VERMIN, THEN. DONT SUPRISE ME LOVE. IN THE CITY YOU AINT NEVER MORE THAN 3 FEET AWAY FROM A RAT BOY.
REALLY? OH DEAR
LETS SEE WHAT WE'VE GOT HERE THEN. AYE, THIS LOOKS LIKE THE WORK OF ONE OF THE LITTLE BUGGERS
I'LL TAKE A QUICK PEEK
FUK OFF RATBOY WOZ ERE
AYE. YOU'VE GOT A NEST HERE
NO SIGN OF IT, THOUGH. WE MUST'VE SCARED IT OFF
BUT...
CHOMP!
GNNN!!
POUNCE!!
IIIIAAAS!! Y' BASTARD!!
HERE MAN, Y FUCKIN' FUCK, WHAT D' Y' FUCKIN' THINK YER FUCKIN' SAYIN', EH? EH? I'M NOT FUCKIN' SCARED OF YE, ME FATHA'LL TEK Y'OOT, EH? EH?
IT'S AAL MINE, THAT SHIT, AAH FUCKIN' TWOCKED IT MESELF
Hop!
HOPS
EH? EH? COME ON THEN, COME ON... FUCK OFF
RIGHT, I'LL LEAVE THIS DOWN FOR HIM. HE'LL NOT BE ABLE TO RESIST
RAT BOY POISON?
OOH NO, THATS CRUEL. DONT YOU HAVE ANYTHING KINDER?
DIAMOND WHITE
WELL, THERE IS THIS HUMANE TRAP, BUT I'M WARNING YOU NOW, IF YOU DONT KILL IT, IT'LL COME BACK AND BRING IT'S MATES, AND THEN YOU'LL HAVE PROBLEMS
WELL I THINK I'LL TAKE THE HUMANE TRAP, THANKYOU VERY MUCH
SOON...
EEH! I THINK I'VE CAUGHT IT.
HERE MAN Y'FUCKER. LERRUS OOT MAN, AAH'VE DONE FUCKIN' NOWT, ME, EH? EH? Y'FUCKER JUST YE FUCKIN' WAIT, AAH KNAA PEOPLE, ME, AND AAH'LL BE OOT HERE BY FUCKIN' LUNCHTIME, AND Y' CANNAT DE FUCKIN' OWT, YE, AND AH'LL TELL Y' THIS, THE FUCKIN' INSTANT AAH'M OOT AAH'LL BE STRAIGHT ROOND TO TORCH YOUR FUCKIN' HOOSE DOON, EH, EH? EH?
HE'S QUITE SWEET UP CLOSE
I'LL SET YOU LOOSE IN THE COUNTRY
THE COUNTRYSIDE
SO...
CHUCKLE! THERE YOU GO, FREE TO PLAY IN THE FIELDS AND MAKE NEW FRIENDS
LEAP!!
SCURRY SCURRY!
VROOOOOOOOOM!
HA HA HA HA FUCK OFF!
TOWN 100 MILES
3 DAYS LATER...
Puff pant, Puff pant
DUMPH DUMPH DUMPH DUMPH
Wheeze!
FUK OFF NOW
SMASH!
BURST!

HERE MAN, Y' FUCKIN' RADGE TEK A CHILL PILL, WE'RE DEEIN' NOWT MAN
SHAG SHAG SHAG!
JUMP ON!
JUMP OFF!
BLEACH
ROLL!

GILBERT RATCHET
COR
TOWN HALL
GRAND NEW YEAR'S EVE PARTY TO-NITE TICKETS - £10
I WISH I COULD AFFORD A TICKET TO THAT NEW YEAR'S EVE PARTY

I'D LIKE TO GO TOO, GILBERT — BUT I'M SIMPLY TOO BUSY HAVING SEX TO GO TO ANY PARTIES
GOSH — IT'S COMEDY PIMP-A-LIKE NIGHTCLUB OWNER PETER STRINGFELLOW

DON'T WORRY, MR STRINGFELLOW
TOOLS
I'LL BUILD YOU A PARTY-CAL ACC-CELEBRATOR THAT WILL COMPRESS A WHOLE NEW YEAR'S EVE PARTY INTO JUST 30 SECONDS

SQUEAK
FOR AULD LANG'S SYNE...
COMPRESSED AIR
ON
OFF
SAUSAGE ROLLS
FIZZY POP
PHEW! IT'S BEEN ONE HECK OF A 30-SECOND PARTY, GILBERT — YOU'D BEST LET ME OUT NOW

OH CRIKEY! MY PARTY-CAL ACC-CELEBRATOR MUST'VE GOT THE MINNELLIUM BUG
WE'LL TAKE A CUP O' KINDNESS YET...
COMPRESSED AIR
ON
OFF
SAUSAGE ROLLS
I CAN'T MAKE IT STOP

TWO HOURS LATER
THAT EXCESSIVE PARTYING HAS LEFT YOU LOOKING A BIT RAGGED
WHAT YOU NEED IS A NICE REJUVENATING FACE-LIFT

STRETCH
HEAVE!
MY FACE-LIFT-O-MATIC WILL SOON HAVE YOU LOOKING YOUNG AGAIN

SSH-LRIPP!
OOPS! THAT WASN'T MEANT TO HAPPEN

YOU LITTLE TWERP! YOU'VE GONE AND RIPPED ALL MY SKIN OFF
NOW MY ENTIRE BODY IS AN AGONISINGLY PAINFUL MASS OF RAW PEELED FLESH

EXCUSE ME — I'M AN ECCENTRIC "SILENCE OF THE LAMBS"-STYLE PSYCHOPATH MILLIONAIRE, AND THAT 'SKIN SUIT' IS JUST WHAT I WANT
I'LL GIVE YOU TEN QUID FOR IT

HOORAY!
TICKETS £10
NOW I CAN AFFORD A TICKET TO THE NEW YEAR'S EVE PARTY

BUT THERE YOU ARE, GILBERT — THERE'S YOUR DAD, EATING HIS EARLY EVENING MEAL, ON NEW YEAR'S EVE
RACING POST
HP
OH NO! IT'S THAT SORT OF NEW YEAR'S EVE "PA TEA"!

LetterBocks

It's the page that doesn't want any trouble, but ends up getting glassed

Smiles better?

Letterbocks,
P.O. Box 1PT,
Newcastle upon
Tyne, NE99 1PT
Fax:
2414244
0191 281 0049
email:
viz.comic@virgin.net
VIZ.CO.UK

■ They say that laughter is the best medicine. My grandad has got Parkinson's disease and we've been laughing at him for months and he hasn't got any better. So much for that theory.

D. Smoog
Paris

■ I've just sat through Janet Street-Porter's TV series 'As the Crow Flies' where she walked in a straight line from Edinburgh to Greenwich. What a pity she didn't start from my house in Haddington, just 16 miles to the east. That way, her walk would have taken her slap bang through the middle of the army's firing range at Otterburn, and she might have been shot. Now *that* would have been good telly.

D. Dick
Haddington

■ I had to laugh the other day when I saw a very crude letter about internet porn I'd sent to Viz published on the letters page. Imagine my surprise when I saw it had been printed with my real name in full instead of the pseudonym I'd supplied. My now ex-boss, who used to pay my home phone bill, has clearly failed to see the funny side. You utter, utter cunts.

Neil Weatherall
e-mail

Taking stock

■ It must be great having your own corner shop. Any time you want anything, you just help yourselves from the shelves. And it's all free! No wonder shopkeepers are always smiling and drive around in Volvo estates.

A. Berry
Grimsby

■ I've just run out of skins, but unfortunately I'm too minced to go out on my own. If anyone is going past the Esso station on Great Western Road in Glasgow, could you get me some Rizlas? Oh, and six packets of Space Raider crisps and four Topics.

Douglas B.
Glasgow

■ Congratulations to Nick Ross for managing to use his catchphrase "Do Sleep Well" on his flowers for Jill Dando. But what a good job Jill wasn't the co-presenter of *The Generation Game*. "Didn't he do well" would have struck entirely the wrong note on the flowers from Bruce Forsyth.

F. Peters
Hull

■ Why do farmers always put their gates right next to the muddiest parts of the field?

Neil Bye
e-mail

■ Esther Rantzen said in the Sunday Telegraph that an unpleasant child is a contradiction in terms, and that she'd never met a child she didn't like. Obviously she's never come home and found some 13 year-old Rat Boy shitting on her living room carpet with her video under his arm.

Mrs A. Hedley
Byker

Onion ladder

■ In this century Britain has only made war with countries whose capital cities begin with the letter 'B' - Germany *(Berlin)*, Argentina *(Buenos Aires)*, Iraq *(Baghdad)* and Serbia *(Belgrade)*. China change the name of Peking to Beijing and we bomb their embassy. One hopes in the new century we will show a little more imagination when making war with other nations.

Martin Harwood
Bradford

■ I haven't got a letter but here's a joke; *Question:* How many women does it take to change a light bulb? *Answer:* Two. One to change the bulb, the other to suck my cock.

E. Groin
Walsall

Mum's the work

■ Why don't all these so called single mothers employ another single mother as an au-pair? Then they could all get proper jobs.

M. Withkids
Surbiton

■ Vauxhall reckon they have made 2500 changes to the new Vectra. Well the original must have been a crock of shite.

Jack Roman
e-mail

■ Rob Thompson's suggestion (page 10) about the publishers of the Big Issue introducing a subscription scheme would have another advantage. It would mean that the hard working vendors could stay at home in front of the fire with their feet up, or make use of their new-found leisure time by going to the opera or ballet.

Don Swan
Nottingham

■ Jerry hall says that to keep your husband keen, you must be a 'maid in the parlour, a cook in the kitchen and a whore in the bedroom." I recently decided to follow her advice. I kept the house very clean, I prepared delicious meals every night, and I allowed dozens of fat businessmen to have sex with me for money in the marital bed. Surprisingly, my husband left me. Did I follow her advice correctly?

Pauline Riley
e-mail

■ With regard to Pauline Riley's letter (above), Jerry Hall is talking out of her Texan arse. The perfect woman is obviously going to be a whore in the parlour, a whore in the kitchen and a whore in the bedroom. And then she can think about getting my tea on.

R.T.
Kilburn

■ Why are tortoises allowed to hibernate for several months and I'm not? I quite fancy October to February in bed but my work won't let me have the time off. I thought we lived in a time of equal opportunities.

C. Mappley
Surrey

WARNING!
THIEVES OPERATE
IN THIS AREA
BEEP!
BEEP!
BEEP!

See You, Jimmy

■ Jimmy Hill seems to be manifesting himself everywhere. Not content with appearing in the Viz or brandishing phallus-shaped cucmbers on saucy postcards, he appears on the pages of popular Scottish cartoon 'Oor Wullie' dressed as a rabbit. Thankfully, Wullie hadn't dropped acid, he'd only eaten cheese the night before.

Alan Donnelly
Croydon

■ Jonathan Ross should be ashamed of himself. All the money he's got and his daughter gets bitten off a snake. I earn just over £100 per week and my daughter has never been attacked by a reptile. My son once got stang off a wasp, but that was when I was on income support.

Mrs G. Yarwood
Halesowen

■ The death of Rod Hull has proved to be a bit of a disappointment for me. I originally misheard the news report and thought they said ROY HUDD. Imagine

how sad I was to hear that the old cunt was still alive.

G. McKendrick
Glasgow

Muff justice

■ If a woman says no she **means** no, but if she tells me she's over 16 then it's my call. Where's the justice?

S. Partridge
e-mail

What's the naughtiest thing you've ever done?

YOU CONFESS

Steve Jenkins, 22, dispatch rider
"When I was 16, I borrowed my dad's car without permission. I crashed it, and said it had been stolen."

Richard Turd-Burglar, 12, ad-sales manager
"When I was a teenager in Australia, I used to steal women's underwear from washing lines and wear it in bed."

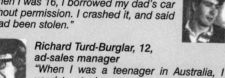

Peter Sutcliffe, 53, lorry driver
"Between the dates of February 1977 and November 1980, in the counties of West and South Yorkshire, I attacked and killed 13 women"

Andy Turnbull, 32, coffee machine engineer
"Once while stopping at my granny's, I used her false teeth to wipe my arse with, then put them back in her mouth."

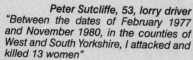

Just ask Walt's head

Each week, you put your questions to Walt Disney's head in a fridge

Dear Walt's head... **Where is the coldest place on earth?**

Rusty Junior III
Talahassee, Georgia

Well, I sometimes think it's the end of my nose! Brrrrr! But seriously, Rusty, it's probably Alaska or Iceland, or some place real chilly like that.

Dear Walt's head... **Why do stars twinkle?**

Mary Beth Kozwalski
Hell's Kitchen, NYC

That's a tough one, Mary Beth. I guess it's all the dirt and pollution and stuff in the skies that makes those little fellers twinkle so. Ahtchooooo!

Dear Walt's head... **Why does a snail leave a silver trail?**

Chuck Jerkoff Jnr.
Des Moines, Iowa

Well it helps them slide right along. See, those little critters, why, they carry their houses around on their backs, and that's a mighty tall order when you've only got one foot. Jesus H. Christ, it's cold in here.

Dear Walt's head... **Does the light go off in a fridge when the door is closed?**

Junior Ableman III, Jnr.IV
Flagstaff, Arizona

Well, little buddy, If I had a dollar for every time someone has asked my head that question...! Yes, it sure does.

Well, my head is starting to thaw out, so we'd best close the old fridge door for this week. Keep those questions coming!

Walt

TOP TIPS

SPREAD the cost of an expensive monthly bus pass by paying for each journey individually.

Mr Teats
Croydon

BLIND date losers. When receiving a consolation kiss from Cilla, use the opportunity to bite her on the eye.

M. Edwards
Surrey

HAVING to read subtitles can be irritating when watching a foreign film. Win brownie points in the cinema by reading the subtitles aloud for others.

Eddie O'Hanlon
e-mail

BREAST feeding mothers. Not enough time to make a nice brew-up? Simply hold a tea bag to your nipple and hey presto! A warm, milky mug of tit-tea.

Ruth Shearing
Wood Green

DRIVERS for Victoria Taxis of Hebburn. When picking up a fare at 3am, try getting out of the car and ringing the doorbell instead of sounding your horn, you fat, sweaty, lard-arsed bastards.

Rooster
Hebburn

SAVE money on expensive digital cameras by simply building models of your friends and family out of Lego and then taking pictures of them with a normal camera.

Orson Cart
Cullercoats

BOB Carolgees. If Spit the Dog asks you to adjust your TV aerial, tell him to fuck off and do it himself.

Hapag Lloyd
Runcorn

FEELING unattractive? Simply watch Robot Wars. Seeing all those spotty geeks paying more attention to a twin armature 12v motor than Phillippa Forester in a skin tight top bending over to pick a washer up off the floor is bound to make you feel like a super-stud.

Richard Harrison
Tywyn

CREATE your own solar eclipse by attatching a football to a broom handle and holding it in front of the sun. For a lunar eclipse, simply substitute a banana.

P. Less
e-mail

PRETEND you're on the Jerry Springer show by sitting in your dentist's waiting room and punching the first person who comes through the door.

Hapag
Runcorn

UNLESS you have a large van or a car with a roof rack, always stress to the taxidermist that you want your pet boa constrictor stuffed in a COILED position.

Joanne Tufnell
Turnbury

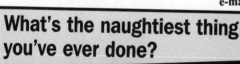

IT'S BALLOONA

START 1

Who wants to be a millionaire? To amass vast fortunes, build busness empires, and then piss it all in the wind vainly attempting to circumnavigate the world in a poxy balloon. Richard Branson's life has been as eventful as his balloon attempts have been farcical. Now you can live that lavish lifestyle, and experience the ups and downs of being Britain's grinniest deathwish millionaire, with this fabulous boardgame. As well as a thrilling race around the world, it is also a dazzling insight into the life of Richard Branson, as told in his recent autobiography.

You have not tied the neck of your balloon properly, and all the air comes out. *Go back to start.*

Congratulations. A perfect take off! Your balloon sails skywards. Unfortunately you're not in it. Niether is anyone else. *Miss 2 turns* while recovery teams try to find it.

4

POP! Your balloon has burst. Grab a lifejacket and go back to square 1.

"CHEESE!" Photo call. Miss a turn while you dress up as a woman

21

Freshly circumcised, you unwisely settle down to watch the sexy sci-fi film Barbarella. Your banjo snaps. Return to the Banjo Hospital.

You're allergic to your first wife's fanny batter and your cock swells up like a balloon. Go to Portland Street Banjo Hospital to have your Kojak's roll-neck removed.

"CHEESE" Photo call. Miss turn while you dangle off a helicopter.

In recognition of your contribution to enterprise Mrs Thatcher awards you the honour of picking up some litter. *Go back 2 spaces* while you look for a womble outfit.

24

CHEESE' Photo call. *Miss a turn* while you dress up as a Long John Silver.

At Princess Diana's funeral you badly misjudge the mood of the nation, grinning and waving to the crowds as if you were arriving at a Royal Variety Performance. Go back 2 spaces.

27

POP Your balloon has burst. Grab a lifejacket and go back to square 1.

CY! THE LIFE & TIMES OF RICHARD BRANSON

A ROUND THE WORLD SUICIDAL, SELF-PUBLICISING, GRINNING BILLIONAIRE BOARD GAME FOR 2 OR MORE PLAYERS.

Instructions

Cut out the 4 counters below and fold back the tabs. Take turns at throwing the dice and move the appropriate number of spaces. Do not start until you throw a six to be born with a silver spoon in your grinning gob.

Whilst at Stowe public school you start writing your very own strum book about a young Scandinavian school matron. Miss a turn while you and your fag have a milk race.

10

The headmaster expels you from public school, aged 13, for making nocturnal visits to his 18-year-old daughter's bedroom. Go back 2 places for being a fucking liar.

At University you develop an unhealthy interest in Family Planning, don a pair of Joe 90 glasses and open your very own hippy clap clinic. Business booms - go forwards 2 spaces.

H

Portland Street Banjo Hospital

7

... fourth
Miss a *turn*
... ur mother
... u walk on a
... building 50
... e trek to
... emouth, on
... our own.

13

"CHEESE!"

Photo call. Miss a *turn* while you dress up as a Zulu warrior.

POP!

Your balloon has burst. Grab a lifejacket and go back to square 1.

Knock knock! You're caught smuggling records from Belgium. Miss 2 turns while the Customs & Excise lock you up.

17

After only weeks in the bookshop your £20 attempt at an autobiography is reduced to £16. Miss a turn

31

CHEESE!

Photo call. Miss a *turn* while you lie on top of an aeroplane.

At the Virgin Cola launch you pose for pictures with Pamela Anderson. Woops! You've burst your banjo again. Return to the Banjo Hospital.

SPLASH!

You have ditched into the sea. *Start again.*

The Mrs Brady Bunch
DOLLY
ADA
ENA

SNORE! K-GGGSK SNORE! WHISTLE...

HUB HUB HUB
CYPRESS GARDENS REST HOME

HUB HUB HUB
...SNORE! RATTLE SNORE..!

HUB HUB HUB

EEH. LOOK AT THAT. 3 IN THE MORNING.
EEEH. THAT'S A DISGRACE. WHEN I WAS A GIRL IT USED TO BE 1 OR 2.
1 OR 2. YES.
THEY OUGHT TO DO SOMETHING.

THEY'LL NOT DO ANYTHING. THEY NEVER DO. IT'S THE SAME IN THE AFTERNOONS. YESTERDAY IT WAS 10 PAST 4.
IT NEVER.
IT WAS. THAT'D NEVER'VE HAPPENED BEFORE THE WAR.
THE WAR. YES.

DON'T TALK TO ME ABOUT THE WAR. I DID MY BIT. I WORKED IN SHELDONS GROCERS. IF I HADN'T DONE THAT, MR. SHELDON WOULDN'T HAVE BEEN ABLE TO JOIN THE NAVY AND GET DROWNDED IN THE ATLANTIC.

I DID MY BIT AND ALL, ADA. I INFORMED ON YOUR SIDNEY TO THE MILITARY POLICE WHEN HE WAS AWOL IN THE LOFT.
THAT'S RIGHT. YOU DID.
THERE'S SOMEONE COMING.

WELL, IT'S ABOUT BLOODY TIME. WE'VE BEEN SAT HERE SINCE 5-AND-20 PAST.
I'M BEFORE THEM. I'VE GOT A WEEPING CYST IN ME OXTER AND I'M HAVING TROUBLE WITH ME VAGINA, DOCTOR.

LOOK AT THAT. HE CAN'T EVEN SPEAK BLOODY ENGLISH. TCHOH
AYE. GREEN AS THE ACE OF SPADES.
I'M NOT RACHELIST. BUT WHITE FOR WHITE. THAT'S WHAT I SAY.

WELL I AM RACIST AND PROUD OF IT. MY ALBERT WAS OUT THERE AND WHEN HE COME BACK, HE'D NEVER EAT ANOTHER BANANA.
WELL, YOU COULDN'T GET THEM, COULD YOU.
I COULD. I WORKED AT SHELDONS. I USED TO PINCH 'EM.

NOW, ME TOP PLATE'S BEEN GIVIN' ME SOME RIGHT OLD GYP, DOCTOR. I USED TO 'AVE LOVELY TEETH. I HAD THEM OUT FOR ME 21st. 'COURSE, I WAS STILL A VIRGIN THEN. I'D MET SIDNEY - BUT WE'D DECIDED TO WAIT. YOU DID IN THEM DAYS.
THERE WAS NONE OF THIS FREE LOVE - WITH COMDOMS AND WHAT-NOT. OH, NO.

THESE DAYS IT'S ALL THESE POCKET FANNIES, FRENCH TICKLERS AND TWIN-SPEED NON-DOCTORS, ISN'T IT.
AYE. TEN-INCH STRAP-ON COCKIES, STALLION DELAY CREAM AND VIETNAMESE LOVE-EGGS.
THAT'S RIGHT. GIMP MASKS, 'BACKDOOR SPECIALS' EJACULATING BUTT-PLUGS. AND CLITS.

NEXT DAY...
EEH. LOOK AT THAT.
THEY OUGHT TO DO SOMETHING.
THEY'LL NOT DO ANYTHING. THEY NEVER DO.

NORBERT COLON

SPOILT BASTARD

I'VE BEEN THINKING MOTHER. THERES MORE TO LIFE THAN MONEY AND MATERIAL THINGS

YES... YES DEAR, THATS RIGHT, THERE IS...

THINGS MONEY CANT BUY- THE FLASH OF A KINGFISHERS WING...
YES!
...A BABY'S FIRST SMILE...
YES!
...THE FRESH SMELL OF A GARDEN IN AUTUMN...
YES YES!

...HEARING THE SONG OF THE LARK... WRAPPING UP WARM ON A CRISP SNOWY DAY...
YES!
...WATCHING THE SUN GO DOWN...
YES YES!!!
Tremble!

...OVER SAN FRANCISCO BAY.
NO!

AND...

LAST CALL FOR FLIGHT BA 302 TO SAN FRANCISCO

IF YOU THINK I'M TRAVELLING ECONOMY CLASS YOU CAN BUMMIN' WELL THINK AGAIN, YOU TIGHT ARSED FAT OLD BITCH

GPD. ST. SD. DJ. AC. V1295.

Not got the bottle to buy a jazzmag...?

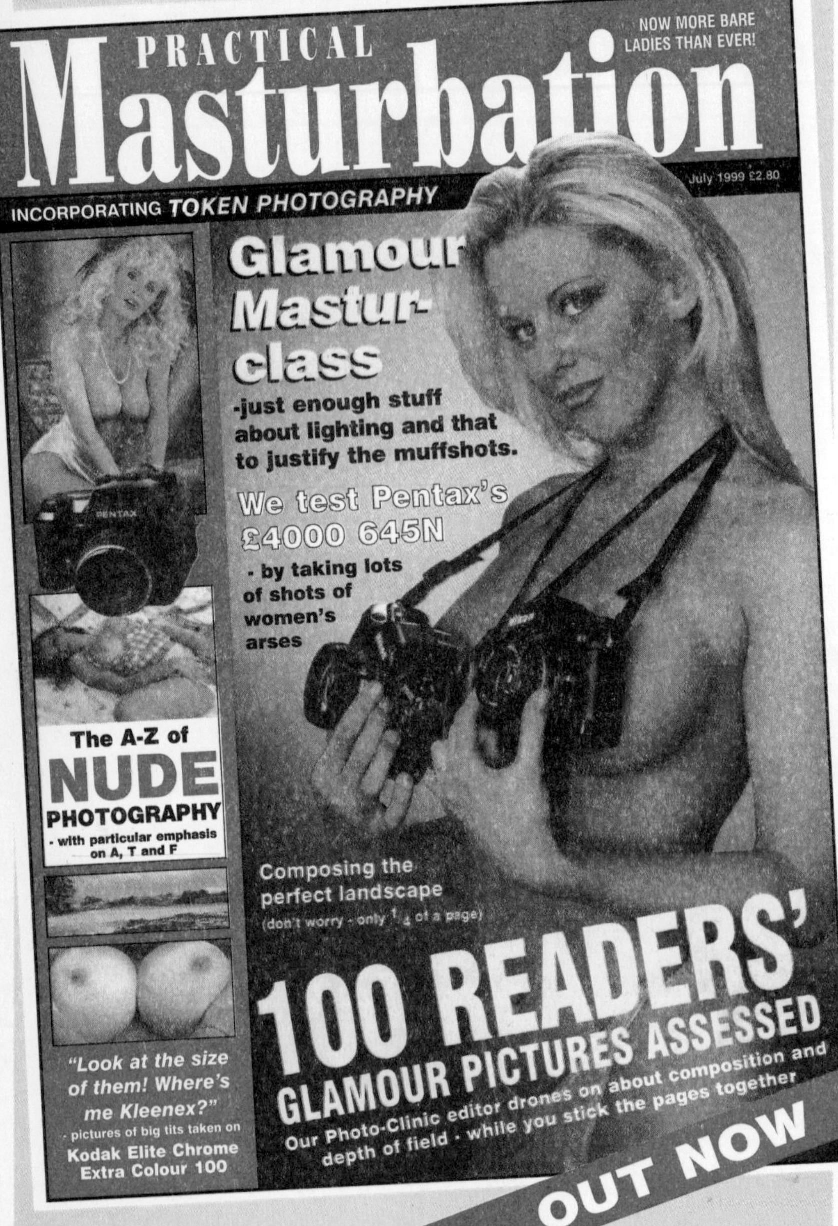

Save the Moyle

Protest launched on Radio 1 airwaves

GREENPEACE campaigners in rubber dinghies yesterday swamped the airwaves surrounding Radio One in protest at the Norwegian Government's policy of Moyle hunting.

A beached Moyle floundering on an episode of 'Never Mind The Buzzcocks' recently.

Moyles, the largest animals on radio, are an endangered species after being extensively hunted for their blabber. The Moyle is also a precious source of ego, a commodity which is used extensively in the entertainment industry.

Victor

Because of their size Moyles are an easy target. They inhabit the shallow airwaves of daytime Radio One and cannot remain undercover for more than one record, before surfacing to spout shit for several minutes. Moyles attract symbiotic parasites who attach themselves to their big, fat, sweaty arses and laugh sycophantically at the constant, incoherent, high pitched sounds which they emit. Some experts believe that these sounds are a form of intelligent communication, although no-one has yet been able to decipher them. Despite its vast bulk the Moyle exists entirely on a diet of cheese and onion crisps which it scoops up in vast quantities in its huge mouth as it gracelessly manoeuvres itself around the airwaves.

Viva

Now protected by international law, the hunting of Moyles is strictly regulated and licenses are only granted for the purposes of scientific research.

Astra 1.3 GL

Despite being the largest animal that has ever lived, Moyles have the smallest penis, at a mere three quarters of an inch - when erect.

Hitchcock Horror Threat to Stars

Beefcake Fabio after the attack by the 11lb goose

STARS were in hiding last night after a spate of attacks sparked fears that Alfred Hitchcock's 'The Birds' was coming true.

In the film, people in a small fishing port are subject to a reign of terror by birds which mysteriously turn savage.

goose

In a chilling echo of the film, American beefcake star Fabio was hit in the face by an 11lb goose whilst on a rollercoaster in Williamsberg, Virginia. Only two months later, Italian screen siren Sophia Loren was viciously pecked at by a cockatoo whilst opening the Harrods sale in London.

"After these two incidents, the stars are taking no chances." said spokesman for the stars Artie Fufkin. "They're all absolutely terrified.

grope

"They've locked themselves in a house and nailed planks across the windows. They're taking this very seriously."

The panic has left the entertainment industry

SHOWBIZ EXCLUSIVE!

at a standstill, with TV studios, concert venues and film sets around the world left deserted.

frotter

Meanwhile, industry chiefs issued assurances to stars that they have nothing to fear, and urged them to return to work. "Please come out. The birds are not going to get you," said Disney boss Michael Eisner.

feel up

Speaking from the four bedroom house in Cape Cod where the stars have been holed up since Tuesday, a nervous Charlton Heston said: "This whole birds thing has got us all on edge. The Artist formerly known as Prince has just heard a noise in the attic and Cilla Black has gone up to investigate. I don't mind admitting, we're real scared and we're not coming out."

Raffles
The Gentleman Thug

D'OILEY CARTE Theatre
The PINAFORES of PENZANCE

I'M ON THE STAGE AND SINGING BUT THE LYRICS ARE REPETITIVE.
HE'S ON THE STAGE AND SINGING BUT THE LYRICS ARE REPETITIVE. REPETITIVE REPETITIVE REPETITIVE REPETITIVE... HE'S ON THE STAGE AND SINGING BUT THE LYRICS ARE REPETITIVE!

LORD ALMIGHTY, BUNNY. THIS SHOW IS INDUCING A CERTAIN AMOUNT OF LONGEUR.
INDEED, ONE IS BORED FUCKING SHITLESS.

SK-K-KK... F-NNNNF!

I SAY! DO YOU MIND?
NOT AT ALL, SIR. FEEL AT LIBERTY TO GO AND FUCK YOURSELF.

OH GOD, BUNNY. WILL THIS TORTURE NEVER END?
WE SHOULD HAVE STAYED IN. I'VE GOT A COUPLE OF RED-HOT PORNO MAGIC LANTERN SHOWS AT HOME.

BOR-ING! BOR-ING!
SHH!

AH - HALF-TIME, BUNNY. FORMIDABLE. LET'S HIT THE CRUSH BAR...
...I CAN'T FACE ANOTHER FOUR ACTS OF THIS UNLESS I'M RODENT-BUTTOCKED.

I SAY, RAFFLES - LOOK AT THE QUEUE. WE'LL NEVER GET SERVED AT THIS RATE.
WATCH AND LEARN, BUNNY OLD THING.

COME ON! COME ON! OUT THE THOROUGHFARE. MY STOMACH IS LABOURING UNDER THE MIS-APPREHENSION THAT MY OESOPHAGUS IS SEVERED.

A PINT OF MADEIRA TOP AND A BAG OF VENISON SCRATCH-INGS, MY GOOD MAN.
YES, YOUR LORDSHIP.

OH - AND COULD YOU BY CHANCE FIT A SMALL CREME-DE-MENTHE IN THERE AS WELL?
CERTAINLY YOUR LORDSHIP.

THEN MIGHT I SUGGEST THAT YOU SHOULD HAVE PLENISHED THE FUCKER UP IN THE FIRST PLACE, PAL.

EXCUSE ME, SIR - DID YOU SPILL MY KILDERKIN?
I'M SORRY?
YOU WILL BE, SUNSHINE. YOU FUCKING WILL BE.
DID... YOU... SPILL... MY... KILDERKIN?

NO. I BELIEVE NOT. BUT IF SUCH A HAPPENSTANCE OBTAINS, I WILL GLADLY REINSTATE YOUR BEVERAGE.
ARE YOU CALLING ME A SODOMITE?
POSH!

SCRUNCH!
AAAARGH!

DING-A-LINGGGG!
AH, BUNNY - I AVER THAT I'LL SIT OUT THE SECOND HALF IN HERE. THEN, AFTERWARDS, I'LL ATTEND THE STAGE DOOR TO PRESENT MY COMPLIMENTS TO THE LEADING ACTRESS.

INDEED. SHE HAS MOST SPLENDID SOPRANO TONES.
YES. AND TITS LIKE TWO PUPPIES ALTERCATING IN A PORTMANTEAU.

AFTER THE SHOW...
AH, MISS KEPPEL. ALLOW ME TO BE THE FIRST TO CONGRATULATE YOU ON YOUR SPLENDID THEATRICAL PERFORMANCE...
... AND FURTHERMORE I SHOULD LIKE TO REQUEST THAT YOU JOIN ME THIS EVENING FOR DINNER AT THE RITZ.

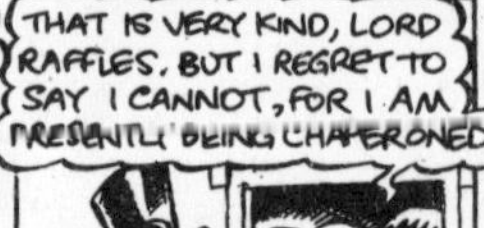
THAT IS VERY KIND, LORD RAFFLES. BUT I REGRET TO SAY I CANNOT, FOR I AM PRESENTLY BEING CHAPERONED...

...BY THE 7th EARL OF NAILS.

'ERE - ARE YOU CHATTIN' UP MY BIRD?

AND WHAT CONSEQUENCES WOULD ENSUE FROM THAT EVENTUALITY...
FUCKFACE?

GO ON, YOUR GRACE! KICK HIM WHILST HE'S RECUMBENT.

SPOILT BASTARD

LORRA, LORRA, CHUCK! LOOK AT ME HURR.. LORRA, LORRA, LORRA!
Cilla's MOMENT OF TRUTH
HA! HA! HA! HA! HA!

NOW THIS WEEK, JOBLESS MR. COLLINS FROM HULL IS TRYING TO BUY HIS CHILDREN'S LOVE BY STICKIN' A LORRA LORRA PINS IN HIS EYES... A HUNDRED IN EACH EYE...
...WHILE TAP DANCING ON A UNICYCLE, CHUCKS!

LOOK AT HIM... MAKING A FOOL OF HIMSELF AND HIS CHILDREN BY IMPLICATION. I'M GLAD IT'S NOT ME
AAARGH! AAARGH! TIPPITY TAP! TIPPITY TAP!
IT'S EMBARRASSING ENOUGH HAVING TO SHARE YOUR NAME WITHOUT WATCHING YOU HUMILIATE YOURSELF IN FRONT OF THE NATION

WELL DONE, MR COLLINS. WORRA LORRA PINS! AND HERE'S YOUR SON'S PRIZE... A REMOTE CONTROL HELICOPTER
POP!

HELLO!? CARLTON TELEVISION? I'D LIKE MY MOTHER TO APPEAR ON 'CILLA'S MOMENT OF TRUTH'...

SO...
ON THE STUDIO FLOOR IN TWO MINUTES, MRS. TIMPSON, AND JUST A COUPLE OF THINGS TO REMEMBER...
...WHEN YOU MEET CILLA, DON'T LOOK HER IN THE EYE, SHE DOESN'T LIKE IT. DON'T SAY 'HURR' OR 'LORRA' AND FOR GOD'S SAKE DON'T TOUCH HER.

OH, DEAR.. I REALLY DON'T WANT TO DO...
DON'T YOU DARE LET ME DOWN, WOMAN... REMEMBER...
LORRA! LORRA! LORRA!
...THIS IS YOUR CHANCE TO WIN MY LOVE

NOW THE NEXT FAMILY TO MEET THEIR MOMENT OF TRUTH ARE CISSY AND TIMMY. THEY ARE THE TIMPSONS FROM FULCHESTER

WELL, TIMMY. YOU LOOKED AT THE PRIZES IN CILLA'S DREAM CATALOGUE, DIDN'T YOU, CHUCK? .. TELL US WHAT YOU CHOSE
WELL, CILLA...
...THE PRIZES WERE SO GREAT, I FOUND IT HARD TO CHOOSE JUST ONE... BUT IN THE END, I DECIDED TO HAVE ALL OF THEM

NOW, CISSY, YOUR CHALLENGE IS TO BALANCE 15 PENNY COINS ON EDGE ON YOUR NOSE, WHILE POGOING FOR 20 BOUNCES
YES, CILLA
LET'S HAVE A LOOK AT YOUR VIDEO DIARY AND SEE HOW YOU GOT ON, SHALL WE?

SO..
OH, TIMMY... SOB!... I CAN'T EVEN BALANCE THE COINS!

MON 10·30
REC
WILL YOU SHUT UP, WOMAN? .. I'M TRYING TO CHOOSE MY PRIZE FROM CILLA'S DREAM CATALOGUE

BOING! BOING!
TUE 07·14
REC
BOING! CHINK! CHINK!

DON'T YOU DARE BREAK THE YOLK... AND DON'T LET IT GO HARD...

THU 9·06
REC
...I WANT IT JUST RIGHT. AND ANY MORE CRISPY BITS ROUND THE EDGE AND YOU'RE DEAD!

BOING! BOING!
WOAH!... ARRGH!
FRI 03·32
REC
CRASH!
FOR FLIPS SAKE, WOMAN, WILL YOU KEEP THE NOISE DOWN. I'M TRYING TO SLEEP UP HERE.

WELL, THAT'S HOW YOU AND MUMMY GOT ON, TIMMY. AND THESE ARE YOUR PRIZES... SO NOW IT'S TIME TO WISH MUMMY 'GOOD LUCK'

LET'S GO!

READY, CISSY? ..
...GO!

BOING! BOING! BOING! BOING!
1...2...3...4...

BOING! BOING!
...5...6...7...8...9...10...
WHIZZ!!

...11...12...13... 14...15...16...
BOING! BOING!

...17...18...19...
YES! YES!

VWOOOSH!
SMACK!
CHINK! CHINK!

OOH, WORRA WORRA SHAME, CHUCK! NINETEEN BOUNCES... PUT THE TOYS BACK, SON...
...YER MOTHER'S LET YOU DOWN

ER... CAN I JUST TAKE THIS OPPORTUNITY TO SAY... HOW ASHAMED I AM... TO CALL THIS WOMAN MY MOTHER...

...IT'S DIFFICULT TO FIND THE WORDS TO EXPRESS MY LOATHING FOR HER, EXCEPT TO SAY...

...THAT I DESPISE HER TO THE PIT OF MY STOMACH... AND I ALWAYS WILL
RADIOS

ESTHER RANTZEN'S
HEART of GOLD
ROARING ACROSS THE ATLANTIC OCEAN WAS THE MOST INCREDIBLE FLYING MACHINE YOU EVER SAW...
BUILT BY TV PERSONALITY ESTHER RANTZEN, IT WAS A HUGE MECHANICAL TURBO-DRIVEN HEART, BEDECKED WITH GOLD-LEAF AND PRECIOUS JEWELS

ACCOMPANYING ESTHER IN THE REMARKABLE FLYING HEART WAS HER CROSS-EYED CHUM CYRIL FLETCHER
ENGAGE VENTRICLE THRUSTERS, CYRIL
AYE-AYE, ESTHER

CYRIL, LOOK - SOME DISABLED CHILDREN ARE MAROONED IN AN OPEN BOAT
WE MUST SAVE THEM!

CLIMB ABOARD MY BIG GOLDEN HEART, CHILDREN

WE'D BETTER STOP AT THIS UNCHARTED ISLAND TO RE-FUEL THE SHIP
DO YOU THINK YOU'LL FIND PETROL ON THE ISLAND, MR FLETCHER?

NOT PETROL, YOUNGSTER — COCK-SHAPED VEGETABLES
YOU SEE, THE ENGINE OF THE HEART OF GOLD IS FUELLED BY ORGANIC PRODUCE WHICH RESEMBLES HUMAN GENITALIA

ESTHER'S CARDIOVASCULAR AIRCRAFT LANDED ON THE MYSTERIOUS UNCHARTED ISLAND
WE'RE SURE TO FIND SOME HILARIOUS VEGETABLES HERE.

ESTHER ~ WE'VE FOUND A POTATO THAT LOOKS LIKE A BIG HAIRY FANNY
THAT'S GREAT, CHILDREN

SUDDENLY
GOOD HEAVENS! AN EIGHT-FOOT-TALL BUTTERFLY!
THIS ISLAND MUST BE AN ISLAND OF GIANT INSECTS!

YES - AND THAT GIANT DADDY-LONGLEGS COULD SPELL TROUBLE
IT MIGHT POSSIBLY TRAMPLE ON OUR AMUSING VEG-FUEL WITH ITS BIG CLUMSY FEET

ACTING SWIFTLY, ESTHER WHITTLED THE END OF AN OLD TREE-TRUNK INTO A SHARP POINT

MOMENTS LATER THE IMPROVISED SPEAR HAD BEEN LOADED INTO THE SHIP'S PULMONARY ARTERY
STAND BY TO FIRE, CYRIL

WHOOMPH! OUT OF THE DEOXYGENATED BLOOD VESSEL ROCKETED THE DEADLY PROJECTILE

BULLSEYE!
GOT THE BASTARD RIGHT THROUGH THE WING

WORKING AS A TEAM THE FOUR FRIENDS BRAVELY PULLED OFF THE GIANT CRANE-FLY'S UNGAINLY LEGS

THE MONSTER'S TORSO TWITCHED FEEBLY ON THE GROUND
AND FINALLY, CYRIL
AND FINALLY, ESTHER...

CYRIL FLICKED A SWITCH AND A LARGE MAGNIFYING GLASS EMERGED FROM THE SHIP'S RIGHT ATRIUM

HOORAY!
THE DADDY-LONGLEGS IS BEING BURNT ALIVE

THE FIRE SPREAD RAPIDLY TO THE SURROUNDING UNDERGROWTH
QUICK - GATHER UP THE SIDE-SPLITTINGLY FUNNY VEGETABLES. IT'S TIME FOR US TO LEAVE

WITH A ROAR OF ENGINES THE SHIP LIFTED AWAY FROM THE BLAZING ISLAND
GOSH! LOOK AT ALL THE GIANT INSECTS DYING!
IT SEEMS ALMOST A SHAME THAT THE ISLAND HAD TO BE DESTROYED, ESTHER

CAN'T BE HELPED, CHILDREN ~ AFTER ALL THAT'S LIFE!
HA HA HA HA HA HA
AWAY ACROSS THE SEA THUNDERED ESTHER RANTZEN'S BIG GOLDEN HEART, BOUND FOR NEW LANDS, AND NEW ADVENTURES

STUDENT GRANT

CAT FOOD
CAKES & TAMPAX
OPEN 'TIL LATE
...NOW LOOK HERE. MY FRIEND TARQUIN HAS DONE NEARLY A TERM OF LAW AT UNI AND I KNOW FOR A FACT THAT I AM PERFECTLY WITHIN MY RIGHTS TO INSIST ON PAYING FOR THIS 20p PACKET OF CIGARETTE PAPERS WITH THIS CREDIT CARD...
JUST A PINT OF MILK
NO FRILLS CAT FOOD
...AND IF NECESSARY I'M PREPARED TO STAND HERE ALL DAY TO PROVE MY POINT...

www.double.d

Mid-west Mom expects massive Net interest

REPORTS that an American woman is planning to open her blouse and reveal her bra on the internet have led to calls for a tightening up of laws governing the worldwide web.

Mother of eight Draylene Shinz, 49, of Illinois expects over *30 million* computer enthusiasts to log onto her home page www.ladyinabra.com to see her in her brassiere on December 18th.

Popular

Moral watchdogs fear that if her plan proves popular, it may spark off a trend for even harder material on the internet - *including ladies exposing their nude bosoms or even knickers.*

And home secretary Jack Straw has been swift to join in the debate.

"If left unchecked, I could envisage a situation where a young man who isn't even old enough to get married could buy a computer, and look at pictures of ladies in bras, whilst he slaps the back of his neck and steam comes out of his collar," he told us.

Shinz - exposure on internet

"This must not be allowed to happen."

Meanwhile Mrs Shinz, speaking from the stoop of her mobile home in Trashville, Carbondale, was unrepentant.

Escort

"It ain't no big thing," she told reporters. "Going on the internet in my bra is the most natural thing in the world. I'm just going like, 'here's my brassiere', that's all. I'm only going to show it for a couple of seconds, anyhow."

Fiesta

And she had harsh words for the people who have complained about her plan.

"They're only sore because their woman ain't showing them no bra at home, and that's for sure. Uh-huuurh."

SHITTY DICK
THERE'S NO FLIES ON HIM

HELLO, READERS! I'VE COME TO THE SWIMMING POOL TODAY

OH, NO! I'VE CRIMPED A LENGTH OFF...
...AND HERE COMES A VICAR!

HELLO, MR. RICHARDS. SWIMMING IS IT, TODAY?
ERM...YES

YES. ME TOO. TODAY IS THE DAY THAT THE BISHOP GIVES SWIMMING LESSONS TO ALL THE VICARS IN THE DIOCESE...
...WHAT'S THAT IN YOUR TOWEL?
OH... ERM... IT'S... IT'S MY SPARE PAIR OF TRUNKS!

WELL PRAISE THE LORD! FOR I HAVE FORGOTTEN MY VERY OWN TRUNKS...
SPLAT!
WOULD YOU BE SO KIND AS TO LEND ME THEM?

SO...
THEY REALLY ARE A MOST GENEROUS TRUNK, MR. RICHARDS
ERM..
SPLAP!

OH, CRUMBS! LOOK AT ALL THEM VICARS...
MALE CHANGING

...GOOD JOB I BOUGHT THIS!
IMMODIUM

GLUG! GLUG! GLUG! GLUG!

THAT SHOULD BIND ME UP GOOD AND PROPER. I'LL NOT BE DOING A SHIT OF ANY SORTS FOR...

...WEEKS!
EH!?

OH, NO!
I MUST HAVE BROUGHT THE WRONG BOTTLE
NOT IMMODIUM
GUARANTEED NOT TO HAVE ANY EFFECT ON THE DOING OF BIG SHITS

EXCUSE ME, THERE, YOUNG MAN...COULD YOU THROW ME THAT INFLATABLE RING, PLEASE?
OOER!

I HOPE IT FLOATS
BLESS YOU, MY SON

B-LOIK!

OH DEAR-A DEPTH CHARGE. I FEAR THAT VICAR HAS PAID DEARLY FOR MY SUPPER OF TREACLE TART, BLACK PUDDING AND TWO POUNDS OF UNLEAVENED FUDGE

I'M OFF BEFORE SOMEONE LINKS THAT BIG TURD TO ME!

OUTSIDE...
LOCAL POOL

OOER! IT'S THE ARCHBISHOP OF CANTERBURY, THE MOST IMPORTANT VICAR IN THE WORLD
THANK GOODNESS I'VE GOT NOTHING IN THE BOMB BAY...

...CHRIST ALMIGHTY!! HOW ON EARTH DID I DO THAT!?!
IT'S THE BIGGEST SHIT I'VE EVER DONE!

OH, LORD... I... ERM... I... ...I... ERM... ERM... ER...

...IT'S NO GOOD. THIS TIME I'M DONE FOR!
THE ARCHBISHOP'S HERE, AND NOTHING CAN DISGUISE THE FACT THAT I'M STOOD RIGHT HERE NEXT TO A BIG FAT SHIT!

DANNY BAKER!..
?

...HOW MARVELOUS TO MEET YOU, ME AND MRS. THE ARCHBISHOP OF CANTERBURY ARE BIG FANS OF YOUR DAZ ADVERTS

COURT CIRCULAR

SANDRINGHAM

Yesterday, HRH The Prince of Wales attended the opening of Camilla Parker-Bowles' legs inside the Royal Bedroom and afterwards wiped his dobber on the State curtains.

BALMORAL

Yesterday, Her Majesty The Queen spent the morning in a council house in Glasgow, failing to conceal her contempt for her host. In the afternoon, she spent two hours pulling miserable faces like someone was waving a turd under her nose. Afterwards, at a garden party given in her honour by the Peebles Townswomen's Guild, she wore gloves to shake hands with some proletariats, before removing the gloves and burning them.

CLARAENCE HOUSE

HRH Queen Elizabeth The Queen Mother drank four bottles of gin and watched the racing on Channel 4. In the evening she ran up another £1m debt and didn't give a shit.

Yesterday, HRH The Princess Margaret burnt her fat arse in the bath whilst ripped to her big saggy tits on champagne.

BUCKINGHAM PALACE

HRH The Earl of Wessex minced into work at 11.50 and spent the rest of the afternoon with his head in his hands remembering'It's a Royal Knockout.' He later gave an interview on American Television where he managed to imply that his multi-million pound-losing company was successful and that everyone in Britain was a twat.

FRU T. BUNN the MASTER BAKER & HIS GINGERBREAD SEX DOLLS

POSTMAN PLOD

Bishop Fined

MAGISTRATES yesterday fined the Bishop of Merseyside £250 after he pleaded guilty to a charge of failing to clear up after a priest.

The court heard that the bishop allowed his priest to repeatedly foul the pavement outside the home of Mrs. Ethel Acetate, 82, of The Wirral. She told the court that when she remonstrated with the Bishop, he became abusive, telling her to "Wind her f***ing neck in".

The court was shown video evidence, shot by Mrs. Acetate, which clearly showed the bishop encouraging the priest to defecate on the path before walking off.

The Bishop admitted the charge and apologised to the court. The priest has since been destroyed.

Shiner for ER Indoors!

KEEN eyed stampithologists may notice something unusual about this year's Christmas stamps. For on the second class stamp, the Queen's head is facing in the wrong direction! And that's because she's sporting a *right royal shiner!*

By our Royal Correspondant Tamara Banana-Pyjama Thompkinson

EXCLUSIVE!

Huntley Palmer, the artist responsible for this year's designs, was quick to explain why he had been forced to make this break with tradition.

"Her Majesty came in on the Tueusday to pose for the first class stamp," he said.

carriage

She kept saying she had to get back to the Palace quickly. Prince Philip was going out carriage driving with his mates that evening, and she had to get his tea ready. But I couldn't get her nose right and it took ages," he added.

According to Palmer, the Queen left in a hurry. When she returned the next day to do the second class stamp, she was wearing sunglasses.

"She took them off and I saw she had a livid purple bruise around her left eye.

"I was reluctant to draw her the other way round, but in the end I had no choice, as her eye had come up like a tennis ball."

alarm

The Queen was reluctant to say what had happened at first, but eventually

broke down, and told Palmer that The Duke of Edinburgh had 'pasted her one.'

"I was shocked. I asked why she didn't leave him. She said that it was her fault because his tea wasn't ready, and anyway, if she left, he would probably find her."

grandfather

Ethyl Franklyn, a neighbour of the Queen's who lives just across the Mall said she heard raised voices coming from the palace on the Tuesday.

The 1st class (above above) and the 2nd class (above) and the Queen (left) looking miserable again

"I saw The Duke get home from his engagements at about 5.30," she told us.

"He'd been in the palace about a minute when an almighty row broke out. It went quiet, then he came storming out with a face like thunder, got into a Coach and Four and drove off."

We called the Palace and asked if The Duke had clocked Her Majesty a fourpenny one up the bracket.

"She walked into a door, alright? It's all sorted now so leave it, eh?" said The Queen's Secretary, Sir Robert Fellowes.

ROGER MELLIE
THE MAN ON THE TELLY

...AND THAT'S ALL FROM 'LOOK FULCHESTER' FOR TONIGHT...
LF
...SEE YOU SAME TIME TOMORROW. GOODNIGHT

ROGER! WHAT THE HELL ARE YOU DOING? THERE'S STILL FIVE MINUTES TO GO
STICK A FUCKIN TOM AN' JERRY ON. I'M OFF
THERE'S A PINT WITH MY NAME ON SITTING ON THE BAR NEXT DOOR

LATER..
COME ON, TOM. WHAT KEPT YOU? I'M THREE NIL UP ALREADY. WHAT ARE YOU DRINKING?
HELLO, ROGER THERE'S SOMEONE I'D LIKE YOU TO MEET

ROGER, THIS IS MARTIN. HE'S GOING TO BE THE NEW PRODUCER ON 'LOOK FULCHESTER'
HELLO, ROGER.
HI! WHAT'S YOUR POISON?

I'LL HAVE A PERRIER WATER, PLEASE
PERRIER? FUCK OFF!
YOU WON'T GET A CONK LIKE THIS DRINKING THAT PISS!.. I'LL GET YOU A PINT, MARTIN

SHORTLY..
ERM... I'M AFRAID THERE'S GOING TO BE SOME MAJOR CHANGES ON 'LOOK FULCHESTER', ROGER
CHANGES!? WHAT'S THIS CUNT ON ABOUT, TOM?

THE SHOW IS OLD AND TIRED, AND FRANKLY ROGER, SO ARE YOU!
I THINK IT'S TIME TO INJECT SOME YOUNG BLOOD ONTO THE SHOW

OLD AND TIRED?.. THERE'S NOTHING THE MATTER WITH ME! I'VE BEEN DOING THIS SHOW FOR 25 YEARS! I COULD DO IT IN MY SLEEP, TOM
THAT'S THE PROBLEM, ROGER. YOU DID LAST WEEK

NEXT DAY..
SORRY I'M LATE, TOM. GOT CHATTING TO THE BARMAN LAST NIGHT. DIDN'T GET AWAY TILL ABOUT 3:00am.
I'M STILL A BIT PISSED TO TELL THE TRUTH

ROGER. THIS IS GWENDY WIBSON. SHE'S JOINING US ON THE 'LOOK FULCHESTER' TEAM
MORNING, PET
...MINE'S WHITE WITH FOUR SUGARS

SHE'S NOT HERE TO MAKE THE TEA ROGER! FROM NOW ON, GWENDY WILL BE YOUR CO-PRESENTER!
FUCK OFF! THIS IS MY GRAVY TRAIN AND I DON'T WANT SOME BLOND BIMBO DIPPING HER BREAD INTO IT

I'M SORRY, ROGER. THE PRODUCER'S DECISION IS FINAL
HERE'S YOUR HALF OF THE SCRIPT

HEY! FUCK THIS, TOM! SHE'S GOT THE FIRST LINE!
I ALWAYS SAY "GOOD EVENING..."
...THAT'S MY FUCKING CATCH PHRASE. SHE CAN'T SAY THAT!

NO, ROGER. LOOK! YOU GET TO SAY IT AS WELL... THERE!.. SEE? FIRST GWENDY SAYS "GOOD EVENING, I'M GWENDY WIBSON" THEN YOU SAY "GOOD EVENING, I'M ROGER MELLIE"

FUCK THIS, TOM! I'M BIGGER THAN THIS SHOW. LOOK FULCHESTER WOULD BE NOTHING WITHOUT ME
IF THAT TROLLOP SAYS "GOOD EVENING" BEFORE ME...
...I'M WALKING OUT, DO YOU HEAR ME, TOM? I'M FINISHED!

THAT EVENING...
GOOD EVENING. I'M GWENDY WIBSON...
LF

THAT'S IT! FUCK YOU!
I'M OFF

IN THE PUB...
THAT WAS A BIT HARSH OF THE PRODUCER, SACKING YOU AFTER 25 YEARS OF SERVICE
DON'T WORRY. I'LL GET 'EM BACK, TOM
I'M GOING OVER TO THE OTHER SIDE - FT3 - AND I'M TAKING MY AUDIENCE WITH ME

I'M AN OLD PRO. I KNOW THIS GAME INSIDE OUT. I MAY NOT BE A YOUNGSTER ANYMORE, BUT I'VE GOT EXPERIENCE...

...FT3 WILL APPRECIATE THAT. IT'S WHAT'S UP HERE THEY'RE AFTER, TOM. NOT GOOD LOOKS!

YOU'RE WATCHING FT3. AND NOW, FULCHESTER TONIGHT, WITH OUR NEW HOST...
FT3
...ROGER MELLIE

GUZ EEBENING
FT
FT3
CLICK! CLICK!
CLICK! CLACK!
ANG TODAYS TOC SHTORY- TWO NUNDREG JOGS LOSK AS NACTORY CLOJES ING VHU NREEGION...

FRU T. BUNN the MASTER BAKER & HIS GINGERBREAD SEX DOLLS

Tearooms in crisis...Tearooms in crisis...

Ooh! Betty's!

BRITAIN'S cake-strapped tearooms are reaching crisis point as a record demand for light refreshments stretches resources to the limit. And now Tea Service bosses fear that many pensioners may have to go without the nice cup of tea and cakes that they so desperately feel like.

By our tea service writer ***Alan Bennett***

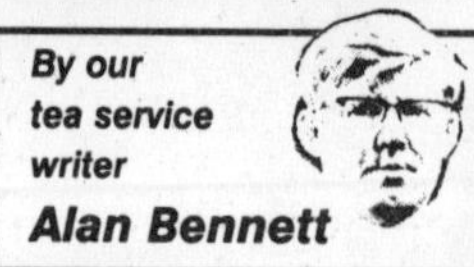

A British tea room working at full strength.

The position has become so bad that Tea Service bosses may consider refusing waitress service for certain OAPs because there simply aren't enough tables.

Dr. Clive Foot - Elevenses

That's one of the recommendations of a controversial report leaked from the Mr. Kipling Institute, an independent Tea Service think-tank.

National Tea Service faces Meltdown

"Unseasonably normal weather has led to elderly people pottering around spa towns," says Dr. Clive Foot of Harrogate University's Department of Elevenses.

"Inevitably a good proportion are going to fancy a nice bit sit down with a cup of tea and a cake, and unfortunately our teashops cannot cope. If the weather doesn't get a bit parkier, and demand continues at this rate, I can see the whole system collapsing in the next three months."

The report cites shocking examples of cases where the system has already broken down under the strain:

Journey of Despair

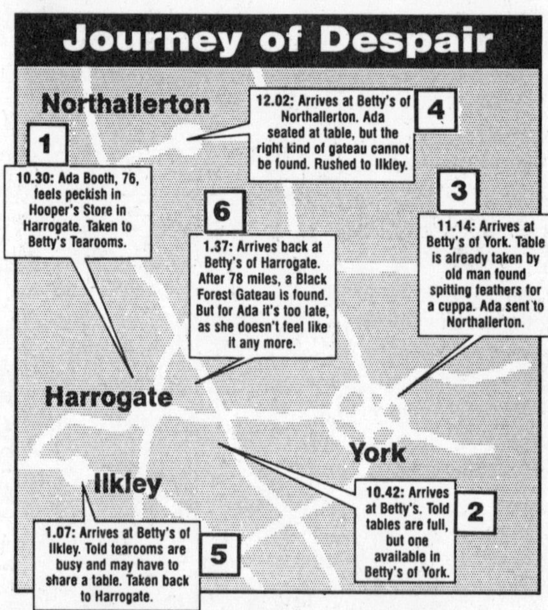

Northallerton
Harrogate
York
Ilkley
1
10.30: Ada Booth, 76, feels peckish in Hooper's Store in Harrogate. Taken to Betty's Tearooms.
2
10.42: Arrives at Betty's. Told tables are full, but one available in Betty's of York.
3
11.14: Arrives at Betty's of York. Table is already taken by old man found spitting feathers for a cuppa. Ada sent to Northallerton.
4
12.02: Arrives at Betty's of Northallerton. Ada seated at table, but the right kind of gateau cannot be found. Rushed to Ilkley.
5
1.07: Arrives at Betty's of Ilkley. Told tearooms are busy and may have to share a table. Taken back to Harrogate.
6
1.37: Arrives back at Betty's of Harrogate. After 78 miles, a Black Forest Gateau is found. But for Ada it's too late, as she doesn't feel like it any more.

*A junior waitress forced to work a 10 hour shift, who miscalculated the amount of sugar in a cup of tea, leaving an 80-year-old lady PULLING A FACE and muttering to her sister.

*An old man of 82 being seated at a table that was still covered in CRUMBS from the previous occupant's scones.

*A plate of biscuits left for 3 days on a cake trolley in a CORRIDOR because staff were unable to find a table for it.

*A 76-year-old woman, taken on a 78 MILE round trip to find a tearoom serving Black Forest Gateau.

A spokesman for Betty's, one of Britain's biggest tearoom chains confirmed last night that stocks of Earl Grey were low, but there was no cause for alarm as yet. "Every old person who genuinely fancies a cup of tea and a bite to eat will be served. They just may have to be a little more patient," he told us.

Where are they *NOW?*

Take That!

Groundbreaking boy band Take That! were never out of the headlines in the nineties, but after their dramatic split, they slipped from the public eye. Whatever happened to those lively lads, asks 15 year old Ada Trousers from Braintree in Yorkshire.

(Clockwise from top left)

Gary Barlow, the bozz-eyed tubby one who penned the band's hits, was declared bankrupt in 1997, after blowing an estimated £40 million on fizz bombs and sherbert dips. He now runs a small newsagents shop at Four Lane Ends in Newcastle upon Tyne.

Robbie Williams, the first to leave the band bought a milk round in Ashby de la Zouch, Staffordshire.

On the band's break-up, **Howard Donald** took the opportunity to realise a lifetime ambition and walk around the world. On his return, his dad got him a job at Boulby Potash mine in Cleveland, where he is presently deputy overman.

Jason Orange left the band with an estimated £10 million which he invested in a revolutionary scientific process to extract gold from sea water. He now lives in a bus shelter in Peterborough.

Mark Owen sank his money from the band into a gas-turbine mobile sex library specialising in under-the-counter farmyard pornography. Business has boomed and he now earns up to and in excess of £100 per week.

Tasha SLAPPA
woz ere
9T9
...AYE, SUR AH FUCKIN' PACKED HIM IN COS HE WAS WEARIN' TWO STRIPE GEAR
SHOCKIN'!
SHADEY!
SHAN!!
...ER...
...EMM...
COULD Y' NOT JUST TWOCK THREE STRIPE?
WHEY- COS IF Y' NICK FOUR STRIPE THEN YER CAN TEK ONE OF THE STRIPES OFF, BUT IF YER TWOCK TWO STRIPE- WHEY- THEN YER SCARRED FOR FUCKIN' LIFE!
ER...
...HOW- DO Y' THINK YER FUCKIN' CLEVVAH?
HAD ON- IF YER TEK YER SPARE STRIPE FROM THE FOUR STRIPE AND GLUE IT ON YER TWO STRIPE, THEN YER GET TWO PAIRS OF THREE STRIPE
OH AYE.
LOOKA!! IT'S FUCKIN' DONNA SHEREE SHERAN! FRIGGIN' HELL- LOOK AT THE NUMBER OF THEM FUCKIN' SCRUNCHIES
EEH, AYE! I'LL SEE WHAT THEY MEAN, I GOT A DECODER FREE WITH 'JUST 17'
...RED, RED, YELLOW, BLUE...
EEH!!
SHE'S SHAGGED NINE BLURKS, FOUR OF EM BLACK, 3 IN A BUS STOP: CHEEKED UP FOUR COPPAS, SHAGGED TWO OF THEM; DONE A SHITE ON A DOORSTEP, SHAGGED THE OWNER, AND SUCKED HIS GREASY COCK...
HERE, GET IN! SHE SHAGGED LURDS, THE JAMMY COO
JUST 17's INTERNATIONAL CODE OF SLAPPERS
...AYE, AND SHE'S SEVEN MONTHS GONE
EEH!! Y' MEAN SHE'S PREGNUNT? THE FUCKIN' DORTY BITCH! HAS SHE GOT NEE FUCKIN' MORALS?
AYE, IT'S A FUCKIN' DISGRACE THAT
-WHICH REMINDS US- HOW ARE YOUR BAIRNS?
WHEY- AAH'VE LEFT SHELLY CARENZA AT ME MAMS, KYLIE MARIE'S AT ME NANNA'S, THE LITTLE BABBIES LEFT AT YEM WITH SOME COLA CUBES, BUT HE CANNAT WAALK, SUR IT'S AALREET, AND BROOKLYN CAPREE GHIA'S DOON THE PUB WITH IT'S FATHA...
THE TRIPLETS WUH IN CARE LAST I HEARD...
OH- AND IT'S AGANEMNOM MARIE'S LAST DAY AT SCHOOL
HAD IT- THAT MEANS IT'S OUR LAST DAY IN SCHOOL AN' AALL.
FUCKIN' HELL,
AYE. WE'D BEST GAN, AAH CANNAT AFFORD TU GET EXPELLED, ELSE THEY'LL STOP GIVIN' ME MAM THE MONEY WHAT AAH NICK OOT HER PURSE.
DO YER KNA HOW TO GET TU SCHOOL?
AH THINK AAH CAN REMEMBER FROM THE LAST TIME AAH WAS THERE
AND SO...
FUCKIN' HELL... SCHOOL... THE BEST DAY OF MY LIFE
FULCASTLE INFANT SCHOOL
HOO RAGGYTASCH!
STOT!
HOY!
MR MASTERSON CLASS 2
Aa Bb Cc
BURST!
WHAT IS THE MEANING OF THIS?
DIVVINT RADGE MAN. WE 'WUH GOING TO 'EGG' YUH, BUT WE NEWAH HAD NEN EGGS, SUR WE THOUGHT WE'D 'BRICK' YUH
AYE
Aa Bb Cc
IT'S THE LAST DAY- IT'S ALLOWED
OH, I REMEMBER YOU. YOU CAME HERE TEN YEARS AGO. WENT OUT TO THE TOILET HALFWAY THROUGH REGISTRATION AND NEVER CAME BACK
AYE. YUH WAS INSULTIN' ME FUCKIN' INTELEGENCIA
AYE
I SEE YOUR BEHAVIOUR NOW IS JUST AS IMMATURE AS IT WAS THEN
IMMA-CHOORE-UH?
DIVVINT CAAL ME IMMA-CHOORE-UH RAGGYTASCH. AAH'VE HAD MORE COCKS THAN YEE'VE HAD HOT DINNAS
GET OUT! GET OUT! NEVER DARKEN THIS SCHOOL AGAIN!!
HERE- WE DIDN'T WANT TU FUCKIN' COME ANYHOO. SCHOOL'S SHIT!
AYE
AAH'M NEWAH STEPPIN' FOOT IN SCHOOL ENVAH AGAIN, NOT EVEN IF YUH FUCKIN' BEGGED US TO
THE NEXT DAY...
DUMPH DUMPH DUMPH DUMPH! DOOBA DOOBA DOOBA DOOBA DOOBA! DUMPH DUMPH DUMPH DUMPH! DOOBA DOOBA!
THIRTY YEARS LATER...
DUMPH DUMPH DUMPH DUMPH! DOOBA DOOBA DOOBA DOOBA DOOBA! DUMPH DUMPH DUMPH DUMPH! DOOBA DOOBA!

LeTtERBOX

It's the letters page who's grandad smoked 60 a day... and lived to be 94!

Star Letter

☞ These so-called speed humps are a joke. If anything they slow you down.

Tim Wakefield
Surrey

☞ "I wouldn't trust him as far as I could throw him" my mother used to say about my father. But then we are a familly of travelling acrobats, so I assume it meant she could trust him quite a lot.

Chris Mapperly
e-mail

Highland fling

☞ What a rip-off these so called Scottish Widows are. The one they advertise on telly is a real gorgeous, classy tart, but when I fixed myself up with one from the 'Encounters' section of the *Glasgow Herald*, she turned out to be a right old boiler living in a council flat in Motherwell.

Jamie McSporran
Glasgow

Do YOU have something to say? No? Then write to Letterbox. There's a Royal Consummation mug for every letter and tip we print.

Letterbox
P.O. Box 1PT
Newcastle-upon Tyne
NE99 1PT
Fax 0191 2414244
email VIZ@VIZ.CO.UK

☞ My favourite sexual fantasy is to be tossed off by Jeremy beadle *with his deformed hand*, whilst 70s novelty popsters *The Wurzels* sit around watching, occasionally moaning "Oo-aaaaaar" to heighten the erotic ambiance. Can any of your readers beat that?

N.N.
North Yorkshire

☞ These so called boffins who keep telling us not to look directly into the sun during the eclipse are talking out their arses. Don't they know that during an eclipse nobody can look directly into the sun as a fucking great big moon is in the way.

P. Moore
Selsey

Only fools in arses

☞ My dog has just had a nine inch worm removed from its arsehole, which bears a striking resemblance to Nicholas Lyndhurst. And it was probably better at acting.

Jenny Al-Fayed
Welton

My old Dutch oven

☞ Now I've been going out with my girlfriend for some time, it seems to be okay when I break wind in bed. It's when I follow through that the petty arguments begin. I will honestly never understand women.

Chris Mapply
Carshalton

☞ How about a *Lonely Hearts* section on the letters page? I'll start the ball rolling.
"Male, 26, non-smoker, seeks attractive girl, 18-25 for good times and possible romance. Single parents welcome. Sorry, no DSS."

John Bush
Oldham

☞ Hi. How it going? Lars Grenninger is my call. The Viz is my funny read ever since years three ago. Laugh! Yes my sides broken good with the giggle. I search friend to write. My likes are cycling, read books and dinosaurs, ten inch cock. Bye.

L. Grenninger
Spitsbergen

☞ Whilst watching Hale and Pace the other day, I couldn't help noticing that my toenails needed clipping.

B.H. Albion
Gillingham

☞ I was just wondering if they served *Walls Viennetta* at the last supper as we always have it on special occasions.

CGB
e-mail

Dust to Dusty

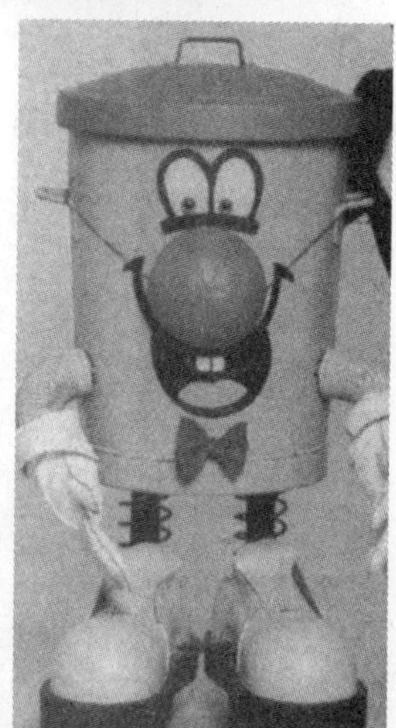

☞ Our upstairs neighbour's cat, Dusty died the other day. And what with Dusty Springfield throwing a seven the other month, I reckon Ted Rogers should get the measuring tape out for Dusty Bin.

Simon Onion
St. Chives

Poxy moron

☞ On the subject of Esther Rantzen claiming an unpleasant child is a contradiction in terms (letterbox, p50). If this is true, I can only conclude that she has never met her own son, Josh. I was at school with him, and never before have I met such a twat in my entire life.

Chris
Bristol

HELLO GIRLS!

The Kirk Douglas Chin Bra Collection

Big 'C' down under

☞ It's nice to see a star like Robbie Williams fronting the British 'Testicular Cancer Awareness Campaign'. Here in Australia, we have to make do with a cartoon of Mark Hughes checking his pills in a shower.

Mick Noble
Brisbane

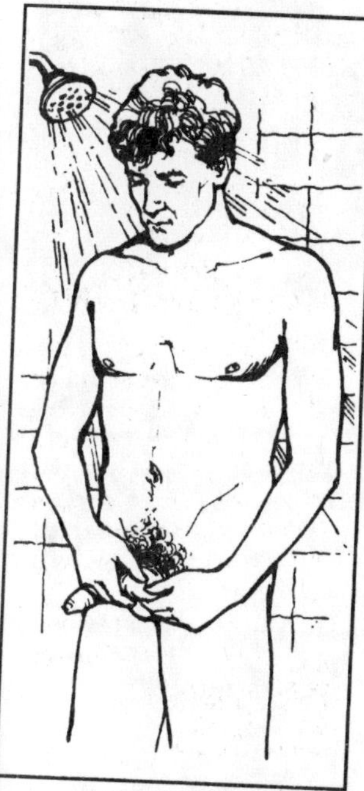

☞ Surely all the speculation of the nature of 'black holes' and 'anti-matter' in Professor Steven Hawking's book *A Brief History of Time* is just a lot of fuss over nothing.

P. Mower
e-mail

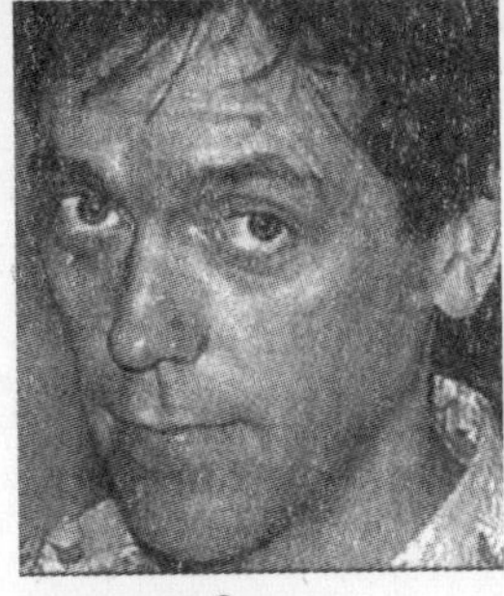

Laurie passes bus

☞ On Saturday 3rd July whilst driving in Hampstead, I saw Hugh Laurie riding a push bike. He decided to overtake a parked bus, and pulled out without looking over his shoulder. A Renault Clio coming up behind nearly dispatched the thespian to actors' heaven. He wasn't even wearing a crash helmet. I know he makes a living playing upper class idiots, but what can I say? Have any other readers seen a celebrity have a brush with the Grim Reaper?

Tony Jauncey
e-mail

☞ Talking of two wheeled celebrities, we passed Ron Haslam in our Saab 900 on the M18 on Saturday 10th July, and we were only doing about 70. 'Rocket' Ron, my arse. Mind you, he was driving a Luton van.

M. Walker
Northampton

SHAGWATCH

WE ASKED you to tell us about any stars you've shagged, what they were like and anything kinky they asked you to do. The response was, however, a little disappointing - just a handful of anecdotes including one about Philippa Forrester which we didn't believe and one about Leslie Ash which we did. Maybe you're a little shy, or maybe the stars aren't the sex machines we all imagine them to be. Or maybe you just forgot you shagged them.

here's one he made earlier

I haven't shagged anybody famous, but I've done the next best thing. I went up town on the piss one night with my mates and pulled this bird with enormous tits. I got back to her hotel and shagged the arse off her. Anyway, it turned out that she was going out with that John Leslie off Blue Peter, which made it an all the more pleasurable experience, I can tell you.

J.Taylor
Crawley

I've never shagged anyone famous, but I once met this Canadian bird who told me the worst shag she ever had was off Phil Collins' keyboard player. Apparently, she was ripped to the tits on drugs in a Toronto hotel room and he was in and out in two pumps.

Pete
London

MOBILE phone users. Call somebody on your phone, leave it switched on and put it in your lunch box. In a few minutes you will have lovely toasted sandwiches.

F. Lenehan
e-mail

OLD people in supermarkets. A polite "excuse me, please" is much more effective than glaring theatrically at someone's back, tutting to yourself.

Mark Glover
Coventry

ANTIQUE owners. Get a realistic value for your item by taking it along to Ronnie Barker's antique shop and multiplying whatever he offers you by ten.

B. Hawkes
Chester

SAVE money on expensive in-car air conditioning by holding a seance in the vehicle. The poultergeists invoked will result in the car interior being several degrees cooler than the outside air temperature.

R. Warskji
Dundee

LADIES. Once you've established that your husband definitely has had an affair, don't make his life a misery by continually questioning him about it.

Lorenzo Brown
Leicester

WHEN struggling to multiply numbers by 8, just multiply them by 10 instead. Then take a bit off.

Paco Temple
Leamington Spa

FLAT pack furniture buyers. Be careful not to throw away any packaging. That flimsy bit of cardboard may well be an integral part of your new wardrobe.

Paul Allen
Manchester

THE ICEMAN COMETH

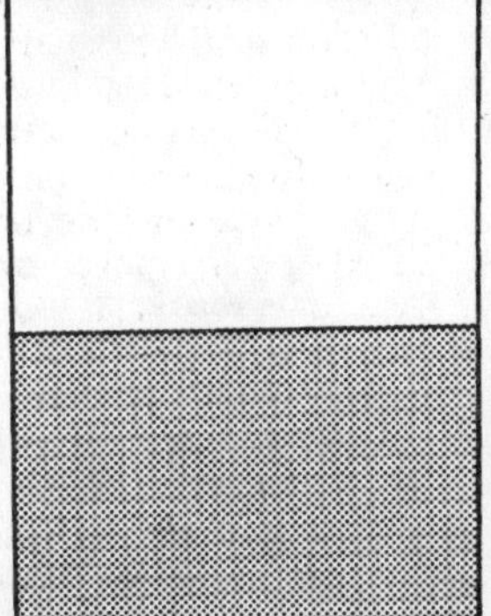
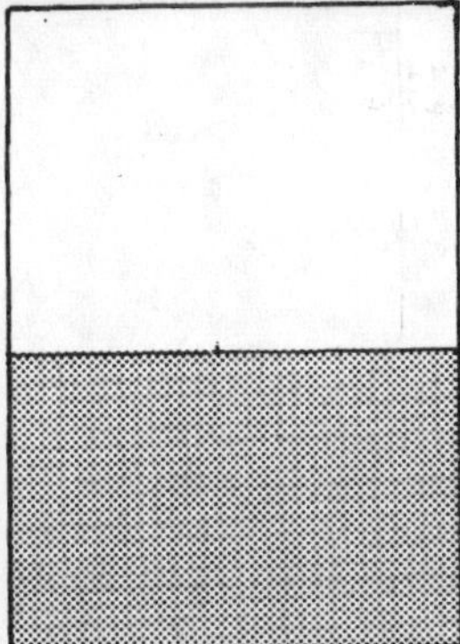

RENEGADE OF SALVATION

Hello, Jeremiah. It's been a long time.
Save your breath, Colonel. I've told you before, I'm not coming back. I've finished with the Salvation Army. I gave them 15 years of my life.

Just one last job, Jeremiah. You're the only one who can pull this one off. One of our men is trapped in the snug of the Dog and Duck...
If some kid bites off more than he can chew, that's no business of mine, Colonel.

It's not some kid, Jeremiah ...it's Kozwalski... Ezekiel Kozwalski. Remember him, Jeremiah? Middlesbrough precinct, December '87...
You don't have to tell me about the precinct...
Oh no! I've dropped my trombone mouthpiece into a dog dirt... and we're on the last verse of 'The Old Rugged Cross'
Here, Jeremiah. Take mine!

...he gave me his mouthpiece.
And now he needs you, Jeremiah.

Jeremiah was soon being briefed in the back of the staff car as it sped towards headquarters.
It was a routine recce. Kozwalski had done it a thousand times before. It was in - sell the Warcry - and out. We don't know what went wrong, but the next thing we knew he'd walked right into a nest of the faithless. He was surrounded.

Our people managed to get this out.

We've worked everything out. There's only one route, and if anything goes wrong, you're on your own.

You come in over the wall at the back. Through the beer garden and into the snug. We think Kozwalski is being held here - next to the fag machine...
GARDEN
SNUG
POOL TABLE
BAR
What's wrong with the front door?

No way. It would be madness to try it. There's a pool table, two blokes playing darts and a barmaid collecting glasses. You'd never get through.
I'm going in the front door!

I'll do it my way... or not at all!

That night, the unsuspecting faithless continued to keep Kozwalski imprisoned in the snug of the Dog and Duck.
Sally Army, eh. Well it keeps you off the streets, eh? Ha! I say it keeps you off the streets, eh? Do you geddit?
Erm...ha! Yes. Erm... I'd better get going...
No, stop a while. Look, why don't you have a drink?
KER RASH!!
PRAISE THE LORD, UNREDEEMED MOTHERFUCKERS!
AIEEE!
TISH!
TISH!
AAAARGH!
CHINKA!
CHINKA!
OOM-PAH-PARP! OOM-PAH-PARP!
SCREAM!
CRASH!
Go on, just have a half of...
What the...?
Instinctively, Jeremiah reached for his last weapon. It was now or never...
TAKE THIS YOU HEATHEN S.O.B.'S
War Cry
AIEEE!
SLAP!
CRASH!
Jesus H. Christ, Jeremiah. That was the most stupid goddamn thing I ever saw. It was also the bravest. The Salvation Army needs men like you, Jeremiah. Whaddaya say?
No thanks, Colonel. He gave me his mouthpiece when mine fell in a turd. Now I reckon we're just about quits. Now if you'll excuse me, I've got some logs to chop.
The number of Salvation Army Soldiers lost or missing, presumed trapped in pubs is unknown. But thanks to Jeremiah Bloodfire, it's one less now.
THE END.

GILBERT RATCHET
I COULD DO WITH A NEW SET OF TOOLS FOR EASTER
TOOLS
THESE'VE JUST ABOUT HAD IT

COR — AN EASTER EGG ROLLING COMPETITION
FULCHESTER HARDWARE SHOP AND THE CHURCH OF ENGLAND — PRESENT —
GRAND EASTER EGG-ROLLING CONTEST
> FIRST PRIZE <
CORDLESS ELECTRIC SCREWDRIVER & A BAG OF NAILS
AND JUST LOOK AT THAT SMASHING PRIZE

ATTENTION! EGG-ROLLING WILL TAKE PLACE AT NOON — THE PRIZE GOES TO WHOEVER'S EGG PASSES THE FINISHING POST FIRST
START
JUDGE
FINISH
I'VE GOT AN HOUR TO FIND MYSELF AN EGG BEFORE THE COMPETITION STARTS

OH DEAR. MY THREE LITTLE DOGS ARE RATHER DISOBEDIENT
YAP YAP YAP YAP
TOOLS
I WILL GIVE THIS LARGE EGG IN MY EASTER BONNET TO ANYONE WHO CAN TRAIN THEM TO BEHAVE PROPERLY

YOU NEED TO SHOW A DOG WHO IS BOSS BY SPEAKING TO IT IN A LOUD, FIRM VOICE
I'LL RIG UP A DEVICE WHICH WILL DO JUST THAT, WITH THE AID OF SOME POWERFUL STEREO EQUIPMENT

THERE
SUPER AMP
MY BARBARA-WOODHOUSE-O-MATIC WILL DELIVER 24 KILOWATTS OF LOUD CLEAR VOICE — THAT SHOULD MAKE LITTLE TRIXIE HERE PRETTY OBEDIENT

SIT!

TRIXIE APPEARS TO BE VIBRATING AT A VERY HIGH FREQUENCY, AND HIS INTERNAL ORGANS ARE SEEPING OUT HIS ANUS
I DON'T CALL THAT PARTICULARLY OBEDIENT

DOGS RESPOND WELL TO LOVE AND KINDNESS
WATER

I'LL CONSTRUCT A MACHINE THAT WILL GIVE YOUR TWO REMAINING POOCHES ALL THE AFFECTION THEY NEED

...AND VOILA! THE HYDRAULIC POWERED PET-PATTER

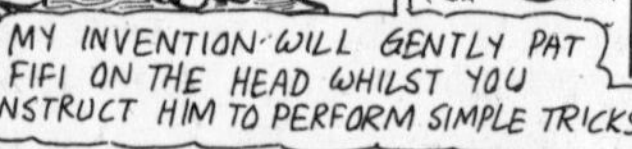
MY INVENTION WILL GENTLY PAT FIFI ON THE HEAD WHILST YOU INSTRUCT HIM TO PERFORM SIMPLE TRICKS

BEG, FIFI.
KER-SHUNK!

NEVER MIND. I'VE AN IDEA HOW TO TEACH THIS THIRD LITTLE FELLOW TO 'FETCH'...
...USING AN OLD LAWNMOWER, A LENGTH OF RUBBER TUBING, AND A STAPLE-GUN

KEEP YOUR CRACKPOT CONTRAPTIONS AWAY FROM MY LAST DOG
THE ONLY "EGG REWARD" YOU'LL GET FROM ME IS IN THE SHAPE OF THIS BUMP ON YOUR HEAD

OI, YOU! MISTER SO-CALLED DOG EXPERT!
PARKIE
IF YOU'RE SUCH AN AUTHORITY ON THE BLOODY ANIMALS, YOU CAN INVENT SOMETHING TO CLEAR UP ALL THESE DOG TURDS

I'LL NEVER BE ABLE TO ENTER THE EGG-ROLLING CONTEST NOW — IT'S NEARLY NOON, AND I'M EGGLESS
HMMMM
SUCK
HOOVER
>SNIVEL< I DID SO WANT TO WIN THAT PRIZE

SH-BLURT!
OOPS!
CLICK
HOOVER
I'VE ACCIDENTLY SWITCHED MY AUTOMATIC POOPER-SUCKER TO 'BLOW'

THE WINNER!
FIRST PRIZE GOES TO THE OWNER OF THAT "EASTER DOG'S EGG"
START
JUDGE
FINISH
HURRAY! THAT'S ME
SPLAT!

STEP THIS WAY, GILBERT, AND COLLECT YOUR PRIZE...
JUDGE
...ONE CORDLESS ELECTRIC SCREWDRIVER AND A BAG OF NAILS
TERRIFIC!

RIGHT THEN. HERE'S THE ROBOT CHAUFFEUR WITHOUT ANY CORDUROY TROUSERS WHICH CONVEYS PRISON OFFICERS AROUND IN A CAR....
JUDGE
SPEECHLESS
HA! HA! IT'S THAT SORT OF "CORDLESS ELECTRIC 'SCREW' DRIVER"

...AND HERE'S JIMMY NAIL'S SCROTUM
JUDGE
HA! HA! IT'S THAT SORT OF "BAG OF NAIL'S"
UMBERTO ECO'S VOICE

MIMESTOPPERS

in association with Humberside Police

POLICE on Humberside would like your help in identifying this man who entered the Sproatley Road, Bilton branch of the Co-op at around 3pm on Monday 8th March. He was captured on security cameras pretending to be trapped in a big glass box and sewing his fingers together. He is believed to be the same man who entered the post office at nearby Burton Constable earlier that week, where he walked against an apparently strong wind and was unable to move a suitcase. Police warn the public not to tackle him as he may be extremely embarrassing if approached.

If you have any information about this, or any other mime, call MIMESTOPPERS now on...

005690 6145

LUVVIE DARLING
BREAK A LEG! x

LUVVIE IS "RESTING" BETWEEN JOBS...
AUDITIONS TODAY

OH, I NEVER PREPARE FOR AUDITIONS. NOT SINCE THE TIME NOEL COWARD WAS CASTING THE FIRST PRODUCTION OF CAVALCADE.
HMM?
SCRIPT

WELL I'D JUST COME OUT OF "A MID-SUMMER NIGHT'S DREAM" AND I HAD NOTHING READY. SO I SIMPLY GAVE HIM MY BOTTOM IN THE REHEARSAL ROOM AT THE NATIONAL.
DID YOU GET THE PART?

IN A WAY. I COULDN'T SIT DOWN FOR A WEEK...
BLIDDIP! BLIDDIP! BLIDDIP! BLIDDIP!
EXCUSE ME. THAT'S MY MOBILE.

LUVVIE?... IT'S LOUIS. LISTEN. FORGET THAT AUDITION - ITS A FOREGONE CONCLUSION LEWIS COLLINS'LL GET THE GIG ANYWAY; HE'S GOT HIS OWN GOOSE COSTUME. HOW DO YOU FANCY A SPELL IN THE WEST END?
ITS THE CARETAKER! AT THE PRINCE OF WALES.

THE PRINCE OF WALES? THE ACOUSTICS IN THERE ARE AMAZING! I'LL MAKE THE STALLS ECHO WITH MY STENTORIAN TONES!

JESUS! THAT'S THE BIGGEST TURD I EVER SAW!
UP THE ARSENAL
FUCK OF

MANUFACTURED BOY BAND SENSATION
BOYZ 'R' UZ
SAUSAGE MACHINE RECORDS
SAUSAGE MACHINE RECORDS NEW BOYBAND AUDITIONS HERE TODAY!
AUDITIONS TODAY!
HEY I'M SO EXCITED! I'VE BEEN WORKING TOWARDS THIS MOMENT FOR YEARS-GOD-I HOPE I'M GOOD ENOUGH TO GET PICKED!
RIGHT, FIRST FOUR IN THE QUEUE, CONGRATULATIONS, YOU'RE HIRED. NOW GET INSIDE.
WOW!
INSIDE...
KER-CHUNK!
HI, ANDREW! YEAH- WE'VE GOT A SHIT HOT BAND HERE- IT'S GONNA BE 'BOYZ-R-UZ' MANIA!!
-THEY'RE JUST GOING THROUGH THE STYLE PACKAGE NOW.
SLICE!
STYLE
RIGHT SID- THAT ONE'S HAVING PIERCINGS, CUT EYEBROW & GOATEE; THAT ONE A MAORI TATTOO; AND THAT ONE'S SENSITIVE, CUTE & GAY;
...THE GAY ONE DOESN'T LIKE THE TALL ONE...
...AND THE ONE WITH THE YORKSHIRE ACCENT COMES FROM BROOKLYN - RIGHT, INTO FASHION.
OOH, YES- I SEE IT- MOODY, LONG, LEATHER! YES! OVER ARMANI!
PHOTOSHOOT NEXT, BOYS.. I NEED THE TALL ONE AT THE BACK TO DO THIS WITH HIS HANDS, THE SENSITIVE ONE TO KNEEL & THE OTHER ONE TO CROSS ARMS AND LOOK OVER HIS SHOULDER. DON'T TRY TO FORCE IT, IT HAS TO LOOK PERFECTLY NATURAL
FLASH!
YEAH, ANDREW, THE PHOTO'S ARE DONE, THEY LOOK FAHKING GORGEOUS. THE FILMS OFF TO SMASH HITS NOW. IT'LL BE ON THE COVER IN FIVE MINUTES
LISTEN, I'VE GOTTA GO, WE'RE DOING THE ACCOMPIANING IN-DEPTH INTERVIEW NEXT
HEY NOW OKAY LA TO KNOW FAVOURI
HEY, YE
SORRY I MISSED YOUR SHOOT LADS, ME AND ANDREW WHERE JUST CELEBRATING ≡SNIFF SNIFF≡ YOUR SINGLE WENT ON SALE LAST WEEK AND WE THINK IT'S GONNA BE NO.1 TOMMORROW!
THATS IF THOSE BASTARDS "999" OR WHATEVER THEY'RE CALLED DONT TRY TO OUTBID US AGAIN
RUB! RUB!
RIGHT, PREPARE YOURSELVES, WE'VE GOT A HASTILY ARRANGED PRESS CONFERENCE TO ATTEND NOW
PRESS ROOM
THANKS FOR COMING CHAPS. GREAT REGRET THAT I HAVE TO THE BREAKUP OF 'BOYZ-R-UZ'. DUE TO MUSICAL DIFFERENCES HELL, BLAH BLAH, SOLO PROJECTS...

GHT- YOUR CONTRACTS HAVE
READY BEEN SIGNED. DONT DO,
Y OR THINK ANYTHING WITHOUT
EING TOLD TO FIRST
OOK! HERES MY PORTFOLIO- IT'S
OT 18 YEARS WORTH OF ORIGINAL
ONGS - ALL MY RAW FEELINGS AND PURE
MOTION WENT INTO THESE
BRILLIANT SONGS

OH-WE HAVE AN ACTUAL SINGER/SONGWRITER- PLEASE- STEP THIS WAY.

SLAM!
FUK OF

OKAY, YOU THREE, ON THE CONVEYOR BELT
BIN
CLUNK!

...mmm-SPORTY!
YES! YES! VERY ACTIVE!
YOU! PINSTRIPES!
YES YES YES!! PINSTRIPES!!
RRING! RRRING!!

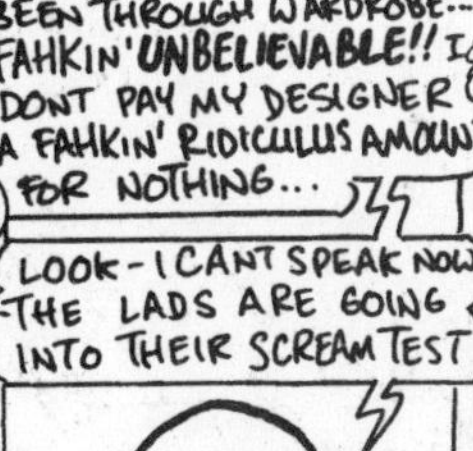

ANDREW! THE LADS'VE JUST BEEN THROUGH WARDROBE-- FAHKIN' UNBELIEVABLE!! I DONT PAY MY DESIGNER A FAHKIN' RIDICULUS AMOUNT FOR NOTHING...

LOOK- I CANT SPEAK NOW THE LADS ARE GOING INTO THEIR SCREAM TEST

WHIRRR!
LIFT!

WAAAARGHHH! SCREAM SCREAM! SQUEAL!
ITS BOYS!
EEEH! YOU FANCY THAT ONE!
EEEH! NO I DONT, YOU DO!
I LOVE YOU FOREVER!
SQUEAL!
ME TOO!
BOO HOO. SOB! CRY. BOO HOOOO!

EAT!
L WANT
S YOUR
UR?
BLUE
IS RED
E QUITE
BLUE

WE'RE GOING TO SHOOT THE VIDEO NOW. YOU'RE VERY LUCKY LADS, WE'VE GOT AN EXOTIC MEDITERRANIN LOCATION. THE SONG'LL BE DUBBED OVER, SO DONT SING AND FOR CHRIST'S SAKE DONT TRY TO DANCE

GIRLY GIRL, YOU ARE LOVELY, GIRLY WHIRL, LIKE A DOVELY, LAH LAH LAH etc...
ACTION!
YES! YES! BEAUTIFUL! KEEP IT UP!!

EXIT
TH
NCE
NFORTUNATLY
DRUGS

CLUNK!
CLUMF!

RIGHT, NEXT THREE, CONGRATULATIONS WELL DONE, GET INSIDE.
SAUSAGE MACHINE RECORDS TOP NEW BOY BAND ADDITIONS HERE TODAY!
YOU'RE CALLED "UPSIDE ORANGE"

Ladies! Nip Tumescence in the Bud...with the

SEXUAL TEMPERANCE SPOON

Guaranteed to soften even the most optimistic ardour!

SCHOOL nurses have known for centuries that a sharp blow from a cold spoon is the best way to tame an unwelcome erection. Now at last, these spoons are available to the public. If you finished with all that nonsense twenty years ago, but it still raises its ugly head, then this spoon is for YOU!

ONE WHACK AND IT'S ON THE SLACK!

Stop it before *he* starts!

Made in Sheffield from finest quality stainless steel, the Sexual Temperance Spoon is kept nice and cold in its own miniature chilling cabinet. Measuring only 6ins x 6ins x 10ins, the cabinet fits easily on the bedside table, ready for any nocturnal emergency.

"My hubby got ideas one night after watching 'Carry On Camping'. A quick flick with the Temperance Spoon sent him scampering to the spare room with his tail between his legs. Thanks!" **Mrs. R Barnsley**

"It's a SPOON!" **Mrs. B Essex**

It's the only spoon that STOPS stirring!

only £24.99 from all good shops

Please note: *Extremely turgid erections may require more than one whack on the lid.*

'Down, Boy' Chastity Products. Unit 6. Fulchester Industrial Estate. Leeds

DOCUMENTARY

Are you a

DAFT SLAPPER

aged 18 - 20 with big tits, who fancies a free holiday?

Or a

PISSED BLOKE

aged 18 to 20, desperate for a shag?

We are an unimaginative TV production company currently auditioning for another so-called documentary about drunken twats acting up to camera whilst on holiday. If you would be interested in appearing, please send a video tape of yourself getting drunk, being sick or lying in bed with a headache, to:

Arsehole Productions, 8th floor, Pisspoor House, 29 Dross Lane London W1

THE UN-INTELLIGENT CARTOON CHARACTER

HELLO READERS! I LOVE IT HERE ON MY UNCLE'S FARM. I'M MILKING DAISY THE COW.
SQUIRT! SQUIRT!

YOU'RE NOT ON A FARM, YOU SHIT-THICK BASTARD. YOU'RE AT MY MOTHER'S FUNERAL, AND YOU'VE JUST WANKED OFF THE PRIEST!

!

OH NO! CAN YOU BELIEVE I'VE JUST DONE THAT?! FUCK ME! I'VE MADE A MOCKERY OF THE WHOLE SERVICE!

WELL, NOT REALLY TERRY. I WOULDN'T HAVE BECOME A PRIEST IF I DIDN'T LIKE THAT SORT OF THING.
HERE'S TEN POUNDS OUT OF THE COLLECTION PLATE.

WHAT THE BLOODY HELL IS GOING ON HERE?! YOU'RE SUPPOSED TO BE MILKING DAISY THE COW, NOT WANKING A PRIEST OFF!...

... HOLD ON. WHAT ARE YOU LOT DOING HAVING A FUNERAL IN MY COWSHED?!
?

HOLD ON, IF THE PRIEST'S BEING 'MILKED' IN THE COWSHED, THEN WHO'S BURYING MY MUM?

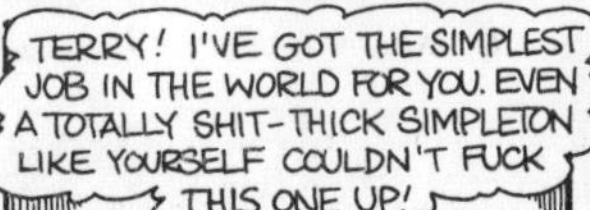

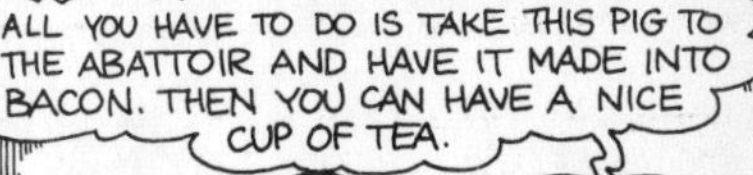

MUM R.I.P. 1920-1999

FUCK ME! I DON'T KNOW WHAT WENT ON THERE. ANYWAY NOW TO SPEND THIS LOVELY LOLLY.

CARE IN THE COMMUNITY DENTIST
SALE NOW ON

ALL YOUR TEETH PULLED OUT WITH RUSTY PLIERS AND STUFFED UP YOUR ARSE ONLY £10
MICK JAGGER ESTATES
DIVORCE FORCES SALE
HOUSE IN MUSTIQUE (FULL OF NAKED BIRDS WITH NO GAG-REFLEX) JUST £10

SPHUCK ME WWEADERS! I AMAYSHZZ MYSHELF SHUMTYMZZ!
CHOMP! NASH! CLACK! CHOMP!

TERRY! I'VE GOT THE SIMPLEST JOB IN THE WORLD FOR YOU. EVEN A TOTALLY SHIT-THICK SIMPLETON LIKE YOURSELF COULDN'T FUCK THIS ONE UP!

ALL YOU HAVE TO DO IS TAKE THIS PIG TO THE ABATTOIR AND HAVE IT MADE INTO BACON. THEN YOU CAN HAVE A NICE CUP OF TEA.

HAVE YOU GOT THAT TERRY?

HO-HUM. NO PROBLEMS SO FAR.
ABATTOIR

LEG OF THICK CUNT £1.50 lb
MINCED SHIT-FOR-BRAINS
RUMP OF FUCKWITT £2 lb
SCRAGG END OF DAFT TWAT

OH. LORDY! IT'S.. THE

FAT SLAGS

Tracey, could you send a fax to...
Right. That's the booze, the balloons, the johnnies and the dildos sorted out. Now to book a strip-o-gram.
'Ere's one. 'Seymour Dick. Your wildest fantasies come true'. Fancy calling somebody Seymour Dick.
Excuse me...
'Ello. Is that Mr. Dick? We're havin' a hen-night. How much to come as An Officer and a Gentleman, do a strip an' wave yer cock in 'er face?

Yeh!...yeh!...*'ow much!?!...*
I don't care if it is a foot long...
You'll have no trouble sticking it up yer arse then, will yer!

He wanted sixty quid, the greedy bastard. That's five quid an inch. At that rate we could get Baz to do it for a tenner.
If you wouldn't mind sending...
Excuse me. I've got an appointment...
For fuck's sake shut up! I'm tryin' to organise a fuckin' hen-night 'ere!

That night...
So anyway, Baz, 8 o'clock on Friday, you comes in to the King's Head dressed as a copper or a fireman or summat, drop yer kecks and wave yer gut-stick in Miss Bishop's face.
She'll fuckin' love it.
That's fine girls, but I'm a bit worried that I might not measure up- a little stage fright, if you know what I mean.

Don't fret, Baz. I saw a documentary about men strippers on Sky. What you do is, before hand, y' go into the bogs wi' a copy of Razzle an' you tug yerself a semi-on. Then you put a tight elastic band around the base before you get the droop.
Cracking idea!

Friday night...
THE KING'S HEAD
C'mon, Miss Bishop. Yer nowhere near pissed enough, yet.
I'll get the drinks in.
Na-aa-aa-aa! Na-aa-aa-aa! Na-aa-aa-aa! Na-aa-aa-aa!

There you go. They didn't have any pineapple juice, Miss Bishop, so I got you a triple Pernod and double Southern Comfort.
VIRGIN
Hey, look! Who's that!?!

It's a copper... come f'you, Miss Bishop!
COOO-EEE! Over 'ere, P.C. Baz!
BAR
SPORT

Erm... Miss Bishops, I'm afraid you're going to... I mean... I'm going to have to take down your particulars... er... I mean my particulars.
Na-aa-aa-aa! C'mon, Baz. ***Geddemoff!***

OFF! OFF! OFF! OFF!

OFF! OFF! O......
Eh!?!
..hunh!?!

Jesus Christ, Baz. What's up wi' it? It's gone all black! An' it's stinking even more than it usually does!
I don't know. I did what you said. I got it on the bone an put a lakky band on it just after you went...
Just after we went...!?! But that was ***five days ago***, Baz. Look at it! It's gone ***rotten!***

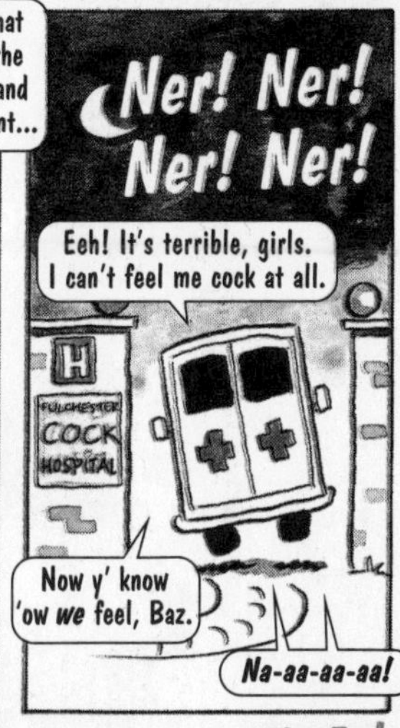
Ner! Ner! Ner! Ner!
Eeh! It's terrible, girls. I can't feel me cock at all.
COCK HOSPITAL
Now y' know 'ow ***we*** feel, Baz.
Na-aa-aa-aa!

The End

THE ADVENTURES OF MAJOR MISUNDERSTANDING

KNOCK KNOCK

I'M FROM THE ELECTRICITY BOARD. WE'RE REPAIRING A CABLE AND YOUR POWER'S GOING TO BE OFF FOR A COUPLE OF HOURS

I'M GIVING YOU NOTHING
I WAS OVER THERE FOR TWENTY YEARS. I KNOW WHAT THEY'RE LIKE

SHOW THEM HOW TO DIG AN IRRIGATION DITCH AND THEY WON'T BOTHER LOOKING AFTER IT
TOO LAZY, YOU SEE. SHIFTLESS. NO BACKBONE.

STEAL ANYTHING THAT WASN'T NAILED DOWN, YOU KNOW.
OH YES, THEY'D BE PILFERING FROM THE TRUCKS AS SOON AS YOUR BACK WAS TURNED.

INGRATES, THE LOT OF THEM. DIG THEM A LATRINE AND THEY'D NEVER EVEN USE IT. JUST SHIT IN THE BUSHES LIKE BLOODY ANIMALS.
NO, SIR. YOU WON'T BE GETTING ANYTHING FROM ME

SLAM!

BLOODY LIGHTS HAVE GONE OUT NOW

DIRTY GARY!

GARY BARLOW charmed fans as Take That's Mr. Clean - but today he exposes the filthy truth behind his squeaky-clean image by admitting: "I have sometimes been to the toilet and then not washed my hands afterwards."

Soap-shy superstar comes clean

In an exclusive interview, the ex-star revealed he has been less than scrupulous with regard to personal hygiene HUNDREDS of times.

Wild

Gary, 28, said: "Take That was a wild roller-coaster ride. We were so out of control that by the time Robbie left the band, I was regularly eating biscuits before bed-time... AFTER brushing my teeth."

Austin

In an amazing outburst the singer, whose new single 'Angel Delight Lady' is released on Thursday confessed: "Everybody thought Robbie was the wildman of the group, but I ran him a close second. He may have blown a fortune on cocaine and fast cars, but once I didn't wash my hair for a whole week.

Dallas

"If you'd read our publicity, you'd have thought we were saints. But nothing could be further from the truth. I remember after one gig on our last tour I crashed out in the hotel. I woke up the next morning and put the SAME UNDERPANTS back on. That was the state I was in. I was like a zombie. When Howard Donald asked me why I was scratching my knackers, I knew I needed help."

Allied

The frank admission of not being particularly clean sometimes will shock those who saw Gary as the well-scrubbed sanitary one in the band. But Gary says his unhygienic days are through. He said: "I've been clean for three years now. When I marry my long-time fiancee, Dawn, in July, I'll make sure I'm spotless from head to toe. I'll even wash behind my ears! And under the bridge. You will mention my new record won't you?"

Barlow - bathing and (below) Barlow -bozz-eyed

TOMORROW: "THE NIGHT MY FINGER WENT THROUGH THE TOILET PAPER - AND I SNIFFED IT."

Julie Burchill

My name is Julie I am 39 and three quarters I live in Brighton I have a cat it is called fluffy it is nice. I dont like boys I had a boyfriend he is called Tony he tried to kiss me at the NME on the lips it was horrid I hate him he smells. My granny died I was sad I cried the vicar put her in the ground there was ham sandwiches and sausage rolls and cake and crisps it was nice she was a communist.

My best friend is Charlotte we go out to play she let me look down her pants I saw her foofoo I showed her my foofoo.

I dont like John Peel I hate him lots all the others think John Peel is nice I hate him Charlotte says he did a poo in his pants and a wee. He smells. Tony likes John Peel I dont like Tony and I dont like John Peel they are smelly fat pigs. I write stories nobody likes my stories its not fair.

SPOILT BASTARD

RIGHT! I'VE FINISHED MY CHRISTMAS LIST FOR SANTA

WELL DONE, TIMMY... IT'S NOT QUITE AS THICK AS LAST YEAR'S
THAT'S THE INDEX...
SLAM!

...THIS IS THE LIST! I'VE SENT ONE TO SANTA AND KEPT A COPY FOR YOU...
I THINK WE BOTH KNOW THE REASON WHY

...BUT DON'T YOU DARE TELL ME
OH, TIMMY. I DON'T THINK SANTA WILL HAVE ROOM ON HIS SLEIGH FOR ALL THIS. HE HAS TO DELIVER TO ALL THE CHILDREN IN THE WORLD
THAT'S TYPICAL OF YOU! ALWAYS THINKING OF OTHERS BEFORE MYSELF

ANYWAY, A LARGE PROPORTION OF THE WORLD'S CHILDREN ARE MAKING TOYS IN THIRD WORLD SWEATSHOPS. THE MORE I ASK FOR, THE MORE GRAINS OF RICE THEY GET
THEY SHOULD BE GRATEFUL I WANT SO MUCH FOR CHRISTMAS. IT'S BASIC ECONOMICS, WOMAN.

CHRISTMAS MORNING...

MERRY CHRISTMAS, MY LITTLE DARLING BOY... MERRY CHRI...

PRESENTS!

YES, ER...

...LET ME EXPLAIN

YOU SEE, SANTA'S REINDEER WERE POORLY, BUT HE PROMISES TO COME JUST AS SOON AS I GET MY.. MY... DISABILITY BENEFIT
BUT I GOT YOU THIS PRESENT. I'VE BEEN SAVING IT UNTIL YOU WERE OLD ENOUGH TO APPRECIATE IT, TIMMY

IT'S A FIRE ENGINE. MY GRANDAD CARVED IT FOR MY DAD WHEN HE WAS A POW WORKING ON THE CHANGI RAILWAY...
...HE...SNIFF!...FINISHED IT THE DAY BEFORE HE DIED

HE WOULD HAVE BEEN BEHEADED IF THE GUARDS HAD FOUND IT. HE HAD TO DISMANTLE IT EVERY NIGHT AND HIDE THE PIECES UP HIS..

SMASH!

STOMP! STOMP!

OH, MOMMY... LOOK WHAT I'VE DONE. DO YOU THINK YOU CAN MEND IT?
YES! YES! I THINK I CAN!

STAMP! STOMP!
HOW ABOUT NOW!?
MATCH-WOOD

BOXING DAY...
STOMP! STOMP!
GULP! GULP!
SAWDUST

Your guide to the Royal Copulation Ceremo

ROMP and CIRCU

At 5pm on the 19th of June, Britain's church bells will peal to celebrate the wedding of HRH Prince Edward to Miss Sophie Rhys-Jones. And at 11 pm that evening, Prince Edward's bellend will *peel* as the Royal marriage is consummated in a ceremony which has remained virtually unchanged since the days of William the Conqueror.

St. George's Chapel (above), scene of the wedding, and the Majestic Nuptial Chamber (left), scene of the knobbing

By our Royal Correspondent

Tamara Pyjama Banana-Tompkinson

Royal consummations have traditionally been secretive affairs taking place behind closed doors, the details being known only to a privileged few insiders. But in the post-Diana spirit of openness, the palace has for the first time released details of the happy couple's wedding-night itinerary.

Posh

After the service at St. George's Chapel, the Royal newly-weds will attend a posh reception hosted by the Queen at Windsor Castle.

At 10.55pm, they will retire to the magnificent Nuptial Chamber in the East wing. At 11.00pm, the ceremony begins in earnest as the couple make their way into twin en-suite bathrooms to disrobe.

Baby

It falls to the Archbishop of Canterbury - the only onlooker allowed inside the royal bedroom - to help the bride into the majestic Arm Summers split-crotch panties and peep-hole negligee first worn by Queen Mary in 1554. In time-honoured tradition, The Archbishop performs this duty wearing oven gloves so as he can't feel her tits.

The new Princess proceeds through the doorway at 11.01, beginning the five-yard walk to the marital bed, followed closely by the Archbishop.

Scary

As the procession passes the glorious mirror-fronted built-in wardrobes, Princess Sophie may pause briefly to dig the itchy, nylon knickers out the crack of her arse. She then waits while the Archbishop draws back the duvet before she climbs gracefully onto the bed to await the arrival of her husband.

Sporty

At 11.02 precisely, the Prince steps out of his bathroom and for the first time Princess Sophie sees him resplendent in ceremonial poly-cotton pyjamas.

Ginger

The Prince approaches the bed from the opposite direction and pauses. The Archbishop then steps forward and, in a scene that has been repeated for hundreds of centuries, stoops onto one knee and lowers the royal pyjama bottoms.

Danny

Like many Princesses before her, Sophie may struggle to keep her emotions in check as, for the first time, she claps eyes on the royal wedding tackle. The Archbishop then retires discreetly to the end of the bed from where he witnesses the proceedings as the official representative of the Church of England.

At 11.03, the ceremony begins in earnest again as the Prince signals his intentions by rubbing her knockers once... twice... three times.

He then holds aloft the Imperial penis - known for centuries as Pink Rod - which slowly makes its way towards the entrance of Sophie's lavishly-pubed beefy drapes. After pausing to bang about a bit, at 11.04 precisely, the curtains to the inner chamber are slowly parted and Pink Rod leads the procession along the vaginal passage, flanked by two hairy knackers.

Taking 'STEPS' to Modernise the Monarchy

THE POMP and Pageantry Of Royal Consummations have served the Country well for over a thousand years. But as the new millennium approaches is the time right to break with tradition and modernise the ceremony?

After eating strong cheese at bedtime, our royal correspondent had a dream, in which he asked top teen pop sensations 'Steps', whose latest record, 'Blancmange Baby', is currently storming up the charts, if and how they would modernise the ceremonial nookie habits of the Royal Family.

"The Royals have to keep their dignity," said singer **Clare, 20**. "Fancy sex is all well and good, but we look up to our Royal Family to set an example."

Hunky keyboard wizard ***Lee, 20,*** wasn't so sure. "If they were a little less prim and proper twixt the sheets, Royal consummations would attract even more tourists into the country than they do," he said.

"Edward and Sophie should be allowed to do whatever they like in bed," said singer ***Faye, 20***. "Old fuddy-duddies shouldn't be allowed to tell them what to do."

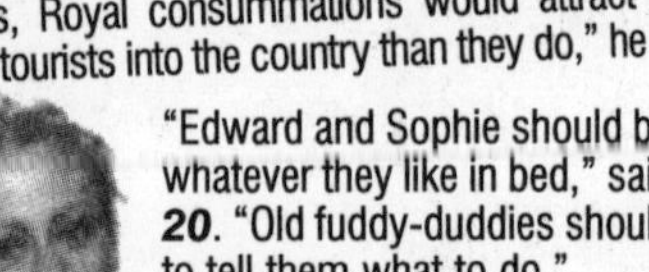

"They should take a leaf out of Queen Juliana of the Netherlands's book," said **Lisa, 20**. "She is more in touch with her subjects because she rides around on a bike and has common everyday sex."

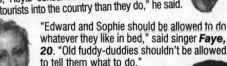

Heart-throb hurdy-gurdy Player **H, 20**, was more specific. "Our Royals are far too boring in the sack. They want to get with the Programme and do more sexy stuff. I reckon they should do S&M, A&O, DVDA and ESD," said H.

everybody's talking about
MSTANCE

We take you behind the bedroom curtains on Edward's big night in

At 11.05, the ceremony reaches its magnificent climax, when the Royal Pods bang three times on the Princess's Biffin Bridge, signalling that the royal wad has been spent. The majestic ritual over, the procession quickly withdraws and the Prince rolls over, emitting a fanfare fart. At this point the Archbishop, now resplendent in a purple and gold trouser-tent, steps forward and invites the Prince and Princess to sign the official deed of Coitus Completus.

Richard

On the stroke of midnight the bottom sheet is raised on a flagpole high above the battlements of Windsor Castle. This is greeted by a deafening cheer from the thousands of spectators who have waited for hours on the Chapel Hill lawns hoping to be amongst the first to see Edward and Sophie's map of Africa.

That Royal Wedding Night Root in full

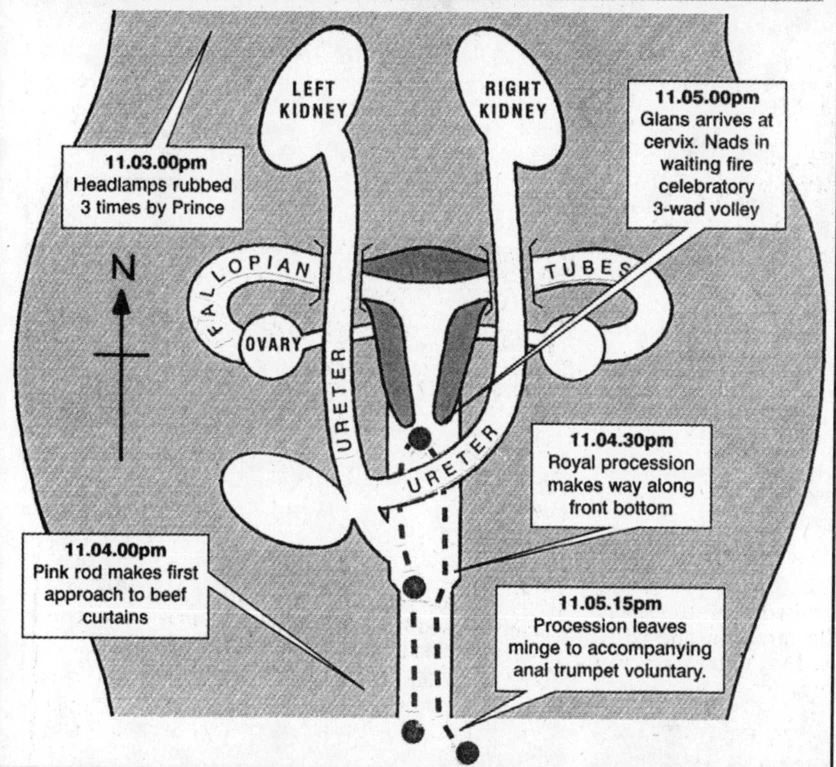
LEFT KIDNEY
RIGHT KIDNEY
11.05.00pm
Glans arrives at cervix. Nads in waiting fire celebratory 3-wad volley
11.03.00pm
Headlamps rubbed 3 times by Prince
N
FALLOPIAN
TUBES
OVARY
URETER
URETER
11.04.30pm
Royal procession makes way along front bottom
11.04.00pm
Pink rod makes first approach to beef curtains
11.05.15pm
Procession leaves minge to accompanying anal trumpet voluntary.

It's a right Royal COCK-UP!

THANKS to the meticulous planning, Royal Consummations usually pass off without a hitch, but over the years there have been a few times when it's not been 'Alright on the Wedding Night'.

• In 1981, it wasn't all plain sailing on Charles and Diana's big night aboard the Royal Yacht Britannia when the Prince accidentally locked himself in the bathroom. The ceremony was delayed by three minutes whilst the then Archbishop of Canterbury, Dr Robert Runcie kicked the door in.

• King Henry VIII was so disappointed in the size of Anne of Cleves's tits that he was unable to raise Pink Rod, and the

ceremony had to be postponed. But it wasn't his fault, as that evening he went on to 'pollute the bed' not once, but twice!

• In his eargerness to consummate his marriage to Queen Victoria in 1840, Prince Albert

rushed the disrobing ceremony and caught the metal bolt fastened through his bobby's helmet on his zip. He spent the rest of the night with the Windsor Fire Brigade trying to free his chopper with a hacksaw.

• Another of Henry VIII's six wedding nights went pear shaped in 1536. During the consumation of his marriage to Anne Boleyn, the hapless Queen let rip with a thunderous fanny fart, blowing batter-bits into the King's beard. She was beheaded later that year.

Sad Death of Lucy the Viz Elephant

REGULAR readers of Viz will be saddened to hear of the death of Lucy, the Viz elephant. She became a firm favourite in the late seventies, making numerous public appearences where she gave rides to children, but quickly outgrew her home, a lock-up garage in Huddersfield, and eventually retired from the limelight.

In the mid eighties, Lucy once again hit the headlines when she was found, still in her Huddersfield lock-up garage - now seriously malnourished and neglected. She was moved to a slightly larger lock-up garage in Leeds, where she spent a further twelve years, before being chained up and left on a piece of waste ground near Wakefield, where she was found dead earlier this month, after youths had repeatedly driven a stolen Landrover into her legs and pelted her with bricks and bottles.

In a sombre funeral ceremony, cheering crowds paid up to £5 each to watch as Lucy was winched on a crane to a height of over 250 feet before being dropped to the ground.

VIZ

SEAN FREE!

Bond to be wild!

- Connery campaigners want star returned to Scotland

AN ambitious attempt to release Sean Connery back into the wild is being scheduled for early next year.

The 68 year old actor, who was taken away from his native Edinburgh by film producers almost 50 years ago, is currently being kept in Marbella, Spain, where he spends much of his time playing golf. He is still flown to Hollywood occasionally to perform for film crews.

After 50 years in showbusiness Sean Connery (inset) could soon be returning to the wilds of working class Edinburgh.

star

Conservationists and film fans alike feel that the ageing star should be returned to his natural working class environment after a lifetime spent in showbusiness.

bounty

Working class Scotsmen are fast becoming an endangered species as a result of New Labour's classless society. The reintroduction of ex pats like Connery back into run down inner city areas could be the only way of maintaining a breeding working class population for the future.

mars

Last year brown nosing comedian Billy Connolly was released back onto the streets of Glasgow. 'Free Billy' campaigners successfully loaded the banana booted comic into a canvas sling at his mansion in Los Angeles and throughout a 12 hour flight to Glasgow the bloated comic was hosed down with champagne.

anti-roll

The "Big Yin" was strapped to the top of a Land Rover for the final leg of his journey home from the airport to the Gorbals district of Glasgow. After an emotional farewell from his showbusiness pals, including a tearful Sir David Frost, the bewildered looking star walked nervously away from the vehicle. For few moments he seemed unsure of himself, then suddenly he bounded off and was quickly lost amongst the tenements.

paralell

The same team will be handling Connery's release. Dr Jennifer Goodall, Professor in Proletariat Conservationism at Heriot Watt University, will be in charge of the operation.

gay

"The main danger is that working class celebrities struggle to adapt to their natural environment after spending too long in showbusiness", said the Professor. "But in the run up to Connery's release we will be taking special measures to ensure that the transition goes as smoothly as possible".

gold

For the next 12 months the millionaire actor will be weaned off playing pro-celebrity golf, and encouraged to make his own breakfast, preferably fried eggs and bacon. "We will also be encouraging him to wear his socks twice before they are washed, and to be less condescending to people on lower incomes than himself", Dr Goodall explained.

musclebound

Connery's return to the wild is set for Spring of 2000. After his release onto the back streets of Edinburgh his progress will be monitored by scientists using an electronic tagging device attached to his Rolex watch. For his first few weeks of freedom luxury food items such as smoked salmon and quails eggs will be dropped off near to his release point to help the star's transition to self sufficiency. Gradually the quantities will be reduced, encouraging the star to fend for himself.

true

Scientists hope that Connery's release will be more successful than that of Billy Connolly, whose freedom lasted less than a week. He was found beaten up in the Bells Hill area of Glasgow where he had been scavenging for caviar in dustbins outside a chip shop.

primary

"Unfortunately in Billy Connolly's case the other working class males appear to have rejected him", Dr Goodall explained. "They probably noticed a foreign scent - like the smell of Prince Andrew's shit on his nose - and reacted violently."

Raffles The Gentleman Thug

RAFFLES & BUNNY ARE SPENDING X'MAS DAY AT GADSHILL, THE COUNTRY HOUSE OF OLD DAYS AUTHOR CHARLES DICKENS...

"...GOD BLESS US EVERY ONE!" THE END.
A FORMIDABLE RECITATION, MR. DICKENS!
INDEED. BRAVO!
FUCKING RUBBISH!
WANKER!

WELL I THOUGHT IT WAS AWFULLY GOOD, RAFFLES. I WAS ELECTRIFIED BY HIS ERUDITION.
TESTICLES, BUNNY OLD CHAP. HE'S JUST A BIG, SHOW-OFF PONCE.
AH, LORD RAFFLES AND LORD BUNNINGTON, WE ARE ABOUT TO COMMENCE A GAME OF 'CHARADES'.
CAPITAL!
JESUS.

YOU GO FIRST, RAFFLES. YOU'RE TERRIBLY GOOD AT THIS.
TCHOH

...SOUNDS LIKE... KISS?
ERM... MISS..?
HISS?
...SOUNDS LIKE KISS..?

POPULAR PHRASE...5 WORDS FIRST WORD SOUNDS LIKE 'KISS'...
SECOND WORD.

YOU! THIRD WORD YOU! OH, I AM ENJOYING THIS, LORD RAFFLES!
FOURTH WORD...

SOUNDS LIKE...EMPTYING..? NOT EMPTYING...POURING..? SOUNDS LIKE 'POURING'...
I'VE GOT IT! BORING! FOURTH WORD, BORING!

FIFTH WORD. SOUNDS LIKE 'ROWING'...? PUNTING?... PUNT?
MORE THAN ONE PUNT..? PUNTS! FIFTH WORD SOUNDS LIKE PUNTS!

I MUST CONFESS MYSELF MOST PERPLEXED BY THIS CONUNDRUM: SOUNDS LIKE KISS... OFF... YOU... BORING... SOUNDS LIKE PUNTS.
A POPULAR PHRASE..? HMM.

MEDIA 'IT' TART

Tara Palmer Banana Pajama Thomp Kinzon

SUNDAY TIMES
HELLO TARA - IT'S SUNDAY TOMORROW AND I WAS WONDERING IF YOU'VE FINISHED YOUR 100 WORD WEEKLY COLUMN YET?

BAH! I'VE NOT EVEN STARTED IT YET. I'VE BEEN FAR FAR TOO BUSY THIS WEEK ASLEEP TO SHOW OFF MY BRAND NEW 'RALPH LAUREN' NIGHTIE ...
NOW I'M GOING TO HAVE TO FIND SOMETHING TO WRITE ABOUT.

I KNOW! I'LL GO TO A PARTY AT THE 'K-BAR' IN SOHO IN MY NEW £60K HONDA AT 90MPH WITH THE ELECTRIC ROOF DOWN - RIGHT NOW!

SO...
MY FATHER ONCE MET PRINCESS ANNE AND I'M WEARING VERSACHÉ - LET ME IN!
BAR

IMMEDIATLY...

DRINK DRINK! SNORT SNORT! DRINK DRINK!

NEXT DAY...
GOR! MY POOR HEAD - OH NO! I'VE GOT FIVE MINUTES TO WRITE 100 WORDS ABOUT THE PARTY AND I CANT REMEMBER A THING!!
I KNOW! I'LL JUST WRITE MY NAME - IN FULL!

SO...
PHEW! THATS IT FAXED OFF. IT'S QUITE EXHAUSTING BEING AN AWARD WINNING JOURNALIST - STILL, IT'S IMPORTANT TO KEEP ON THE RIGHT SIDE OF THE PRESS
CLICK!

BUT...
GASP!!
EWSAG
READ ALL ABOUT IT! TABLOID EXCLUSIVE! STUPID POSH TART PISSES KNICKERS ROUND HER ANKLES WHILE ON BENDER
MORE PICTURES INSIDE

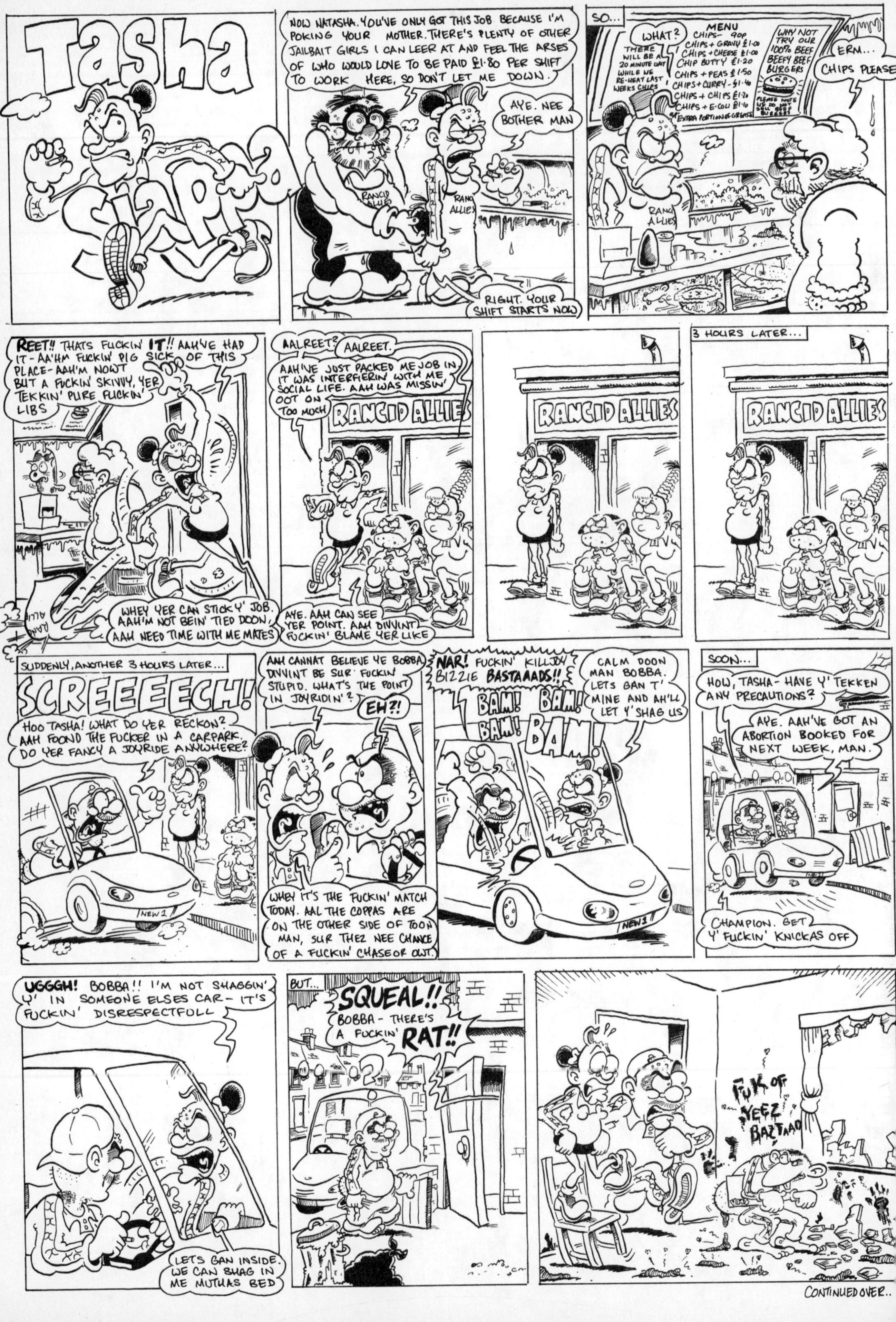

Tasha Slappa

NOW NATASHA. YOU'VE ONLY GOT THIS JOB BECAUSE I'M POKING YOUR MOTHER. THERE'S PLENTY OF OTHER JAILBAIT GIRLS I CAN LEER AT AND FEEL THE ARSES OF WHO WOULD LOVE TO BE PAID £1·80 PER SHIFT TO WORK HERE, SO DON'T LET ME DOWN.

AYE. NEE BOTHER MAN

RANCID ALLIES

RIGHT. YOUR SHIFT STARTS NOW

SO...

THERE WILL BE A 20 MINUTE WAIT WHILE WE RE-HEAT LAST WEEKS CHIPS

WHAT?

MENU
CHIPS- 90P
CHIPS + GRAVY £1·00
CHIPS + CHEESE £1·00
CHIP BUTTY £1·20
CHIPS + PEAS £1·50
CHIPS + CURRY - £1·40
CHIPS + CHIPS £1·20
CHIPS + E-COLI £1·10
5P EXTRA PORTION OF GREASE

WHY NOT TRY OUR 100% BEEF BEEFY BEEF BURGERS

PLEASE NOTE WE DO NOT SELL BEEF BURGERS

ERM... CHIPS PLEASE

REET!! THATS FUCKIN' IT!! AAH'VE HAD IT- AA'HM FUCKIN' PIG SICK OF THIS PLACE- AAH'M NOWT BUT A FUCKIN' SKIVVY, YER TEKKIN' PURE FUCKIN' LIBS

WHEY YER CAN STICK Y' JOB. AAH'M NOT BEIN' TIED DOON, AAH NEED TIME WITH ME MATES

AALREET?

AALREET.

AAH'VE JUST PACKED ME JOB IN. IT WAS INTERFIERIN' WITH ME SOCIAL LIFE. AAH WAS MISSIN' OOT ON TOO MUCH

RANCID ALLIES

AYE. AAH CAN SEE YER POINT. AAH DIVVINT FUCKIN' BLAME YER LIKE

RANCID ALLIES

3 HOURS LATER...

RANCID ALLIES

SUDDENLY, ANOTHER 3 HOURS LATER...

SCREEEEECH!

HOO TASHA! WHAT DO YER RECKON? AAH FOOND THE FUCKER IN A CARPARK. DO YER FANCY A JOYRIDE ANYWHERE?

NEW 1

AAH CANNAT BELIEVE YE BOBBA. DIVVINT BE SUR FUCKIN' STUPID. WHAT'S THE POINT IN JOYRIDIN'?

EH?!

WHEY IT'S THE FUCKIN' MATCH TODAY. AAL THE COPPAS ARE ON THE OTHER SIDE OF TOON MAN, SUR THEZ NEE CHANCE OF A FUCKIN' CHASE OR OWT.

NAR! FUCKIN' KILLJOY BIZZIE BASTAAADS!!

BAM! BAM! BAM! BAM!

CALM DOON MAN BOBBA. LETS GAN T' MINE AND AH'LL LET Y' SHAG US

NEW 1

SOON...

HOW, TASHA- HAVE Y' TEKKEN ANY PRECAUTIONS?

AYE. AAH'VE GOT AN ABORTION BOOKED FOR NEXT WEEK, MAN.

CHAMPION. GET Y' FUCKIN' KNICKAS OFF

CONTINUED OVER...

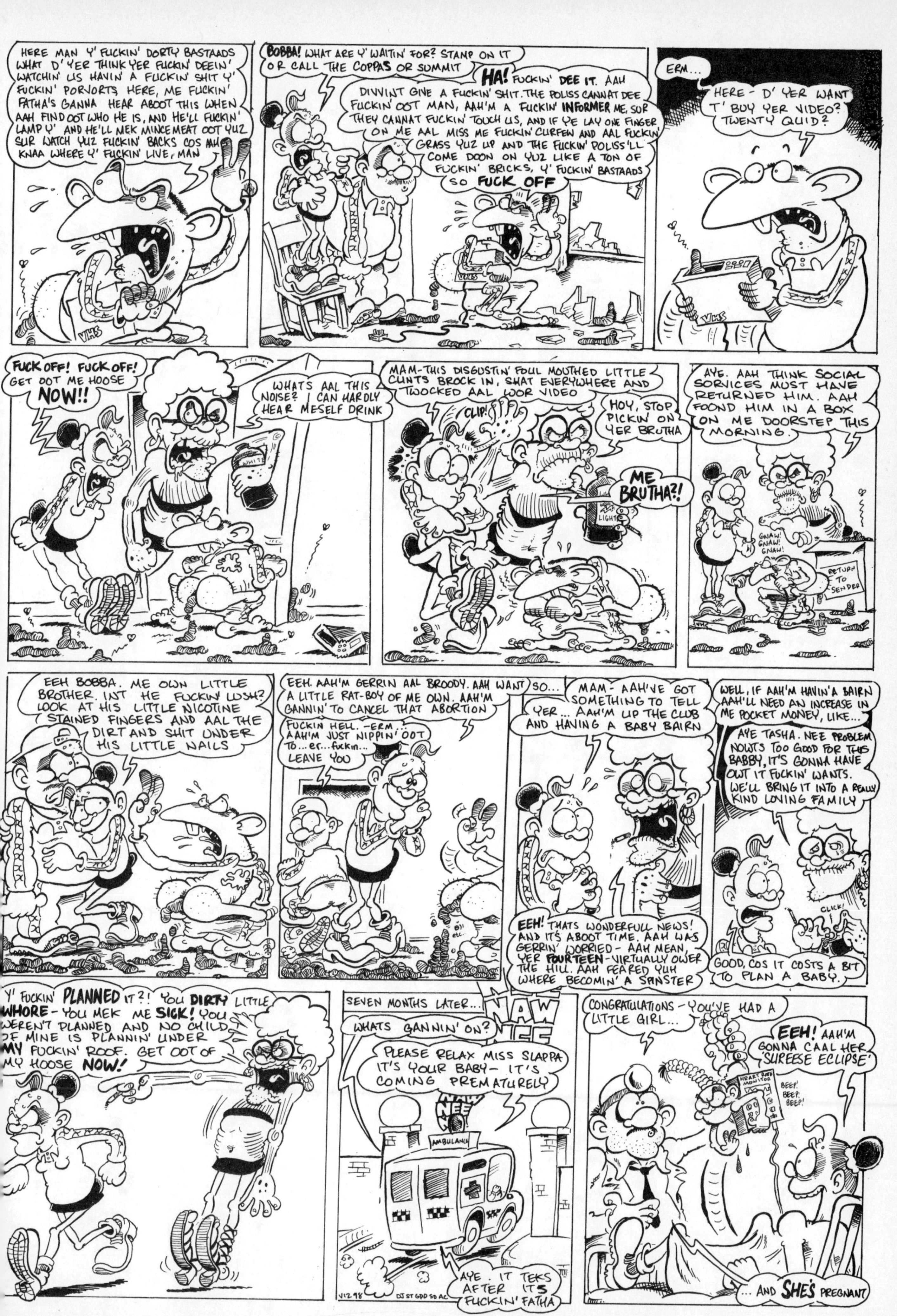

HERE MAN Y' FUCKIN' DORTY BASTAADS WHAT D'YER THINK YER FUCKIN' DEEIN' WATCHIN' US HAVIN' A FUCKIN' SHIT Y' FUCKIN' PORVORTS HERE, ME FUCKIN' FATHA'S GANNA HEAR ABOOT THIS WHEN AAH FIND OOT WHO HE IS, AND HE'LL FUCKIN' LAMP Y' AND HE'LL MEK MINCE MEAT OOT YUZ SUR WATCH YUZ FUCKIN' BACKS COS AAH KNAA WHERE Y' FUCKIN' LIVE, MAN
VHS
BOBBA! WHAT ARE Y' WAITIN' FOR? STAMP ON IT OR CALL THE COPPAS OR SUMMIT
HA! FUCKIN' DEE IT. AAH DIVVINT GIVE A FUCKIN' SHIT. THE POLISS CANNAT DEE FUCKIN' OOT MAN, AAH'M A FUCKIN' INFORMER ME, SUR THEY CANNAT FUCKIN' TOUCH US, AND IF YE LAY ONE FINGER ON ME AAL MISS ME FUCKIN' CURFEW AND AAL FUCKIN' GRASS YUZ UP AND THE FUCKIN' POLISS'LL COME DOON ON YUZ LIKE A TON OF FUCKIN' BRICKS, Y' FUCKIN' BASTAADS SO FUCK OFF
ERM...
HERE - D'YER WANT T' BUY YER VIDEO? TWENTY QUID?
FUCK OFF! FUCK OFF! GET OOT ME HOOSE NOW!!
WHATS AAL THIS NOISE? I CAN HARDLY HEAR MESELF DRINK
MAM-THIS DISGUSTIN' FOUL MOUTHED LITTLE CUNTS BROCK IN, SHAT EVERYWHERE AND TWOCKED AAL OOR VIDEO
CLIP!
HOY, STOP PICKIN' ON YER BRUTHA
ME BRUTHA?!
AYE. AAH THINK SOCIAL SERVICES MUST HAVE RETURNED HIM. AAH FOOND HIM IN A BOX ON ME DOORSTEP THIS MORNING.
GNAW! GNAW! GNAW!
RETURN TO SENDER
EEH BOBBA. ME OWN LITTLE BROTHER. INT HE FUCKIN' LUSH? LOOK AT HIS LITTLE NICOTINE STAINED FINGERS AND AAL THE DIRT AND SHIT UNDER HIS LITTLE NAILS
EEH. AAH'M GERRIN AAL BROODY. AAH WANT A LITTLE RAT-BOY OF ME OWN. AAH'M GANNIN' TO CANCEL THAT ABORTION
FUCKIN HELL. -ERM... AAH'M JUST NIPPIN' OOT TO...er...fuckin... LEAVE YOU
SO...
MAM- AAH'VE GOT SOMETHING TO TELL YER... AAH'M UP THE CLUB AND HAVING A BABY BAIRN
EEH! THATS WONDERFULL NEWS! AND IT'S ABOOT TIME. AAH WAS GERRIN' WORRIED- AAH MEAN, YER FOURTEEN- VIRTUALLY OWER THE HILL. AAH FEARED YUH WHERE BECOMIN' A SPINSTER
WELL, IF AAH'M HAVIN' A BAIRN AAH'LL NEED AN INCREASE IN ME POCKET MONEY, LIKE...
AYE TASHA. NEE PROBLEM NOWTS TOO GOOD FOR THIS BABBY, IT'S GONNA HAVE OWT IT FUCKIN' WANTS. WE'LL BRING IT INTO A REALLY KIND LOVING FAMILY
CLICK!
GOOD, COS IT COSTS A BIT TO PLAN A BABY.
Y' FUCKIN' PLANNED IT?! YOU DIRTY LITTLE WHORE- YOU MEK ME SICK! YOU WEREN'T PLANNED AND NO CHILD OF MINE IS PLANNIN' UNDER MY FUCKIN' ROOF. GET OOT OF MY HOOSE NOW!
SEVEN MONTHS LATER...
NAW NEE
WHATS GANNIN' ON?
PLEASE RELAX MISS SLAPPA IT'S YOUR BABY- IT'S COMING PREMATURELY
AMBULANCE
AYE. IT TEKS AFTER ITS FUCKIN' FATHA
CONGRATULATIONS - YOU'VE HAD A LITTLE GIRL...
EEH! AAH'M GONNA CAAL HER 'SUREESE ECLIPSE'
HEART RATE MONITOR
BEEP! BEEP! BEEP!
... AND SHE'S PREGNANT

Letterbox

Star Letter

Viz Letterbox
P.O. Box 1PT
Newcstle upon Tyne
NE99 1PT

Fax: 0191 241 4244
email viz@viz.co.uk

➧ On our wedding aniversary this year, my husband promised to treat me like a princess. And he was as good as his word. He took me out for a meal, got completely pissed and on the way home crashed the car into a concrete pillar at 120mph, killing me instantly.

Mrs B.
Essex

➧ Something ought to be done about Britain's so called Fat Cats. My husband works a seventy hour week as a security guard and comes home with less than £150. Meanwhile, the woman next door has got a cat that weighs three stones and never does anything, just eats butter out of the fridge and shits in our flower bed. Where's the fairness in that?

Mrs B. Kramer
Hull

Top of the pop-shots

➧ I was interested to find out that the 70s pop group 10cc derived their name from the average quantity of semen produced in a human ejaculation. I feel this is appropriate, as I've always thought they were a pile of wank.

C. Spencer
Battersey

➧ You think you were worried about the Millennium Bug buggering your washing machine or video on New Years Eve, 1999. What about Steven Hawking? I bet he was shitting fucking bricks.

D. Hypergrade
Cambridge

False romance

➧ So this film *Romance* claims to be the first in Britain to contain scenes of actual, rather than simulated sex. What a

load of rubbish. I saw *Confessions from a Holiday Camp* in 1978, which contained a scene where scouse actor Tony Booth shagged a woman in a toolshed so much that the shed actually fell to pieces. If *that's* not real sex, I don't know what is.

P. Mackay
Fife

Rip-off Van Rental

➧ I needed to move a wardrobe last week and telephoned a van hire company to ask the cost. I was staggered when I was told it would be £8000. How I laughed when I realised I had misdialled, and by com-

plete coincidence had rung Van Morrison's agent. Do I win £10?

S. Hayes
Wigan

➧ So Michael Portillo has come out of his filthy closet and now intends to stand for the seat left vacant by the sad death of Alan Clark MP. I am a life-long Tory, but I will not be voting for this bouffanted nancy boy. I don't want to see the Mother of Parliaments defiled by the sight of a man wearing false breasts and a dress mincing up to the dispatch box, dragging a chair and limply examining surfaces for dust.

T. Kavanagh
Canary Wharf

no.use@all

➧ This internet thing will never catch on. Only the other day I needed a hair cut. After several wasted hours searching the net, I gave up and had to walk down the road to the barbers. Home shopping my arse.

Donny Gall
Donegal

➧ I've got 58 pence to my name and I live in a cardboard box behind a bus shelter in Peterborough. With her huge overdraft, the Queen mum is £4 million worse off than me, yet she lives in 5 castles. I'm not a communist or anything, but I wonder if someone could offer me an explanation.

Charlie
Peterborough

➧ If the waitress in the Bardon Mill Little Chef is reading this - please will you clear away our empty plates and take our pudding order?

S.L. Marston
Table 6

➧ Now that the war in Kosovo is over, we can thank the Red Arrows for their contribution. If at any stage in the conflict, the alliance had needed planes to fly very close together, perhaps in a 'V' formation with coloured smoke coming out of the back, they would have been right there. But they didn't, so they weren't.

L.T.
Leeds

Grumble grumble

➧ Why do pornographers insist on using the term 'amateur' when what they really mean is 'ugly'.

J. Deegan
Australia

➧ No wonder Patrick Moore is so good with a telescope, what with that fucking great wonky eye of his.

M. Partridge
e-mail

➧ Why is it that people never seem to fight on top of trains these days?

Justin D.
Cobram, Australia

Desert island dish

➧ It seems you cannot open a newspaper these days without seeing the results of a survey that names Carol Vorderman as the woman most men would want to be stranded on a desert island with. A more sensible choice of 'Girl Friday' would be Sharron Davies, as she could suck you off and then swim for help.

Spud
Luton

➧ I was watching golf on telly the other day and I realised that even the top players take two or three swipes at the ball before being able to hit it. I'm not one to complain, but I'm not sure they are completely worth the millions they receive.

Dave
e-mail

Gas bag

➧ When I was nine, my best mate Jon and I threw a Calor gas container into a bonfire for a bit of a laugh. My next door neighbour phoned the Fire Brigade who arrived just in time to pull the canister out before it exploded. She's always been an interfering old bitch, but as for the Fire Brigade - haven't they got anything better to do?

L. Andrews
Surrey

EEH - IT DOESN'T SEEM 5 MINUTES SINCE YOU WERE THIS HIGH
ARTHUR ASKEY'S MUM
OPERATING THEATRE

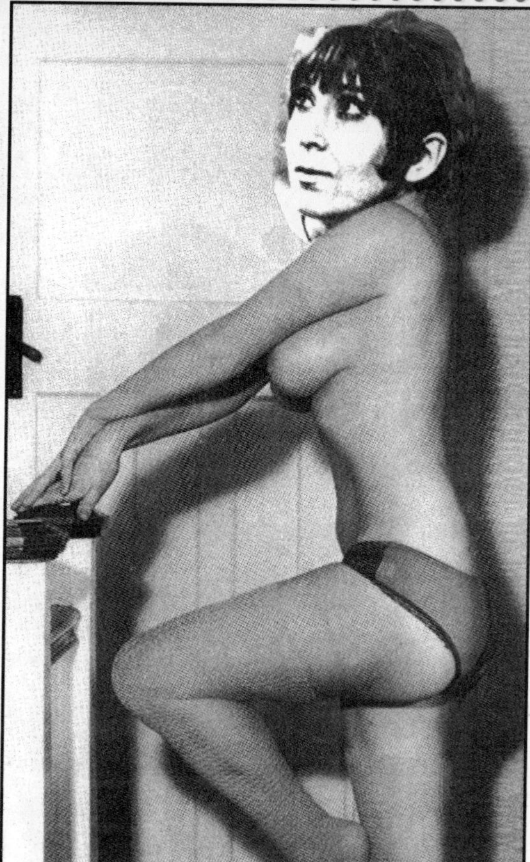

➧I'm a bunch of squaddies stationed in Bratislava and I...erm, we are dying to see a picture of the lovely Anita Harris with her kit off. Failing this, is there any chance you could cleverly graft her head onto any naked bint using that computer stuff. I... we have searched the internet for the above, but to no avail. Can you help?

Tom Spaghetti, 18/30 Lancers

** Here you go, Tom. All done with scissors and glue, and 'Anita' job you couldn't wish for.*

Monkey business

➧I recently paid £10 to drive around The Marquis of Bath's Safari Park at Longleat. What a farce. If any of your readers see the marquis, perhaps they might like to clamber all over **his** car, waving their arses in **his** face, pull the rubber trim off **his** windscreen and shit on the back of **his** window, see how he likes it.

J. Kidd
Frampton on Severn

➧My daughter got married last year, and I called a company to enquire about the cost of hiring a marquee for the day. I was staggered to be quoted a price of £8000. How I laughed when I realised I had dialled the wrong number and was actually talking to the agent of 'Mark. E.' Smith out of *The Fall*. I'm sorry to go on, but I really do need £10, honest.

S. Hayes
Wigan

➧I would just like to say a big thank-you to all those wonderful young people who stand on motorway slip-roads (in any weather, mind you) holding up boards telling us motorists where they lead to.

B. Bollockbrain
Braintree

Billy no-mates

➧I don't have any friends. If any reader has one they don't want or don't particularly like, could they please pass him/her onto me?

C. Mapperly
Surrey

Top Tips

AVOID being spotted by the police when drinking and driving by fitting net curtains to your car windows

A. Jones
Telford

RUNNING out of paper in the office? Simply take your last clean sheet, place it on the photocopier and, hey presto! As many blank sheets as you need.

P. & T.F.
Leek

KIDS, This Halloween, make big, hairy spiders out of two kittens sellotaped together.

S. Partridge
e-mail

MAKE your own smokey bacon flavoured crisps by slicing the soles from an old pair of slippers and frying them with the contents of an ashtray.

Mrs. M
Norfolk

CREATE a 'fly's eye' view of the telly by watching your favourite programmes through a dimpled beer mug.

K. Monkey
South Shields

PUBLIC toilet operators. Wind your customers up by installing wash basin taps which have to be held down at the same time as you are trying to wash your hands. remember not to put plugs in the sink as well.

Ollie McCarthy
Caerphilly

HAVING a pool party? Feed your guests beetroot. Anyone pissing in the poolwill then be identified by the large crimson cloud hanging around them.

Sam Alcock
Brisbane

OLD candle holders off birthday cakes might work as golf tees for golfers who've fallen on hard times.

O. McCarthy
Caerphilly

BALDIES. Regain your social credibility by lightly sketching a complete circle around your head with a pen and claiming that your baldness is a joke costume.

Eddie O'Hanlon
Somewhere

CULTIVATE a reputation as a cannibal by grilling streaky bacon on foil under the grill, laid out in a hand shape, and then leaving the stained foil out where visitors will see it.

D. Nelson
Broadway

DON'T throw away old leather jackets. Sewn together they make ideal 'skin suits' for psychopathic cows.

I. Ball
Low Cocken

CAN YOU LEND ME A TENNER
TILL I GET BACK ON MY FEET

Cheese Football Results

Wensleydale **1**	Cheddar **2**
Red Leicester **0**	Dairylea **1**
Cracker Barrel **1**	Stilton **1**

European Cup 3rd Round 2nd leg

Gorgonzola **2**	Parmesan **2**

(**3-2** on aggregate)

IT'S ALRIGHT, FORTESQUE. IT'S NOT A REAL LION. IT'S MERELY A SHALLOW WALL CARVING PRODUCING A CONVINCING ILLUSION OF DEPTH.
PHEW! THAT'S A RELIEF.

THE CRITICS

John Fardell '99

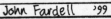

ROYAL COURT THEATRE

From veteran playwright, Arnold Usbourne, comes a deeply moving monologue...
An angry rant against injustice...
BASTARDS!! STABBED IN THE BACK! YEARS OF MY LIFE WASTED!!

ROYAL COURT THEATRE BAR

How tragic it is that his latest play has closed after just one performance.
Closed thanks to your bloody review, you hypocrites!.. You never even came to see it!!
Usbourne's new play is his worst yet
STATE OF THE NATION by Arnold Usbourne
CANCELLED

It's well known that you haven't written anything worth seeing for years, Arnold.
One didn't want to cloud ones professional judgement by getting too close to the production...

Well no-one'll get the chance to see it now... I suppose you've come to gloat.
Not at all... We've come on professional business...
We've come to interview you for The Sunday Chronicle.

An interview?.. With me?... Right! I'll tell 'em a thing or two...
Well, er.. not so much of an actual interview as a sort of profile of your life and career...
We need to check a few details...

You see, our editor's heard how you're drinking yourself into an early grave and she wants to make sure that we've got an up-to-date obituary on disc.
To be ready for when we need it...

Obituary?!! You can write your own bloody obituaries!! I'm going to ram this review down your throats with a broken whisky bottle till you choke to death on your own words!
Using typically hyperbolic language, Usbourne attempts to set up a completely unconvincing dramatic scenario....
ludicrously far-fetched...

Ten minutes later...
Who would have thought that this writer still had it in him to produce scenes of such Greenawayesque horror? Shocking and deeply affecting... Cough cough!

So who have we got coming up next?
Natasha and Crispin Critic, your saintliness...
N. and C. Critic Life Record
PEARLY GATES
ST PETER

Ah yes... Both born in 1959...
Congratulations! It's a boy!
Congratulations! It's a girl
MATERNITY WING

One emerges from this almost womb-like installation feeling that the whole tedious experience has been at least 9 months too long...

...A rather lacklustre delivery by the mother-figure, not helped by an inadequate and uncharismatic supporting cast.

Both children showed an early interest in the arts...
PLAYGROUP
Come on, Crispin. Let's paint a picture like the other boys and girls, shall we?

There! Mine's the best, isn't it?
It's rubbish!
Crispin's made a mess!
No no, it's..er.. lovely... For a first attempt... Why don't you have another go, Crispin?

..Crispin?...
One no longer feels the need to waste ones talent as a mere practitioner.... One has a higher calling...

Ah yes, one has rarely had the misfortune to encounter such a putrid heap of mediocrity... This entire exhibition is made up of the worthless daubings of a particularly immature school of painters...

CONTINUED OVER...

Aren't you going to play in the Wendy house with the others, Natasha?

Frankly, one is reluctant to become involved in a production where an ill-conceived group casting decision has dictated that *I* am not allowed to be the mummy.

I mean, what can one say about this second rate attempt at kitchen-sink realism?... The plot is entirely devoid of any narrative drive, the actors fail to bring any emotional depth to their roles and the set lacks any sense of gritty urban decay...

They continued to develop their craft as critics throughout their time at school...

Though it was at University where their work took on a new subtlety,...

Robertson's clumsy use of the chalk medium against the nihilistic black canvas results in an ultimately uninspiring piece...

Bland and incomprehensible

$a^2+b^2=c^2$

a

b

c

Tcha! Another evening wasted at a terrible student theatre production... I'll just rattle off my review for the Cambridge Arts Soc. Magazine...

"In Toby Tompkinson-Smythe's new play, badly written dialogue and laughable over-acting combine to make a totally ridiculous production."

CLICK CLICK TAPPITY TAP TAP

Ahem... Isn't Toby's father the Arts Editor on The Sunday Chronicle?

Ah.... I'll just re-write this slightly...

"In Toby Tompkinson-Smythe's new play, bravely experimental dialogue and an almost Brechtian, declamatory style of acting combine to make a truly remarkable break with the conventions of naturalism."

CLICK TAP TAPPITY CLICK

...a subtlety which gave them a real edge in the competitive world of arts journalism...

Ah, Natasha! Crispin! I've heard **so** much about you from Toby... How'd you like to take on the theatre and film pages?

The Sunday Chronicle

...And the rest of their *pretentious, self-serving, parasitic* little career is all too well known...

So do we let them in, or what?

ST PETER

Hmm... It's a *tricky* one... On one hand they haven't actually committed any *mortal sin* which I could send them **down below** for...

I suppose that's true.

On the other hand, I don't think I could *stand* having them up here

This entire space seems to lack the gritty pain and suffering so essential to great art...

Indeed... One finds the relentless beauty and perfection rather *shallow* and *decorative*...

PEARLY GATES

ST PETER

OSWALD "MIND MY BROLLY" MOSLEY

The Blackshirt Funnyman

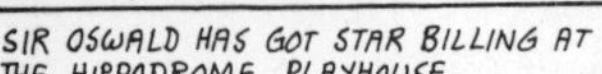
SIR OSWALD HAS GOT STAR BILLING AT THE HIPPODROME PLAYHOUSE

I'VE REHEARSED A CORKING ACT FOR THIS AFTERNOON'S SHOW
HIPPODROME
SCRIPT
TO-DAY OSWALD "MIND MY BROLLY" MOSLEY BLACKSHIRT FUNNYMAN
'ERE — MIND M' BROLLY, CHUM

MATINÉE PERFORMANCE BEGINS IN ONE HOUR, MOSLEY
RIGHTY-O, GUV'NOR — I'LL TODDLE OFF HOME AND SPRUCE UP ME COSTUME

YOUR BLACK SHIRT'S NEARLY WASHED, SIR OSWALD
DE-DAH, DE-DAH. THAT'S GRAND, MRS MITFORD

LUMME! I MUST'VE USED TOO MUCH BLEACH IN THE WASH!
JIGGLE ME JACKBOOTS WITH A JAVELIN! MY BLACK SHIRT HAS TURNED A BLOTCHY GREY

I CAN'T APPEAR ON STAGE IN AN OFF-BLACK SHIRT
MY ACT'D BE FLOPPIER THAN A FLATFISH

I'LL SOON BLACKEN IT UP WITH A DAB OR TWO OF COAL DUST

MIND MY BROLLY, CHUM, WHILE I POP DOWN THIS COAL CELLAR

THAT'S NOT A COAL CELLAR, MATE — IT'S A TALCOM POWDER CELLAR
CHEMIST
WHUMP!
TALC
I'M JUST DELIVERING SOME SUPPLIES TO THIS CHEMIST SHOP

SWIVEL ME SWASTIKA ON A SWIZZLE-STICK!
THAT'S MADE MY BLACK SHIRT WHITER THAN EVER

TSSCH!
HOW AM I SUPPOSED TO WRITE MY NEW NOVEL WITH A BROKEN PEN?
PG WODEHOUSE
I WOULDN'T WALK PAST THERE, PAL — P.G WODEHOUSE KEEPS SHAKING HIS LEAKY FOUNTAIN PEN OUT THE WINDOW

I'LL HOLD ME SHIRT UP IN FRONT OF PG WODEHOUSE'S WINDOW
IT'LL BE ALL LOVELY AND BLACK FROM INK STAINS IN NEXT TO NO TIME

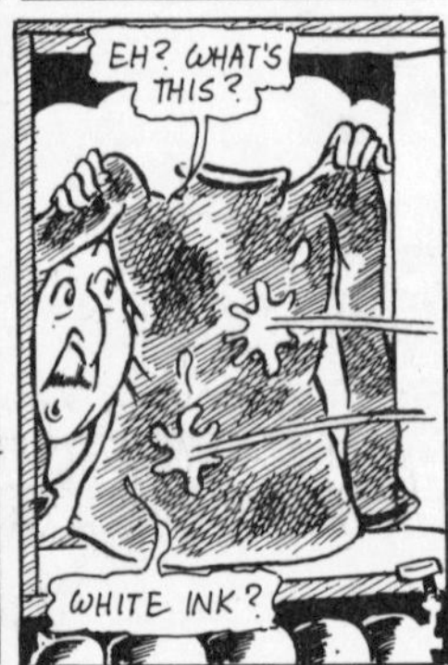
EH? WHAT'S THIS?
WHITE INK?

UH! UH! UH!
NOTHING LIKE A QUICK PULL ON ME P.G TIP
FROTTER THE FÜHRER WITH A FRISBEE! 'PLUM' HAS TAKEN A BREAK TO EMPTY HIS PLUMS

BAH! NOW LOOK AT THE STATE OF ME
MY SHIRT IS SPATTERED WITH WODEHOUSE'S 'JEEVES & WOOSTER SAUCE'

A DIP IN THIS TAR SHOULD DO THE TRICK
TAR
THERE — BLACK AS THE ACE OF SPADES. NOW TO PUT IT ON

DANGLE IL DUCE FROM A DRAINPIPE! THE TAR IS BOILING HOT
WOW! OW! OOH!
I'LL COOL THAT CHAP DOWN WITH THIS BUCKET OF WATER

SPLOSH
COO! IT WASN'T WATER — IT WAS WHITEWASH
GLUG! MIND MY BROLLY, CHUM

CALL YOURSELF A BLACKSHIRT MOSLEY? YOU'RE AS WHITE AS A SHEET
YOU'RE NOT GOING ON MY STAGE IN THAT STATE — I'LL HIRE A REPLACEMENT ACT TO TAKE YOUR PLACE

NOBBLE ME KNIGHTHOOD WITH A KNOBKERRY! THE DAY'S BEEN A COMPLETE WASHOUT

YIKES! A GHOST! I'M GETTING OUT OF HERE
SWAG
?

WELL DONE! THAT CROOK HAD JUST ROBBED MY SAFE
FASCIST OUTFITTERS
SWAG
PLEASE HELP YOURSELF TO ANYTHING FROM MY SHOP

HI! YOU CAN PUT MY ACT BACK ON THE BILLING, MR MANAGER
HIPPODROME
BRAND NEW
NEVILLE "WHERE'S ME PIECE OF PAPER" CHAMBERLAIN
A SONG, A SMILE & A POLITICAL APPEASEMENT
I'M ALL BLACKSHIRTED UP AND RARING TO GO!

AND
...WE MUST HARNESS MODERN MACHINERY AND SECURE A MOBILISATION OF ENERGY, VITALITY AND MANHOOD TO SAVE THE NATION...
HA HA HA HA HA
MIND MY BROLLY, CHUM

Owen de-Compo-ses

COMPO, scruffy star of the BBC's longest running comedy 'Last of the Summer Wine' was yesterday reeling from the news that, Bill Owen, the actor who played him for 25 years, had been axed from real life.

EXCLUSIVE!

The wooly-hatted character, 25, was last night too upset to comment after

Cancer

Owen, 85, was sensationally written out of being alive by cancer docs at a London hospital. He told us: "I have been Bill Owen for a quarter of a century, and now that he's been written out, I'm not quite sure what I'll do. I suppose I'll probably have to go back to not existing like I used to before I was invented."

Derry & Thoms

Meanwhile Owen, dead, was putting on a brave face. "I suppose it's a blessing in disguise," he told us from his coffin. "I've been typecast as a living being for 85 years, and I think it's time to move on to something different. I've already had a few interesting offers, including being eaten by worms."

Compo (above) - uncertain future
Owen (left) - looking forward to a well earned rest in peace.

Food & Drunk

With JILLY GOOLDEN

This week, Jilly recommends her favourite hangover for under £15

3 bottles of Nigerian Cabernet Sauvignon. 1/2 bottle Woods Navy Rum. 4 tins of White Lightning. 1 bottle of cooking sherry.
Morrissons £14.49

I AWOKE with this hangover with a distinct taste in my mouth. I was getting cupro-nickel, like sucking a handful of old two-pence pieces. The back of my front teeth were coated with sulphurous fur, like on a bee's back.

I tried to lift my head from the pillow, but I was getting rhythmic pulsating throbs, as if an all-in wrestler was trying to force sausage meat behind my eyes.

And there was a strong bouquet. I was getting Parmesan cheese and bad eggs, a sort of putrid, acrid smell, like a dairy farmer's slippers.

Then I realised my hair and ears were stuck to the pillow with congealed vomit. I swung my legs over the side of my bed and sat there waiting for my brain to catch up. I became aware of a strange feeling in my stomach. It was like Marlon Brando wearing a jumper soaked in sea water, trying to kick start a diesel Harley Davidson Fat Boy in two feet of porridge. I was getting hippopotamus's tongue licking canal water off my kidneys mixed with The Keystone Cops made out of omelette being chased out of my arse by a jelly tube train full of lead bricks. It was all in there.

And I was sweating like a Mother's Pride processed cheese sandwich wrapped in cling film and pressed into a driving instructor's arse stuck in a traffic jam on a hot bank holiday.

When my brain caught up with my eyes, I was in a kaleidoscope. There was an increasing pressure in my head, culminating in an explosion of hot light behind one eye. I was getting a sudden massive increase in heart rate accompanied by a terrifying spiral of anxiety, like a shark in a washing machine eating its own tail.

And for such a spicy hangover it had a very long finish. I was spewing Fairy Liquid till after tea time, and the feelings of depression and remorse lasted well into the next day.

Obviously for £15, it's not the most explosive hangover I've ever had, but it was cheeky and unpretentious and the ideal accompaniment to a few tentative sips from a cup of water. Very good value. ***

By jove! – it's a heartache without...
Bonnie Tyler's
"Total Eclipse of the Heart" Bonnocle
Bonnie
11th August
1999
The Sun
Moon

On the 11th of August the world will stand still and, as the sky darkens owls will hoot, cockerels will cock, and chinese people will bang saucepans.

It can only be a total eclipse and what better way to view this once in a lifetime celestial extravaganza than with Bonnie Tyler's Bonnocle™. Using state-of-the-art corrigated cardboard technology developed by NASA for space biscuit boxes, the Bonnocle™ was designed by top fashion icon, Jean-Claude Galtieri and combines functionality with high chic.

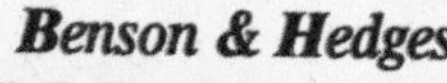
Benson & Hedges

MONKEY FAGS

Government Health Warning
SMOKING FAGS CAUSES BLUE ARSES ON MONKEYS
6mg Tar 0.5mg Nicotine 8mg Bananas

MILLIE TANT
WE ARE ONE SISTERS!
and her radical conscience

START! START! START! YOU DISGUSTING PENIS EXTENSION!
A-HUF! A-HUF! A-FLUF! A-FLOOF! PUP! wheeeeze!

HMPH!

HELLO! ARE YOU HAVING TROUBLE? I KNOW A BIT ABOUT CARS. I USED TO BE A MECHANIC MANY YEARS AGO. WOULD YOU LIKE ME TO....

STEP BACK! STEP BACK NOW!
CAN'T YOU SEE I'M A LONE WOMAN?
I'M VULNERABLE!

YOU ARE INVADING MY PERSONAL RAPE-PREVENTION PERIMETER!

ZAP!
CATTLE PROD

HELLO? ASSISTANCE? I'D LIKE A ROADSIDE RECOVERY LESBIAN...
... I SAID LESBIAN!

WHAT DO YOU MEAN YOU HAVE NO FEMALE MECHANICS?! THIS IS AN OUTRAGE!
I AM CANCELLING MY MEMBERSHIP AT ONCE!..
WELL, NOT QUITE AT ONCE, YES. ONCE YOU'VE SENT SOMEONE TO FIX IT, YES.

AND I WANT LONE WIMMIN EMERGENCY PRIORITY.
I AM A WOMAN. WHAT DO YOU MEAN 'DEEP VOICE'?

THE PROBLEM? THE PROBLEM IS THAT IT HAS BEEN BUILT AND DESIGNED BY MEN FOR THE SOLE PURPOSE OF OPRESSING WIMMIN.
YES, IT WON'T START. YES. RIGHT, HALF AN HOUR, GOOD.

30 MINUTES LATER...
AAAA

DEAR, DEAR. BAD PLACE TO BREAK DOWN, MIDDLE OF A BUSY STREET.
BREAK DOWN? THIS IS WHERE I PARKED IT LAST NIGHT, IT WOULDN'T START THIS MORNING.

FIRSTLY, ARE YOU SURE YOU HAVEN'T RUN OUT OF PETROL?
AAAA

WHAT DO YOU TAKE ME FOR!? YOU MUST THINK I AM SOME KIND OF FLUFFY-HEADED BIMBO!

YOU ASSUME I KNOW NOTHING ABOUT THE VEHICLE AND IT'S MECHANICS SIMPLY BECAUSE OF MY FEMININITY!
AAAAA
SORRY. YES, I'M A BIT OLD-FASHIONED.

RIGHT THEN. IF YOU JUST POP THE BONNET AND TURN THE IDLE SCREW CLOCKWISE A COUPLE OF TURNS FOR ME AS I TRY TO TURN IT OVER.
RIGHT!...HA!...YES!...RIGHT! I'LL DO JUST THAT!

!?!

YOU PATRONISING BASTARD! YOU THINK YOU CAN TREAT ME AS A SLAVE SIMPLY BECAUSE YOU HAVE A PENIS. YOU ARE TRYING TO MAKE ME DO YOUR FILTHY WORK FOR YOU BECAUSE YOU FEEL THREATENED BY MY MENSTRUATION!

HERE'S YOUR PROBLEM.
I HAVEN'T GOT A PROBLEM! ...YOU'VE GOT A PROBLEM!

IT'S DAMP IN YOUR ELECTRICS. BIT O' THIS W.D. 40'LL SORT IT OUT, YOU CAN DO THIS YOURSELF. JUST SPRAY IT ALL AROUND IN THERE. JUST PRETEND IT'S HAIRSPRAY DARLIN'.

SPRAY IT HERE? YES. I SEE.
FSSHHHHHHHHHhhh!
PAT!
GROPE!
MIND YOU'VE GOT A LOVELY ARSE. I LIKE A BIRD WITH A BIG ARSE.

BOOM!

HMMM.
MILLIE'S BRAIN
SQUEAK! SQUEAK!

MARRIAGES

Mr. WAYNE CURTIS to Miss. KYLIE-MARIE DUFFY

The wedding of Wayne Curtis and Kylie-Marie Duffy took place at Fulchester Registry Office on Saturday.

The bridegroom, 38 year-old son of Mr and Mrs. Les Curtis was sporadically educated between suspensions at Fulchester Comprehensive School, and now works as a free-lance tarmac operative.

The 16-year old bride is the eldest daughter of Mr. Bert Duffy, a dodgem car mechanic from Barnton Pleasure Beach.

She was given away by her father who spent the ceremony glaring at the groom and muttering obscenities under his breath.

Wearing a pure white, veiled maternity wedding dress made of Duchess Satin, she carried a large bunch of Esso Mini-mart flowers held in front of her abdomen.

The groom's brother, Frankie 'Dirtyarse' Curtis was the best man, and the ushers were made up of several of the best man's friends from 'The Roadfuckers,' a motorcyling enthusiasts association.

During the reception, which was held in the function room upstairs at 'The Dog and Hammer' public house, the bride's father repeatedly interrupted the groom's speech, calling him a 'cradle snatching cunt'.

A vicious fist-fight broke out between them, culminating in the knocking over of the wedding cake, which was made by the bride's auntie, Mrs. Vera Brody.

The groom's mother, wearing a salmon-pink ballerina length dress and clashing scarlet pill-box hat, took off one of her white court shoes and attacked Mr Duffy, screaming at him to 'less it for fuck's sake, for fuck's sake less it, will you?'

Order was restored and the two families re-grouped at opposite ends of the room for an afternoon of heavy drinking.

At the evening reception, music was provided by 'The Diamond Nites Experience', a mobile discotheque operated by the groom's brother, Terry.

Tensions again boiled over into ugly scenes of violence during a raucous singalong rendition of Jeff Beck's 'Hi-Ho Silver Lining'. Fists flew after the groom waggled his tongue and pushed his face into the cleavage of the chief bridesmaid, 14-year old Tracie-Marie Duffy, the bride's sister.

The bride's father, wearing an ill-fitting brown suit and training shoes, broke a chair over his son-in-law's back, and was immediately glassed in the throat by the Head Groomsman, Mr. Edward 'Psycho' Foster, wearing a traditional motorcyclist's outfit of torn, oil-soaked jeans and a leather waistcoat.

The ensuing mellee was broken up by a guard of 20 officers from the Fulchester Police Rapid Response Unit, led by Sgt. William Howse, who wore a dark blue serge tunic with silver buttons, matching trousers and a protective hat, all set off by a highly polished teak truncheon. In attendance were Sheba, Saracen and Simba from the Barnton Constabulary Canine Unit.

The couple, who intend to live at his mum's, honeymooned on a sofabed in his mum's spare room in Shit Street, Fulchester.

Animal cruelty man fined

A WIMBLEDON man has been fined £600 and banned from keeping pets for a year after being found guilty of organising illegal Womble fights.

Terry Freeman, 26, pleaded guilty to 8 counts of illegally trapping Wombles, hunting them with a Jack Russell terrier, and causing unnecessary suffering to 14 of the litter gathering rodents.

video

The court was shown shocking video evidence of one of the fights, filmed secretly by an undercover RSPCA officer and narrated by Bernard Cribbins.

Sickening scenes showed the blood-covered animals being goaded by jeering crowds before being thrown into a small arena to tear each other apart.

decline

"Wombles have been a protected species since 1919 after snaring and fighting caused the breeding population to decline to just a handful of individuals" said Adrian Street, Chief Inspector of the RSPCA.

"Unfortunately, Womble fights have not stopped, they've just been driven underground, overground."

After the fight, the video was handed to the police, but three of the Wombles involved, Tomsk, Orinoko and Madame Cholet had to be destroyed by RSPCA vets.

MICHAEL WINNER GETS HIS DINNER

I WANT MORE SOUP! I'M MICHAEL WINNER, I DIRECTED DIRTY WEEKEND AND I'M A CLOSE PERSONAL FRIEND OF CHARLES BRONSON AND I... WANT... MORE... SOUP!

IS MR. WINNER'S SOUP READY YET, GASTON?
ZUT ALORS! ZAT EES HEES 'OW YOU SAY THIRD BOWL! 'EE MERST ZINK A AM MADE OF SPERNK!

JANET STREET-PORTER CRUSOE
AND HER RESEARCHER FRIDAY

THE ATLANTIC OCEAN....
WE'VE HIT AN ICEBERG!
THE SHIP IS SINKING!
GOD SAVE US ALL
HOOOOOOOOT
WOMEN AND CHILDREN FIRST!

RESEARCHER! OIA'M FEELING RATHER THIRSTY. BVRING ME A GLARSS OF CHAMPAGNE
SMASH HITS
THE SHIP HAS STRUCK AN ICEBERG, MA'AM—PERHAPS WE SHOULD FIND A LIFEBOAT

DOWN'T TELL ME ABAHT ICEBERGS. OI DOWN'T PAY YOU TO TELL ME ABAHT FAHKING ICEBERGS
SMASH HITS
ICEBERGS ARE NOT A SUBJECT WHICH INTERESTS ME IN THE SLOIGHTEST. JUST BVRING ME A GLARSS OF FAHKING CHAMPAGNE!

LOOK AT ALL THESE DVREADFUL PEOPLE BOBBING AROUND IN THE WATER! GET THEM OUT OF MOY SIGHT AT ONCE!
YES, MILADY
ONE THING OI CANNOT TOLERATE IS A LOAD OF FAHKING PEOPLE BOBBING AROUND IN ICY COLD WATER

THREE DAYS ADRIFT LATER
THAT'S NOT A SALMON! THAT'S A COD. THVROW IT BACK
OI HATE COD. BVRING ME A FVRESHWATER SALMON
I REGRET, MA'AM, THAT THAT SPECIES IS UNAVAILABLE IN THE ATLANTIC OCEAN

DOWN'T TELL ME ABAHT THE ATLANTIC OCEAN! OI WANT A FVRESHWATER SALMON! JUST TAKE ME TO THE GVROUCHO CLAB BEFORE I GET VERY CVROSS!
STAMP
BREAK

WHOY IS WATER POURING INTO THIS BOWT? OI DIDN'T ARSK FOR A BOWT FULL OF WATER
OI HAVE ABSOLUTELY NO INTEREST IN WATER-FILLED BOWTS. OI WANT THIS BOWT FILLED WIV CHAMPAGNE

THANK GOODNESS, MA'AM — IT'S A DESERT ISLAND. WE'RE SAVED.
IN MOY EXPERIENCE OI HAVE ALWAYS FOUND DESERT ISLANDS TO BE A MOST DISAGVREEABLE FORM OF LAND MASS

FIRST OF ALL, I'D BETTER BUILD US A SHELTER, MA'AM — IT LOOKS LIKE THERE'S A STORM COMING
OI HATE STORMS

OI HATE TYPHOONS, MONSOONS, HURRICANES, CYCLONES AND GALES
BUT OF THE MANY TYPES OF WEATHER OI REALLY DO NOT APPRECIATE, OI CANNOT ABIDE STORMS

OAW FOR GAWD'S SAKE!
OI DISTINCTLY TOLD YOU OI WANTED MY SHELTER BUILT IN POST MODERN STYLE — THIS IS FAHKING NEO-VERNACULAR!

OI DOWN'T PAY YOU TO BUILD ME FAHKING NEO-VERNACULAR ARCHITECTURE
BOOT
IF OI TELL YOU TO BUILD IT POST MODERN, THEN YOU FAHKING WELL BUILD IT POST MODERN

AND BVRING ME A SAHNDWICH, OIA'M HUNGRY. AND OI DO NOT WANT ANY OF THIS TVROPICAL FRUIT
YES, MA'AM. BUT I SHALL HAVE TO GROW SOME WHEAT TO MAKE THE BREAD FIRST...
JUST DO IT!

SO, 3 MONTHS LATER

SIX MONTHS LATER

EVENTUALLY
HERE IS YOUR SANDWICH, MA'AM
THIS SAHNDWICH IS MADE WIV WHITE BVREAD!

DOWN'T GIVE ME A SAHNDWICH MADE WIV WHITE BVREAD. OI HATE WHITE BVREAD
FLING
STAMP
STAMP
IF THERE IS ONE FING THAT MAKES ME LOSE MOY TEMPER, THAT IS BEING GIVEN WHITE FAHKING BVREAD SAHNDWICHES!

AHOY THERE, CASTAWAYS!
LOOK, MILADY — A RESCUE SHIP!
WHO ARE THESE DREARY PEOPLE? OI CERTAINLY HAVE NEVER SEEN THEM IN THE GVROUCHO CLAB

DO YOU KNOW WHO OI AM? OIAM JANET SVREET-POR-TAH. OI AM AN INNOVATOR OF TELEVISUAL PVROGRAMMING
OI PERSONALLY REVOLUTIONISED ENTERTAINMENT FOR. YAHNG PEOPLE

SHIP BOARD ENTERTAINMENT
KICK JANET STREET-PORTER'S FUCKING TEETH OUT
ME FIRST
HERE

mr. LOGIC
hmm
HE'S A PAIN IN THE ARSE

WE'RE LOSING ALTITUDE!... WE'LL HAVE TO JETISON ONE OF THE HEAVIER ANIMALS!
FUT! FUT!
ZOO TRANSPORT
FUT! FUT!

CASINO
LUCKY LUCAN'S
24 HOUR GAMBLING
hmmm...

INSIDE...
FEELING LUCKY TONIGHT SIR?
CASH DESK

FEELING LUCKY? LUCK IS MERELY A SUPERSTITIOUS CONSTRUCT, MADE TO DESCRIBE FORTUITOUS COMBINATIONS OF CIRCUMSTANCE.
THEREFORE YOUR QUESTION MEANS NOTHING TO ME.

LUCK, AS PROVIDENT SERENDIPITY IS AN ABSTRACTED CONCEPT AND THEREFORE NOT APPLICABLE TO SUBJECTIVE PSYCHOLOGICAL STATES, OR "FEELINGS".
YES. FINGERS CROSSED, THEN.

A ONE POUND CHIP, PLEASE.
THAT'S A POUND, THEN.
NATURALLY.

FEITES VOUS JEUX MADAMES ET MONSIUERS.
hmmm...

VOL-AU-VENT LA PLUME DE MA TANTE

WHRRRRR!
TINK! TINK!
KLAKKETY KLAK!

NUMBER ONE.
OOOOH!

10 MINUTES LATER...
I SAY, DO YOU MIND IF I JOIN YOU? PERHAPS SOME OF YOUR LUCK WILL RUB OFF ON ME ... ONE WAY OR ANOTHER IT'S YOUR LUCKY NIGHT.

WELL, WHO, APART FROM A VERY CLEVER GAMBLER LIKE YOU, WHO'D HAVE BET ON THE NUMBER ONE COMING UP SIX TIMES IN A ROW? THE ODDS ON THE SIXTH ONE MUST HAVE BEEN HUGE.

THE ODDS ON ANY CONFIGURATION OF SIX NUMBERS COMING UP ARE EXACTLY THE SAME. THE ODDS ON MY SIXTH BET ON THE NUMBER ONE COMING UP WERE 33-1. EXACTLY THE SAME ODDS AS EVERY SINGLE SINGLE-NUMBER BET EVER PLACED ON A ROULETTE TABLE.

YOU AIN'T HALF CLEVER, I BET YOU COULD WIN ON CARDS AS WELL ... COME ON, LET'S SEE YOU TRY, EH?
hmmm...

WHAT? YOU'RE BETTING YOUR WHOLE LOT ON ONE HAND OF CARDS?

YES. YOU SEE I HAVE A STRAIGHT FLUSH. THE ODDS AGAINST ANYONE HAVING AN EQUAL HAND (AS NONE BETTER CAN BE ACHIEVED), ARE 54 OCTILLION TO ONE. APROXIMATELY.
COR! YOU DON'T HALF KNOW SOME BIG WORDS. WHAT'S AN OCTILLION?

A THOUSAND THOUSAND THOUSAND THOUSAND THOUSAND THOUSAND THOUSAND THOUSAND THOUSAND.
OOOH! I ALWAYS GET HORNY WITH A MAN WHO KNOWS LOADS OF STUFF ABOUT NUMBERS AND BIG WORDS AND THAT. AND GAMBLING GETS ME GOIN' AN' ALL. ARE YOU BETTING SOME MORE?

I SUMMISE THAT YOU ARE MAKING A PROSPECTIVE SEXUAL ENTREATY BASED ENTIRELY ON MY PRESENT FINANCIAL ENGORGEMENT, AND AS AN OPPORTUNITY FOR SEXUAL GRATIFICATION HAS NOT BEEN FORTHCOMING FOR SOME TIME, NOTWITHSTANDING MASTURBATION, I FIND THE PROSPECT OF PENETRATIVE VAGINAL INTERCOURSE, LEADING TO EJACULATORY ORGASM, NOT UNWELCOMING.
I SHALL CEASE GAMBLING FORTHWITH, AS TO CONTINUE WOULD RISK THE CHANCE OF PLACING MY TUMESANT MEMBER INTO YOUR REPRODUCTORY TRACT.

I KNOW A LOVELY LITTLE HOTEL AROUND THE CORNER, ARE YOU GOING TO BUY ME SOME BUBBLY?
I ENVISAGE CHAMPAGNE AS BEING A WISE PRE-COITAL INVESTMENT AS THE IMBIMBENDUCATION OF AN EFFERVESCENT INTOXICANT MAY HELP FACILITATE SUCCESSFUL INTRAMISSION.

OOOH, DON'T WALK UNDER THAT, IT'S BAD LUCK.
THE ONLY ALTERNATIVE WOULD BE TO DIGRESS FROM THE PERAMBULATORY CAUSEWAY AND ONTO THE CARRIAGEWAY DESIGNATED FOR MOTOR-VEHICLES. THE STATISTICAL PROBABILITY OF INJURY OR DEATH BY AUTOMOTIVE IMPACT IS FAR GREATER THAN ANY RISK CONCOMMITANT WITH SUB-LADDERANT WALKIFICATION.

MEEEEEEP!!
HMMNEEOOAAW!!!
THERE. I TOLD YOU.

BOOM!

THIS DOES NOT NECESSARILY INVALIDATE MY ORIGINAL PREMISE.

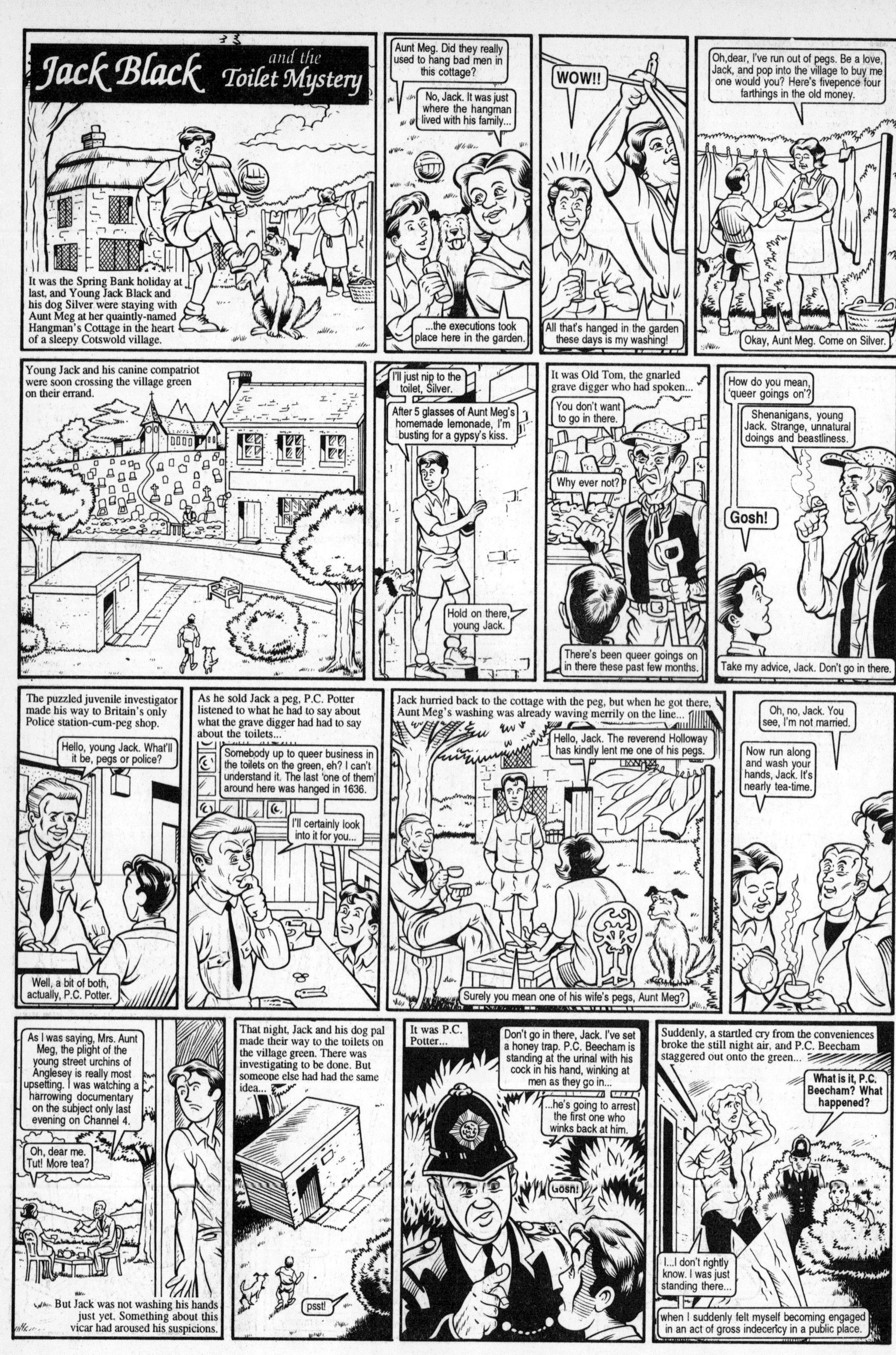
Jack Black and the Toilet Mystery
It was the Spring Bank holiday at last, and Young Jack Black and his dog Silver were staying with Aunt Meg at her quaintly-named Hangman's Cottage in the heart of a sleepy Cotswold village.
Aunt Meg. Did they really used to hang bad men in this cottage?
No, Jack. It was just where the hangman lived with his family...
...the executions took place here in the garden.
WOW!!
All that's hanged in the garden these days is my washing!
Oh,dear, I've run out of pegs. Be a love, Jack, and pop into the village to buy me one would you? Here's fivepence four farthings in the old money.
Okay, Aunt Meg. Come on Silver.
Young Jack and his canine compatriot were soon crossing the village green on their errand.
I'll just nip to the toilet, Silver.
After 5 glasses of Aunt Meg's homemade lemonade, I'm busting for a gypsy's kiss.
Hold on there, young Jack.
It was Old Tom, the gnarled grave digger who had spoken...
You don't want to go in there.
Why ever not?
There's been queer goings on in there these past few months.
How do you mean, 'queer goings on'?
Shenanigans, young Jack. Strange, unnatural doings and beastliness.
Gosh!
Take my advice, Jack. Don't go in there.
The puzzled juvenile investigator made his way to Britain's only Police station-cum-peg shop.
Hello, young Jack. What'll it be, pegs or police?
Well, a bit of both, actually, P.C. Potter.
As he sold Jack a peg, P.C. Potter listened to what he had to say about what the grave digger had had to say about the toilets...
Somebody up to queer business in the toilets on the green, eh? I can't understand it. The last 'one of them' around here was hanged in 1636.
I'll certainly look into it for you...
Jack hurried back to the cottage with the peg, but when he got there, Aunt Meg's washing was already waving merrily on the line...
Hello, Jack. The reverend Holloway has kindly lent me one of his pegs.
Surely you mean one of his wife's pegs, Aunt Meg?
Oh, no, Jack. You see, I'm not married.
Now run along and wash your hands, Jack. It's nearly tea-time.
As I was saying, Mrs. Aunt Meg, the plight of the young street urchins of Anglesey is really most upsetting. I was watching a harrowing documentary on the subject only last evening on Channel 4.
Oh, dear me. Tut! More tea?
But Jack was not washing his hands just yet. Something about this vicar had aroused his suspicions.
That night, Jack and his dog pal made their way to the toilets on the village green. There was investigating to be done. But someone else had had the same idea...
psst!
It was P.C. Potter...
Don't go in there, Jack. I've set a honey trap. P.C. Beecham is standing at the urinal with his cock in his hand, winking at men as they go in...
...he's going to arrest the first one who winks back at him.
Gosh!
Suddenly, a startled cry from the conveniences broke the still night air, and P.C. Beecham staggered out onto the green...
What is it, P.C. Beecham? What happened?
I...I don't rightly know. I was just standing there...
when I suddenly felt myself becoming engaged in an act of gross indecency in a public place.

But we've been watching from the bush. We didn't see anyone go in or come out.
I know. That's the strangest part of all. After I shot my bolt, I turned around... and there was **no-one there**. It's all most perplexing.
The three made their way inside the toilets
There's no other way in or out, except for this window. And that's far too small for anyone to fit through. Hmm!
Woof!
What is it, boy? What have you found?
Jack picked up what his faithful feline friend had found, and held them in the beam of P.C.Potter's torch.
A banana skin, a little fez, some tiny trousers..? I just don't understand it.
I think I do.
And if you make your way to reverend Holloway's service tomorrow, everything will be explained.
The next morning, an expectant congregation crammed into the ancient pews of the church...
Good morning everyone. I'm delighted that a young visitor to our village has asked to read the lesson for this service.
Jack eagerly took the pulpit...
The lesson today is taken from Leviticus. Chapter 14.
"And he that lies with the bottom of another man, he shall be unclean in the eyes of the Lord for he is an abomination...
...and the Lord spake in a terrible voice saying I hath nothing against them personally but, it's just not natural, is it? I mean, continueth the Lord, it's just not right. For they are unclean and vile and filthy in Mine eyes and hanging is too good for them if you asketh Me. It turneth My stomach, it really doth."
Many of you I am sure, will have been shocked to hear about the recent goings on in the toilets. Well, I am here to name the guilty party, for he is here today... in **God's house**.
The congregation gasped as Jack made his announcement...
It is the vicar! The Reverend Holloway!
P.C. Potter sprang into action...
Well done, Jack! But how did you know?
Easy! Whilst having tea at my Aunt Meg's, he made **two very** simple mistakes.
First, he let slip he isn't married, and then he said he watches Channel 4.
Brilliant. So you knew that he was 'one of them'. But how did he get up to all that filthy malarkey in the toilets. We never saw him go in or out.
That was the **clever bit. He** didn't... But anyway, it's time to sing a hymn, isn't it, Reverend Holloway?
How about 'We Plough the Fields and Scatter'?
No! Not that one!
Yes, Reverend. The only Hymn that contains the note middle C. The only note that is **never** played on this church organ.
Gosh! A little monkey!
Yes. Reverend Holloway perverted this little creature. He trained it and sent it out to enter the mens toilet through the tiny window, there to do his queer bidding by simian proxy.
Shame!
Back at Hangman's Cottage...
Well done, Jack. Thanks to you, Reverend Holloway is off to an island surrounded by sharks, where the RAF can use him for bombing practice.
Yes. **And further!**
What's going to happen to the monkey? Can I keep it?
I'm afraid not. It's been queered up and there's a chance it could be catching. We're going to have to hang the wretched creature.
Can I be the executioner?
Well, as owner of Hangman's cottage, that duty really falls to Aunt Meg, Jack.
Oh, go on Jack! You do it.
After all, it was your hard work that solved this mystery.
Thanks Aunt Meg!
Hooray!!
THE END

The THREE SHAKESPEARES

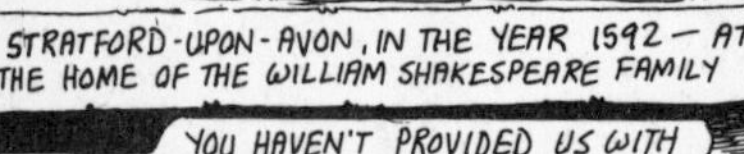

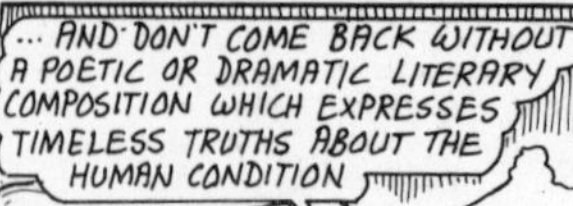

Cacko Jacko

THAT ACTOR who plays Jacko out of Brush Strokes was celebrating with friends last night after being presented with the 1999 BAFTA award for lifetime non-achievement.

The award is given in recognition of unremarkable contributions to showbusiness, and past winners have included such theatrical pot-boilers as the thin bloke who worked at the paint company with Terry Scott in Terry and June, and him out of On the Move. Not Bob Hoskins, the other one.

winner

Last year's winner, the woman with the big nostrils who looks a bit like Lynda Bellingham, but isn't, presented Jacko out of Brush Strokes with the award at a Gala Dinner at London's swanky Grosvenor House Hotel.

SHOWBIZ EXCLUSIVE

Last night, the actor recalled some highlights of his sparkle-free 21-year career in film and television.

douglas

"I was definitely in the last series of *Get Some In* and someone once saw me opening a bowling alley in Scotland. I often played a general purpose villain in The Sweeney, Minder or The Professionals, that sort of thing," he told us.

angelo

"I look quite like Terry, the chef out of Fawlty Towers, but I don't think that was me. I think my my name is Kevin or Keith or something like that. My wife just calls me Jacko out of Brush Strokes or sometimes him out of the Flash adverts."

That actor - no great shakes

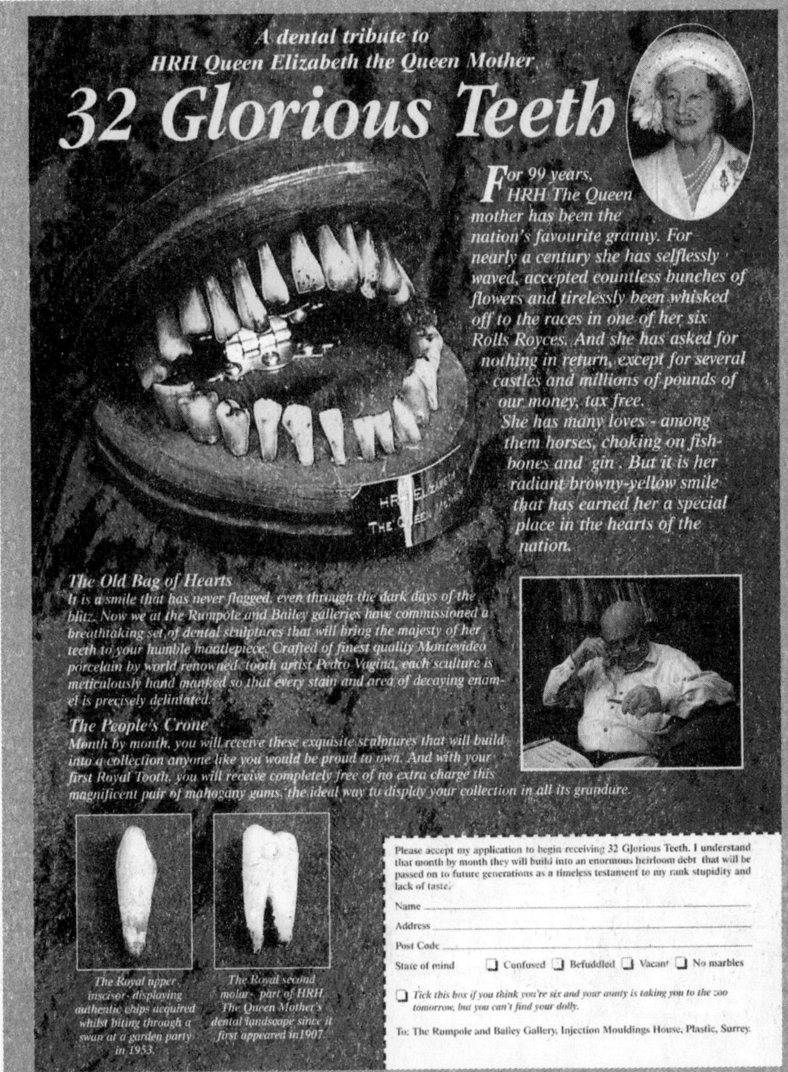

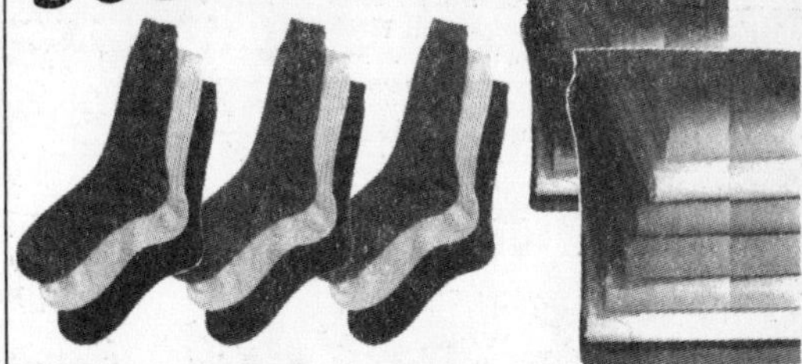

You can't hurry love...

16-year-old Lydia Chambers had been going steady with Matthew Marshall for nearly 4 months. They had become very close, but Lydia could not help thinking that there was something missing from their relationship.
You see, if you put a little away each week into a Building Society savings account, it soon mounts up. Before you know it, you'll have enough to take out your own pay-as-you-go tax-free ISA, or perhaps invest in some low risk unit trusts.
Yes, Matthew.

God! Do you have to be so *sensible* all the time?
Blah, blah... safe... blah, blah... sensible... blah, blah... low risk... blah, blah...

Later that day, Lydia met her best friend Danielle for a cup of coffee.
...I mean, Matthew is very nice, Danielle, but he does go on and on about Building Society accounts and stuff like that.
Bor-RING!! You want to give him the push, Lydia. There's plenty of time for that *safe* stuff when you're old.

I've been seeing Jed for a month now, and we've already dabbled with some *high risk stocks* and stuff......now he's asked me if I'll play the FT share index *futures market* with him, and I've agreed.
Wow! Matthew has never suggested any-thing that *daring*.

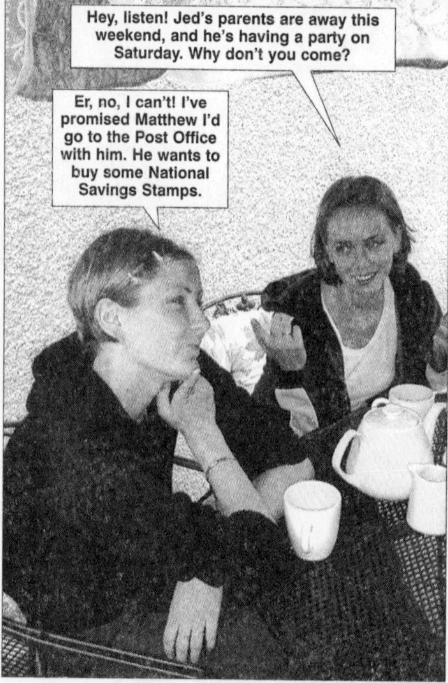

Hey, listen! Jed's parents are away this weekend, and he's having a party on Saturday. Why don't you come?
Er, no, I can't! I've promised Matthew I'd go to the Post Office with him. He wants to buy some National Savings Stamps.

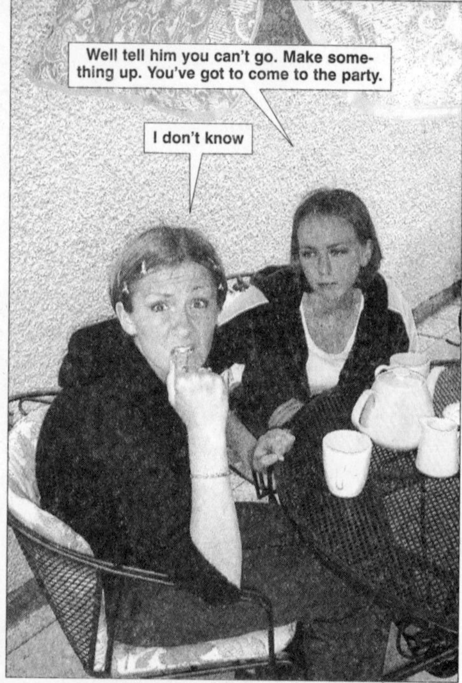

Well tell him you can't go. Make some-thing up. You've got to come to the party.
I don't know

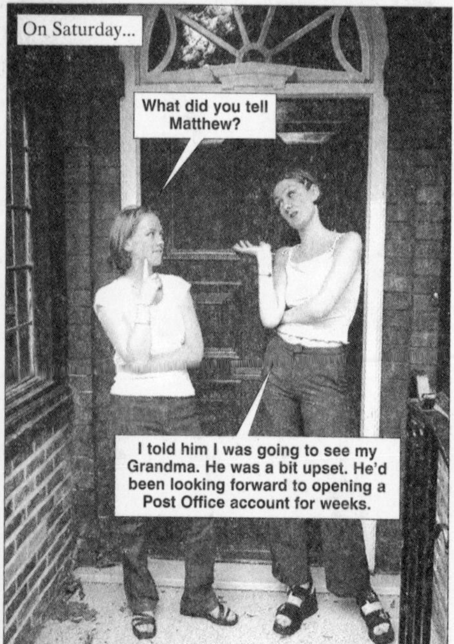

On Saturday...
What did you tell Matthew?
I told him I was going to see my Grandma. He was a bit upset. He'd been looking forward to opening a Post Office account for weeks.

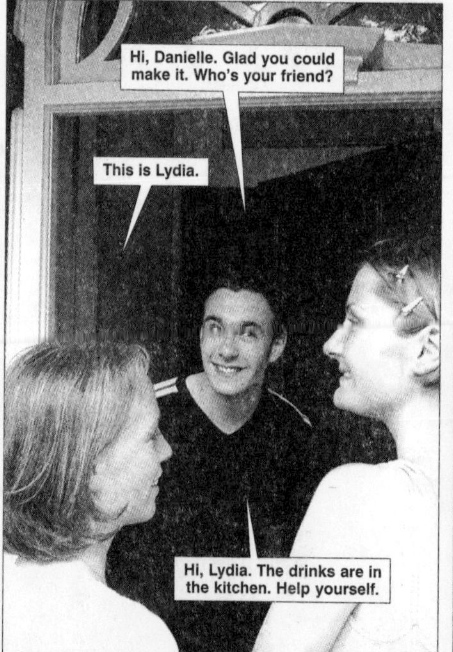

Hi, Danielle. Glad you could make it. Who's your friend?
This is Lydia.
Hi, Lydia. The drinks are in the kitchen. Help yourself.

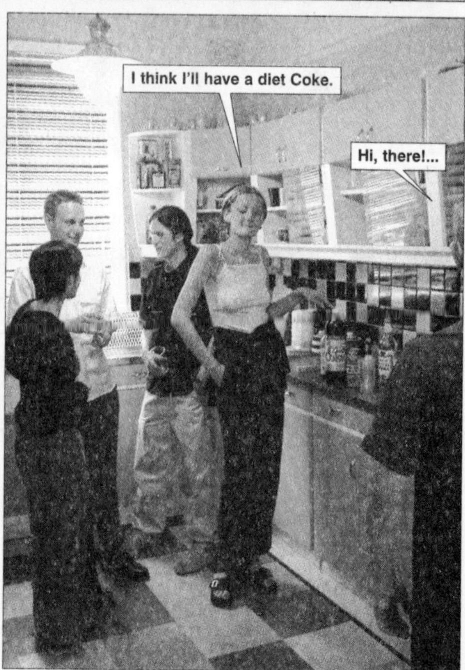

I think I'll have a diet Coke.
Hi, there!...

...I'm Nathan. I saw you come in with Danielle. Let me get you a drink.
It's okay, I've...

Here, shotgun this.
No. I don't really...
Oh, come on. It's a party. Enjoy yourself!

You look a bit sad, Lydia. Is everything okay? Is it money worries, uh?
No, not really... well, sort of.

Thought so. Well don't worry, I'm not going to tell you what to do with your cash.
Hey, he seems okay!
Here. Try some vodka.

As the evening went on, Lydia found herself pouring her heart out to Nathan.
...you see, I'm not sure I want it to just sit there in a 90-day notice account.
Of course you don't.
I mean, I might want instant access or something.
Yeh, sure you might. Here, have some meths.

You see, a girl like you should try and spread your cash around a few high risk ventures. Maybe a Pacific Rim trust fund or something.
Wow! Nathan's financial advice is *LUSH!*

Listen. We can't talk here. Why don't we go upstairs?
There's a little desk where you can sit down and get more comfortable.

I... I feel a little... a little... woozy!
Yeah, sure, Baby. Come and sit down.

Shortly...
GO ON! YOU KNOW YOU WANT TO! You *HAVE* to take risks if you want to see higher percentage returns! Look at the performance of these ultra high-risk trusts. You could make a fortune in weeks!
Will I ...regret this... in the morning?...

Cont. page 35

THE ADVENTURES OF

MAJOR MISUNDERSTANDING

Stars in their 'ice'

BRITAIN'S showbiz agents are in for a bad year as an unusual combination of climatic conditions has caused many of their frail celebrities to perish.

A touch of frost catches failing stars

A mild winter followed by an early spring tempted many agents to bring out their elderly stars, only for them to be caught out by a late cold snap. Now the agents face the summer season with dangerously depleted stocks of stars.

Freak

Ernie Wise, Dirk Bogarde and Johnny Morris are just a few of the less resilient performers who have fallen victim to the freak conditions.

Blues

"It's the worst year I can remember for a long time" one agent told us. "It's not affected me too badly, but I deal mostly in pop stars and alternative comedians, and they're fairly hardy. But a colleague of mine who specialises in song and dance men has lost fifty percent of his stock since February."

Chuckle

This latest blow will be the last straw for many agents, some of whom are still recovering from the hurricane of 1987, which wiped out many stars including Eamonn Andrews, Irene Handl and Patrick Troughton. A spokesman for Equity, a sort of Oxfam for celebrities, said "It's the same story every year. When will agents learn that stars should be kept indoors until the middle of May at least."

Grace

We phoned Buckingham Palace to ask how the Queen mum was. "She's in the porch wrapped in an old blanket with a paraffin heater to keep the frost off," her agent said.

Morris - Animal Tragic

Wise - little urn

Dirk - wears white shroud

FUCK PEAS!
BEANS make MY day!
For more information about beans phone the Bean Information Council

ravey davey gravy

THUMP! THUMP!..
EEK! SCREECH!..
THUMP!..THUMP!
THUMP!..

SCREEEEEEECH!
THUMP! THUMP!
SOUNDS LIKE SOME PHAT WAXNESS COMING FROM NEXT DOOR
YEAH! BEEFY!

EEEK!...EEEEEEEK!
THUMP! THUMP!
IT'S THE BEST NEW-ON RAWKUS I'VE EVER HEARD
FUCK OFF! IT'S PROGRESSIVE BRIT HOUSE!
BRIT HOUSE!? IT'S MORE LIKE MASSIVE PUMPING EURO TRANCE THAN BRIT HOUSE!

TRANCER? - MORE LIKE A SMOKER'S BEAT IF Y' ASK ME
IT'S GIVIN ME THE FULL RUSH! IT'S A SORTED BIT OF TACKLE!

I WANNA KNOW WHAT IT IS!.. IT'S MASHIN' ME FUCKIN' SWEDE
LET'S GO AN' QUIZ THE BOSS MAN
NOW YER SPARKIN'

THUMP!
EEEEEEK!
EEK! EEK!
DING! DONG!
MASS-I-I-I-I-I-VE!!

BOO YAKKA! WE'VE BEEN SPECKIN' YER CHOONS, BOD. I RECKON IT'S BOUNCY HOUSE
...BUT HE RECKONS IT'S A SHARP STYLE HOUSE GROOVER

AH, YOU'RE BOTH WRONG, LADS...
YOU SEE, I'M HALFWAY THROUGH MURDERING MY WIFE WITH A HAMMER

Portrait of EVIL!

ANDY McBride knows only too well the horrors commited by the world's most depraved dictator. For Andy, an 18 year old trainee shoe shop assistant, was a member of the crack Sea Cadets during the 1990 Gulf War, and attended weekly training sessions in a church hall near his home in Buxton. Now, in these extracts from his bombshell new book, we expose the true terror of Saddam Hussein's evil reign.

'A massive military convoy rumbles through the streets of Baghdad towards the national TV station. Tanks surround the building and armed guards storm inside. *But this is not a military coup.*

On a whim Saddam Hussein, the self-styled butcher of Baghdad, has decided that tonight he is going to appear on 'Al Gamani Generihad', Iraqi TV's version of the Generation Game.

Spaghetti

Not surprisingly Hussein wins every game. A terrified judge awards him ten out of ten for making spaghetti, even though his soggy lump of dough is stuck to his shoes. His folded table napkin looks more like a dead duck than a swan, and in the next round he ends up on his backside attempting to dance the Lambada.

Best

But, surprise surprise, at the end of the game Saddam Hussein is the winner. In the control room nervous TV producers mop sweat from their brows. ***All is going well until - at the climax of the show - a nervous Saddam forgets one item from the conveyor belt... a sandwich toaster.*** His face floods with rage.

Great

Minutes later the show's host Jimrihim 'Nick Nick' al Davidson, his assistant, seven other contestants, plus 250 staff and technicians at the television centre are all dead - ***slaughtered in a warped act of bloody revenge exacted by the world's most evil man'.***

Later in his book Andy gives a spine chilling insight into life - and death - in the torture chambers beneath Saddam's Presidential Palace.

'Ahmed Salih ran a small hairdressing salon in a fashionable area of Baghdad. One day he received a call summoning him to the Presidential Palace. Saddam had been watching telly again, and after seeing some seventies repeats on Iraqi Gold he decided he wanted a moustache like Jason King.

It was an unusual request, but one which Ahmed dare not refuse.

Eastern

The barber's hands trembled as they trimmed the tyrants trademark black moustache. When he was finished there was a nervous silence as Saddam stared sternly into the mirror, then suddenly his face beamed with delight. The moustache was perfect.

In a fit of generosity the mad mullah gave the barber a million pound tip. But the hapless hairdresser never got to spend it.

Escape

The following day Saddam heard that in 1973 Jason King actor Peter Wingard had been convicted of a sex offence with a crane driver in a bus station toilet in Glousestershire. He exploded with rage.

Scenes similar to this are common place in the labyrinth of torture chambers beneath evil Saddam's Presidential Palace.

That night Ahmed Salih was dragged from his bed and taken to the notorious torture chambers beneath Saddam's palace where he was chained to a dungeon wall and left there - ***until his beard was two feet long and his trousers were all raggedy at the bottoms.***

The Butcher of Baghdad weilds a gun as he prepares to embark on yet another orgy of death, yesterday.

The terrifying truth behind the nightmare of the horror of the DICTATOR of DEATH!

Then he was stretched on a rack until his body was 15 metres in length.

Suprendo

Ahmed then pleaded for mercy as he was pushed into an iron maiden. But his cries were in vain. ***The sharp metal spikes glistened as the heavy door was slammed shut.***

Balls of Fire

Somehow the unfortunate barber was still alive when the door was opened. For a moment it seemed he had survived his ordeal - until the guards gave him a drink. ***Suddenly water began to spurt out of tiny holes which riddled his entire body.***

Chariots of Fire

Saddam is obsessed with security. Even his own government ministers are blindfolded before they meet their President, then they are shot immediately afterwards. Evil Saddam then breaks open their skulls with a solid gold teaspoon, before dipping real soldiers - ***terrified teenage conscripts*** - into their heads and feasting on their still-warm brains.

Local Hero

But as their grey matter churns about in Saddam's madcap stomach, their ordeal is far from over. For the instant his hapless victims emerge from Saddam's deranged rectum, they are scooped up, blindfolded, and shot again.

Memphis Belle

Saddam then invites the ministers wives to a banquet to feast on the twice shot dead shit remains of their husbands. After the feast Saddam jumps out of a giant cake and guns down all the guests. ***Their lifeless bodies are then liquidised before the power hungy dictator mixes them with strawberry Nesquick and drinks them through a giant straw.***

Memphis Slim

So mistrusting is Saddam of his faeces the following evening all of his nocturnal ablutions are rounded up in the dead of night, and folded into a souffle which is then cooked at high temperature. After thirty minutes of agony the twice shot, eaten, liquidised, twice shitted, drank and pissed out souffle finally collapses when evil Saddam opens the oven door allowing cold air to rush in.

© Copyright Andy McBride 1998. Andy McBride's book 'Saddam Insane -The Butcher of Baghdad - Portrait of a Monster Painted in Blood on a Canvas of Fear' is published by Guillemot Books, priced £19.99.

THE ADVENTURES of BILLY CONNOLLY

OCH, AH'M AAL O' A FLUTTER
BUSTLE
HER MAJESTY THE QUEEN O'ENGLAND IS COMIN' ROOND FER AFTERNOON TEA

DING DONG
JINGS! THAT'LL BE HER NOO
AN' AH'M LOOKIN' MUCKLE SOPHISTICATED IN MA BRAW NEW SMOKIN' JACKET AN' MONOCLE

GUID AFTERNOON, YER MAJESTY
AH'M TRULY HONOURED BY YER PRESENCE HERE IN MA HUMBLE WEE CASTLEY THING

Y'ALRAIGHT, BIG YIN?
CRIVVENS! IT'S NO' THE QUEEN — IT'S YON GEET BIG HAIRY-ARSED WELDER FRAE DOON THE ROAD

YE'LL NO' MIND IF AH NIP IN TAE USE YER LAVVY, BIG YIN?
AH'M ABSOLUTELY BURSTIN' TAE TAKE A CRAP, YE KEN

OCH M'BOAB! HERE COMES THE QUEEN! AH CANNAE LET HER SEE ME IN THE COMPANY O' THIS WELDER
IT DISNAE BEFIT A PERSON O' MA SUCCESS AN' SOCIAL STAUNDIN'

QUICK — HIDE YERSEL' UNDER THE SOFA AN DINNAE MEK A SOOND
BUT BIG YIN, IF AH DINNAE GAE TAE THE NETTY SOON AH'LL SHITE MA TREWS

DAE SIT DOON, YER MAJESTY, AN AH'LL POUR YE A CUP O' EARL GREY
HIGH NICE. THENK YEW.

SNIFF SNIFF AY SAY — THERE'S A DISTINCTLY PROLETARIAN ODOUR EMANATING FROM BENEATH THE SETTEE
IT SMELLS LIKE A SHOP GIRL, OR A FECTORY WORKER PERHEPS

HIGH STRANGE — AY SHELL JUST TAKE A PEEK...
CRASH
JINGS!

..ERM.. ALLOW ME TAE ADJUST YER HAT, YER MAJESTY
YANK
WHAT'S GOING ORN? AY CAN'T SEE A THING

AH'M GAE'IN THE TURTLES HEID HERE, BIG YIN
MICHTY ME! SHE'S NEARLY PRISED HER HAT OFF — QUICK, PIT THIS SHEET AWA' YE

THAT'S GOT IT ORF ... ?! WHAT ON EARTH IS THET, MR CONNOLLY?
THIS? ERM... IT'S A GHOST, YER MAJESTY. AAL THE MUCKLE POSHEST HOOSES ARE HAUNTED BY GHOSTIES AN' GHOULIES, YE KEN

WELL AY DON'T LIKE IT. IT SMELLS WORKING CLARSS
GET RID OF IT BEFORE IT STARTS OFFERING ME CHOCOLATE BISCUITS
RICHT AWAY, MAJESTY

AHEM AWA' WI' YE, YE SPOOKY WEE GHOSTIE!
PSST FIND YERSEL' A HIDIN' PLACE IN THE KITCHEN AN' KEEP YER HEID DOON

NOO PARDON ME WHILE AH JIST FETCH THE CAKE TROLLEY YER GRACIOUS HIGHNESS
VERY WELL

PHEW! YON WELDER SEEMS TAE HOV MADE HISSELF SCARCE
CAKES
NOO AH KIN CONTINUE WI' MA REGAL AFTERNOON TEA

HERE YE ARE YER MAJESTY
CAKES
A BRAW SELECTION O' MOOTH-WATERIN' DELICACIES FRESH FRAE FORTNUM AN' MASONS

OCH. SORRY, BIG YIN
CAKES
AH SEEM TAE HOV SHAT AAL AWA' THAE POSH LASSIE WI' THE FACE LIKE MA WORKBENCH
CRIVVENS!

Letterbox

It's the page that can't shake the dewdrop off its Herman Gelmet

Viz Letterbox
P.O. Box 1PT
Newcstle upon Tyne
NE99 1PT
Fax: 0191 241 4244
email viz@viz.co.uk

Star letter

★ These so-called disposible cameras are such a farce. Now I have absolutely no record of a perfectly lovely holiday.

S. Partridge
e-mail

★ British readers may be interested to know that the other day I saw 'Harold' off *Neighbours* walking around Melbourne. And I can tell you he looks a very different person. Off screen he is painfully thin, a foot taller and sports a moustache, but he still wears his unmistakeable coke-bottle glasses. At least I *think* it was Harold off *Neighbours.*

Justin Deegan
Cobram, Australia

Phoney lines

★ The girls on the 'Live 1-2-1, 30 second instant cum lines' are not really 19-year-old blonde Swedish nymphos with a 38-22-36 figure. They're more likely to be fat 49-year-old boilers with saggy tits, big arses and treble chins. I should know, because my missus is one.

A. Berry
Grimsby

★ I am left handed, and I have to laugh, because every time I have a wank, it feels like somebody else is doing it.

L. Vincent
Stoke

★ May I just say that not everyone who watches the Miss World contest on television is a slobbering sexist. Some of us think that in these cynical times it is refreshing to hear beautiful girls so concerned about the environment, elderly people and world poverty. The fact that they are wearing skimpy costumes barely concealing their vibrant, rounded breasts and tantalising us with the briefest glimpses of shaven bikini lines covering their mounds of pleasure is totally irrelevant.

Paul Dixon
Northumberland

He's got the hump

★ I was recently on holiday in Morocco, and I took this photograph of what must surely be the world's most miserable man. I mean, if he isn't happy giving camel rides to tourists, why doesn't he get another job?

S. Gill, Gateshead

BRONX ACCENT JOKE
SAY BUD - HAVE YOU JUST SOILED YOUR UNDERPANTS?
SOILED THEM? WHY - I ONLY JUST BOIGHT THEM!

The reverie's a bastard

★ Since I won the Football Pools, my life has been like a dream come true. Only the other day I gave my girlfriend a cuddle, but she turned into my dead grandad and started to chase me, and it was like I was running through treacle. And then I realised my maths 'A' level was about to start in ten minutes and I'd done no revision and couldn't find a pen.

R. Baker
Stroud

★ I am amazed at the poor state of driving in this country. Only yesterday, in dense fog, I passed dozens of motorists who were doing in excess of 90 miles per hour.

Tony English
e-mail

Opportunity knockout

★ They say that in a fight, you should use your opponent's weight against them. That's all very well, but it didn't do my uncle any good when he was attacked in a pub by Lena Zavaroni.

P. Miller
London

Blue blood

★ So your Royal Family are worth the millions they cost because of all the tourist dollars they bring into the country? If they were really committed to boosting tourism, they would strip naked and perform depraved sex shows on the balcony of Buckingham Palace. I wouldn't travel round the block to see your Queen changing the guard, but I'd fly halfway round the world to see Lady Melons Windsor licking out Sophie Rhys-Jones whilst getting ridden up the ass by Zara Philips with a 10-inch strap-on. **Hot diggety!**

Chuck Schwartzheimer
San Francisco

Well hung over

★ Despite all I've had to drink over the past years, my cock still does a bloody good job. Let's hear it for my knob.

Craig Parks
Wimbourne

★ When will greengrocers stop referring to 'New Potatoes'? They've been out for years now, so isn't it about time they just called them potatoes?

T. Doyle
Dagenham

★ People often complain about how American culture and tradition is being imported wholesale to Britain, changing the face of our nation. I agree that we are turning a little 'Americanised' in our outlook, but there are many charming customs that arrive from 'over the pond'. Halloween for instance used to be a non-event over here. Now I can look forward to gangs of threatening looking fifteen-year-olds in plastic 50p horror masks demanding a quid each not to overturn my dustbin or snap my car aerial.

S. Marsden
Barnsley

Hopping mad

★ I am a Flea Circus owner and recently decided to groom my performers for a big show. I chose 'Johnsons Dog Flea Shampoo', but far from cleaning my fleas' hair, it actually killed them. Let this serve as a warning to other flea keepers.

D. Miller
Kiphill

★ I think astrology is a pile of shit. My girlfriend is an Aries and she's got tits like two thruppenny bits on an ironing board. Meanwhile, her younger sister, who is also an Aries, has got the biggest pair of paps I've ever seen. I'd like roly-poly astrologer Russell Grant to explain that if he can.

Andrew nesbit
e-mail

★ Would S.L. Marston (letterbocks, p90) mind waiting his turn? I was here before him and I still haven't had my 'Early Riser' breakfast yet.

B. Corry, Table 4
Bardon Mill Little Chef

Top Tips

SAD blokes. When attempting to get into a barmaid's knickers, why not 'playfully' pull back your tenner just as she reaches to take it when paying for a round. It really turns me on.
Rosie
Bristol

BELL RINGERS. Don't waste time raising money to save your church bells. Get the same teeth-grating effect by simply dropping different lengths of scaffolding pipe off the roof of the church at 8 o'clock every Sunday morning.
Mark Smith
Wantage

OFFICE managers. When leaving your office desk for any length of time, make sure you leave your mobile phone on and unattended. Set it to play 'The Yellow Rose of Texas' loudly, instead of just ringing, then complain loudly when you return and find it in pieces in the bin.
Damian O'Neil
Heaton

MUMS over 50. Don't forget the last date for boiling Christmas carrots and sprouts is the 5th of December.
Pete O'Bog
West Bromwich

ASTHMATICS. Avoid going on holiday to places where the scenery is described as breathtaking.
J. Cloth
Bedside Manor

PARENTS. Baffle everyone your baby daughter will ever meet by calling her 'Shivorn' but insist it is pronounced 'Sea O'Ban'.
A. Delarosa
Hove

TIRED of being nagged to walk the dog? Pretend you've already taken it out by unrolling a turkey rasher out the side of its mouth whilst it lies by the fire to give it that shagged out look.
D. Pickering
Whitehaven

AMERICAN locomotive drivers. When confronted with a car obstructing a rail crossing, the brake pedal is the one that slows the train down, not the one that sounds the fucking horn.
Jim Gearbox
Lamesville

SURPRISE your wife by tidying her underwear drawer when she's out. Try on stockings to check for ladders, and try on bras and suspenders to check for broken clasps. Keep defective lingerie hidden in the shed as it can be used to clean up paint or tie garden canes, etc.
R. Leigh
Rayleigh

A PAIR of fox terriers, one strapped to each foot make ideal 'organic' rollerskates.
Justin Deegan
Victoria, Australia

BIG ISSUE vendors. Have blonde hair and big tits. That way you'll sell more copies.
G. Rice
Liverpool

SINGLE people. Pretend you're having sex by parking your car in a secluded country lane and steam up your windows using a 'travel kettle' plugged into the cigarette lighter.
Alastair Green
e-mail

ANOTHER BRONX ACCENT JOKE

SOILED? WHY DIDJA JES' BUY A PAIR OF SOILED PANTS?
WELL THEY WEREN'T SOILED TILL I BOIGHT THEM!
BAH- FUCK OFF!
AYE MAN
WILL YA LOOK AT THAT?! THEY'RE TALKIN' AT CROSS PORPOISES!

WHAT'S YOUR FUCKING PROBLEM? Miriam SORTS YOU OUT

Dear Miriam... I started a new job about a year ago and became friends with this wonderful young woman. About three months ago, our friendship turned into something more affectionate. The trouble is, we are currently in a pub, and I'm trying to get back from the bar with two pints, a gin and tonic and a bag of crisps under my arm. The room is very crowded. Do you mind if I just squeeze past you there?

Miriam says... **Hoy! What's your **fucking game?** You've spilt me fuckin' pint. It was a full 'un an' all, you clumsy wanker.*

Dear Miriam... Oh! I'm sorry.

Miriam says... Aye! You fuckin' **will be, son. Outside, **now!***

Dear Miriam... Look, I really don't want any trouble, I just...

Miriam says... Come on. You start it. **Stick one there. Come on!*

Cyril Fletcher's Photo Corner

I am indebted to **Mr. Calvin Evans** for this bi-month's photograph, taken whilst enjoying a day at Uttoxeter Racecourse. Mr. Evans advises anyone using the public conveniences there for defaecatory purposes should ensure they wipe properly as they are liable to have their anus inspected by one of the course officials. I would at this point like to ad some witty little pun concerning equestrianism and anuses, but sadly I am unable to think of one on account of my being almost certainly dead.

Esther...

Our Teacher's a Microbe

CHRISTMAS WITH
BIFFA
FATHA
MUTHA
THE
BACONS

HOWAY! LET'S GAN OOT F' WOR BIT CHRISSMUS DRINK, EH, BIFFA SON?

WHAT'S GANNIN' ON 'ERE!? ...A FUCKIN' CURT!?
EH?
NEE SON OF MINE GANS OOT IN A FUCKIN' CURT!

FUCK YEE! IT'S FROZZEN OOT THERE! THERE'S TWO FOOT O' SNEDGE
SNEDGE!?
Y' GEET PUFF! SNEDGE IS NOWT! WUZ'RE GEORDIES!

I NEVER THOUGHT I'D SEE THE DAY WHEN YUZ'D BRING SHAME ON THE NAME O' THE FUCKIN' BACONS

INSIDE.
HOO, FATHA! THERE'S A CANNY TABLE BY THE FIRE
NO, SON.
WUZ'RE GANNIN' OOT IN THE BEER GARDEN

F-F-F-FUCKIN' 'ELL. IT'S F-F-FREEZIN!
BIFFA! STOP SHIVERIN' LIKE A FUCKIN' HUR-MUR!
AYE!
IT'S NOT FRIGGIN' CAD, SON. IN FACT IT'S FUCKIN' WAAAM, THIS

Y' REET, MUTHA. IT'S FUCKIN' BOILIN'. I MIGHT 'AVE T' TEK ME FRIGGIN VEST OFF SOON
PHEWF! I CANNAT GET ME BREATH, I'M THAT FRIGGIN' HOT

IT'S NEE GOOD. I'M GANNA HAVE T' SIT IN THAT FISHPOND AWA THERE FO' T' COOL DOON

STOMP!
HEH! HEH!
SMASH!

AAAH! THAT'S BERRA!
HOO, BIFFA...

I'M THAT FUCKIN' WAAAM, I'M 'AVIN' T' LOB SNEDGE DOON ME KEX T' COOL US DOON A BIT
I'LL TELL Y' WOT, THOUGH, THIS SNEDGE IS SO FUCKIN' HOT, IT'S SCAAALDIN' ME FUCKIN' PILLS

AYE, FATHA! SNEDGE AALWAYS BORNS GEORDIES. AANLY PUFFS THINK SNEDGE IS FUCKIN' CAALD!

HO, BIFFA. WUZ'RE AAAL GEORDIES TOGETHER, EH? WHADYEE THINK ABOOT SNEDGE THINK IT WAAAM D'YE, EH?
NO! I'M F-F-F-FUCKIN' F-F-F-R-R-F-F-FROZZ!
FUCK ME! I'VE GINVEN BORTH TO A FRIGGIN HEEMASEX!
REET!
I'LL SHOW YEE WHO'S A PUFF! GET OOT THAT FUCKIN' POND!

SPLOOSH!

HA! HA! HA! THE STUPID SOFT SHITE!

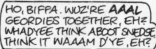

SHORTLY...
HOWAY, SON. WUZ'LL GET YUZ AAAL THAWED OOT
HYPOTHERMIA HOSPITAL

HEH! HEH!. THIS IS CANNY. I'M AAAL COMFY CURZY, LIKE.
AYE, SON
YEE KEEP YERSEL NICE AN' WAAAM!
WUZ'RE OFF F'WU'CHRISSMUSS DINNAH! IF Y'NEED OWT, RING FO'THE NORSE!

HOY, NORSE!.. ...NORSE!...
TINKLE! TINKLE!
CAN I HAVE A NICE MUG OF CUR-CUR!?

CUR-CUR!?.. CUR-CUR!?
I'LL FUCKIN' CUR-CUR YEE IN A MINUTE, SON!
EH!?

NEE PATIENT OF MINE DRINKS CUR-CUR AN' SLEEPS UNDER A IDA-DOON LIKE A FUCKIN' BIG HOM!
DOKTA IS A CUNT
FWIP!!

AN' WUZ'LL 'AVE THIS WINDEE ORPEN AN' AAL!
SMASH!
Y'NEED FRESH AIR, Y' FUCKIN' LITTLE TWAT!

HEH! HEH! MERRY CHRISSMUS, SON!

SPAWNY GET

HI, READERS! I'M BUSTING FOR A PISS, ME, BUT I CAN'T FIND NO LAVVY

EXCUSE ME, I'M A URINE SCIENTIST BUT I'M AFRAID I'VE RAN OUT OF PISS TO DO EXPERIMENTS ON... ... I DON'T SUPPOSE?...

WOW! THAT'S LOADS! HERE'S FIFTY QUID

ZZZZZ-ZIP!
CHOP!
RATS! I'VE GONE AND CHOPPED ME COCK OFF!

GREAT! I'M A DIRTY FILM PRODUCER AN' I'M DOING A FILM ABOUT LADYBOYS, BUT I CAN'T AFFORD TO GO TO BANKOK. PUT THESE PLASTIC TITS ON AN' I'LL GIVE YOU £500

SO...
...AND... ACTION!
HA!
TAP! TAP! TAPPITY! TAP!
DIRECTOR

SHORTLY...
ROYAL VICTORIA COCK HOSPITAL
COCK TRANS-PLANTS FROM £500

I'M SORRY, SPAWNSWORTH, BUT WE'VE RAN OUT OF MENS COCKS...
BAH!
COCK DOCTOR
I'M AFRAID ALL WE'VE GOT LEFT ARE THE GENITALS OF A KANGAROO...

...AND AS EVERYONE KNOWS, A KANGAROO HAS GOT TWO COCKS!
HEY, SWEET!...
...I'LL TAKE THEM!

SO...
THERE!...FINISHED!
WOW!
THEY'RE GREAT!

EXCUSE ME...WE'RE THE SINDY TWINS AND IT'S OUR SEXUAL FANTASY TO BE SHAGGED BY ONE BLOKE....
...AT THE SAME TIME!
WE WONDER IF...YOU'D...?

WHAHAY!
UGH! UGH! OOH, YES! OOH, YES!
BOING! BOING! BOING!

SPECKY TWAT
the LOW QUALITY DEFECTIVE EYESIGHT HUMOUR CARTOON

HELLO READERS, TODAY I'VE ...
NO SPECKY, YOU BLIND BASTARD WE'RE OVER HERE.
READER'S VOICE

AH, YES. HELLO READERS, TODAY I'VE HEARD OF A TWO-FOR-ONE OFFER AT TOP OPTICAL SUPERSTORE 'SPEXPRESS'.

I COULD WEAR ONE PAIR ON TOP OF THE OTHER. I'LL GO DOWN THERE RIGHT NOW.

AH YES. 'LIQUORICE ALLSORTS AVENUE', THIS IS THE STREET WHERE THE SHOP IS.
WHEELBARROW RD

AH YES. HERE WE ARE.
OPEN

HELLO MADAM, I SAW YOUR OFFER IN THE NEWSPAPER OF TWO PAIRS FOR THE PRICE OF ONE.

RIGHT. THAT'S TWELVE PENCE THEN PLEASE.
VERY REASONABLE. I'LL WEAR THEM STRAIGHT AWAY THANKS, NO NEED FOR A BAG. GOODBYE.

DEAR ME. WHAT A FOUR-EYED WANKER.

NOT SURPRISINGLY...
GREENGROCER
AAAH THAT'S BETTER NOW. GOD'S GIFT OF SIGHT HAS BEEN RENEWED.

JUST THEN...
HELLO. I'M DAVID DAVIES OF THE FOOTBALL ASSOCIATION. YOU'RE JUST WHAT WE NEED FOR THE F.A. CARLING PREMIERSHIP.

NEXT DAY...
GET STUFF FROM
BEER
PUNT!

PHEEEEEEP!
BEER IS GRE

GET STUFF FROM SHOPS
HANDBALL.
WHAT?!
BEER
HO FUCKING HO HO HO!
READERS VOICE

SUICIDAL SYD
HE'S ALWAYS TRYING TO POP HIS CORK!
PULL

GREAT! A FREE FACSIMILE OF THE VERY FIRST ISSUE OF THE VIZ. I'M GOING HOME TO READ IT STRAIGHT AWAY.
I'LL PROBABLY SPLIT MY SIDE LAUGHING!
NEWSAGENT
VIZ 99 ON SALE
GPD·SJ·SD·DT·AC / LEW STRINGER

THIRTY SECONDS LATER.
JESUS WEPT!
I THINK I'LL GO AND KILL MYSELF!
GLOOM

AHA! HERE IT IS. MUM'S BLEACH.

SYD! STOP!
GLUG GLUG GLUG

THAT'S MY HOME MADE LEMONADE! I'VE BEEN KEEPING IT IN THERE SINCE I RAN OUT OF POP BOTTLES.

BAH! I'M DESTINED NEVER TO BUY THE FARM.
DINK!

SUDDENLY
EXCUSE ME. I'M A NYMPHOMANIAC AND I'M CHOKING FOR A SHAG. DO YOU FANCY COMING IN AND OBLIGING?
ERM... YES, ALRIGHT!

HEY, THIS IS GREAT! YOU KNOW, LIFE ISN'T SO BAD AFTER ALL.

WHAT'S GOING ON HERE?
OH NO! IT'S MY HUSBAND, O.J. SIMPSON.

Smile if you had it with Tony

All the women who have ever shagged Tony Blackburn have been invited to turn up in Regents Park next month to pose for a special commemorative photograph to celebrate the Millenium.

Organisers of the ambitious event, 'Blackburn 2000', which is being funded by the Lottery Heritage Fund, hope that around 2000 women will attend their record breaking photocall on November 16th.

shagged

"The idea is to create a unique record of all the women Tony has ever shagged, and one that can be handed on to future generations", said photographer Sven Aruldssen yesterday.

knackered

Former Radio 1 DJ Blackburn confessed to having slept with over 250 women in his autobiography fifteen years ago.

knockered

Assuming he has kept up his rate of intercourse since then, the turn out on November 16th should be around the 2000 mark. Police will stage their biggest operation since last year's countryside demonstration to control the enormous crowds of women who have shagged the heart-throb DJ.

APOLOGY Mr. Arthur Finlay Plywood

On August 2nd 1994 we published a 12-page article headed "Horror of paedophile school head's cannibal frenzy", which reported allegations that Mr. Plywood had murdered and eaten children in his care, had dug up war hero Sir Douglas Barder's corpse in order to make a skin suit, and made repeated threats to 'bugger the Queen mother inside out' whilst injecting crack cocaine into the shaft of his penis and masturbating onto a severed head. We now accept that these allegations were wholely without foundation and ought not to have been published. We apologise to Mr. Plywood for any embarassment or distress they may have caused.

OBITUARY

SIR ALGERNON SPENCE-PERCIVAL

Sir Algernon Spence-Percival, OBE, KG, Playground Poet Laureate 1968-1999, died on September 26th aged 98.

ALGERNON SPENCE-PERCIVAL was born on March 6th 1901, youngest son of Hector Spence-Percival. Himself a minor playground poet in his own right, Hector made a comfortable, if not lavish living from the royalties on his ever popular composition: *" Who wants to play/ At Cowboys and Indians?/ No girls."*

The young Algernon was educated at Marlborough where he first developed his own love of playground poetry. His early effort: *"Milk, milk/ Lemonade/ Round the back/ Chocolate's made"* caught the eye of Professor Gowens-Whyte at Trinity Hall, Cambridge who immediately offered him a scholarship.

After an unremarkable accademic career, Spence-Percival took up a post as Visiting Professor of Playground Poetry at Durham University, and it was during his twenty years there - which he later recalled as the happiest of his life - that he wrote his masterpiece, and the poem by which he will surely always be remembered. *"My friend Billy/ Had a ten foot willy/ And he showed it to the lady next door./ She thought it was a snake/ So she hit it with a rake/ And now it's only five foot four,"* was published to commemorate the death of George VI in 1952, earning Spence-Percival immediate critical acclaim.

He was appointed Playground Poet Laureate in 1968, and his first work under Royal patronage: *"Georgie Best/ Superstar/ Walks like a woman/ And he wears a bra,"* was written a year later to mark the investiture of Prince Charles as Prince of Wales.

In contrast, his final official composition, comissioned to mark the funeral of The Princess of Wales, was perhaps his finest work, perfectly capturing the mood of a nation united in grief: *"Ip, dip, doo/ Doggy does a poo/ Cat does a wee-wee/ Out goes you."* He is survived by his wife, Celia and their two sons.

The Adventures of
MAJOR MISUNDERSTANDING
ERM... EXCUSE ME...
YOUR WALLET... YOU JUST DROPPED IT BACK THERE
THERE'S NO POINT IN SHAKING THAT TIN AT ME
WE ALL KNOW WHAT THOSE PEOPLE GET UP TO. DISGUSTING.
HIJACKED THE PERFECTLY GOOD OLD ENGLISH WORD 'GAY'
I REMEMBER WHEN 'GAY' USED TO MEAN 'HAPPY'. NOT ANY MORE. BLOODY SODOMITES HAVE TAKEN IT AWAY FROM US.
YOU CAN SPOUT YOUR 'POLITICALLY CORRECT' JARGON 'TILL YOU'RE BLUE IN THE FACE
THE HUMAN BODY ISN'T DESIGNED FOR THOSE PRACTICES. SIMPLE FACT OF NATURE.
BLOODY BBC IS CRAWLING WITH THEM.
CAN'T SWITCH ON THE WIRELESS NOWADAYS WITHOUT HAVING IT FORCED DOWN YOUR THROAT
DIRTY BUGGERS HAVE ONLY GOT THEMSELVES TO BLAME
YOU'LL NOT GET A PENNY OUT OF ME.

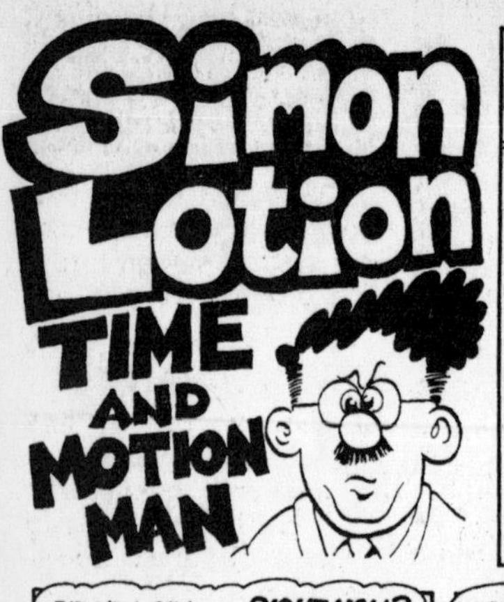
Simon Lotion
TIME AND MOTION MAN

HE'S HOME! HE'S HOME!
DADDY'S HOME! DADDY'S HOME!

DADDY! DADDY! WE'VE GOT A BIG SURPRISE FOR YOU!
YES! YES! WE'RE GOING ON A PICNIC!...
!
RIGHT NOW!

DID YOU SAY... RIGHT NOW?
YES! YES! MUMMY'S PACKED EVERTHING IN THE CAR ALREADY!

WHAT? BUT WE HAVEN'T HAD TIME TO PLAN THIS. THERE HASN'T EVEN BEEN TIME FOR ME TO DRAFT AN ITENERARY.
COME ON DARLING, LET'S JUST GO. WE CAN BE ON THE BEACH IN TWENTY MINUTES.

NUMBER ONE. THE CAR BOOT IS FACING AWAY FROM THE HOUSE. THE CAR IS TWELVE FEET LONG. THAT IS AN EXTRA TWENTY-FOUR FEET FOR EVERY TRIP CARRYING PICNIC EQUIPMENT AND PROVISIONS.

NUMBER TWO. WHERE'S THE RUG?
WHAT DO YOU MEAN?
THE RUG. WHERE IS IT?

IT'S IN THERE. IN THE BOOT.
YES. IT IS IN THE BOOT. BUT WHERE IN THE BOOT?
... AT THE BOTTOM.
HURRY UP DADDY! WE'RE ALL READY!

YES! I'VE GOT MY SWIMMIES UNDER MY CLOTHES!
YES! YES! BUT LET'S LOOK AT THIS RUG PROBLEM. WHEN YOU TAKE OUT THE BASKET AND THE BEACH TOYS, WHAT ARE YOU GOING TO PUT THEM ON?

WELL... DOES IT REALLY MATTER? CAN'T WE JUST MAKE THE MOST OF THE SUNSHINE?

OF COURSE IT MATTERS! REMEMBER... 'LAST IN IS FIRST OUT. FIRST IN IS LAST OUT.' ... SAY IT.

SAY IT AND IT WILL HELP YOU REMEMBER WHEN YOU RE-PACK. ... SAY IT!

LAST IN IS FIRST OUT... FIRST IN IS LAST OUT... LAST IN IS FIRST OUT... FIRST IN IS LAST OUT...
GOOD. RIGHT. YOU BEGIN TO RE-PACK USING THE SYSTEM I HAVE OUTLINED, AND I WILL BEGIN MY 2,114 POINT SYSTEMATIC CHECK OF ALL THE VEHICLE'S SYSTEMS.

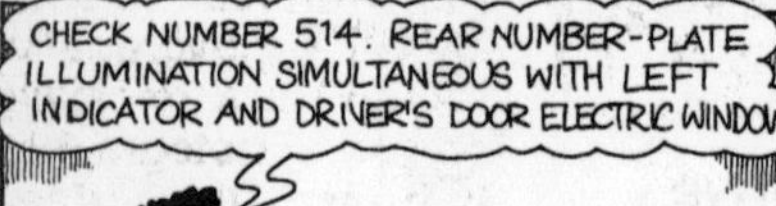
CHECK NUMBER 514. REAR NUMBER-PLATE ILLUMINATION SIMULTANEOUS WITH LEFT INDICATOR AND DRIVER'S DOOR ELECTRIC WINDOW.

RIGHTY-HO! COME ON THEN! IT'S PICNIC TIME! LET'S GET MOVING... WE'VE GOT SANDCASTLES TO BUILD!
GREAT DADDY! LET'S GO!

THINK ABOUT WHAT YOU'VE DONE. YOU'VE DUG OUT THE SAND FOR YOUR CASTLE, LEAVING A HOLE. NOW YOU ARE DIGGING A SEPARATE MOAT - YOU SHOULD OF COURSE HAVE DUG THE MOAT FIRST AND USED THE SAND PRODUCED TO BUILD THE CASTLE.

JOHNNY BALL REVEALS ALL!

Johnny lifts the blue T-shirt over his head.

He strips for some grass-cutting action

JOHNNY BALL reveals all his charms as he strips off whilst mowing the lawn of his Buckinghamshire home.

The gorgeous telly babe slipped his blue top over his head to reveal a fine set of assets.

Bubbly 'Think of a Number' presenter Johnny, 61, showed that he has certainly got ONE figure worth thinking about.

One neighbour said: "All the men here go topless when doing their lawns, but Johnny really shone. He looked fantastic."

Johnny - taking a break after quitting T.V.'s 'Play School' in 1983 - later sat with wife Diane and had a nice cup of tea.

Pictures: ENRICO RATZORIZZO

PHWOOAR! *Show us some MOWER Johnny*

PERV FALLS FOR BEAUTY

A PEEPING Tom fell 90ft to his death from a tree as he tried to spy on a topless beauty who was mowing the lawn.

Pervert

The filthy pervert had inched his way along a branch overlooking the garden, as he tried to snap pictures of the unsuspecting stunner.

Sicko

"We all go topless when mowing our lawns round here", said neighbour George Fisher," but you don't expect to be spied on by sickos."

Filthy

Another neighbour said: "I heard a scream from the tree, and saw a man desperately grabbing at a branch. Then he disappeared and the scream got fainter until I heard a thump. Serves him right."

OBITUARY

Enrico Ratzorizzo 1974 - 1999

VIZ SNAPPER Enrico Ratzorizzo - who has been killed in a tragic accident on an assignment in Buckinghamshire - had in his short but illustrious career earned himself a reputation for fearless professionalism and cold, ferret-like persistence, writes Picture Desk Editor, Ronnie Shit.

Loved

Over the past few years Enrico earned himself the title 'The People's Parasite' for his brutal disregard for the privacy or feelings of his victims.

Sensitive

Three-times winner of the prestigious Chuck Berry Award for Intrusive Photojournalism, Ratzorizzo was the lensman behind many front page scoops, including the first shots of Arthur Askey's legs in a hospital incinerator, and his sensational pictures of Christopher Reeve fighting for his life, taken from inside the air-conditioning system of the Intensive Care Unit.

Caring

But he will be best remembered for his sensitive coverage of Benny Hill's decaying corpse, photographed through the dead star's letterbox over the four day period he lay undiscovered.

Charity

He leaves a camera with an absolutely enormous lens, and a high-powered motorcycle with white Fiat Uno paint down the side.

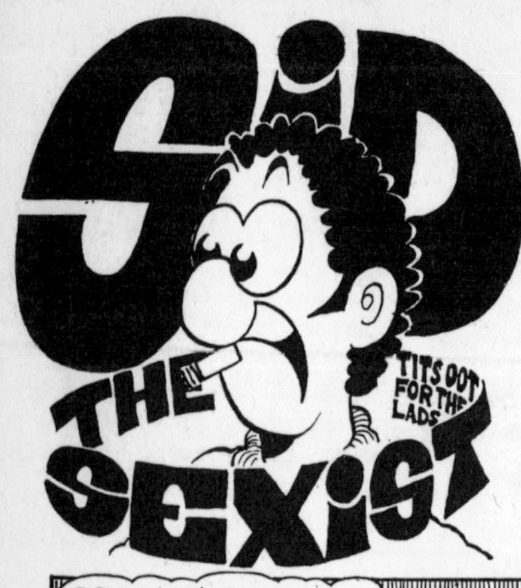

AYE. MEBEEZ SUR. BUT THAT NEW ONE, I SEEN 'ER IN THE SUN, IT'S FUCKIN' CHARLES ATLAS IN A FROCK, MAN. YOU'D HAVE TO BE A PUFF TO FANCY HOR LIKE ...ERM ... I THINK.

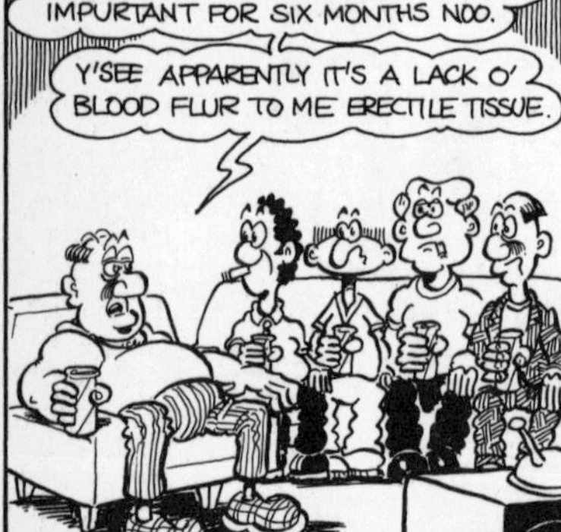

WINNING FORMULA

It's the pits as Ferrari race aces bend the rules

THE WORLD OF FORMULA 1 was rocked to its foundations last night after allegations that the Ferrari team CHEATED in order to secure this year's constructors' title. The Italian team faced disqualification from the Malaysian Grand Prix after after pieces of wood on the side of its cars breached stringent technical specifications, but the latest allegations, if proved correct, could mean that far more serious rule-breaking has been commonplace throughout the season.

SHOCKING SPORTS EXCLUSIVE!

According to Ferrari insider Ray Savage, team drivers Michael Schumacher and Eddie Irvine have regularly employed under-hand tactics, including;

- Setting up *fake diversions*
- Spreading *quick-drying glue* on the track.
- Running into back markers, and *cutting them down the middle with an enormous circular saw,* which comes out of the Ferrari nose cone.

A big red car going very fast - yesterday

witnessed

Michael Schumacher smiles and touches his ear, yesterday

ONE shocking instance of cheating, which Savage claims to have witnessed, happened at this year's British Grand Prix: "Irvine was trying to overtake Hakkinen, but the flying Finn was not letting him past.

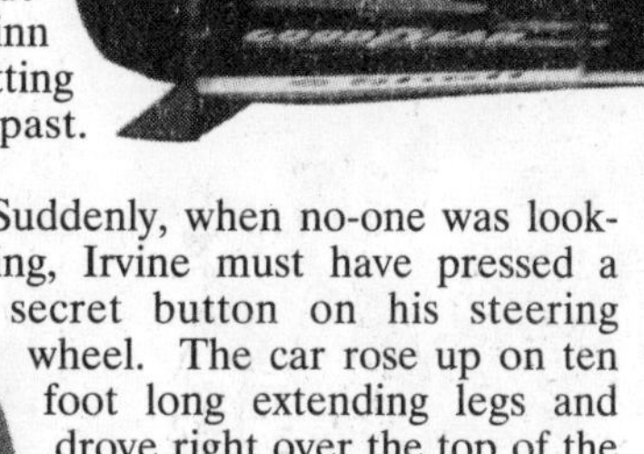

"Suddenly, when no-one was looking, Irvine must have pressed a secret button on his steering wheel. The car rose up on ten foot long extending legs and drove right over the top of the McLaren. It was a disgrace."

judged

Loyalty to his own team prevented Savage telling race marshals what he had seen, but after another incident later in the same race, Ray felt that he could hold his tongue no longer. "Schumacher rounded the first corner with a hefty lead over Coulthard. Then, quick as a flash, he pulled up, jumped out of his car and painted a false tunnel onto the side of a wall, and a length of false road leading up to it.

juried

"Then he put up a shortcut sign, pointing at the 'tunnel' and waited behind a bush. Coulthard and the rest of the pack were heading round the corner by now, and when they saw the shortcut, they naturally went straight for it. However, to Schumacher's amazement, they simply drove into the tunnel as if it was real, leaving the German in last place.

barristered

"Quickly, he jumped into his car, and set off at full speed in pursuit, only to crash immediately into the painted wall. Staggering out of the wreckage, Schumacher was then run over by a steam-roller which came out of the tunnel. That's how he broke his legs - and it served him right. That was me and Ferrari finished as far as I was concerned."

Father of eight Savage was later forcibly ejected from the Silverstone circuit, after being seen by security guards entering through a hole in the fence, and attempting to sell bootleg Michael Schumacher hats to racegoers.

IRVINE 'MADE LOVE LIKE A RABBIT' - Model

Irvine at home yesterday

A FORMER model who once got banged off of Formula 1 race ace Eddie Irvine, claimed last night that he 'made love like a rabbit.'

"It was amazing," said 49-year-old Bridie McO'Dougle, from Belfast. "We met in a hotel bar, and he took me back to his room. He made love to me 150 times that night. He was insatiable. He would hop about on the floor, sniffing at a load of sawdust.

burst

"Then he'd jump onto my back for a frantic five second burst of love-making, before hopping off to nibble at some vegetable peelings in the corner of the room. It was the most incredible sex I've ever experienced."

grumbling

McO'Dougle is presently undergoing DNA tests in an attempt to prove that the 28-year-old racing driver is the father of the twelve, hairless blind babies to which she gave birth three weeks after their night of passion.

Millions of us buy a newspaper every day to keep us abreast of what's going on in the world. We read them and we throw them away, but who amongst us ever stops to think about how they are produced? Let's take a look behind the headlines at a typical day in the life of a newspaper.

READ & LEARN A DAY I

The story of your morning paper starts a whole 24 hours before it hits the streets, when an editorial meeting is held. Stories may come from many sources; press agencies at home and abroad; correspondents filing eye-witness reports from war-zones around the globe; investigative journalists doggedly pursuing tip-offs and leads. Here the editor and his staff go through the early editions of their rival papers looking for stories about celebrities to rip off

Back in the pub, the journalist manages to snatch a few seconds between trebles for a quick sandwich and six bags of crisps. Then it's back to work, leaning on the bar spouting opinionated libellous gossip to anyone who'll listen.

It is the job of the campaigning journalist to expose injustice and root out corruption in high places. Woodward and Bernstein's Watergate cover-up story was responsible for bringing down a president, whilst John Pilger's fearless reporting has led to the exposure of many human rights abuses. Here, an investigative journalist with a hidden camera is being wanked off in a massage parlour by a woman in suspenders.

His heart attack over, our reporter is racing against time. There are only thirty minutes left before his copy must be on the sub-editor's desk, but circumstances are conspiring against him- the business desk of the Financial Times has just come in and they're six deep at the bar.

Journalism, as with many professions, has its less enjoyable sides. Here, a junior reporter has been threatened with the sack unless he 'doorsteps' a recently bereaved mother in order to suggest that her son died of AIDS. It's a job that requires sensitivity, tact and nimble fingers to pocket a school photograph from the mantelpiece.

THE LIFE OF A NEWSPAPER

Once the story has been decided upon, it is assigned to a reporter. Deadlines are tight and he knows there is no time to lose. Within seconds he's in the pub guzzling trebles and fiddling his expenses.

Newspapers not only inform, they also make us laugh. It is the job of the editorial cartoonist to take a humorous look at one of the day's stories. Here we see the artist hard at work. His caricatures are instantly recognisable as, with a few deft lines from his pen, he writes who it is supposed to be on their shirt.

n the pub, it's 2.30 and me for a heart attack.

In the world of newspapers, a picture is worth a thousand words. Don McCullin's harrowing photographs have been credited with hastening the end of the Vietnam war. This gin-soaked old smudger, however, is up a tree in the South of France trying to get a picture of Posh Spice's tits.

With just seconds to go, the story is finally filed. It is now the job of the sub-editor o change the facts and quotes made up by the reporter, in order to suit an amusing punny headline that he thought of earlier that morning.

9.00pm and the editor finally 'puts the paper to bed'. The presses start rolling, printing the first of millions of copies that will find their way onto our breakfast tables. For the printers, there is a long evening's work ahead. For the journalists, there is just enough time to nip to the pub all night before the whole dismal process starts again the next morning.

Practical Serial Killer

Incorporating MODERN CANNIBAL

December 1999 £1.75

Celebrity Interview

Jeffrey Dahmer

– "A Fridge full of Heads of my Own"

SPLEEN CUISINE

Cooking up a Three Corpse Dinner-

Our 'Head' chef's favourite recipes

RESULTS OF OUR BIGGEST SURVEY EVER!

You don't *have* to be a long distance lorry driver

...but it helps!

FREE SKIN SUIT PATTERN

Part 2 -those tricky Sleeves

PLUS

Keeping yourself to yourself-

We show you how!

KILLING TIME!

10 hobbies to explain away those whiffy drains

FREE CD "Voices in my Head"

Start collecting the coupons this week!

In your newsagents now

GPD ST SD AC DJ

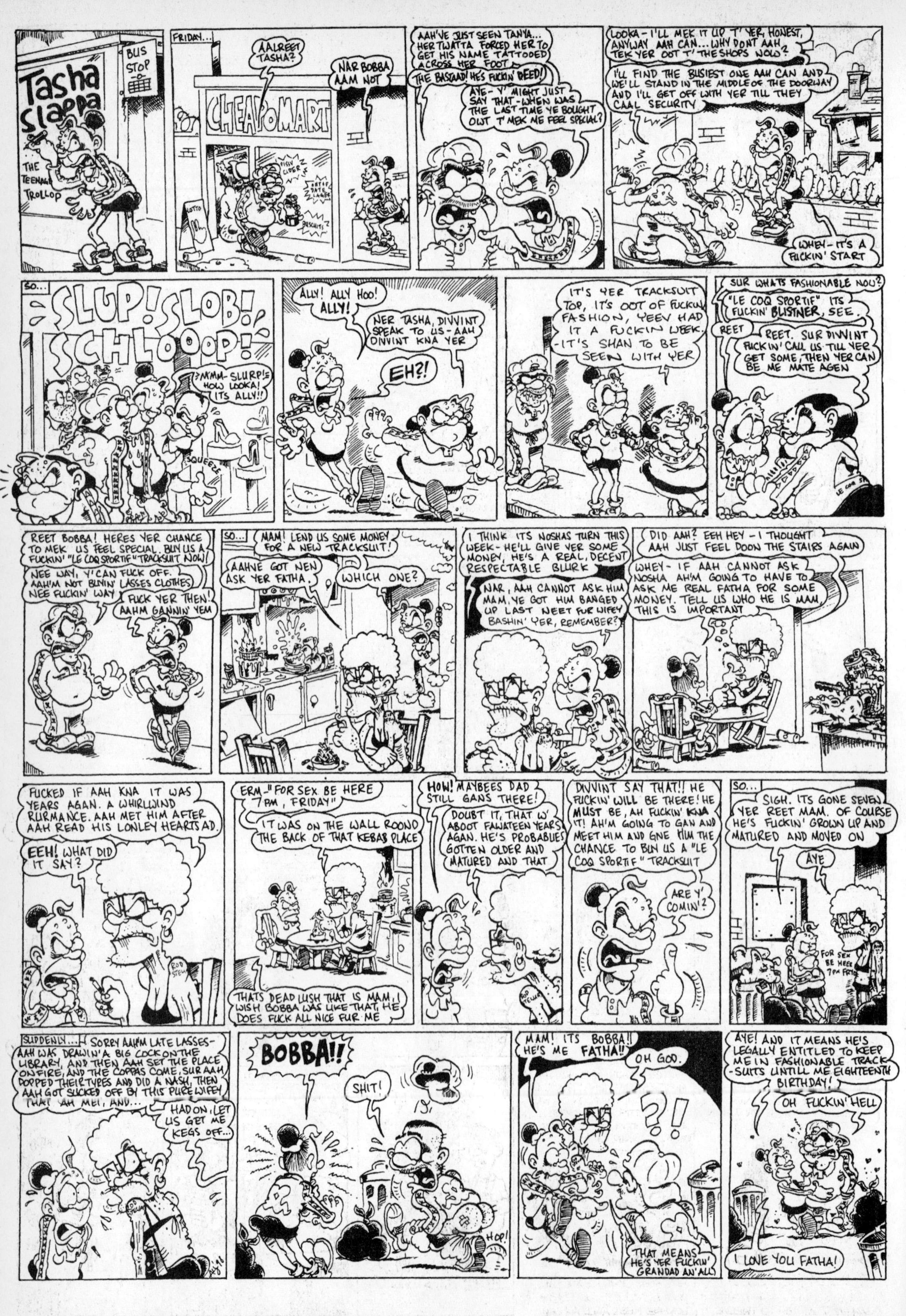
Tasha Slappa
THE TEENAGE TROLLOP
BUS STOP
FRIDAY...
AALREET TASHA?
NAR BOBBA AAM NOT
CHEAPOMART
PISSY CIDER
BISCUITS
AAH'VE JUST SEEN TANYA... HER TWATTA FORCED HER TO GET HIS NAME TATTOOED ACROSS HER FOOT
THE BASTAAD! HE'S FUCKIN' DEED!
AYE- Y' MIGHT JUST SAY THAT-WHEN WAS THE LAST TIME YE BOUGHT OWT T' MEK ME FEEL SPECIAL?
LOOKA - I'LL MEK IT UP T' YER, HONEST, ANYWAY AAH CAN... WHY DONT AAH TEK YER OOT T' THE SHOPS NOW?
I'LL FIND THE BUSIEST ONE AAH CAN AND WE'LL STAND IN THE MIDDLE OF THE DOORWAY AND I'LL GET OFF WITH YER TILL THEY CAAL SECURITY
WHEY- IT'S A FUCKIN' START
SO...
SLUP! SLOB! SCHLOOOP!
MMM-SLURP! HOW LOOKA! ITS ALLY!!
SQUEEZE
ALLY! ALLY HOO! ALLY!
NER TASHA, DIVVINT SPEAK TO US-AAH DIVVINT KNA YER
EH?!
IT'S YER TRACKSUIT TOP, IT'S OOT OF FUCKIN FASHION, YEEV HAD IT A FUCKIN WEEK. -IT'S SHAN TO BE SEEN WITH YER
SUR WHATS FASHIONABLE NOW?
"LE COQ SPORTIF" ITS FUCKIN' BLISTNER, SEE.
REET
REET. SUR DIVVINT FUCKIN' CALL US TILL YER GET SOME, THEN YER CAN BE ME MATE AGEN
REET BOBBA! HERES YER CHANCE TO MEK US FEEL SPECIAL. BUY US A FUCKIN' "LE COQ SPORTIF" TRACKSUIT NOW!
NEE WAY, Y'CAN FUCK OFF. AAH'M NOT BUYIN' LASSES CLOTHES NEE FUCKIN' WAY
FUCK YER THEN! AAHM GANNIN' YEM
SO...
MAM! LEND US SOME MONEY FOR A NEW TRACKSUIT!
AAHVE GOT NEN ASK YER FATHA.
WHICH ONE?
I THINK ITS NOSHAS TURN THIS WEEK- HE'LL GIVE YER SOME MONEY, HE'S A REAL, DECENT RESPECTABLE BLURK
NAR, AAH CANNOT ASK HIM MAM, YE GOT HIM BANGED UP LAST NEET FUR WIFEY BASHIN' YER, REMEMBER?
DID AAH? EEH HEY - I THOUGHT AAH JUST FEEL DOON THE STAIRS AGAIN
WHEY- IF AAH CANNOT ASK NOSHA AH'M GOING TO HAVE TO ASK ME REAL FATHA FOR SOME MONEY. TELL US WHO HE IS MAM, THIS IS IMPORTANT
FUCKED IF AAH KNA IT WAS YEARS AGAN. A WHIRLWIND RURMANCE. AAH MET HIM AFTER AAH READ HIS LONLEY HEARTS AD.
EEH! WHAT DID IT SAY?
ROD STEW
ERM-"FOR SEX BE HERE 7PM, FRIDAY"
IT WAS ON THE WALL ROOND THE BACK OF THAT KEBAB PLACE
THATS DEAD LUSH THAT IS MAM, I WISH BOBBA WAS LIKE THAT, HE DOES FUCK ALL NICE FUR ME
HOW! MAYBEES DAD STILL GANS THERE!
DOUBT IT, THAT W' ABOUT FAWATEEN YEARS AGAN. HE'S PROBABLIES GOTTEN OLDER AND MATURED AND THAT
ROD STEWA
DIVVINT SAY THAT!! HE FUCKIN' WILL BE THERE! HE MUST BE, AH FUCKIN' KNA IT! AH'M GOING TO GAN AND MEET HIM AND GIVE HIM THE CHANCE TO BUY US A "LE COQ SPORTIF" TRACKSUIT
ARE Y' COMIN'?
SO...
SIGH. ITS GONE SEVEN YER REET MAM. OF COURSE HE'S FUCKIN' GROWN UP AND MATURED AND MOVED ON
AYE
FOR SEX BE HEER 7PM FRID
SUDDENLY...
SORRY AAH'M LATE LASSES- AAH WAS DRAWIN' A BIG COCK ON THE LIBRARY, AND THEN AAH SET THE PLACE ON FIRE, AND THE COPPAS COME, SUR AAH POPPED THEIR TYRES AND DID A NASH, THEN AAH GOT SUCKED OFF BY THIS PURE WIFEY THAT AH MET, AND...
HAD ON, LET US GET ME KEGS OFF...
BOBBA!!
SHIT!
HOP!
MAM! ITS BOBBA!! HE'S ME FATHA!!
OH GOD.
?!
THAT MEANS HE'S YER FUCKIN' GRANDAD AN' ALL!
AYE! AND IT MEANS HE'S LEGALLY ENTITLED TO KEEP ME IN FASHIONABLE TRACK-SUITS UNTILL ME EIGHTEENTH BIRTHDAY!
OH FUCKIN' HELL
I LOVE YOU FATHA!

SID the SEXIST
TYNESIDE'S SILVER-TONGUED CAVALIER
TITS OOT for the lads

IN THE PUB...
1999 THEN, EH?
AYE. YE CAN SAY THAT AGAIN.
AYE. WUZ'LL AALL BE IN THE FUTURE NEXT YEAR.

AYE. WE'D BEST START WOR PLANS FOR THE BIG NEET.
ROOND TU MINE, MAN. BIGGEST PARTY THE WORLD'S EVER SEEN.
SCROGG RURD, WAALKER. GET YASSEL'S DOON.

EXCELLENT IDEA SID. JUST LIKE LAST YEAR, EH?... US FAWA AN' HALF A BORREL O' EGG-NOG, WATCHIN' CAROL FUCKIN' SMILLIE ON THE FUCKIN' BOX AAL NEET.
OH AYE. AN' THE LASSES... SID'S MAM AN' 'EEZ AUNTIE DOLLY, PISSED UP ON LEM-SIP LIKE THERE WAS NAE TOMORRO'.

AYE. GREAT PARTY SID. WUZ ARE AALL STILL COMIN' DOON OFF IT, MAN.

LISTEN. WE'VE GOT TU GERRIT PLANNED. IT'S ABSOLUTELY VITAL THAT WUZ GET MORE PISSED UP ON THE MINELLIUM NEET THAN ANY OTHER NEET EVER.
AYE, AN' TAXIS ARE GANNA COST A THOOSAND POOND.

AYE. COZ O' THE MINELLIUM BUG.
IS THAT THAT NASTY FLU WHAT ME MAM'S GOT?
NAH. IT'S A COMPUTA VIRUS. AALL MACHINES WHAT RUN OFF THE 'LEKKY ARE GANNA GAN WRANG. MURST O' THEM'S GANNA SET A'HAD THEY RECKON, LIKE.
AYE. AALL THE NEWKULEAR BOMBS IS GANNA GAN OFF BY MISTAKE, AYE, THERE'S GANNA BE NOWT THEY CAN DEE ABOOT IT.
AYE. IT'S GANNA BE THE END O' THE WORLD. FUCKIN' APOCALYSE AN' THAT. WE'RE GANNA WAKE UP ON NEW YEAR'S DAY AN' WE'RE AALL GANNA BE DEED.

IT'S AAFUL THAT. THEY SHOULD DEE SUMMUT ABOOT IT, MAN, ... A THOOSAND POOND FOR A TAXI!!
SUR WHAT'S THIS MINELLIUM DURM ABOOT?
WHY, IT'S GANNA BE LIKE MAD MAX INNIT? COZ IT'S AALL GEET PURST HOLOCAUST AN' AALL THAT.

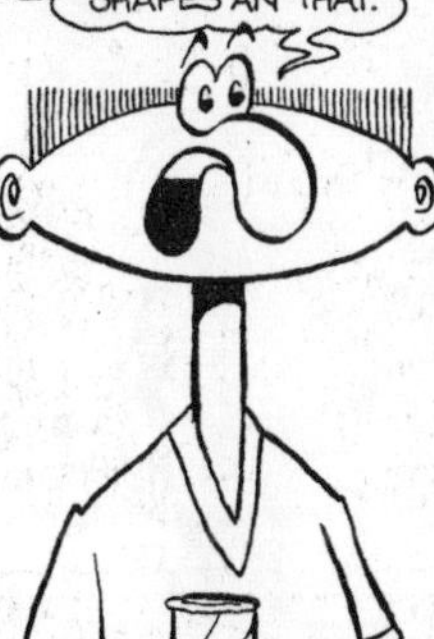
AYE. WUZ ARE AALL GANNA BE MUTANTS. AALL WOR HEEDS'LL GAN FUNNY SHAPES AN' THAT.

AYE, SUR THE DURM'S GANNA HAVE TINA TORNA IN IT FLEEIN' AROOND ON A GEET BIG LAKKY BAND.
AYE. AN' A DWAARF'S GANNA BE DRIVIN' ROOND ON BIG DADDY.

HAD ON. DIVVEN'T TAALK YA SHITE. THAT CANNAT BE REET. BIG DADDY'S DEED.
AND GIANT HAYSTACKS.

AYE. BUT THIS IS THE FUCKIN' NEXT MINELLIUM, WE'RE MOVIN' INTU THE TWENTIETH CENTURY... THEY'LL JUST CLURN HIM.
AYE. THEY'LL BE ABLE TU CLURN OWT, SHEEP, COOS, BEER, EVEN GOOD LOOKIN' BORDS.

AYE. THEY RECKON IN A HUNDRED YEARS TIME WUR AALL GANNA BE RURBOTS.

ERM... AYE JOE. THIS TIME NEXT YEAR YE'LL BE ABLE TU GAN INTO BOOTS WITH A HUNDRED POOND, AN' COME OOT WITH A SEXY BORD YE'VE DESIGNED YERSEL' OFF A MENU.. PICK YA BEST BITS AN' THAT, BIG HAIRY FANNY, MOOSE'S LUG, OWT YE WANT, Y'KNAA.

THEN THEY JUST MIX THE D AN' A UP IN A FUCKIN' JAR, AN' THERE Y'GAN, BINGUR! YER AAN CLURN BORD.
...OR TWO FOR A HUNDRED AN' FIFTY POOND, Y'KNAA FORRA LESBIAN SHOW.

AYE. AN' IF YA WIFE'S GORRA HEEDACHE AN' SHE'LL NOT LET YE ON, YE JUST GAN AN' GERRA CLURN OF 'ER OOT THE CUBBAD, AN' BOB'S YER UNCLE, ... EH? EH?

NAAH MAN... CLURNS ARE MADE OOT O' THE SAME JEANS... THAT MEKS THEM EXACTLY THE SAME...
...SUR SHE'LL HAVE A HEEDACHE AN' AALL.

HOW MAN. NEW YEAR'S EVE 1999 IS GANNA BE UNBELIEVABLE! WE'VE GOT A WHOLE YEAR FOR TU MEK WOR PLANS.
AYE. AN' GET IN WOR DRINKIN' PRACTICE.
WHY MAN, THE WHOLE WORLD'S GANNA BUILD ITSELF INTO A FRENZY!

JUST THINK, ANY FIT YOUNG BORD THAT'S NOT HAD IT YET, ISN'T GANNA WANT TU GAN INTU THE NEW MINELLIUM WITHOOT 'ER VORGIN STRING POPPED...
...IT'S GANNA BE A WORLDWIDE SHAGFEST AT TEN TU TWELVE.

PICTURE IT LADS, WUZ ARE THE MOST PISSEDEST EVER. GORGEOUS VORGINS CHEWIN' DOON ON WUZ WHILST WU NECK CHAMPAGNE. THEN AALL THE ATOM BOMBS START GANNIN' OFF.
EEH HELL! BORDS, BOOZE AN' BOMBS, IT'LL BE LIKE EVERY BONFIRE NEET AALL AT ONCE.

FUCKIN' HELL.

NEW YEAR'S EVE 1999, 11·59pm...
A-CHOO!
SIDNEY, GO AND FETCH ANOTHER LEM-SIP FOR YOUR AUNTIE DOLLY.
A GLASS OF EGG-NOG ANYONE?
10-9-8-7-6-5...

FUCKIN' HELL.

ROGER MELLIE
THE MAN ON THE TELLY RADIO
BOLLOCKS!

ROGER HAS BEEN THROWN A CAREER LIFELINE - HE'S TAKEN OVER FROM THE AGING JOHN DULL AS HOST OF BBC RADIO 2's 'DRIVE TIME SHOW'...
...AND THAT WAS... THE SMALL FACES WITH...'LAZY SUNDAY AFTERNOON'
REMINDS ME OF MY DAYS ON CAROLINE, THAT ONE...
...CAROLINE MY SECRETARY AT RADIO 1, THAT IS...

...WENT LIKE A TRAIN SHE DID. I REMEMBER ONCE AT A PARTY AT TONY BLACKBURN'S HOUSE... ON HIS WATER BED, ACTUALLY... I'D HAD A FEW DRINKS, BUT I WAS STIFF AS A ROLLING PIN...
LEAVE IT ROGER. GO TO THE TRAFFIC!

...ANYWAY... ER... WHERE WAS I? ...AH, YES. SPEAKING OF LAZY SUNDAYS AND SMALL FACES, IT'S NOT SUNDAY - AND HERE'S SOMEONE WITH QUITE A BIG FACE - AND AN ARSE TO MATCH... IT'S OUR TRAVEL GIRL ...SALLY P.
ERM... THANK YOU, ROGER...
...I DON'T KNOW IF THAT WAS A... ER... COMPLIMENT OR NOT
HEY! TOUCHY! TOUCHY! THERE'S NOTHING WRONG WITH BIG ARSES... I'VE SHAGGED FATTER THAN YOU, SAL AND ENJOYED IT! SO... TELL US ABOUT THE TRAFFIC

LATER...
I'VE TOLD YOU, ROGER! TAKE IT EASY WITH SALLY... I THINK YOU'VE UPSET HER AGAIN
STUDIO

COME ON, TOM. YOU CAN'T MAKE AN OMLETTE WITHOUT RUFFLING A FEW EGGS - SEXUAL CHEMISTRY - THAT'S WHAT IT IS...
...AM I, OR AREN'T I POKING HER!?! THAT'S WHAT THE LISTENERS WANT TO KNOW... PUTS EARS ON SEATS, TOM

ANYWAY, I CAN'T STAND HERE GABBING ALL DAY. I'M MEETING SOME BLOKE IN THE HOTEL ACROSS THE ROAD... SOME SORT OF SPONSORSHIP DEAL TO DISCUSS...
... SEE YOU LATER, TOM

Hotel de Posh

RECEPTION
BAR
BLAH BLAH BLAH

MR. ROGER MELLIE?
THAT'S ME
HI! I'M... ER... MR. SMITH. I CALLED YOU YESTERDAY

NOW, YOU MAY BE WONDERING WHY I ASKED YOU HERE...
YEAH...
...LISTEN. BEFORE WE TALK BUSINESS, LET'S NIP UPSTAIRS FOR A BIT OF A FRESHENER, EH?

ER... NO... I DON'T THINK...
C'MON. I'VE GOT A ROOM BOOKED UPSTAIRS
STAIRS TO ALL FLOORS

I CAN'T TALK BUSINESS WITHOUT A TOOT OF THE OLD MARCHING POWDER INSIDE ME
FLOOR 1
BUT...

I'VE ORDERED A COUPLE OF RUSSIAN PRO'S FOR US. THEY SHOULD BE IN HERE READY!
NO... I JUST WANTED TO...
REDS IN THE BED, EH!?

WOOF! WOOF! THEY LOOK TASTY! THE LAST LOT THEY SENT ME WERE A RIGHT LOAD OF SHOT-PUTTERS! WHICH ONE DO YOU WANT FIRST, EH?
GIGGLE!
NO... ERM... REALLY... I... ...I JUST...

COME ON, GET STUCK IN OR I'LL HAVE 'EM BOTH MYSELF. HEH!
NO, ROGER, YOU SEE...

...ACTUALLY, WHAT I CAME HERE TO SAY, WAS...
I'LL DO A LINE OFF ONE OF HER TITS... WATCH THIS!

...ROGER MELLIE... ANCHORMAN, BROADCASTER AND T.V. PRESENTER... TONIGHT... ...THIS IS YOUR LIFE!
SNORT!

EH!? ...I... I DON'T BELIEVE IT!... I. CAH!... I DON'T BELIEVE IT!
THIS IS YOUR LIFE

I CAN'T BELIEVE I FELL FOR IT... YOUR DISGUISE!... I BET THAT TOM WAS IN ON IT EH? HEH! HEH! FUCK ME RAGGED!
THIS IS YOUR LIFE